first

D1209665

Breakdown

JOHN BRATBY

Breakdown

THE WORLD PUBLISHING COMPANY

CLEVELAND AND NEW YORK

Published by The World Publishing Company
2231 West 110th Street, Cleveland 2, Ohio

Library of Congress Catalog Card Number : 61–6560

FIRST EDITION

PR
6052
.R3
B7
1960

Please let it be understood that all the characters in this book are entirely fictitious, have no connection with people alive or dead, and are drawn completely from the author's imagination. Any resemblance between living persons and the characters in this book is entirely coincidental.

Furthermore, any resemblance between situations and settings in this book and situations that actually happened in actual settings is accidental.

John Bratby

Contents

PROLOGUE

Brady painted a painting of ten oranges, seventeen pieces of orange peel, and two lemons on a table-top. Behind the table was a pair of french windows. Brady painted the painting in the mountains outside Rome, in a village called Anticoli. He had been rather angry with the painting when it was finished, and had slashed the canvas, a badly primed Italian canvas, with a carving-knife. Remorsefully he had patched up the tear from behind with a piece of sticking-plaster used for cut fingers.

He had an old Lambretta at the time: a light green Lambretta that was battered and which spent most of its declining life in service stations. The Italians were rather hard on Lambrettas. One put them in for servicing, and the emotional garage boy would take out all the good parts, put them on his spares shelves, and replace the good parts with very ancient and worn ones. So Brady's Lambretta was very inefficient indeed.

It was a task of no remarkable simplicity to get an Italian carpenter to make a box for the painting, so that the painting could be carried in its wet state on the back of the Lambretta: Brady spoke no Italian.

Brady drove the painting down to Rome from the hills, and Raviano and Anticoli, during the night. The painting bumped up and down in its box, and its wet surface smeared against the inside of the box. Brady worried as he drove down the olive-tree-bordered road that led to Rome.

.   .   .   .   .

After being exhibited in the Tartaruga Gallery in Rome the painting was eventually shipped to England, where it was exhibited again.

9

It was a small painting, and Brady had painted it in the sweltering Italian summer when the sky was unbearably blue; and the paint seemed too liquid, as he applied it to the canvas, because of the heat. 'Why so many oranges?' you might ask; with a quite unnecessary curiosity, and insistence upon the existence in your novel of explainable statements: This is not a detective novel, dear reader, and you won't find every statement checked and re-checked for accuracy and credibility, as you would undoubtedly find in the excellent books by Dorothy L. Sayers. But we perceive you are suffering, dear reader, and that will not do at all. We hate to think of your needing explanations and justifications, and suffering with the hunger for them. So read on, please, and explanations will follow, to soothingly ointment the pain in your over-questioning brain.

Brady's eyes had become yellow. Now that statement only makes things worse, doesn't it? There is no explanation there, for the existence of so many oranges in Brady's painting. But those of you who are worried will obviously be readers of detective fiction, for it follows that such minds would be drawn to detective fiction. All readers of detective fiction are amateur detectives so they say: so, dear readers, with minds of logic and reason, please try to work out why Brady's yellow eyes explain the existence of many oranges in the painting he did, when his eyes, and the eyes of his wife, were yellow. It is a simple problem and will be answered very soon.

·　　·　　·　　·　　·

In the painting, amongst the oranges, was a packet of Quaker Oats. While shopping in Rome Brady had seen some packets of Quaker Oats on sale. He didn't like Italian food: so the sight of this good English food made his eyes shine—and the withdrawn coins in his hand shine also—in the artificial light of the chromium-bespattered grocery shop, as he passed them over the counter to the Italian grocer, his arm jostled by the pushing and shoving Roman housewives. With three packets in his hand he departed from the shop, squeezing past the bumping bumpy ladies.

·　　·　　·　　·

Here we are, you budding Sherlock Holmeses. The food was unhygienically sold in Italy. In Brady's butter he had found tape-worms. The butcher's finger-nails were extravagantly dirty, and the fruit was sold unwashed. So Brady picked up the germs from the fruit.

His eyes became yellow like mustard and thin gravy. His skin yellowed, and he felt that characteristic depression that accompanies the sickness of yellow jaundice. No illness makes its sufferer feel more depressed than jaundice does, and suicide becomes a good idea. The doctors, who don't work under a National Health scheme, charge many lire in romantic Roma, and suicide becomes a good idea again as one's money runs out and one's skin yellows more.

You have to drink orange juice in great quantities, and fried food and fat are banned from your diet. So Brady's kitchen became filled with orange peels, and when he had somewhat recovered he began to paint them.

One hundred marks in one hundred if you got the problem right, dear reader. And ten marks for ingenuity if you thought that Brady's eyes were yellow because he had smudged them with some yellow paint used in the painting of the oranges (yellow plus red makes orange). Twenty marks for possibility if you thought his eyes were yellow because of orange juice squirted upon them from a badly and recklessly squeezed orange.

.   .   .   .   .

Mr. Carter had long, curly, yellow hair, horn-rimmed spectacles, a swarthy complexion, and busted deltoids. Every winter he suffered from epilepsy, and every winter he was sure would be his last. Back at his home Mr. Carter had a collection of matchboxes filed away in alphabetical order. Mr. Carter had a recurring sense of humour which was practically smothered by his everlasting and non-ceasing verbosity. His verbosity didn't cease when the intelligence departed from it: it would continue about subjects of a non-thoughtful nature with as much vigour as it dealt with thoughtful subjects. His verbosity was sometimes amiable and sometimes angry, but it was never non-existent.

Sometimes Mr. Carter would talk with an intense intelligence of a very high order, about subjects ranging from the workings of the mind to the glories of matchboxes. It was when he was talking about his wife's intelligence (she was an M.A., B.Sc.), and her myopia (she was in actuality a woman of the finest vision and non-bespectacled), that his conversation became lacking in conviction. Mr. Carter was driving his little car—it was useful for his hobby hunts—along Piccadilly, and became involved with the car of a certain Mrs. Crumpet. Mrs. Crumpet was a typically hopeless woman driver, and the result of the movements of her car, in relationship to the movements of Mr. Carter's car, was that Mrs. Crumpet turned down Old Bond Street when she had no intention of doing so.

Mrs. Crumpet was vast, hatchet-faced, rounded as regards her figure, full-breasted, and the sophisticated-affected type of middle-class married woman, who is everlastingly bored; who orders her groceries by telephone; and who is fed up with just being a housewife, while her husband is away enjoying himself at sweating blood to earn the forty a week to keep her in dresses and to pay for home help and other luxuries; and who always wants more and more and more.

Mr. Crumpet was a managing director who loved his work, and in his spare time went to bed with his wife or wrote his book—*The Life of Mrs. Jane Gordanghauser, O.B.E.*, who was his aunt. He peered through half-inch-thick glass spectacles with green myopic lizard's eyes; was shy and retiring and obedient to his wife, until he broke out pettishly and started to threaten to burn her petticoats. A thoroughly nice admirable chap. Mr. Crumpet married late in life, and will never get over the horrors of the next war.

Dear Mrs. Crumpet wore gold-rimmed spectacles; had fine curly hair in little wisps all over her head and curling over her bumpy forehead; had big soft hands with birthmarks all over them; had little grey eyes that sparkled wetly; wore clusters of imitation flowers on her ear-lobes, around which pretty golden hair curls abounded; had a fat yellow tummy and a fat, bright vermilion backside, both encased in the most powerful corsets buyable; had cheeks like rosy apples, with hairs all over them, covered with layers of sweet-smelling powder; plucked eyebrows of two fine lines curving unconvincingly across her lower forehead; a double chin in which sank a choker of pearls; a red rosebud mouth piled high with shiny, red, sticky stuff; and a large mole nestling charmingly amongst the little black hairs on her vast powdered chin. Mrs. Crumpet was six feet two of irresistible femininity. She was extraordinarily good at whist drives, arranging flowers, keeping fat Persian cats, sending Christmas cards, going to the pictures, seeing ghosts, buying corsets, going to cocktail parties, being ambitious for her husband to become a Sir, writing to her M.P. about bananas floating in the river, spending money, getting rid of her children at boarding-schools, and burning toast. She changed her home help regularly every month, changed her gardener every two months; went to bed with toy alligators in short satin skirts and red silk blouses, got up at midday, sat at her dressing-table for an hour, slopped around in pom-pom slippers and a violet silk dressing-gown till teatime; was scared stiff of when she would experience her change of life—she was forty-five; adored air force officers and Americans; drove the milkman, the dustman, and the baker barmy; practically lived in the local beauty shop; smashed a car up once a year; was sadistic to her cats; ate too much pastry; read every woman's magazine published; lived by astrology; knew the lives of the film stars by heart; adored Christmas; belonged to a black-magic club; and had seven birthdays a year.

She parked her car off Old Bond Street and went back on foot to do some window-shopping. Mr. Fattish on his Lambretta swerved to avoid Mrs. Crumpet as she crossed the road, and he found himself caught in a stream of traffic, which forced him away from his destination and along Old Bond Street in the wrong direction.

Mr. Fattish had a bald head with golliwog hair rising high on either side of it and far outwards from above the ears. His face looked as if he made himself up with brick-dust every morning, a face blazing with unhealthy fire. Gold spectacles, bent and crooked, were in front of closely set eyes; a toothbrush moustache resided like an accumulation of gold dust below his yellow and red nose; he never washed and his red face was greasy; when he bent his head forward the nude crown could be seen to be very lightly covered with fine gold hairs on skin of brown tinged with bottle-green. His jaw seemed disconnected from the upper part of the face, and the area round the mouth suspended disconnectedly with monkey poutings and gestures. Large ears protruded from the sides of his face, competing with the golliwog's hair for attention; hair of the same kind made its unkempt way from the balding top, back of the high cranium, down over the unwashed collar, a collar frayed and greasy, beneath a coat collar speckled with dandruff. Beneath a waistcoat too small for him swelled a potbelly, and, within the confines of clothes a few sizes too small, a bumpy, weird, fat body was attached to legs that were never exercised. His eyes were wide open with innocence that was not innocent, and his mouth curved in an over-amiable crescent, both features hiding a character wise, sensitive, and deeply hidden. A fantastic alizarin-crimson cloak hung on his shoulders, tied at the neck, in front of a spotted bow-tie of yellow and green. The cloak could be anchored against the wind by strings tied across the belly (a feature of his own design), the trousers were vivid sky-blue, the waistcoat pink with white buttons, and the shoes blue suède. No funnier or more magnificent sight was to be seen in London than Mr. Fattish, crash-helmeted, driving on his motor-scooter.

James Frail was in Mr. Fattish's bad books. Fattish didn't approve of Frail, and was not reticent regarding making that fact known to Frail. When Frail was walking in Old Bond Street, and saw Mr. Fattish coming down the road, he quickly hid from his enemy by going quickly into an art gallery called the Mazford Gallery, which was at the corner of Haze Street and Old Bond Street.

He looked round at the exhibition of James Brady's work that was upon the walls. Many of the paintings were sold and the exhibition had the measles.

Of the unsold paintings the one he particularly liked was one called 'Jaundice in Italy', a painting known to my readers rather intimately.

By the way we thought our more particular readers—the

ones who like to know the why and wherefore of everything—would like to know just what led up to, and caused, the entry of Mr. Frail into the Mazford Gallery. So we have explained in great detail the cause and effect, and the links in the chain. Our statements regarding character and appearance were inserted because we didn't want to leave anything out that might, unknown to us, have been a contributory factor: for we know how demanding our 'detective story' readers are, and how they want *all* the facts, be they relevant or *seemingly* irrelevant: we do wish to be as co-operative as possible. We are sure that our more perceptive readers will detect, amongst the facts about character and appearance just given to them, certain things which we had not realized were contributory causes for directly or indirectly making Mr. Frail enter the gallery wherein our prologue story really begins.

.   .   .   .   .

Mr. Frail 'bought' the painting and owed all the cost to the gallery. He gave his name and address, and took in return the painting, which he carried home with him.

The gallery waited a long time for the money but none was forthcoming. So they wrote. Getting no answer, they called at 17 Bloodbury Street, the address Frail had given, but his landlady said he had moved. So the gallery and Brady gave up the chase.

Some time later the following advertisement appeared in *The Times* personal column: 'Typical Brady still life for sale. Write BOX. . . .'

The gallery asked a friend of theirs to write inquiring after the painting, as they were curious to know who was selling a Brady painting in this way, and they had faint suspicions anyway.

Receiving a reply the friend went to see the painting and was shown it by a friend of the owner. It turned out to be 'Jaundice in Italy'.

So the gallery contacted the police, and a bailiff went and took the painting away.

The gallery was not allowed to have the painting, because legally it belonged to Frail, peculiar as it may seem.

The powers that be put it into an auction sale. That is the procedure in such cases. The painting, because it was badly advertised, and auctioned at an auction room that didn't normally sell paintings, sold for ten pounds, which Brady eventually received, minus auction-room commission. The painting was originally priced at seventy pounds.

2

The Royal Academy of Arts had its Summer Exhibition every year. Professional painters and amateur painters submitted their work to the Selection Committee, and if it passed that, the work was subject to the hazards of the Hanging Committee. The Hanging Committee were hanging the work of James Brady.

'It is so big, this painting: it takes up enough space for thirty smaller paintings. Do you think it really deserves to be hung?' said a retrograde member of the old guard, who painted innumerable pictures of Mary Queen of Scots with a very flashy and smooth technique. He looked at the huge painting before him with obvious distaste, and puffed at his pipe to ease away the pain.

'Of course it deserves to be hung. I think it ought to be in the main room,' replied a young man with a big black beard and grubby corduroy trousers.

'Oh no! We can't have it here. Why, when we have our great dinner in the main room, all the dignitaries will have to sit and look at it while they eat. It will put them completely off their food, I think,' said the painter of Mary Queen of Scots, bursting into laughter which transformed his blotchy old face and revealed his decayed and nicotine-stained old teeth: a laugh which seemed to distress his face; giving one the feeling that the old man should really keep from laughing, because his face couldn't stand the strain of so much contortion and movement upon it. His face collected itself once more, and after the storm came the calm. He puffed once more at the pipe and tried not to look at the painting before him.

.   .   .   .   .

16

The Selection Committee had been predominantly radical that year, and despite the protests of members, like the Mary Queen of Scots painter, Brady's painting was hung right above the spot where the hierarchy sat on the Great Dinner Day.

The Press made a great fuss about Brady's ugly painting, and they complained about its being hung just above the head of the Prime Minister when he attended The Great Dinner.

But Brady sold it: and for a great sum too.

.   .   .   .   .

Brady had not seen his painting in the Royal Academy and he rather wanted to. But he was scared to go and look at it for he felt that everybody would recognize him.. So he spent some of the money he had got from the sale of the painting, a multiple self-portrait picture, at a theatrical-costume shop in London. He bought a wig with flowing waves of golden hair. He went also to his optician and procured a pair of pince-nez. Then he settled down to grow a beard, which he treated with hydrogen-peroxide when it was fully mature.

Adequately disguised, and with a Peterson curly pipe stuffed between his golden moustache and his golden beard, Brady managed to make his way round the Royal Academy without being identified.

3

'Oh, Mr. Brady! I adore those paintings of "Still Water in a Blocked-up Guttering"—numbers twenty-three, twenty-four, and twenty-five. I have always wanted someone to paint guttering water *con amore*. How much are they?'

'Well, the big one—the six feet by five feet one—is three hundred, and the other two are two hundred each.'

'I wonder if my daughter Grace would like one for her bed-room. Or do you think that one called "Clogged-up Carburettor" would please her more?'

'I don't know, Lady Mavis, I'm sure.'

'Hullo, James. This private view of yours is producing a few sales. How many have you sold so far? Let's count the red spots: one . . . two . . . three . . . isn't that one behind Lady Mavis? Yes! That's four . . . and five . . . six . . . why seven already James. Good for you.'

'Well, Sam, the critics have got to have their go at them yet. Those critics are parasites, you know: where would they be without us artists? Heaven knows what Arthur Fascetious-gas will write about them: the last time he did an article on my paintings he devoted three-quarters of the article to writing how he was such an intelligent chap. Then I remember Bernard Haveathem writing that long column of vicious twaddle: they are all frustrated painters those painting critics, you know: they can't paint themselves so they write about painting instead, and don't hide their jealousy either. Oh I say! Look who's come in.'

'Yes, I suppose you are right, James. By the way, did you see that wonderful breakdown lorry outside the gallery? I don't know why it's there, but wouldn't it be wonderful to paint?'

'Screech! Screech! Ooh! Ooh! Mr. Brady! How wonderful to see you in person. I've never seen you at one of your private views before. I've always wanted to meet you. I just *love* your paintings. They *all* remind me of the Alps and I've spent some of my happiest days in the Alps: that lovely thick paint with all those valleys and mountains in it. *Lovely*. I don't care what the subject is—I just love the paint!'

'Excuse me, Mr. Brady. I'm from the *Daily Puerile*. Can I take a photograph of you with one of your paintings. Look, I've brought along a huge advertisement paint-tube for you to hold, and a paint-brush.'

4

Brady frowned over the statement he had received from his gallery. It was a statement of what the gallery owed him, what pictures he had sold, and what items the gallery had charged him for. It looked like this:

18

Proprietors: Mazford Limited.   Directors: V. Mazford,
                                             P. D. Cluckenwell.

Telephone: MAYFAIR 876823

In Account with James Brady, Esq.

Dr.	£.	s.	d.
Frame for 'Multiple portraits of Mrs. Brady' & 6 small frames for early paintings	24	0	0
20% commission on Mural for American Steel and Copper Company	500	0	0
Cartage	10	6	0
Frame for 'Dead Sailor'	10	0	0
" " 'Self Portrait with books'	5	0	0
" " 'Mrs. Brady & donkey'	7	0	0
Structure on back of 'Lady Diana Slade' ..	3	0	0
London Group fees	3	0	0
Commission on portrait of Lord Hoorish ..	45	0	0
33⅓% on £3609 12 9	1203	4	3

April 7th. Cheque

At this point Brady lit a cigarette and leant back in his
chair exhausted. Then he added up the figures and checked
wearily the total given by the gallery. It didn't seem to be
correct so he went through the figures again. Then he turned
to the adjoining column.

		Cr.	£.	s.	d.
Dec.	8	Balance owing	523	0	0
"	20	'Multiple portraits of Mrs. Brady' ..	100	0	0
"	20	'Dead Sailor'	100	0	0
"	20	'Mrs. Brady & donkey'	105	0	0
"	20	'Lady Diana Slade'	105	0	0
Jan.	6	'Bert Sand & ball'	157	10	0
"	7	'Jennifer & doll'	157	10	0
"	10	'Baby & roses'	1000	0	0

. . . Brady could not make head or tail of it all and leaving
the statement he went to bed.

PART ONE

1 James Brady: Painter

JAMES was a painter of pictures in oil-colours. The paintings were large, perhaps ugly, vigorous, and brutal. He was a success and made money from his so-called 'awful' giant creations on canvas or hardboard.

James Peter Alfred Brady was uncouth, fat, bespectacled, and balding. James Brady had a frowning, glowering, egotistical appearance; brutish, alive, and selfish was James, with a receding forehead curving back nakedly over the top of his head, between greying hair on the sides. Bull-necked, heavy in body, a constant cigarette inserted in his full lips amidst the ugliness of his piggish face, Brady looked perpetually self-conscious, and looked sometimes intelligent and sometimes purely animal, uncontrollably emotional. He was a child emotionally, but sometimes very adult intellectually. Sometimes Brady's emotions ruled him and he became impulsive, dictatorial, overbearing, arrogant, and debased. It is not to be said that our Brady was unaware of this failing. On the

23

contrary Brady was aware of it. When his emotions were calm and passive Brady used his intellect a great deal. Often when his emotions were not calm Brady would control them with his higher self. But there were times when Brady's emotions ruled him, and then Brady was a fool, any man's mug, and in the hands of Fate.

Let me try and explain Brady the animal, Brady the lustful emotionalist, Brady debased.

Once upon a time, as the story-books used to say, Brady stood in front of his painting, a big bulging figure in the midst of the agonies and emotions of creation. His eyes were alive, feverish, full, and dark. Above his eyes were to be seen contracted muscles on the lower forehead, above and between the eyebrows. His forehead was corrugated with worry lines, and some distance away his ulcers hurt terribly.

Angry brush-strokes covered the canvas in front of him. He picked up on his brush some Prussian blue, and drew with it into the sticky wet mass of paint intended to be a door. He felt very uncomfortable. Cigarette smoking, he dimly thought, was not as good as it was cracked up to be. The smoke got into one's eyes, behind one's spectacles, and the cigarette burnt one's mouth. Then he realized his cigarette was all used up, and that the stub was very very short, burning him. Unhappily he relieved himself of the cigarette, and lit another one, by holding the old to the new.

Wearily, his eyes aching, his stomach burning with acid, the artist rushed to the kitchen to get a glass of milk. He drank it hopefully but his stomach still hurt, the milk had not absorbed the acid. He stood for a while, motionless, thinking.

Back at his canvas he drew some more with Prussian blue, wiped his hands on a turpsy rag, and went over to the telephone. He looked for a moment at the black shapes, with the gleaming punctured circle, and lifted the speaking and hearing part. He inserted his finger in the chromium holes, and drew his finger down. He watched the letters and numbers, as the chromium holes revolved back across them to their original places. He repeated this six times, and then listened impatiently.

Very often when he was fed up he rang his gallery, on some pretext, just so he could talk to someone. The relief of talking to someone was short, because his impatient manner bored the person in the gallery, and that person soon terminated the conversation.

Brady listened to the impatient ringing, and the sound jarred on his taut nerves, making the acid run into his stomach even more. Lines of pain were across his face, and his eyes burned in his head. His full mouth was compressed into a vicious brutal line, and his eyes stared fixedly.

The line rang and rang, and Brady stood tense with mounting disappointment. Jamming the hopeless thing down into its cradle, the man stood unhappily smoking his cigarette, glancing now and again across the room at his painting. He looked bitterly at the huge Victorian sideboard in front of him, littered with ashtrays, a diary, concertina letter-files, a roll of drawing-paper fixed with an elastic band, a record-player dusty with a Louis Armstrong long-player on it, a round tin of antiseptic ointment (he was very afraid of impetigo), and writing materials. From the flat top of the carved wood sideboard rose three mirrors set in carved wooden verticals and topped impressively with more carved wood. He walked round his vast piece of furniture in his studio, and looked guardedly at himself in one of the mirrors. What he saw did not alter his mood, and his soul felt imprisoned, longing to be free, emotionally free and emotionally active. He wished he wasn't so fat. He wished he was this, he wished he was that. But he was satisfied with himself at the same time: was he not a successful painter? Was he not four years before a student living on five pounds a week, most of it spent on depravity? Was he not six years before living on less money with no hope about the future? Yes, he was satisfied; his paintings sold for three hundred pounds each in England, and in New York they were priced at between fifteen hundred dollars and thirty hundred dollars.

He strode out of the large Edwardian room that served as a studio, and walked across the hall, and through the glass-covered corridor that led to the garden. Picking up a butcher's axe, he walked down the garden, to the oddly constructed

26

bird-cages he had built, where he began to savagely attack the cages with his axe. Bearing the detached pieces of wood in his hands, he returned up the garden, to the tiled area outside the windows of his studio, where he began to chop firewood. He sweated easily, and soon his brow was very wet and he chopped wood mistily seen through sweat-covered lenses. He chopped away in frustration, subconsciously seeking a fuller life, an outlet for his high emotionalism.

Down drove the peculiarly shaped axe into the vertical of clean white wood. He enjoyed the sight of the new sides of the split, areas of wood that had never seen the light of day before. A drop of perspiration trickled down his upper lip into his mouth, and steam was in front of his face. Down went the axe to the right of the wood-gripping fingers of his left hand. Brand-new wood was revealed: clean, fresh, yellow-white. Down went the axe, open split the vertical of wood. He selected a new piece of wood, and split it down three times, his vest soaked and clinging to his ribs and spine. Intolerant of his job, and irritated by his sweat-soaked vest and blurred lenses, he swung the axe perilously near his wood-holding left-hand fingers. He checked himself, called himself a fool, and went on carefully.

The chopped wood stacked by his studio fire, he sat down and warmed himself. It was not enough: his life. He must have more. But how?

He was imprisoned in the prison of his successful ordered existence. His marriage was happy, his child of three a delight. Part of Brady, a big part, loved the prison he was in, a self-made prison of his love for his wife, his child, his art, his sound economy. Brady didn't want to bust any of that prison up, but part of Brady longed to break loose for a short spell.

Brady resumed work on his canvas, had a meal; watched his television with his wife, gloomily reviewed his dramaless day, and, taking off his shoes, coat, spectacles, and trousers, placed his fifteen stones of genius-containing personage beside his wife, and assailed her tired mind with uninterrupted speech for three-quarters of an hour, before he finally slipped into the arms of Morpheus.

He had his life all organized. Well organized. He had built

himself a life, by ambition, hard work, and some talent. He had then fitted himself into this life, squeezed himself in, until he was there within the life he had created for himself, kidding himself he was satisfied, but really cramped and suffocated, like a fat waist imprisoned in a tight corset, longing for freedom. His dreams that night were intense, his soul ran free in his dreams, and his body threshed about in the bed, the sheets creased and folded with the forms of his figure. His wife slipped from the bed and went to sleep elsewhere. But his dreams continued. The cell door was open for a while.

Dreamily he heard his wife's voice. Dreamily he saw his paper and letters placed on the half of his pillow that didn't sink beneath his head. Blurred was the image of his tiny son looking at him. Muzzy was the sight of a cup of tea in his wife's hands. Did he want to start another day of frustration and headaches? He tried to find sleep again, but the early-morning noises were against him. He began to sit up in bed, and sourly reached for his cup of tea, looking with jaundice at the letters on his pillow. The cell door clanged shut and he began another day. But not at all eager to begin it he stayed between the sheets for hour after hour, thinking about the cage around him: he did not think of cages or prisons, or of escape, rather did he long for escape subconsciously, and consciously he thought of such things as the monotony of work, of the monotony of his days, of the similarity of his days, of the comfortable life he lived, of its success, of its deadness, of its weary, weary pointlessness.

Another day. He looked from the bed at the bedroom, and called in vain for his son to amuse him. He stared at the Press cuttings on his blanket-covered pelvis, his name in the papers: he should be happy. But he was happy. He had all he wanted. But deep down the animal longed for life, for wild emotionalism, unfettered by controlling sensible thoughts.

He shaved ruthlessly, and the blood ran.

Another day. He came through the bathroom door and entered his studio. He made a fire and started work. But as he worked through the morning, drawing well with paint, a successful man, with money in the bank, and love for his wife and boy, his emotional soul stayed hungry, refusing to be content. Where would it all end? Surely a break-out would come some day. Brady was not really happy.

But Brady loved order. Brady loved a well-ordered life, a life in control. By such loves Brady caged the animal within himself that longed to roam the dark jungles of emotional, lustful experience. The animal writhed in its cage, tearing at the bars, rocking the flimsy cage till it seemed the cage would burst. Would the cage stand the strain? Can we find the answer by looking at Brady's face? As I wrote before, Brady's brow sloped back, his neck was like that of a bull, his eyes were dark and glowering, his mouth was sensuous and full above a relentless chin and heavy curving jowls, and above the eyes bulged contracted frown-muscles. Would the animal come uppermost in such a man, or would the intellect discipline and rule the emotions and lusts, the violence, and the greed for drama and high-powered events? Look at him again. Perhaps the visage, when the man is working at creating a work of art, when the man is trying to create a noble thing, will show signs of the man above the animal. Let us look. The face is changed, it appears. Faces change from one minute to the next. The head is not thrust forward on the neck now in a brutish way. It is held erect, and the eyes are clear and controlled. The brow is clear and the face is calm. The darkness has gone from the face, the face is no longer working angrily, contorting itself brutishly. The chin is up, not sunk on the sternum of the chest. The mouth is composed nicely, and the eyes are clear as glass. The spine is not curved, but it is straight.

Slowly the head sinks forward and down. Slowly the eyes become blurred and dark. The mouth scowls and sulks. The face darkens and begins to work brutally. The shoulders curve and the spine slopes a bit forward.

What will happen? Will this man control himself and remain steady? He has a lot to control. He has to control himself every minute of the day.

Look at this picture: A huge black gorilla in a cage. Seven feet high is this brute, long powerful arms, vast hairy chest, and thick short legs. Nothing holds back his search for the satisfaction of his lusts—if he is in his jungle. His eyes are fierce with an orange light, and he will kill to clear a path to his desires. But he is in a not-too-strong cage. If a person opened the cage door, ever so slightly, for an instant, the beast would be out, free and terrible.

It is not difficult to see why I have shown you this picture.

Brady smoothed his forehead with his finger-tips, lit a cigarette, and angrily went on working. His wife had forgotten to make him any eleven o'clock coffee. Outside his studio windows his son poured sawdust from one toy lorry to another, and chanted the noise of a car's engine incessantly. In one place on the canvas Brady's paint was half an inch thick. He moved the brush in the vermilion on his palette, and thought about it being twenty shillings a tube. The cell door was securely locked, and the huge hands of the gorilla on it could not make any difference—yet. Brady burnt his lips on a neglected burnt-down cigarette, quivered with pain, and stamped out the tiny stub on the wooden floor. He lit another cigarette straight away and went on working. He chain-smoked for ninety minutes.

2 The café

THE café was small, a workers' café, used by lorry-drivers
and road-mending labourers. A bus-driver, a bus-conductor,
and a grey-white-faced middle-aged man, sat at a table in the
corner nearest the door. A youth with teddy-boy tendencies
opened a meat pie at another table, spread sauce over the
contents by moving the heavy slow belt of dark-brown issuing
from the unwiped sauce-bottle opening—by moving this
issuing mass in a graceful curve over the uneven surface of the
opened pie—and then he closed the pie's manufactured-looking
pastry cover on top of the rest of the pie, and began to manipu-
late a knife and a fork, his head bent forward, his hair all over
his forehead. Cups of tea were on a few tables. At another
table sat a tramp, asleep in not the best of positions, a cup of
tea on the table in front of him, his shoulders sagged, his chin
dug into his chest, and the whole of him askew. Behind the
counter, immersed in an atmosphere of flurry, scurry, hurried
orders across the counter, hurried orders to the girl who let

the kitchen know what it should know, smells, and steam, was a typical low-class café owner, his face white like the pickled human flesh of the museum of the Royal College of Surgeons. The place was warm, and it was cosy with the smells of cooking and the feeling that the place was so often full of humanity, eating, talking, smoking, and swearing. The girl was young with no personality, thin yellow hair, watery eyes, and a white apron. Her existence at the time was just a matter of nervously muttering, 'Bacon-and-eggs, bread, butter, and tea for two,' or something similar, after it had been hastily yapped at her by the café owner. As one saw her behind the counter, as one ordered one's cup of tea from the owner, she seemed submerged in waves of instructions and the transmitting of those instructions to the kitchen. She didn't seem to exist, just a ghost and a slave, buried in nervous activity.

The huge chromium tea-container rose gleaming from the counter, where wrapped chocolate biscuits and sandwiches resided, and cups of tea hit the counter top, overflowing, and making seas of orange tea, through which silver and copper coins were wetly pushed.

Bus-drivers loved the café, it was a haven of rest. The only deficiency was that the girl was servile, sexless, and uninteresting. The labourers and bus-drivers would have preferred a confident sex-rushing piece, falsely padded and eager for banter.

Outside the main road hummed and roared with traffic, the pavements were seldom quiet at that time of the day.

Across the road was an attractive waste piece of mud, holed and hilly, covered with bits of grass, cigarette packets, old tins, and old bottles. Cross this dirt- or mud-flat, and you came to the market, on a bigger mud-flat, where big discs of old clothes lay on the ground, and big discs of kettles, oddments, and pieces lay on the dry mud too, surrounded by disreputable people and an encouraging salesman: between the spreads of things for sale were puddles, quite a few of them.

Some people turn their noses up at this sort of thing: are they not right? Or are they right?

Out of the steamy windows of the café the men inside

could see a vast advertisement facing them across the road.
They could also see, if they looked in the same direction, the
back of the menu card in the window, and the typists walking
along the pavements. Odd as it may seem, bus-driver Fred
and errand-boy Marty preferred to look at the 'dollies' on the
pavement, rather than the sweaty back of the menu card. The
window tables were rather popular, and the passing scene
viewed from them was of interest to all the customers; to
those interested in cars, to those interested in lorries, to those
interested subconsciously in the visual aspect of a road, and to
those—the majority—who were interested in the lively young
ladies who passed by and who sometimes reacted favourably
to the meaningful glances aimed at them. The tramp at a side
table could not care less about the glories of the main road to
the city. Perhaps he had not slept well the previous night.

At about eleven in the morning a crowd of workmen
crowded into the small café, and pleased the heart of the
owner because of their company and custom. When it was a
day that was warm enough, the door would be left open. The
girlies passing by would be carefully enjoyed by the relaxing
happy workmen in the café, and, when a forty-inch chest with
a pair of hot eyes above it passed by, a deep guttural noise,
as from the zoo, would swell from the café to the apparition,
who would be embarrassed or smug according to her character.
The particular noise of male appreciation on these occasions
was part yearning, part defensive jeering, part good-humoured
praise, and part Chessington Zoo: a very remarkable sound,
sometimes made by university students, rarely by clerks,
never by the fair sex, and never by clergymen, or boys under
the age of three years. Darwin was right, of course.

At eleven-thirty one morning the café was full of cynical,
open-eyed, smoking workmen, each with his cup of tea and
bun or cake in front of him, and each operating his own paper-
tube chimney. They sat there in a mass, thinking individual
animal thoughts, and reacting to intruders with a solid crowd
reaction, partly hostile: was it not their café after all? Wasn't
the workman with his union behind him the strongest man in
the country with so many rights and more rights he indiscrimi-
nately established whenever he cared to. They had had

C   33

elevenses at this café for two weeks now: whose café was it if it was not theirs? A? What! Anybody else who wanted a cup of tea or coffee at that café, at that time, had better walk in with humility. From 11 a.m. to 11.30 a.m. Jack Barker's Café belonged strictly to the carpenters, plumbers, and labourers from the new building-site one hundred yards away. An individualist walked in, and felt the hostility, and felt therefore nervous. He braced himself and marched stiffly to the counter, halted sharply with nerves, the eyes of the café on him, and briskly ordered a cup of tea. 'Go it, soldier!' reached his ears, and he drank hurriedly, and left quickly amidst titters. So Jack Barker's Café was cruel when it cared to be. The men settled down again to look for some more passing sex, some talking 'pots', back axles, and new cars, some talking about union matters, and some glancing at the strip cartoons in the daily rag.

Suddenly there was silence. A poor poet stood outside. The silence was fierce and like a sheet of steel across the café. But the poet wanted a cheap cup of tea, and he did not realize that the café would soon be empty. Eyes in the café were hard and tinged with jeering. Plumbers and carpenters, when in a crowd together, with union membership cards in their pockets, don't like single individualists, and like even less, sensitive-eyed and gentle-mouthed poets, in corduroy jackets, and high leather boots covered by pale blue jeans, smoking hand-made cigarettes with frightened elegant movements of the arms and hands. They had a name for them, a name used for chaps who drop bricks and drainage pipes baked in heat, a name used for chaps who say please softly and pleadingly, a name used for chaps who mix concrete in the wrong proportions. The men in the café used it clearly as they watched the drip come in for his cup of tea.

His hair was long and over his back collar. His nails were long and very clean. A captivating arty fringe ran parallel with his eyebrows, and his eyes were hazel. He was long, elegant, too graceful, and too soft. A pipe hung in his outer breast pocket, bowl visible, a very nice touch visually. A beard curled well from his chin, and his voice was very high-falutin', and it was listened to by all in the expectant silence that ruled Jack Barker's hygienic food house. Even the spineless girl stood still and watched and waited, mockery in her weak eyes.

A cup of tea was pushed contemptuously through a puddle of stale brown tea on the counter, and the poet looked at his reflection in the side of the big tea-urn of chromium. The poet tried hard to think of the poetry of chromium reflections, steam, and dim hard faces viewed through tears.

'You don't arf get them sometimes, don't you,' jeered a plumber. And his mates laughed too loudly.

'You can't drink soup with them 'airy mouths, Bill. It all gets soaked up in the 'air.'

The poet leant an elegant and bony elbow on the counter, where it was dry, and adjusted himself into a pose Botticelli would have eagerly drawn: he dropped one hip, bent one knee, curved his neck back, and gazed at the far ceiling. He pretended he was deaf. Behind that pose his heart had melted into water. A lorry-driver came in, brushed him rudely, and ordered his drink in a very powerful masculine voice, making it quite clear that he did not approve of girls with beards.

The poet ran a moist finger down the sweating chromium tea-urn and decided not to light his pipe. The grace and elegance of the procedure would be lost on the low creatures in the café anyway.

So I have set the scene for James Brady to enter one day in the future, when the poet has gone, and the union members have used the café for two months.

3 Esmerelda

IN THE staff-room of an art school sat an art mistress, twenty-four years of age, lonely, miserable, and well qualified to teach art students as regards her own personal talent, which was a good sensitive talent. But she was unstable mentally and had had a couple of serious breakdowns in the past, one just after her first year of puberty, and one when she was working in Bayswater in a vast factory-like teashop owned by a man she met in Russia when she was an infant: the teashop was very good, and nothing about the shop's treatment of its employees caused her breakdown. Lack of love from her aunts, a pet terrier's hate, and an unstable background were the causes of her feeble mind. She taught in Malvern.

Dark straight hair cascaded down across her shoulders, and she had the frail pathetic body and arms popular in the art schools. Great dark eyes brooded with melancholy, and she allowed a huge long lock of hair to stay fallen over her face, over one eye and down across one cheek. Bright red calf-socks contrasted with the wickerwork basket at her feet, that held money in a purse, many pencils, a book on Van Gogh, a book on Renoir, a book on Manet, and a diary in leather with a key-locked metal fixture. No make-up was on her face; and it was pale and strained. Her deep dark eyes were crossed now and again with desperate lights. She was writing poetry, very personal poetry, bad poetry, incoherent poetry, about a lover of hers (who didn't exist), who was a lark who flew away across the fields in the dawn.

This lady was a virgin, and virginal ladies of twenty-four who would rather not be so are very often in a bad state of frustration. Her mental frailty, coupled with her longing to be loved, caused her mind to be very near breaking-point. Teaching in an atmosphere of unrestrained adolescent feelings was also a great strain on this poor lady.

The last end-of-term party she had attended had hurt her deeply and shattered her brittle self-containment. She was just getting over it. The end-of-term party was very gay, very uninhibited, rather wild, and displayed rather a lot of released emotions and free love-making. The students embracing each other, the teachers embracing students, and the vague figures behind the dark trees in the dark of the school grounds, had been a hard series of things for her to see.

Now the new term had settled in, and the party was like a bad dream, dreamed vividly long ago.

She wrote poetry in the staff-room, and waited for the lesson that was her responsibility to commence. Other members of the staff came into the room, but she hid her head by bowing it, and the hair down its sides moved further forward, forming an opened curtain over her face. The pencil moved over the paper, and the stupid poetry rushed from her heart in torrents, a slight release of her pent-up feelings. She looked up a bit from her paper, and, still with bowed head, she observed the male trouser legs moving to and fro around her, and she heard the male chatter cut across now and then by a happy flattered female voice, musical and gay. She frowned and scribbled on, her spotty unhealthy face pale between the curtains of greasy dark hair. When she arose to go to her teaching it could be seen that she had a good figure beneath her dark dress, and her face could be beautiful if the joy of being loved was in it, instead of the pain of being so alone. A tragic sad person finding little sympathy from her pupils.

The bell had rung and classes were changing. In the corridor students rushed hither and thither. A beard and a pipe, long skirts and wickerwork baskets, drawing-boards and books, rushed by. Long strings of beads bounced on flat chests and curved with full ones. Pony-tails and long long hair on the girls, greased wavy quiffs and long long hair on the boys. A boy with an easel, a girl with paint on her dress and paint-brushes in her hands. Turmoil after the ringing of the bell. A girl with a dedicated, sincere, heavy face, in a smock covered with paint-brush wipings. A young man with a bow-tie, an imbecilic grin, a burnt-umber oil-colour smeared absent-mindedly on his artistic brow, chattering inanely in sandals and bright yellow socks. Gay, gay student life. The turmoil of changing classes. A fifteen-year-old boy in a lower class, wishing to be back at the telly. The dream-girl of the school, bangles, bracelets, and beads, huge eyes encircled with black, with a pale vacancy inside the encirclement of generously applied mascara, four youths around her, all happy in her personal atmosphere of sex. Flat heels, low low skirt hems, hair in rats'-tails, and some with reddened mouths: the girls. The boys with boxes of paints, and rolls of drawing-paper, some in jeans, some in Marlon Brando leather jackets. Half teddy-girls, half teddy-boys. Part middle-class daughters in appearance and part art-school girls in appearance. Full arty types, veterans of the school, mixed with newcomers just from secondary schools. Gradually the noise died down and the corridor emptied. Classes began: dress-making, the anatomy class, the drawing from the nude-figure class, and the painting classes. The unhappy mad lady began to teach. In the deserted corridor outside, the school's principal joked with an off-duty painting master. The glamour girl of the school hurried to her class, along the quiet corridor. The principal winked at the painting master, and they both stared happily at her until she vanished behind a closing door. They went on talking about the unhappy, mad, lady teacher, but the principal didn't know of her previous breakdowns. The principal suggested to the painting teacher that she needed a man. The man in charge of the painting laughed like rich mahogany through his lemon beard, and swore to himself he would substitute glue for oil paint in the paint tubes that were only for his personal use, so that thieving students who tried to pinch his paint would, upon using it, find themselves in a very sticky situation: theft revealed and hands webbed with glue. Passing across a piece of paper, the principal said he had found a bit of her poetry. The lemon beard read it, fingering a tin of semi-liquid glue filling up his coat pocket, while the principal stood by. Lemon raised his eyebrows significantly and returned the paper. The interview she had before the governors was good from her point of view, said the rotund principal. Then he said she had changed a lot since then. They parted, the principal to his office, and lemon across the field to the dining rooms a quarter of a mile away. A student was drawing a tree by the field.

Far away in London the mad lady teacher's old uncle swore at her aunt, stole from his wife's handbag, and went out to the boozer. His wife looked sadly at the mirror, and fingered her black eye. She looked at a photograph of her niece, taken on a holiday, looking radiant and fine. A smile creased her face as she thought her niece was away from it all and happy.

The name of the melancholy lady who taught at the art school was Esmerelda. She heard the bell ring for termination of afternoon classes and went to the staff-room to collect her coat. Outside the sky promised rain and inside the noise was high. She muttered good night to a teacher and descended the stairs.

Esmerelda left the art school in the winter dark, a dark blue duffel-coat on her form and the wicker basket in her hand. She pulled up the duffel-coat hood and made her way to the bus, in the midst of a stream of art students disgorged from the school. She queued for the bus in the beginning rain, with art students in front of her and lined up behind her.

She let herself in with her key and climbed the stairs to her room. The stairs were ill-kept and ragged and the walls peeled. Her room was covered from floor to ceiling on the

walls with her paintings, some pictures of herself, some of her
room, some of various sitters she had persuaded to sit for
her in her characterful picture-gallery bedroom. Against her
landlord's wishes she had painted the walls bright orange, and
the ceiling the same. A picture hung on the back of the door
clattered as she closed the door and locked it with the secretive-
ness of the eccentric. Most of the paintings were oil-paint on
paper, and piles of drawings lay on the dressing-table by the
window. She lit the gas-fire and began to prepare a meal.

Down below lived her landlord, an ex-street dustman,
old and solitary, living with his television and a table piled
high with papers. Amongst the papers were solitary oranges,
aged and furry with growth. Dust lay thick, and things were
left to rot or stay where they were: such was the result of the
apathy of solitary old age. The whole house was thick with
dust in all the rooms, and the peace of rooms never lived in,
never disturbed, was through most of the silent house: the
house of an old man who had never married and who had
lived with his cousin for years till she died, leaving him helpless
and caring not about himself. Esmerelda had asked him if he
had ever wanted to marry and he had answered fervently
'rather!' 'Faint heart never won fair lady', applies to her landlord, and 'an inviting look sometimes, gives a girl men friends',
applies to Esmerelda, but where the second saying comes from
is a mystery to me.

Esmerelda ate her meal and began to draw the plates and
food remains. Below the old man wished she was living elsewhere. But she had ignored one notice to quit. He looked
through his steel-held lenses and waited for the television
programmes to begin for the evening, munching away at a
huge peanut-butter sandwich.

.   .   .   .   .

Every term the painting students held what was known
as their sketch-club criticism. A well-known artist was
invited to criticize the work of the members of the sketch
club, and paid a few pounds, and his expenses for doing so,
from the sketch-club funds, which mainly came from the sale
of tickets for the annual play, put on by the students and

staff. Paintings and drawings were hung up on the walls of the painting department, over the field by the sculpture house. The visiting critic was given a good dinner, toadied to by the sketch-club president, and escorted over the field to begin his wearisome task of saying something about the array of bad paintings and drawings displayed before him.

The sketch-club president was a small, wiry, energetic, shock-haired painting student with Communist politics, a bright red tie, an awful lot to say for himself, and a captaincy in the army behind him. He sat down to write a letter to James Brady, inviting him to criticize the next sketch-club array of paintings. He eventually posted the letter, and waited for the artist to reply.

Surprisingly, Brady replied with his promise to attend, and the sketch-club president rushed around telling everyone the news.

    .   .   .   .   .

Esmerelda awoke next morning to the suffocating sight of dozens of her paintings everywhere in her room: dozens of self-portraits staring at her as she sat up in bed, naked and refreshed. She stepped out of bed, slung some bacon in the pan, lit the gas-stove ring beneath the frying-pan, and also lit the gas-fire. As the bacon sizzled, she danced around the room with its windows uncovered by curtains.

People who are slightly mentally unbalanced, because of severe unhappiness in the reality of their life, retire as often as they can into an escapist world of their own creation. When they are in their own little private world they naturally lose touch a bit with the world of reality around them. As Esmerelda often escaped from reality into a private world, she often forgot that the real world of people was around her, and that morning she was unaware that people could see her from the street below her window, as she danced nakedly around, slinging a sausage into the bacon fat in the pan, and pushing potential toast beneath the red-hot grill. Only occasionally did Esmerelda close the curtains, and viewing her was becoming a habit with some of the local lads.

Soon her gaiety wore off and her usual melancholy took

over. She prepared for school, and just before she departed she threw last night's paint-scrapings into the lavatory-pan.

When she was away at school that morning, her landlord was to be seen looking into the lavatory-pan for quite a while, looking at all the paint-scrapings diving in the small amount of water in the neck of the pan. He indulged himself for an hour or two in angry thoughts about how the paint could clog up the pipe from the pan to the sewer, for he had plenty of time on his hands, and then, after his pathetic dinner on the rubbish-piled table, he made a ceremony of going upstairs with a bucket, and fishing out the paint, which he put in the bucket, muttering to himself all the while.

It was a funny thing: they both thought each other mad.

One day, it was a Sunday, Esmerelda heard unanswered knocking at the front door. She stood in her room painting a self-portrait on a piece of paper pinned to the wall.

Going downstairs, and realizing that the house was empty but for her, she opened the door, revealing her landlord's younger brother. She had heard of this brother: he had designed his own version of the snooker-pool table, so her landlord had told her with some senile pride. Inside the house she listened to the brother's pity for her landlord and the hopeless way he lived in chaos, squalor, and dust. She agreed politely with the brother about the tragedy of her landlord,

eventually showed him to the door, and resumed painting. They both thought each other mad: Esmerelda and her ancient landlord.

4 The Lambretta

THINKING about his wife's first pregnancy, which was at a time when he had not much money, and she had suffered rather in consequence, and thinking of her second pregnancy which was also a grim affair resulting in a still-born child, Brady wrote out a cheque for two hundred pounds and sent his wife to buy a motor-scooter, so that in her next pregnancy she would be able to do her shopping transportation in comfort, for she shopped at the bottom of a large hill that led up to Brady's home right at the top. Her next pregnancy, he resolved, would be in a setting of warm fires, more housekeeping money, and warmer clothes. While she purchased the red machine from a very casual salesman, Brady went on painting.

Up in Norfolk, Brady and his wife had some friends who lived in a farmhouse. An ex-art student with a huge British-Jap face, topped with piles of crinkly hair, a cleft jaw, a great mouth, and slanty chink eyes, 'ran' the farm with his wife, a dark-haired girl with an intense small face that glittered with charm and energy. The wife had adapted herself to farm life very well, with a resulting surprising change in her: from a sophisticated, much-sought-after, casual art student, gay and party-going, she had changed into a cross between a proper country-woman and a town-bred artist lady, slightly slovenly in appearance, coarser and fuller in character and body than she was before. The husband had lived most of his life on the farm, and the change in him was the change of passing from irresponsible bachelor life to slightly more responsible married life.

The great British-Jap derivative had an old house by his ancient farmhouse, which he transformed into a studio, where he spent most of his time painting terribly good paintings, letting the farm go from bad to worse. Most of the work on the farm was done by another ex-art student who was the third of the trio on the farm. Tall, hunchbacked, and bearded, he had dark curling hair, a bunched-up face, and knobbly forms: he looked like an elongated gnome. Active from morn till night, the backbone of the farm was unmarried, a jack-of-all-trades, and surly.

.   .   .   .   .

His son deposited with a kindly housewife, Brady and his wife went down on their Lambretta to stay at the farm.

Brady's wife was six foot tall, black-haired and with savage, bloody birth-mark blotches all over her face. It must seem inconceivable that such a woman could be beautiful but she was, despite her disfigurement.

Intending to look at some houses in Norfolk, south of Norwich, Brady and his wife mounted the Lambretta, unprotected by crash-helmets, but very well wrapped up, and set off on their journey. Brady stopped at the approach to a town, dismounted, and handed over the machine to his wife, who drove it to a garage for more petrol, while Brady rested in a public garden, reading about how Stirling Moss had lost the world championship by riding the race of his life, in the day's paper.

Refilled with petrol and oil, Brady's Lambretta continued

its journey through country roads, round unsuspected bends, and in between fields and trees. Brady was clothed in a corduroy jacket he had bought in an Italian market in Rome for six shillings, over which was a black leather jacket he had bought for somewhat more at the same place (from a pile on the ground, by the side of a stall selling piles of cigarette ends) and on top of which was a twelve pounds new calf-length coat. On his hands were new, black-leather, fur-lined gloves. Two pullovers, a shirt, and a vest added to the bulk of his originally bulky-enough body. On his legs were a pair of his father-in-law's discarded combinations, held together with a safety-pin, a pair of pyjama trousers, a pair of jeans, and his best pair of trousers. Two pairs of socks and a stout pair of shoes added to his very warm and devastating appearance. His wife had many many clothes on her also.

The pair decided to have a look at the sea, so they followed the signposts, and roared along a straight stretch of road at forty miles an hour. They pulled up at a little village, and the wife purchased some milk and food, while the man wandered around the village on the machine, much to the amusement of two young girls.

Now Brady was in a high-strung state of nerves, due to the strain of driving for so long whilst a learner. The meaningless laughter of the girls angered Brady, and viciously he ordered his wife to remount, whilst he packed away the milk and food in the bag between his knees. Violently kicking the kick-start pedal, he mounted, jammed the handle into gear, and twisted the throttle. Soon third gear was reached, and the machine roared down a straight country road, Brady's hand slowly turning the accelerator twist-grip. Ahead of them the road changed into an old Roman road and went up a hill between dark-brown fields. Where the road changed to a Roman road, Brady suddenly realized that the road he was on continued not into the Roman road but curved on. Realizing his mistake, Brady tore on, laughing to his wife. On went the road straight as far as Brady's myopic eyes could see. The girls in the village: their laughter still angered him, and Brady roared past a man with a shotgun, watching by the roadside. The seeming disapproval of the gun-man regarding his speed, further angered Brady, and, telling himself it was a straight deserted road, Brady did not slacken speed.

Brady lifted his head, told himself he was happy and felt the wind smack into his face. The little Lambretta wheels revolved faster, the speedometer pointer swung over further to the right, where the forty and fifty figures were marked, the explosions in the cylinder became nearer to one another, making a steady roar of high sound. The road was straight, the joy of seeing the sea was ahead, and Brady twisted the twist-grip accelerator with a black-leather hand.

Then there was bend, a very acute hairpin bend, covered with dead wet leaves. Brady entered the bend hoping it was a slack gentle curve. His mind became a block of tension with adding fear. He saw the bend was a hairpin bend, and he saw the trees had kept the sun off the road and that the road glistened with greasy wetness. His brain seized-up with fear, and he braked with back and front brakes—hard. The wheels ceased to move around, but they moved on the slippery road in an uncontrollable skid, turning the machine completely round. Brady was thrown to the road and he rolled over and over, protected by his complete wardrobe. One lense of his spectacles was smashed, and one side piece torn from the myopia correctors. Brady's forehead was covered with blood, which, when he regained his feet and put on his spectacles again, picking them up from the road surface, trickled down behind his lenses and on to his cheeks.

The sight of his wife, unconscious on the road, flat on her back, puffing foam from her lips, drove him crazy. He walked around her yelling for her to come back from the dead. But she was only in concussion.

Brady cried wildly on the deserted road, his hands acting madly. He stared at his wife through one good lens and one shattered lens, blood falling down his face, a mass of blood on his brow.

.   .   .   .   .

You will by now have realized that Brady was an angry man. A man who tried hard to control himself, but who failed sometimes, as he did when he caused the Lambretta accident. His wife in the local hospital with concussion, Brady stayed at the British-Jap's farm, shooting at unfortunate sparrows with his double-barrelled shotgun and sevenpenny cartridges in large numbers. Brady realized how his temper got the better of him and he was sickened by his weakness. He roamed the fields of the farm in great, white, paratrooper's boots, his gun in his hands, safety-catch off, and death to sparrows, blackbirds, pigeons, partridges, pheasants, rabbits, and hares in his eyes. Considering that he could hardly see out of one swollen, blackened, reddened eye, below a dressing on the forehead, and peering through a shattered pane of glass, and considering he was badly shocked and made a lot of noise at the wrong times, it is not surprising that he fired sixty-two five-shot, twelve-bore cartridges, and killed one robin red-breast at a range of two yards, and a sparrow that sat in a tree, singing to him, silhouetted against a clear sky. Brady took it out on the birds, or intended to, and the roar of the gun when the pins hit the metal cartridge-ends went well with his desperate soul.

Why, Brady asked himself, should he have been taunted by the laughter of two village girls, into tearing around Norfolk at speed into a smash-up, that might have killed his large and beloved wife? Who luckily now slept in a hospital bed with a screaming headache and one swollen eye, instead of being in a wooden box waiting for burial. Brady knew the answer. Brady knew why. As he waited for the blackbirds to swarm overhead at a low level in the Norfolk sky, Brady answered himself. He was weak. He had a desperate, eager soul that broke out from the chains of discipline at any opportunity. He was tired of himself. Had he to go on like this, a slave to his emotions? Brady squashed the muddy furrows with his large white boots, and fired excitedly at a sparrow that curved round the top of a hedge and clattered into the safety of the hedge-stems. The noise died away across the brown fields and hedges, and he swung the lever between the stock and barrels, opening the gun, letting curling wreaths of grey smoke issue from the steel circles at the barrel beginnings. He raised the barrels to the sky, and looked down them, or up them to be correct: dirty curls of smoke hung almost motionless in the barrels, and Brady inserted two more red cardboard cylinders with brass ends. The brass detonator-ends rested in the encircling steel-barrel rings, and Brady closed the gun: the safety-catch clicked automatically to reveal a yellow word SAFE, and Brady immediately covered the word with the slide of metal. Weak, weak, weak! He knew it and became petulant, angry. His failure to shoot accurately made him even more petulant, and he staggered on wildly in search of a victim to vent his spite upon. He checked himself and called himself a fool. Digging in his coat pocket he extracted a packet of Player's from down the side of the box of twenty-five cartridges, and lit a cigarette. The cartridges clanked in his pocket in their card box as he stumbled on, fretting with a sense of his inadequacy. His emotional soul ruled him, he thought. One rotten day it would make him do God knows what foolishness. He was wild with the fear of his weakness, and afraid of the future: what would the future bring a man with a soul that might rise up any day and drive him to desperate acts? Why was he so sensitive to laughter? He hated Brady and Brady hated him. They fired a few more sevenpences, watched the birds fly away, and then they went back to the farm, shooting at the blurred dark shapes flying around the hedges in the darkening sky. His feet were soaking wet, his nerves were tattered, he felt drained and worthless, him and Brady, Brady and him.

Did you shoot anything? he was asked. It galled him to have to say that he had shot about twelve shillings' worth of cartridges, and killed only a robin and a sparrow. It brought home to him his inadequacy: he couldn't even shoot little birds near him with a huge double-barrelled gun, firing scattering shot. That inadequacy, coupled with his awareness that he was not master of his emotional soul, made him feel prideless and wretched. Determined to prove to himself that he could shoot like any sensible man, he stood in the disappearing light, outside the farmhouse, shooting at the birds that lived in the trees and bushes around the low, Elizabethan, timbered building. No birds died, however, but the shooting attracted the attention of the passers-by on the road nearby. Weak with his inadequacy Brady waited in the half-light, a bizarre figure in huge white boots, battered spectacles, a plastered forehead, and with a huge, engraved, metal gun in his hands, a heavy box of cartridges sagging down one pocket of his shapeless, dirty corduroy jacket. The talkative hunchback told him for a long, wearing, quarter of an hour, in the gathering night outside the house, that the time to get partridges is at dawn. They sleep in the middle of fields, he said, and if you walk across the fields at dawn, or late afternoon (when they settle for the night), they may suddenly be disturbed, and fly up in front of you, stupid and flummoxed, and then you can shoot them easily. Brady resolved to show himself he was no fool with a gun the following morning, when he would kill a pheasant for his friend's dinner. He did not know the difference between a pheasant and a partridge. Anyway, one of the two birds slept in the fields, and tomorrow he would disturb them, and find out which one did. Brady was a fool with a gun in his own eyes, but he didn't take into account the two facts: he was in a state of shock, and he could only see properly with one eye. But his lack of faith in himself was established, even more than ever before, and he did not trust himself as his own master. This would help the breakdown to occur one day. When he needed faith in his power to control himself, he would have little faith, and the gorilla would break out of the cage, with dire consequences.

The following morning he was out shooting again: partridges or pheasants did not seem to sleep on this farm, and Brady held his gun, stock on the ground, barrels pointing below his chin, as he lit a cigarette, in the middle of a field. After a while of dispirited puffing, Brady's eyes dropped to the two circles looking up at him, two circles of steel from out of which had come many times ten pieces of deadly shot. It took Brady a long time to realize that the safety-catch might be inoperative, and, when he did realize, he hastily examined the catch, to see if he had been such a fool. He discovered that the gun was set to fire, and his self-esteem dropped a few hundred degrees. One day, he told himself, he would make the Big Fool out of James Brady, and he was right! After all, believe you will do a foolish thing, and by believing it you will surely help yourself to do it. Such is the power of faith misdirected.

A huge hare bounded from a hedge as Brady walked. So surprised was he, that Brady let it get across the field before he fired at it. Then Brady reloaded quickly, amidst curling smoke, and fired two barrels again at a far-away dinner, a dinner far out of range by then. Brady felt sick, and fired six barrels into the clear sky, with rage and deafening noise. The trees mocked him, the twirping, chirping, twittering birds flying away from the other sides of hedges mocked him, the great sky laughed, and the dark-brown fields were bored with him: the wrecked harvester stood uninterested in him, and he, Brady, was lonely and futile. A sense of one's futility leads to desperate acts, and Brady's desperate acts were waiting for him in his future, heralded by his own sense of his futility.

How he wished a gorgeous pheasant lay dead at his feet!

.   .   .   .   .

The old Austin car, 1926 vintage, clattered on its way to the hospital. It was cold in the car, fiercely cold, and Brady's face was pink and his eyes watered. He watched the Norfolk fields race by as the British-Jap, with the high, curving cheek-bones and cluttered teeth, rattled the car over bumps in the road with not enough care for the old back axle. The car was a scratched red, painted long ago, and the Jap smoked a curling pipe that was held insecurely in his dirty teeth: it bumped on his great chin and kept sinking deep into his yellowish lower lip. Clinging over his huge head and abundant thatching the Jap wore a yellow Balaclava helmet marked with oil-paint, and on his hands were green woollen gloves with holes in them. He grinned largely with stained teeth, and then snorted clouds of smoke down his mouth and unshaven chin from his Japanese yellow-red nose. The car bellowed and changed gear, and ground surprisingly strongly up a hill. The seats at the back were piled high with rugs and blankets, and the road could be seen through the floorboards at Brady's frozen feet. Driving the great junk-heap round corners, half as if he were driving a tractor and half as if he owned the road, the Jap seemed to hurl the car along.

Brady glanced at the man at his side, and was sure he saw

pieces of soil shake off from the artist's unpleasantly coloured, greasy cheek. The driver's eyes were blue and clear with wind-forced tears: deep in the eyes was a hate of careful driving, of life, be it his own or that of drivers coming towards him. The speedometer in front of Brady on the old wooden dashboard was faulty and registered fifty: the car was going much faster. The Jap kept his car engine carefully attended to and he had recently put very large tyres on the big wheels. The brakes were very good and needed to be.

The car thundered down the main street of the town, seemingly straight at a bus, but was cleverly swerved round it, and on it thundered with its defective silencer. Why didn't the police stop the car? Brady wondered: but they did not stop it as its great width monopolized the street it raced down. Children cheered the old wreck, their cheers mingled with the flying air, and the Jap's face split from ear to ear in a teethy elephantine grin of triumph and embarrassment. Brady was frightened.

Up the hill to the hospital with its high pretentious front-age. The car slowed down and ploughed its front left mud-guard into some metal barrier. The painters on the scaffolding laughed, and the Jap just sat with his eyes lowered and a forced still laugh quivering on his face, as Brady went inside the building to collect his wife. A black male nurse walked out of the main door as Brady went through the glass swing doors, and the Jap watched the Negro's elbows bounce as he walked along to the new X-ray department.

Brady came out with his wife, who was dizzy and weak. They wrapped her in rugs and blankets, put her in the front, with Brady alone in the back, and drove off.

Brady's wife bumped up and down in the car, and her head cried with pain. Tractors, five of them, constantly crashed together in her head, and her face opened with pain, tears in her eyes.

Back at the farmhouse the logs burned with a blue flame in the fireplace: they were roofing beams from an old house, the beams having been covered for decades with slate tiles. Something from the tiles made the logs burn with a green-blue flame. The wattle-and-daub walls of the room showed the straw in them, and a cat was sick with fur balls it had 'cleaned' from its over-luxurious coat. Sweat poured over Brady's face in the heat and his white boots caked with mud dried by the fire, as he sat drawing himself in a rotten scrap of mirror. The Jap sat talking to Brady's wife, his soily bare feet propped near the fire.

The Jap's wife was pregnant and beaming. The hunchback was reading a book on plumbing. The atmosphere was heavy and stifling, hot and thick; Brady wiped his face with a week-old handkerchief, his hair was wet with sweat. The Jap's face was crimson with the heat as he poked the fire: a huge burning log crashed outwards and the Jap said he was sorry. The cat rolled on its back and stretched its legs immodestly. Brady felt bored and yawned loudly. Brady began to sing and everyone tolerated this politely for half an hour. Brady sang well and the Jap and Brady's wife talked in low voices; Brady was jealous for *he* wished to talk to the wife who had been away from him for a week. He yawned rudely again and trouble began.

The Jap's face became full of blood, his mouth became fierce, and he told Brady to stop, in tense, arrogant terms, but he was justified. Brady shouted tersely back, the Jap strode to him, as he sat there, and clasped the hair of Brady's head, Brady sitting, the Jap standing towering above him. Brady rose and pushed the Jap across the room, till the Jap fell on the floor. From then onwards things gradually mended until peace was established with less help from Brady than from the generous Jap. Brady never apologized, and by all this the gorilla had weakened the cage it was imprisoned within.

Before concluding this chapter we must describe the Jap's character completely, for we must not leave out mention of his finer points. The man was in fact deeply intelligent and had an extraordinarily brilliant brain. The profundity of the man was both surprising and enormous; his knowledge of life was that of Sigmund Freud (no exaggeration here); and aged men in the neighbourhood frequently asked his advice on such subjects as 'How to face the nearby threat of death', or 'How to live the last years of marriage in harmony'. A really wonderful man.

5 The gorilla cage is not so strong

THE brand new Lambretta stood in the repair shop, its forks damaged, its front brake damaged, the back carrier dented, the side foot-rest torn off, its paint scratched, and its kick-start mechanism to be repaired. However, Brady's face was clear and a new pair of gold spectacles adorned his face.

The Lambretta repaired, Brady rode on it with his wife to a small group of shops near his home. Stopping by the roundabout, Brady let his wife dismount to go and look in the Red Cross shop, which sold all kinds of things from children's toys to a flying-suit, from books to furniture, and from shoes to fire-tongs, at a ridiculously low price, this all being a great attraction to Brady's wife who loved an extreme bargain; while he sat on his damaged newly purchased motor-scooter by the side of the road, beaming unhappily at the visual beauty of the scene before him, of passing lorries and swanky new cars bought on hire-purchase, of ravishing housewives, of pretty baby-girls, of yellow-lighted shop-fronts, and gigantic

red buses scorned in the evenings by television viewers. Brady leered uncomfortably at the scene before him, and wished his wife back on the Lambretta seat behind him, and he driving her home through the late afternoon dark, to the little boy asleep in his room, while the battered old wireless issued out quietly its various programmes to the deaf ears of the sleeping boy, a toy car on his pillow, another in his hand, and more on the bed he slept within. The combination of Brady's discomfort and his effort to enjoy himself visually, cast a peculiar look on his cold face. As Brady became more and more impatient with his wife, and his discomfort increased, he beamed harder at the cars, women, and lorries.

On the pavement walked a man and his wife, out shopping for a dressing-table: it had to be 'contemporary' but shiny and smart, and obtainable on hire-purchase of course, like their TV set, tape-recorder, record-player, electric cooker, and refrigerator. It had to be glossy. They also were out shopping for a 'television lamp' set in a miniature ship's steering-wheel. They walked towards Brady's back, interested in it.

As they approached, Brady ached for the return of his blotched-face wife: he was fed up with all the cars, buses, motor-cycles, and lorries that noised past him into the roundabout confusion ahead. Waiting never was a much-sought-after occupation, anyway. He felt cold and neglected. But you can't stay miserable, he thought, got to make life into a happy affair. He tried very hard to enjoy the visual material in front of him—he was a painter, a master of the visual world. He twinkled his eyes, looked as interested as he could, stared fixedly, and tried to lose himself in the visual activity before his eyes. As the husband and wife passed they stared hard at the remarkable sight of Brady trying to be happy: they walked ahead of him, their heads turned over their shoulders, fascinated by Brady's face. Their eyes spoke volumes, eyes that scorned, eyes that were critical, eyes that sneered. Brady bridled as he saw them, and his discomfort crystallized into glassy anger. What the blazes do they think they are looking at? He swore. Indignation took over his mind and reason was left at home where nobody criticized him. The two heads still looked at him in unison, two staring faces over two backs and walking feet. His eyes hard with fury, his mind wild, Brady sang out in a brittle voice a word he had learnt from a scaffold-maker when he, Brady, was ten. The word was lost in the car noises, but Brady's wife heard as she came over to the scooter, and she did her best to tell Brady how she didn't like such behaviour. Scared of his temerity, Brady growled at her to get on the seat, and when she was on, he drove to the other side of the road, and made his way home, to a little boy who was maybe awake now and yelling for his mother. Brady felt he should lock himself behind a door: they would lock him up in a place for lunatics if he was not careful, he thought, scared thoughts freezing his mind. His wife's eyes were disapproving.

6 Mounting inferiority complex

THE visitor stood outside as the door opened to greet him, opened in response to the flickering horizontals of the pushed bell on Brady's television screen. The night outside the door was black, softened by paler mists and fog, green and yellow. Amidst the night stood the visitor, smiling amiably at Brady. His nose seemed to refuse to grow downwards from the eye-brow level: it gave one the impression that it was determined to grow from the nose-base upwards, rather than be conventional and give the impression that it was growing downwards like the majority of noses. Obviously his nose wanted to be different and it succeeded in that: it was like the nose of a pig. His mother used to say it was 'tip-tilted', but that was like saying that Cyrano de Bergerac's nose was 'not diminutive'. Everyone said de Bergerac's nose was colossal, and everyone said the visitor's nose was squashed and pig-like. He had tiny eyes with thick, coarse, yellow lashes and brows, that were hard blue and nearly covered by a great yellow fringe of hair that covered his low brutish forehead. Teeth sprang out of his permanently open mouth at all angles:

here, there, and everywhere. The jaw sprouted yellow hair rudely. The jaw was shapeless, gigantic, unpleasantly white, and composed of soggy, unsavoury flesh. Below this hanging monstrosity called a jaw was a bumpy neck as long as a camel's and covered with coarse, yellow hair in the most disgusting manner. Sometimes the fringe of hair would be disturbed and sometimes all the yellow head-hair would sprout uncontrollably in all directions, so that he looked all the time as if he were drying his hair with the hot air from a hair drier.

All this, and yet his mother thought he should be a film star.

As the visitor took off his corduroy coat, Brady saw jeans with the pockets on the rump flapping untethered, and high pink-leather boots half-covered by the jean ends. Tiny gold ear-rings were set in the long lobes of the ears, and a jazzy, dirty, American shirt could be glimpsed, open at the neck, mostly covered by a huge dirty-white pullover, with the name of an American university football team plastered over the front in huge red capitals, and curving over the back in an arc of similar red capitals. On the gross large hands, with huge fat finger-ends below dirty long nails, were a number of rings, one of them an inch-wide gold ring, and another a turquoise ring in an extravagant gold setting, the stone enormous and rectangled. A long cigarette-holder issued from the protruding lips, and a line of smoke went ceilingwards from the end of a fat, king-size, American cigarette. On the wrist, hairy and thick, was a chunky chromium watch, with its bracelet of hinged lumps set deep in long, thick, single, yellow hairs, all of which the tattered black sleeve-end of the white pullover would now and then cover.

A young man of twenty-six, who sold rare books in a little shop in Fulham, and who played the washboard with thimbles in a traditional jazz-plus-skiffle group much in demand at art-school parties. A young man who attended evening painting classes at Esmerelda's art school: hearing of Brady's coming sketch-club talk at the art school, the young man had brought his paintings to Brady's home for Brady to criticize, as he admired Brady's painting. The visitor sometimes set fire to his painting on paper during the evening classes at the art school, much to the distress of the ladies and gentlemen around, earning him a reputation there as a crazed man due to be forbidden to work at the school in the future. His paintings he showed Brady were Action paintings, dribbles of paint, trodden upon and tortured in many ways. Brady did not know what to say, and opened a conversation about the sketch club he was due to visit. The picturesque visitor praised Esmerelda's teaching, and then began to praise Esmerelda, pure sexual admiration, disguised as admiration for her sincerity, open-mindedness, and understanding of Action painting and painting with bicycle wheels.

'Now the Tachistes of the States are Big Men,' enthused the visitor, his eyes fixed on the horrible messes he had brought. 'The tensions in the work of Jackson Pollock are wonderfully created between one ribbon of tar and another. He is an expression of this Age—directly in tune with the Universal Subconscious of the Beat Generation of the U.S.A., the only generation that is up to date,' went on the visitor, getting more and more intense. 'Jackson Pollock was Great, really expressing the basic unrest of the atom-bomb-threatened today. He was in touch. He never Unwound, never rested, kept up the Tension all the time. Now in England most of the artists are working—painting—in the past. It's no good: they are out of touch, they are reversed anachronisms. A few are a bit in touch, take Esmerelda whatsername at the art school, she is intelligent. It's a fine thing to meet a true Child of the last half of the 1950–1960 Decade,' ended the visitor pretentiously and slobberingly. Brady weakly suggested the use of vacuum-cleaner emptyings for use with the bitumen used on the visitor's paintings. The visitor mumbled politely and went on quickly: 'I want my work to have the immediate impact of an emblem on a shield carried by ancient knights. Immediate Impact, that's my aim.' The visitor threw a painting on Brady's floor and squashed his foot over the slightly wet paint. 'You see? Dynamic action paint. Look how the pictorial impact is enhanced!' Brady looked at the splashes of paint on his floor. The visitor seized the tricycle belonging to Brady's child, and wheeled it over the hardboard painting on the floor, crashing his pelvis into Brady as he did so. Brady wailed inwardly. 'Now look at the crossing movements of the tyre-marks against the central paint explosion,' muttered the visitor excitedly. 'They are Active.'

As Brady went to get a large bottle of very old and decayed printers' ink, the visitor attacked his painting with Brady's bread-knife. Brady returned to an atmosphere of creative turmoil and an excited voice shouting incoherent words such as 'Big Men—Stresses of Force—Basic Tensions of this age—Pollock's being was a mess of exposed nerve endings, in Touch—Sam Francis——' The visitor seized the old printers' ink delightedly, and straddling his masterpiece, with legs far apart, the painting on the floor between his feet, he sploshed and splashed the ink down and across his Expression of The Tensions of Today, singing wildly and happily a Charlie Drake rock-'n'-roll hit called 'Splish, Splosh, I'm having a wash'. His face covered with spots of ink, the visitor assailed Brady with: 'Spread those Tensions amongst the Grease and Oil Pools on the Garage Floor—The Power of the Inertia of the Beat Generation—how can we find roots in an Atom-Bomb Explosion?—the Beat Generation has to survive, they will squash us if they can [he squashed his foot descriptively into his painting], so can you blame them for their bicycle chains and flick knives!' Flabbergasted at the incoherence, Brady recoiled. 'Don't be afraid, man. See this razor.

61

I'd use it on any—now don't scare, Mr. Brady, you are all right—I'd use it on any old man who laughed at my clothes. They will not let us live unless we assert our right to live in the New Way.'

He pocketed the razor and sprinkled bread-crumbs into the pictorial blasphemy at his feet.

.   .   .   .   .

Brady wondered why he had allowed the teddy-boy-Tachiste-book-seller to make free within Brady's room. He also wondered about the startling change that came over the visitor: but very many teddy-boy types were like that, he mused, seemingly fine fellows at first, but betraying an underlying hate and wildness as one got to know them. Not that the visitor was a true teddy-boy in dress or appearance: there were many half-teddy-boys in the world today.

Brady resented the now-departed visitor, he felt he had given in to the visitor's will, and it made him feel inadequate once more, as he had felt when he was shooting birds on the Norfolk farm. As Brady watched his television he pondered over this problem. This sense of weakness built up in Brady, and he looked in mental retrospect at his painting achievements, to try and convince himself that he was not weak, but the sense of weakness prevailed. Often naturally violent men, realizing their violence, make a great procedure of controlling that violence, the result being a suppression of the violence and not true control, so that the violence is still alive, but hidden and covered under a false meekness and sweetness. Some criminals have had very sweet angel faces, men who have acted with the utmost cruelty and brutality. Brady always hid his natural violence by a covering of its opposite, meekness, and men treated him as a fireless person, lacking what they considered, falsely, to be a manly agressiveness. Other men tended to bully Brady, as they saw him as a feminine somewhat fawning person. Consequently Brady found it very hard to keep his violence in check, when his good manners were mistaken for lack of manhood, and his gentleness was mistaken for lack of spine. Very often, under such provocation, Brady nearly came to the point of violence:

the behaviour of the visitor had taxed Brady's patience sorely, but Brady had kept his naturally violent, aggressive reaction down.

You may find Brady a somewhat contradictory person, complex and confusing to study: so he was, but few of us are simple characters when the veneers are removed, and few of us are simple to analyse, the underlying causes for our actions being often multiple and contradictory. All we need remember about Brady is this: within him were many frustrated forces, caged by Brady's mental activity; forces which longed to break free, and would break free, given the right circumstances; forces which, when released, would cause havoc on no small scale.

.   .   .   .   .

Brady parked his Lambretta by the side of the market, and locking the machine, he wandered away to a café for a drink of tea. It was eleven-ten in the morning. Brady did not take off his newly acquired crash-helmet, and looked as if he had come from Mars as he crossed the busy road. In his hand was a sketch-book, for he intended to draw the people in the café. As he entered the café the occupants grew silent, and Brady's eyes saw very little behind his glasses, which had become misted in the hot, wet atmosphere. Remarks about his dropping from a flying saucer he did not catch, and he ordered his cup of tea, wiping his glasses on a handkerchief. When he replaced the glasses he saw the café very clearly, and the faces laughing at him. He felt uncomfortable.

Bumped by newcomers, Brady took his cup of tea to a table occupied by two men, and setting his cup and saucer on the slop-covered table, he began to draw, defiantly. Nobody liked this very much and the remarks were loud and insulting. Brady put down his sketch-book, rose from the table, and went across to the chief offender, telling him to keep his remarks to himself. He was generally laughed at, and encouraged by the support the chief offender ventured another comment, feeling it would make him a coward to back down at that point.

Brady knew what would happen at that point if he acted

as anybody else in the café would have acted under such provocation: Brady would begin a fight. Brady was imaginative, and could see in his mind the sequence of events that would follow, terminating in police interference and court action, so, reluctantly and furious, he backed down silently, quickly leaving the café, followed by jeers of childish derision. They use such men for making wars with, he thought, trying to console himself as he walked away. He told himself he had taken the strongest course, and he was right. But a man can't back down in the face of stupid taunts all his life, Brady thought: some day he would have to break loose, he muttered angrily as he unlocked his motor-scooter, and he dreaded that day, because he knew his life would become stupid when that happened; and he did not dread that day because he was physically afraid, in fact part of him longed for that day, as men will long for physical violence, and its greatest manifestation: War.

Brady sat before his studio fire, the evening was late, and the fire was very well alight, with a huge chunk of black, hardly burnt coal on its top. Brady was an economist, and liked to save money at all times: the sight of the huge lump of unburnt coal worried him. If he went to bed in a few minutes' time the fire would burn all through the night to no purpose, and he wished to save the large lump of coal, which was slightly burnt so far.

By the side of the fire, which was built high on a week's ashes and cinders, was a wooden box, containing many sticks of firewood, a large coal scuttle, and slightly further away was a glass jar of paraffin used for immersing the absorbent firelighter block in.

Brady worried about the wasting coal-lump for five minutes, and then took the poker, a bar detached from an old pram, the wheels and base of which were now used as a plaything in the garden for adult children of about twenty to thirty years of age, and began to dislodge the coal-lump from the top of the fire, his idea being vaguely to put it on the tiles in front of the fire to burn out. He didn't think about all the smoke that would fill the room, when the lump was out of the fire, but so much for thoughtlessness. Keeping the piled-up fire in at the front were three bricks dug out of a garden rockery and a large fire-brick.

Brady worried the toppling rock of coal with the original poker, and, as you expected, it rolled off the fire, flaming wildly, breaking open on the tiles in front of the fire, having fallen from the top of the nine-inch-high fire-brick to the tiles below. A tile split across, and pieces of live coal flaming dangerously rolled angularly into the room. As in the Lambretta accident, Brady lost his nerve, his wits, and stumbled about with two sticks of wood used as giant chop-sticks, trying to put the pieces of flaming coal back on to the fire. In his confusion he knocked over the paraffin-jar with a foot, and the paraffin spread over the scattered, burning coals, great tongues of flame leaping up everywhere. Brady was scared stiff, and had visions of a fire-engine, the house burning down, and his wife rushing out into the road with her child in her arms, both in nightdresses, as a burning house caught other houses in the row alight. Rushing into the garden, which was partly illuminated by the light from the studio windows, which were numerous, the crazed man found the garden hose, and fumblingly fitted it to a kitchen tap, through the window by the kitchen sink. Turning the tap full on, he smashed a window in his studio, opened it, and leapt in through the window, the spurting hose in his hand. Before him was no danger—a died-down smouldering emergency and a blackened, hardly charred wood-box, and books on the mantelpiece blackened by soot. He saw the hose spurting vigorously over two armchairs and one giant painting, so he put the hose nozzle into the garden and began mopping up the sea of water.

I mention to you this incident so that you will know the events that led up to, and contributed to, Brady's eventual collapse as a self-respecting man. There is no need to say that this stupid event just related, coupled with his built-up feeling of inadequacy, contributed towards Brady's feeling that he was unable to cope with life, which feeling made Brady less resistant to stress and strain and crisis in the future.

Dispirited, Brady left his wettened and blackened studio, and prepared for bed. Back in the dark, unlit studio, two paraffin stoves burned by the soaking canvas, and they burned there all night, until in the morning the canvas was in a much drier state.

. . . . .

Some time later Brady was painting by an open window which revealed the garden, a lawn, and flower-beds. Birds flew in the garden, from fence to tree, and from tree to lawn. Lighting a cigarette, Brady glanced out of the window at the sparrow occupying the lawn: he started as he saw a fat pigeon on the lawn. He crept to the end of his studio, opened a drawer, and extracted an air pistol. Opening it, he put in a pellet of lead, and screwed in the bolt again: he put the barrel to the floor, pushed down hard, and, straightening his body again, crept to the open window, murderously, with the pistol in his hand. Through the window he aimed at the pigeon, and fired the gun. A sharp snap resounded in the silent studio and garden, and the pigeon flew away, startled but unharmed. Brady reloaded and fired after the flying pigeon, with no success. Brady loaded the gun again and waited for the birds to settle again, so that he could shoot any bird that was a target, while the dog next door barked at the disturbance. Some time later, a sparrow dropped nervously on to the empty lawn. Brady by this time was irritable and impatient and he fired viciously, just as his small son rushed into the garden from behind a projecting wall, talking to himself, and running into Brady's line of fire. The child was unharmed, and went on playing happily after remarking to his father that: 'Daddy go bang, bang, with gun; Daddy shoot boy dead; Boy [his name for himself] go huh, huh, huh, huh [crying noises].' Brady stood by the window for a long time, silent and self-reproaching. He might have killed his son. Later, in an attempt to relieve himself of his state of mind, rather than for any other reason, Brady dramatically related the incident to his wife, while the child played in absorption at the task of loading small lorries with sawdust, to the accompaniment of a babyish monologue about cars and lorries and men in the lorries. Having told his wife, Brady felt somewhat better, and left his wife to worry instead of him. But later on Brady felt self-criticism, and it added more to the pile of feelings of lack of self-respect and inadequacy. He gave away the air pistol

shamefacedly, lying to the receiver about his reason for passing the weapon on.

.   .   .   .   .

About a year previously Brady had bought a wrist-watch. Now it worked tolerably well, but when the twist-screw on the side of the watch was pulled out, it would not turn the hands when it was turned. It didn't connect with the hands properly and the twist-screw could be turned for ever and the hands only moved occasionally. So much may be boring, but what Brady did as a result of this is important to my story: it is one more incident that added to Brady's growing inferiority complex. And I repeat wearily once again the explanation: Brady's inferiority complex caused him, later on in a crisis, to have no faith in his ability to control himself, or the critical circumstances which threatened to break up Brady, circumstances which opened the door of the cage which contained the gorilla described previously, when its symbolism was explained.

Brady could not be bothered to take his watch to the repair shop, to explain the repair needed, and to collect the watch when it was repaired. So he tried the popular 'Do it Yourself' activity with disastrous results. Taking a backed razor-blade, a small gold-coloured safety-pin bent open, and a large safety-pin similarly bent open, Brady set to work. Opening the back plate by pushing it round with a big screw-driver, Brady examined the delicate works revealed. Miniature screw heads and small ticking wheels. After trying to get the mechanism from the case with no success, Brady gave up and screwed on the back plate again, leaving out a fine rubber circle, the loss of which the watch didn't seem to notice. Later on, Brady tried again, this time unscrewing four tiny screws with a razor-blade. His activities then resulted in a spring of some kind flying out suddenly in a surprising and disturbing manner, and darting into the mysteries of his armchair, somewhere around Brady's bottom, where it slipped down a crevice. Realizing that the watch was now well and truly broken, Brady bundled the remains of the watch together, and hid the evidence of his disgusting clumsiness and stupidity in a drawer.

7 Emotional release

BRADY entered the sketch-club room before his dinner, to enable him to have a preview of the work on the walls, so that after dinner he would be able to talk with greater fluency about the hung paintings. The room was heavily decorated with sketch-club work, hung in ghastly confusion, and was empty except for a member of the school staff of teachers, a horse-faced character with tightly curling hair. This member of the staff had a mauve complexion, large, warm, human eyes hidden by half-closed eyelids, a fancy-checked waistcoat, tartan trousers, and chukka boots. A dark-green corduroy jacket covered his tall, muscly body; he smoked small cigars incessantly, and his face was well lined and essentially nervous; his hair was ginger, abundant, and well combed, the front silhouette of the hair mass was uneven, angled, and bumpy; he had an eager look, which sometimes relaxed into a casual slackness that was extreme, and that slackness made him look utterly vulgar, worthless, and disintegrated; in his slack moods, which were mostly to be seen when he was drunk, he got tired of being eager, integrated, and self-respecting, and just let himself go. A naive, riotous person, fond of cigars, this man would teach at an art school all his life, probably at the same art school, getting gradual seniority, until at fifty or sixty he might attain the glorious height of becoming principal of an art school.

Brady ignored him, mainly because this person pretended he didn't know who Brady was: in actual fact he was all too well aware of Brady's identity, and jealous of his achievements and reputation.

Brady wasn't ignored by the girl who then entered; in fact he saw from her ingenuous eyes that she was fascinated by him, and she stared at him a great deal, the thoughts in her eyes being easily readable: 'The Great Mr. James Brady here in person—Golly.'

Looking at the paintings the Great Man despaired, did not look forward to the task of criticism ahead, and went to dinner.

.   .   .   .   .

Students sat on the floor, students stood round the walls, students sat in chairs, and some sat on high stools: some girl students sat on the laps of other girl students and looked hysterically gay; and some girls sat on the laps of boys and looked truly happy and contented, their seats not being able to see Mr. Brady and not caring very much about that factor either, and these male seats looked very happy about it all, too. The atmosphere was expectant, electric, alive, and not very quiet.

Mr. Brady began. He cleared his throat six times, said, 'Good afternoon,' and then cleared his throat three times again. He stammered out how pleased he was to be of service to the new generation of potential artists, and a few more trivialities, then gave up completely, looked wildly around, and lit a cigarette with trembling hands. Gathering his courage he leapt across the room, confronted a painting, and blurted out a great mass of impassioned verbosity. He was off. He went from painting to painting, a surge of mounting speech, pouring relentlessly from his mouth, word after word tumbling fast after each other in a stream of high-pressure talk. His voice monotonously charged on and on, a thick wave of excited, ruthless intellectualism. The students were bored to tears and wondered when it would stop. But Mr. Brady was too frightened to stop, he hid behind the cascade of sound he made, and didn't let up for one and a half hours. Then the head of the sketch club thanked him politely, as Brady stood there nervously, and it was all over. Gay crowd-babble took the place of Brady's surge of monotonous sound, and the students evacuated the room, relieved and free.

He felt a tug at his arm, and looking round saw Esmerelda standing beside him, her morbid eyes filled with an attempt at pleasantry and charm. While she was talking polite nothings to him, he felt a lust for her sweeping over him. He leaned gratefully on the meaningless conversation, amidst the scurrying students, his mind very weak and exhausted after his trying experience of criticism. Because he was so exhausted he allowed himself to lust after this not-too-beautiful girl, and he did not control his mind as he should have done.

Walking with her across the field to the school building, he felt light-headed with nervous exhaustion. The terrific strain of pouring out tirade after tirade of words at the students had after-effects: he felt tired, high-tensioned, out of control, and definitely not himself, slightly intoxicated by the high tension of his battle with nerves and words. At any other time Esmerelda would not have roused his lusts, but now he was a changed man, exhausted and excited, and his eyes surveyed her greedily, as they say in cheap novels such as this.

Esmerelda, as any woman would in the circumstances, sensed Brady's lust, and her virginal soul was excited. She looked curiously at the man at her side as they walked, her eyes ambitious and calculating beneath the dark fringe of hair. When a woman has never had a natural sex life she becomes unscrupulous and selfish when an opportunity of having a relationship with a man becomes presented to her. Esmerelda spared not a thought for Brady's wife, as she began to dig her claws securely into the unsuspecting, tired, weak

71

man walking to the main building of the art school with her. Any woman, however unattractive, when out to secure a man's attention and lusts, if she feels she is not playing a losing game, and has the deck of cards stacked in her favour (as Esmerelda had then), will summon up, from heaven knows where, physical attraction that has hitherto not been evident in her. Esmerelda became transformed; Brady's desires raged within him and he stepped off on to the thin ice with a recklessness born of exhaustion and the fever of over-exertion.

Esmerelda took hold of his arm to emphasize a point in the conversation about art, but her ulterior motive was an evil one. Brady felt the pleasure of the contact, and stopped to talk further and with ease. The girl's years of sexual frustration and misery loomed depressingly in the back of her mind, driving her to desperate measures, now a brief chance of putting an end to those dreary years occurred to her; a brief chance, because when Brady was in the school building her chance of talking privately to him again would be a slender one, he would be in the midst of people, and in his home-bound train in a short while. Esmerelda suggested that they look again at the sketch-club paintings, and they retraced their steps, Brady's mind in chaos, his uncontrolled feelings racing madly, wild immoral thoughts easily playing with romantic, sexual ones. All Brady could think about was that his wife would expect him to stay the night at a hotel near the art school and for him to return in the morning. Brady thought again, and the thought was of the eagerness of the girl playing up to him: her intentions were clear, vulgarly clear. This, Brady began to think, was the entrance to a road that led away from the boredom and claustrophobia of his married life. Why should not he break out and have some cheap fun? Brady thought weakly, drunk with nervous strain and Esmerelda's obvious invitation. His wife would never know.

They entered the now-deserted sketch-club exhibition-room and talked about the paintings. Brady overheated and worked up. Esmerelda determined to let go her one chance of a lifetime in no other circumstances than the sudden bombardment of hydrogen-bomb-carrying bombers, or of the

discovery of an escaped lion sleeping in the life-models' dress-
ing-room. Even if those unlikely things happened, Esmerelda
determined to let go only if she was killed. Such was the terrible
determination of a sexually frustrated girl when given the
Chance of Life. Brady didn't stand a chance, and even if he
did he would have discarded it, because Brady wanted what
Esmerelda wanted, and he wanted it with the lack of self-
control of a drunken and very tired man, who sees a gate
open from a prickly forest afire, leading to a pleasant garden
filled with fire-hoses, and calm lakes, and firemen, and understandably wants to run through the gate into the garden.

You may feel that this description of Brady's being
seduced is lurid, vulgar, and highly coloured. I would agree
with you, but what I write is what happened; and I cannot
apologize for presenting my reader with a truthful description
of the kind of things that happen, in the minds of the participants and outside the minds of the participants, when two
people of opposite sexes get immorally, emotionally, and
sexually involved with each other: vulgarity is the outcome
very often, and when one of the persons involved is emotionally adolescent and the other a frustrated virgin, the chances
of the outcome being vulgar, lurid, and highly coloured are
increased one thousandfold. One cannot write about bestiality in a tasteful way and give the true picture. However,
apologies cost nothing to give, and to give them is often very
profitable to the giver, so I will apologize to those among my
readers who find the previous descriptions hard to digest, and
I will ask them to bear up courageously to face the tasteless
scenes that are to follow. I will add that to the best of my
knowledge—I know, at this point in the book, no more about
the rest of it than my reader does—no more scenes of sexual
depravity will be written to embarrass the more discriminat-
ing and squeamish of my kind and long-suffering readers. To
continue:

In a setting of student-paintings of nude models, apples
and jugs on checked tablecloths, portraits, and landscapes;
chairs in abundance, easels, a model's throne, and many
stamped-out cigarette-ends on the floor, Brady and his
'intended' talked about the paintings in clichés that came

easily to their minds, and gave most of their energies to their separate desires, and working out the best way to achieve their desires.

Brady's mind was building up its weakness as the time passed and as he became surer and surer of Esmerelda's attitude to him. As I said, she made no secret of her attitude, and talked to Brady with her hand on his arm most of the time, standing very close to him, brushing against him at every opportunity, and taking a very friendly attitude towards him. The afternoon changed to dusk.

The conversation changed gradually from art to general intellectualizing and from that to human relationships and people. Highly intellectual conversation can switch from one subject to another very easily, and it soon turned to sex, free love, and morals in this particular case. Both of them helped each other to get on to such subjects. Once on such subjects, it is easy to apologetically use oneself as an example to prove an intellectual point, and both of them began to do this. Esmerelda was talking about sensuality in paintings at first, and from there the conversation turned to sensuality in painters being expressed in their paintings, and so on to sensuality in people, and, for example, Esmerelda's self-explained sensuality, and the expression of it through painting, because of her inability to express it physically. So went the talk.

The conversation became more and more personal and Esmerelda and Brady began to feel strangers no more. At this point there was an interruption and an evening student entered. It was the part-time painter of Tachiste paintings who had called on Brady, and painted a painting on the spot with his feet, some time previously.

Brady and Esmerelda left the room, and Esmerelda invited Brady to her room for a cup of tea, so they walked to the bus together and went to Esmerelda's home.

No reader of cheap erotic fiction will need a description of what happened from then onwards, and for my readers who don't read cheap erotic fiction I will say that Brady and Esmerelda stopped communicating by intellectual conversation but went on communicating, and that Esmerelda learned a lot about life she had previously not known, and that Brady

74

put another nail in his coffin, if you will excuse the cliché. But for the benefit of our readers who will not believe a thing until they see it, I will show you a scene in Esmerelda's room.

Brady sipped a cup of tea, his eyes heavy with passion. He choked out a view of Picasso's position amongst the great masters of painting through the ages. Esmerelda was not listening, and neither was Brady. Esmerelda cut through his talk with a stark invitation for him to spend the night in her room. Brady stopped talking, stood transfixed, and looked imbecilic. Esmerelda looked heated and embarrassed. 'I love you,' said Brady with an outburst of passion. Once the dam is open the waters rush out with a great surge, and Brady suddenly felt like released dam waters. There was no holding him back now. He bounded at her and enveloped her with passion. Ludicrous as it may appear, there is nothing so electric as the first physical contact between two people who desire each other, and Brady felt ecstatic as he kissed the girl. I cannot write about the subtleties of these moments because there were no subtleties: it was all gross and animal. I am as nauseated as you are—but you did want to see for yourself. I know also that I will have disappointed those of my readers who expected a spicy description of the Passion of Esmerelda and Brady, and to those I offer my sincerest apologies and the loan of four books in my private library (for those who wish to take me up on this offer to lend my four most-prized books my phone number is XYZOOOO).

Well, perhaps just to increase the sales of this book: Brady ran his sweating hands tremblingly over her bare shoulder, muttering passionately into her greasy dark hair. She brushed her lips hard across his wet forehead and then took off her shoes. He gasped excitedly and clutched a table for support.

Having removed her shoes, Esmerelda smiled to herself and put them on a chair. Brady quivered with passion, and took off his watch. He moved towards her, crashing into a chair, then grasped her in an amorous embrace, every nerve tingling with excitement. As he pressed his wet face to hers, rivers of sweat coursed down his face: his ears were wet where the spectacles lodged in the crevice between them and the head; his nose was greasy with sweat where the spectacles hung on the nose. Brady caressed her nose with his lips, and his glasses slipped off from the greasy skin, and crashed into her passionate eyes. Inserting his hand between their two faces, Brady pushed on his spectacles again, laughing hysterically. Having seen a love scene on the films, where the male gypsy grasped his love by the throat and then kissed her, Brady felt the occasion called for some originality, so he grasped Esmerelda by the throat preparatory to kissing. Misinterpreting this gesture Esmerelda fought wildly, and some time elapsed before the passionate scene was re-established as before. Clutching her dress, Brady leant down to untie his bootlaces and his glasses slipped off again on to the floor. As he bent down to pick them up, he leered at her ankles possessively: she stroked his balding head, and removing her hand looked distastefully at her hand, wet with the sweat from his head. Sure of his charms, Brady removed his shoes and fingered her spotty face passionately. Back home his wife let the cat out for the night.

Now I will show you another scene in Esmerelda's room, slightly later—when you have recovered from the criminal eroticism of those last heated, torrid, tempestuously gripping sentences. They won't need to borrow my four books now. But no more—here is Esmerelda's room, afterwards:

A cup of tea stood on the mantelpiece, half-full. Esmerelda's dress lay over a chair-back. She was herself in bed, eyes open. Brady sat naked in a chair, a look of suffering on his face. Esmerelda spoke: 'Dear James. It is because I need you that I am blackmailing you with the threat of telling your wife about us. My blackmail is that you should continue to see me regularly. Dear James, I need you too much, so I can't be decent about this.'

Brady felt the world crashing around his ears. What had he let himself in for? He was certainly tied now. If only he had not come for that cup of tea, he thought.

Esmerelda lay in bed, deep in thought. She couldn't let Brady go now. If she did she thought she might never have a lover again, and that her life would go back to what it was prior to her meeting with Brady. She was so afraid of the sadness of her life before, that she was driven by that fear to blackmail Brady into having an affair with her—a permanent affair. She didn't care that she might ruin Brady's life in her attempt to add pleasure to hers.

Brady sat naked and despondent, saying nothing. He then lit the gas-fire and put on some clothes. He stood by the mantelpiece looking at Esmerelda with hate. Then he turned and surveyed the jumble of objects on the mantelpiece. He found a form from a marriage bureau and read it unhappily.

His passion satisfied, Brady's mind became ordered again, and he was very depressed by the situation.

Esmerelda came over to him, throwing off the bedclothes. She held his shoulders in her hands and expected affection. But Brady threw her off and she cried a bit: but she knew she was in control of Brady now and that her life would flower because of it. She dressed silently and began to cook a meal. Brady hit her with the back of his hand and she clung to him pathetically. Repentant, Brady consoled her and his hate began to disappear. He left in the morning knowing he must return.

.   .   .   .   .

Brady sniffed and pulled at his cigarette; then he coughed to clear the irritation in his throat, sending showers of germs over his model who stood near him. Brady laid on strips of paint with his brush, laying a strip down the nose of the model's head on the canvas, a piece of paint down the cheekbone, and a few brush-marks around the eyes. As the art-student model talked of Jackson Pollock painting with chicken wire in the desert and of Pollock's death in a car accident, Brady thought about his affair with Esmerelda, an affair which he would gladly terminate if it was up to him to make the decision. But Esmerelda's desire for him was the governor.

Kneeling down, Brady brushed in the legs, and drew the feet, smoke hurting his eyes, and he coughing harshly. What was he to do? Just how could he throw Esmerelda off? He thought of killing her; he indulged himself in a complicated plan, which he knew he could not put into practice: nobody knew of his relationship with Esmerelda. So one day he went to her room and killed her, slipping unnoticed out of the house again. Or, better still, he gave her potassium cyanide and wiped the froth from her lips: they might not realize it was murder for a few days. But they always caught him in the end, for she had written about him in her diary, and the police found the book. Brady stopped imagining and pulled himself together. He went on painting.

One day when he visited Esmerelda he asked her about a diary, and she showed him hers. He found many mentions of himself, and resolved to steal the book. As Esmerelda opened the curtains, he put it in his pocket, and when she turned towards him he kissed her passionately. As he held her, he thought of killing her then: he released her and swung a punch at her jaw. It missed the jaw and his fist sank into her neck, making her gasp for breath in agony. His second blow knocked her out, and he bent down to kill her. But he recoiled and ran away. Later he received a letter from her, forgiving him, and asking him to visit her again, adding a hint of a threat.

So Brady descended from self-respect, self-control, and dignity, to depths of animal behaviour, sordid and vile. The gorilla had broken from its cage; Brady's lustful emotional side had found a way out, and a means of fulfilment, and also it now ruled him; the finer, controlling side of Brady had died, and he was as much in control of himself as a piece of straw in the wind. Brady even tried his hand at murder: only because he was a coward did the murder not materialize. Brady's self-respect had dwindled gradually; his failure to shoot birds, his Lambretta accident, the swearing in the road, his apparent weakness in the café, his stupidity with the watch and with the fire, not to leave out the near-shooting of his boy—all mounted up together in a great lack of faith in himself, into a great doubt about his balance and worth, which inferiority complex made him vulnerable when faced with a strain, such as the first meeting with Esmerelda after the criticism.

So in this way Brady fell from the state of Grace. As they said in Victorian novels, his Downfall was complete. His weakness had betrayed him. So far his violent nature had broken free from restraint and suppression, in a few incidents culminating in the attempted murder. His emotional lusts

78

had run unchecked. You may think Brady could break up no further; that the breakdown of the well-known painter to a murderer, but for the lack of a spot of nerve, was as far as the breakdown would go. But Brady was not given a chance to pull himself together and recover, for Esmerelda was the trouble and Esmerelda would not let him go. With Esmerelda releasing her hold, Brady might quite well have restored himself, but with Esmerelda determined to hang on, he could only become more and more broken down; the whole situation fed his weaknesses, and they grew on the food, and rapidly, swelling to enormous proportions, because the situation was rich food indeed. This breakdown of Brady may seem over-dramatic, building up to attempted murder after adultery. But such things as murder and adultery happen often—you read in the papers about them—only here in this story you are not only reading about the drama of the murder, or the seduction and adultery, but about the causation of these final dramatic high points, the causation explained carefully and in detail, with relevant incidents related.

Why should Brady's downfall be checked at this point? With a somewhat mad, or shall we say unbalanced, female threatening him, it is surely more likely that he would go on breaking up, going from degradation to depravity.

.   .   .   .   .

Brady sat in the railway carriage, on his way to the town that his Esmerelda's art school was called after. As he looked confusedly at the variety of faces, looking at him and the other people on his seat, he thought about his predicament. He had sensed Esmerelda's instability and unbalanced mind, and was sure that given the slightest provocation she would write to his wife, informing her of the adultery of her husband —Brady. Esmerelda knew her hold and its power over Brady: she was happy now—she had a man. She was not going to give up her new-found happiness easily, and Brady had to pay a very high price for his first act of adultery, on the night after the sketch-club assembly. Brady looked round in the carriage for a 'No Smoking' notice, did not find one, and drawing out his chromium lighter and a cigarette, he put the cigarette in his mouth, clasped its thin paper covering between his over-dry lips, raised the lighter to the end of the cigarette and clicked the lighter; a small oval flame of clean yellow over a flame of blue resulted, and, lighting his cigarette, Brady puffed away, and tried to think amongst the soothing smoke, but with no success. The general situation for Brady was nerve-racking in the extreme, and his ulcer was getting worse: Brady sat in the railway carriage, unable to think of any-thing else but his internal pain. He had no chance, therefore, to think out the situation, and find an answer to his problem. He sucked a tablet for his ulcer, which was an absorbent chalky tablet, supposed to soak up the big amount of acid in his stomach. Folk who get in a mess often cannot get out of it, because they are so nerve-racked all the time, as a result of the worry, that they cannot calm their minds sufficiently to enable them to think about the mess they are in with the intention of clearing up the mess by Thought; their minds are continually in a state of confusion, and as in that state they cannot advise themselves, they need an adviser. Brady was one of those folk, but he had no one to advise him. He tried hard to think clearly and rationally, but his nerves were in a bad state and his attempts at thought were interrupted by violent ulcer pains.

Brady alighted from the train, pushed through the crowds of jostling people, and joined the queue of people fighting to get past the ticket-collector. Brady handed his ticket across a business-man's face, and rushed into the freedom of the station courtyard beyond, where he scattered himself over a taxi-driver's open window, and gave an address to the picturesque face in a tense manner. The taxi-driver looked unintelligently at the somewhat distraught Brady standing amongst the rushing people, and asked for the address again. Having repeated it, Brady collapsed inside the taxi, and stared wearily and fixedly at the people outside the window, as he sat in the doubtful privacy of the taxi, his hand on the shiny leather seat beside him. The little oasis of small and not much privacy drove through the desert of traffic, people, and shops, jerking hither and thither, round corners and in and out of traffic: it *was* all a desert to Brady—if he was amongst all

F   81

those people in that strange town, he would have felt as lonely as a desert traveller and as lost as a desert traveller might feel, and the taxi was a temporary home from home. He looked at the taxi-driver's neck, and the glass panel before it, through which he saw the terrifying mixture of motor vehicles on the road ahead. Brady felt criminal and hunted as he rode to Esmerelda's room. Well he might feel so, for if his secret was revealed, police action would eventually be taken against Brady, or legal action anyway, which was just as bad; and the powers of Justice were a mixture of police authority and legal authority in his mind: his was the mind of an unworldly artist, somewhat childish regarding the power of the law, which it regarded with the awe that a child views the law, and its establishment by the police. Brady lived in his own world, as unrelated to the world around him as he could make it: like most painters. And now his small world was threatened by the intrusion of the law, he was frightened. His two crimes were adultery and attempted murder. He knew his wife would never forgive him for his adultery, such an insult to her as it was; or he thought he knew: perhaps his wife would have forgiven him if he had told her all of it, and put himself at her mercy. But he did not tell her, and his fear of her possible lack of forgiveness drove him deeper into the mess and complications of his affair with Esmerelda—such a one-sided affair: sure he got some physical satisfaction from Esmerelda, but his mind was hysterical with worry, and that coupled with Esmerelda's blackmail made it difficult for him to enjoy Esmerelda. So he went unwillingly to her room in the square taxi.

The old man who owned the house in which Esmerelda's room was had no idea that Brady stayed the night in Esmerelda's room. Brady's departures in the mornings were a matter of creeping down the stairs, opening the front door on to the fresh morning, and closing it after him, silently and gently, after which he quickly went down the road. Most times Brady visited his girl in the daytime, for his wife was more easily deceived that way. But, when Brady visited Esmerelda in the evening and stayed till morning, his stories to cover the visit were invented with great difficulty and great ingenuity. Brady's most-used excuse on these occasions was that he was doing sketch-club criticisms, at various art schools far from his home, which were held in the late afternoon, and necessitated his staying overnight at hotels. When he returned to his wife he invented conversation about the visits, which he found a very difficult mass of lies to invent. Unfortunately, Esmerelda was getting greedy, and increasing the blackmail payments as blackmailers are prone to do, so that Brady had to visit her more than once a week. As you can see, Brady had ample cause for worry, and he was in a desperate state.

Brady descended from the taxi, paid the fare with no tip, and put his key, which Esmerelda had had made for him by the local locksmith, to the front door. It was due to the existence of this key that Brady kept most of his visits a secret from the old man. The taxi-driver swore at Brady as Brady entered, due to the absence of a tip. The shouting of the taxi-driver as the door opened, aroused the old man, who opened his kitchen door, and watched Brady mount the stairs. Brady resolved to leave early the next morning to be on the safe side. If the old man found out Brady's secret he would make a tremendous effort to get rid of Esmerelda from his house, and furthermore Esmerelda would have a witness to her sleeping with Brady, which would make her hold on Brady even stronger: also she would have difficulty in finding another room where she could carry on with Brady, and that might lead to further complications for Brady. He might have to take her to hotel rooms, and then witnesses against him would become many, and, worst of all, one of Esmerelda's many pupils might see them going into a hotel together, or at least they might see Esmerelda and her prisoner going around the town towards a hotel. Brady's mind boggled at the thought, as they say in the cheap thrillers, of which this book might very possibly be one.

Brady entered the room and looked irritably at Esmerelda as she sat painting a picture.

Now Esmerelda's unnatural hold over Brady made their affair one which not many women would enjoy. A one-sided love affair is an unhealthy thing, and only a mad woman would tolerate or enjoy it. Esmerelda knew it was all she could get from life, and she clung to it, but the fact that she went on and on with the sordid business indicated that her state of mind was very peculiar indeed. Furthermore, her madness was developing, due to the inhuman pressure she applied to Brady to keep the affair in existence. At her school they noticed the change in her; they noticed an added desperate wildness and a peculiar joy of life that had arisen within her. She was developing a sexual attractiveness, but it was so wild and crazy and self-contained that the men she taught with kept well clear of her. Imagine what effect it would have on a normal woman, to be attacked by a potential murderer. A normal woman would be shocked for weeks. And to forgive the man, and love him afterwards, would be a very great strain on a normal woman. Esmerelda was not normal, but those things strained her mind just the same, and she was in as bad a mental state as Brady, her unwilling lover. And so, consequently, the two highly strained people, when they met, met in an atmosphere of a lunatic asylum, aggravating each other's mental chaos.

Brady said, 'Hullo,' with reluctant warmth and Esmerelda approached him devouringly. Brady broke from her embrace, and went to look at the painting she had been working on when he entered. She began to nag at him for his lack of affection, and Brady slapped her face. This had happened before, but her unprecedented reaction to his assault surprised him. She ran at him, and scratched his face as they wrestled, saying as she backed away from the shocked man, 'Now explain that to your wife.' It would indeed be a task to explain finger-nail scratches away, and Brady quailed inwardly. If Esmerelda's control of Brady had been cold-blooded and calculating, she would not have scratched him, for such an act might bring their affair out in the open before Brady's wife and result in Esmerelda losing her hold over Brady. But Esmerelda's blackmail was not coldly calculated: the initial thoughts that had made her work out the blackmail scheme had been desperate ones, but not coldly calculating ones. Even after the scratching she didn't realize what a silly thing she had done.

But Brady's reaction was stimulated by the fear of his wife finding out, and he couldn't see how she could fail to do so when she saw the obviously female scratches. Feeling all was to be revealed and that it was only a matter of time before all his life broke up in pieces, Brady went wild with lack of hope. Revenge was his impulse and he beat up Esmerelda for a few mad minutes, chairs overturning, until she lay sobbing on the floor. Brady watched her for a while, and then he felt tenderness within himself for her, and regret. After all they had slept together, and she did love him in her way. He helped her up and kissed her. She mended herself as best she could and they loved each other from then till the morning, with a love born of the beating. Brady was soft. He left her the following morning, bruised and puffy, a pair of black eyes beginning to develop badly on her face. She stayed away from school, writing that she had 'flu, and a fortnight afterwards she went on teaching.

Brady sat in the returning train, watching the scenes outside the carriage windows fly past. His scratches were large and the blood had hardened into long scabs. He wondered what to say to his wife. He invented a story about an art student who had been so incensed by his adverse criticism of her painting, that she had leapt from her seat and attacked him; but he knew it was such an improbable story that his wife wouldn't really believe him, unless he told the story well and with emotion. But he doubted his powers of telling a lie convincingly as the truth, and he knew that his wife would put the scratches together with his night-absences, and think the worst. He tortured his mind for a story that would convince his wife. He knew for a start that the story must be that the scratches came from a girl and that made the story-making very hard. Why not a cat though? thought Brady hopefully. His wife knew he was a bad person with cats, and that they always disliked him: in fact he had been scratched by a cat he had tried to caress, in her presence. His mind filled with relief. He evolved a story about a cat that was always in the staff-room of the art school he was supposed to have gone to. Before the sketch-club meeting he was talking in the staff-room, and lifting up the school cat, an old and bad-tempered male, he had tickled its stomach in an effort to make it purr. Then he had nuzzled it, by pushing his face in its fur, and the cat had attacked him. He invented students and staff apologizing all the following afternoon, and relaxed in his carriage, filling in the details and embellishing his story. Put over with a good bit of acting, he felt sure his story would work, and so it did.

.   .   .   .   .

Esmerelda pointed to the clavicle on the art-school skeleton and asked Brenda Worthington for its name. Brenda, sitting in the semi-circle of students around their teacher and the skeleton (known affectionately as Percy), screwed up her forehead in an effort to appear as if she was thinking; she also stroked her forehead with the balls of her finger-ends and looked at her lap—two more indications that she was thinking. As a matter of fact she was thinking of a soldier at the local barracks, a private in the Royal London Lowlanders Regiment, but she made a great show of pretending to be searching for the name of the bone to be seen at the neck-opening of her blouse. Esmerelda turned to Reg Scott, a lad with a jazz-club membership card sticking out of his coat breast-pocket, and a muddy pair of corduroy trousers on his legs. Reg brightly volunteered the answer of 'scupula', which caused Esmerelda to turn to Dora Frandish, a tall girl of fifteen, blessed with pretty bourgeois glamour, who answered with the smartly produced answer of 'tibia'. Esmerelda welcomed all this, for it gave her a chance to think her own thoughts, as she asked the same question over and over again, getting variations on the wrong answer.

Fred was instructed to demonstrate the action of the biceps muscle, on the skeleton. Fred rose skinnily to his crêpe-soled feet, and pushed his indecent and much-creased jeans forward by the Bernard-Buffet-shaped legs within them. A Sloppy Joe sweater, with no shirt beneath it, revealed a lot of bare neck, a lot of upper chest, and some very bony and protuberant clavicles, the bones no student of Esmerelda's had been able to identify and locate on Percy the skeleton, who was hardly any bonier than Fred. Fred had American-type spectacles, splaying out at the sides, a crew-cut, a wasted face with much evidence of the existence of cheek-bones, teeth, jaw-bones, and forehead bones. Below the evident curving jaw-bone, was a large Adam's apple and completely uncovered sterno-mastoidous muscles (they run from behind the ears to the point where the two collar-bones or clavicles meet: this is a description of an anatomy lesson, you know).

Fred pushed his bony knees towards the skeleton, and his gluteous-medius muscles, mixed up with the other ingredients of rump steak, swelled like two small footballs under the covering of tight jeans. Fred was a black, black Negro.

Esmerelda kept the lesson going to the end, giving out clichéd instructions which required very little of her attention, and left a large part of her mind free for thoughts of Brady. Esmerelda felt very different from the lady teacher who used to sit morosely in the staff-room looking at the legs that passed in front of her downcast and melancholy eyes. Now Esmerelda's life was full to the brim with glorious incident and sexual satisfaction. But, whereas before Esmerelda was just a little bit unbalanced, now she was very off-balance mentally. It was not in the things she said to her class that her pupils saw something that struck them as odd; they saw in her eyes a ragged, jazzy confusion of tensions, and they saw that her jaw was seemingly larger, set more hardly, and that she gritted her teeth often. They noticed she was wilder, quicker-tempered, and fiercer, than before. Also it was readily observed and noted that she had blossomed: the previously sad forms of her face seemed now lifted and reassembled, so that they were almost beautiful, and a joyous look was on them or expressed by them: her breasts seemed higher, firmer, and larger; her back was straighter, her hips larger, and her whole body more vital than before

But the strain of holding Brady against his will was telling on her, and it showed. At her room she was less controlled than at school. When she was alone in her room, she would stand motionless for periods of time up to half an hour, and she would curse and swear, and would break and throw things. In fact, as she taught the anatomy lesson in the school, if we went to her room we would find broken china in pieces all over the floor, a half-eaten breakfast overturned on the gas-stove, and two oil paintings on canvas ripped and slashed. Downstairs her landlord looked through the 'treasures' he had picked up at an auction sale: Lot 629, a broken soldering iron, two great earthenware jars, some pieces of cut glass—15s.; Lot 721, four old curtains—6s.; Lot 7, a primus stove, a collection of books, a chair, 12s.; and Lot 14, a refrigerator (broken)—£20. He looked down the hall at the stain on the dusty hall carpet, that was caused by Esmerelda angrily flinging his inkpot from the kitchen to the hall, and he resolved once again to get her out of his house—but she would stay on.

Esmerelda returned to her room by the bus, her mind buzzing with problems and nerves. She had a row with her landlord when she got in.

8 Chelsea

ELIZABETH lived in Chelsea, and she had a room of her own in a big house. Elizabeth was twenty-two, she cooked on a gas-ring, and attended an art school. Betty, as her friends called her, was small, pretty, dark-haired, and definitely 'arty'. She always carried a sketch-book in her duffel-coat— a blazing red duffel-coat, and often she could be seen walking around with a young gentleman with a black beard, a black fringe, drainpipe trousers, and a very, very, solemn look. Yes, Elizabeth was 'arty' all right.

Let us take a look at Elizabeth on Saturday night last year. She was standing with a group of art students on the pavement outside a coffee-shop called the Bamboo Bar. Betty had a yellow duffel-coat on this time and red trousers with yellow socks to match the coat. Her hair was tied with a yellow ribbon. She was talking to a huge fellow in corduroy jacket and different-coloured corduroy trousers. He was smoking a curly pipe, and was red-faced, comfortable-looking, and shod in sandals with red-and-blue socks showing through. Under his arm was a bottle of beer, a bottle of red wine, and dangling from his hand a bottle of white wine. In his pocket resided five packets of potato crisps. Betty held five portions of fish-and-chips, and they were all going up to her room to eat and drink.

In they all trooped. A little grubby man walked into the house after Betty. He had a brown unkempt beard, a little boy's face, a cigarette in his mouth around which the beard curled wildly, a beret on his head from which protruded wisps of brown hair, and in his hand he held an unwrapped painting of six kippers and a solitary sardine on a white plate. Waving the painting carelessly against his leg, the little grubby man followed Betty. Behind him was a fat girl in a polo-necked sweater of a bright green colour. She had red hair in a fringe which hung in rat's tails all down her very green back. Her eyes were constantly looking at things as objects to paint, and as she went in she said to the grubby little man: 'Gosh, Philip! You would be smashing to paint from the back if you sat on my Indian stool. I say, Philip, would you pose for me?' After her came a big bony girl in a leather coat, who looked very unhappy. She was talking to a man in an Italian-style short coat, a pair of pointed, elegant shoes, a thinly striped Italian shirt, and a very narrow black neck-to-belly tie: he was the new Italian-derivative 'arty' type, the type that has been to Italy and never recovered; he had a Lambretta, of course, and painted on sacking on canvas with thick mountains of house-paint in the Abstract manner, now popular in the land of the Romans, Leonardo the Talented (big All Time, All Round Italian Genius), and Gina Lillipop. When he could afford it he drank espresso coffee, and lived in the Italian-style coffee-bars that have sprung up all round London.

Betty was talking to Harry Hardcastle and Harry was high, heavy and hearty. Harry was a shy man but who would know it? He concealed his shyness beneath an exterior of enormous good nature, a loud cheerful and ever friendly voice and talk about any subject that he had no real feelings about (he felt embarrassed when subjects close to his heart were being discussed). Nobody knew the Real Harry Hardcastle, and sometimes his act deceived himself and he became the Harry that everyone knew. Such a man was far from unique of course, for there are millions like him except that they differ from him physically. Harry didn't stop going till he reached six foot six inches, and he had a thin patch of hair on the top of his head that people said was due to his banging his head on door lintels and country ceilings. When he was ten years old Harry was the same height as other boys of that age. Then adolescence with all its disturbances came to Harry and his relatives watched with wonder as he suddenly grew and grew, higher than his father, and then way out into space. His parents were of normal height, and his relatives said it was all due to his grandfather, who was descended from a tribe of African natives of vast height who peculiarly associated with a pigmy tribe. These tribes, incidentally, came into the news in the autumn of 1959 concerning the Black and White problem in Africa. However, Harry's grandfather didn't look black and he didn't look native.

Harry found that being someone else most of the time was a great strain, the result being that Harry was a hot boy for the Jug and Bottle. Nobody ever remembered Harry without picturing him with a glass of booze in his hand. How Harry had got into the Chelsea set is certainly something of a mystery and nobody knew much about his background. What they did know was that he was generous and good fun, and that was good enough for most of them. Harry tried to make himself look like a Chelsea Charlie, but the short beard, open-necked shirt and sketch book in his hand, just looked ADDED and that was that. Everyone who thought at all—and they were in the minority in Chelsea—felt that Harry belonged in the world of rugger clubs and ancestral homes. Still, everyone liked Harry, for he was harmless and good fun, unless you expected the man to be a REAL person, in which case you found him very irritating.

There was a grave disadvantage in being such as Harry: since people could meet only the OUTSIDE Harry and could not meet the real INSIDE Harry, the outside Harry had many friends but the real inside Harry had none. It can be truthfully said that although Harry had many girl friends he had in fact not one girl friend. The hearty version of this pathetic man had girls galore but the shy real Harry had never had a girl friend in his life and this was enormously sad. As we mentioned before, Harry was far from unique; and every brain doctor knows of the man with the Jekyll and Hyde split personality. We must not say that Harry's secret self was evil in any way: the truth was that Harry's secret self was just sad and inexperienced. He never really experienced anything properly because the things that happened to him didn't really touch his real self: nothing sadder than this can be imagined. On the surface he seemed adult and worldly but really he was a lost child. So he drifted through life, always on the surface, hiding a child beneath a false manliness. Harry would never do anything that was real and significant because to do that in this world a man must be in touch with reality and Harry never was. There was no hope for Harry because his act was perfect: if one day it could be penetrated then his life would change, but there was little hope that penetration of his Oscar-deserving performance would occur.

The room was decorated on its walls with hundreds of colour and black-and-white photographs cut from magazines and newspapers. A fancy Victorian picture-screen was in one corner blocking off the gas-stove, and a pail by its side filled to its very brim with slops consisting of tea-cup emptyings, washing-up water, and discarded custard. A big ornamental mirror covered one wall, and toy cars, steam-rollers, and trains were lovingly placed on the mantelpiece with art-gallery invitation cards.

Drinks were consumed, cigarettes were alight; pipes were pompously waved, pointed stem forward, filled with demonstrative ceremony, chewed hard, and sometimes smoked for smoking's sake; paintings were discussed intensely, love affairs were continued beneath a protective façade of bad arty manners, and a great deal of personal display was put on. On the couch, beneath the fifty-two cut-out photographs of James Dean, a monkey-faced man with black straight hair in abundance, big protruding brows, a table-flat receding fore-head, a squashed-in nose with great, holed nostrils, and hair oil glistening on the edges of his large ears, poured from his mouse-trap line of a mouth romantic drivel to the fashion and dress-making student, dressed absurdly and studiously, a long narrow umbrella leaning on her silk-stockinged knee, who sat beside him.

As the zoo product just described, drank from his glass of beer and acted affectedly, the girl beside him clicked out clichés from her unsensuous mouth, and sparkled her inhuman eyes at him, above which resided nakedly a pair of plucked eyebrows, obscene in their nudity. The slit-mouthed throwback to the days when apes mutated to human beings, intensely confident in his lady-killer assets, enveloped his pinned-together doll in the charm of his deep-set, dark, lovelorn eyes. Flattered, she responded with affected and dead-passion glances, and encouraging movements of her sexless body. Happy in his world of conquests and one more on the way to realization, the son of a dustman, with a yellow vintage Rolls-Royce outside Betty's residence, smacked his knees with his yellow gloves and surveyed his dressy shoes with contentment, telling his companion that he was determined to become a parasite on middle-aged, rich, society ladies, so that he could have the money and time to spend his life loving such gorgeous creatures as his companion. This frank and seemingly tactless line, was put over with such a pantomime of facial contortions of charm and flattery, that it furthered his cause, and made his companion feel eager to enter his unprincipled and racy world.

Pleased at his progress, he started on the softening-up section of his technique, by bringing out an elegant hip flask of high-alcohol whisky. His mother had been won from his father by an Italian nobleman, who used this technique: soon, drunk as a dog in a cellar where the beer tap has been left open, his mother had gone off in the Italian's car, and became the Italian's nine-hundredth love; when discarded, the mother had by then developed a taste for a way of life far above a dustman's, so she went and stood outside the Grand Hotel where the Italian had resided. The monkey-faced offspring of the dustman and the social climber, who fell down the ladder after being whisked to the top in a hotel lift, used the technique his mother had related to him over a glass of gin

in a Paddington apartment, but he never forgave his mother
for the fact that he was the result of her love of a dusty dustman, and not the result of her love of a perfumed Italian
Count that she met while cleaning out the Count's hotel room;
for he found it very retarding to tell his potential conquests
that his father humped dustbins all day, and he was very
sensitive about a scar that ran from his 'widow's peak' to his
ear and from his ear to his mouth, that he had obtained by
falling from his father's dustcart when it was moving; but in
these days of scarred, balding, and Bogart-type screen heroes,
it did not hold him back to be so scarred, in fact it added spice
to his appearance, and helped rather than hindered him.
However, he could never take his girls down Piccadilly at
night, for if he did, a tarted-up old lady would emerge from
the shadows and call him 'my son Jimmy'—and he liked to be
called James; but it wasn't the name that made the girl friend
hail a taxi and drive off alone, leaving James standing swearing at the much-made-up lady by the gates to Green Park,
while the painted lady squeaked endearments to passing
gentlemen who reacted by feeling sick.

James had lost the affections and money of a film-pro-
ducer's daughter in this manner, and it was no soothing
ointment to the wound to receive weekly monies from his
mother—which he never refused.

James watched the concoction of pins, fashion styles, and
short, white-net gloves, beside him, get more and more intoxicated on high-percentage proof whisky, with calm, calculating
eyes.

Sitting by the wall, on the floor, were two artists, two
bottles of beer between them. One was browny-haired, baby-
faced, and with thick, pink, sulky lips; his brown hair covered
his forehead and his eyes were small, embedded in thick white
flesh, like holes in the snow caused by continual drippings
from an over-full guttering. His nose was greatly over-long,
his cheeks baby-full and rosy, his brow frowning with everlasting misanthropic resentment: he was short and awkward,
and waved his long arms around carelessly, knocking things
and people accidentally. Now and then he would run his finger-
tip from his nostril, up his nose side, to push it finally up into

a closed, lidded eye. .... He would comb his hair with his long paint-stained fingers, every now and again, so that the gleaming curves of dislodged hair would cascade down into his eyes. Clutching his head with a clawing hand, he voiced the virtues of Picasso, throwing his shoulders back and flinging out his arms terminating in splayed, long, narrow fingers, when his friend disagreed with him, at the same time passionately and with deep-throated weariness bellowing more of the virtues of Picasso at his friend: a small chair was hit by a back-flung shoulder, and toppled over with a crash. Apologizing profusely and too easily, somewhat casually and with no sincerity, browny head unwound himself, leapt to his feet, barged into someone, and put the chair to rights. His small blue eyes saw Betty: they filled with petulant watery-weak lechery, and were quickly hidden guiltily in an angry frown, the flesh surrounding the eyes bunching around the eyes and concealing the expression in them: his cheeks blushed and his full mouth swelled, and tensed with passion suppressed. Arms, hands, head, legs, and feet everywhere without control, he managed to seat himself on the floor again, here he frowned and glowered like a spoilt child forbidden a desire, a sulky, handsome, eccentric baby of twenty-four years of age, in a small blue raincoat that reached no further than his thighs.

John eased his way past drinking figures. Like a cat that knows it can get through a space if its whiskers can, John knew that if he could get his shoulders through the space between two groups of laughing people, then he could get the rest of himself through: he made progress around the room with the upper part of his body bent forward. John was searching for a bottle of wine: actually beer would have been quite a satisfactory find. He put his empty glass in his coat pocket and burrowed onwards amongst the intoxicated throng.

John Margaret was the son of a wine taster, a wine taster who had had plans for his son. James Margaret had been tasting wine for thirty years, and he hoped his son would go to a university and become a credit to him, make lots of money, marry a good sensible wife who was a good cook and hostess, be a subject James could boast about to his friends, and—a secret hope this one—keep James comfortably in his old age, for

James had no pension coming to him and no insurance policy.

James Arthur Margaret saved hard and sent John to a good school. John was good at art and pathetic at all the other subjects such as geography, English, French, and arithmetic. James looked at the terminal school reports with sad eyes, and made pompous observations to his knitting wife.

John in his adolescence did not go out with girls or spend his time with the lads, but that did not mean that his studies for his General Certificate of Education resulted in better terminal reports. John was a dreamer at home and at school; and he would sit at his school desk, a desk inky and engraved, staring out of the window, as the lessons droned on around him, not penetrating to his dreaming brain.

But John did excel at one thing and that was cross-country running. This was not a sport practised all the year round, and John was only able to shine during the rugby season, when the alternative sport was cross-country running.

At art John was good but not exceptionally so. The art teacher at John's school was old and uninspired, and his teaching did not move John.

Then old Mr. Fargertown retired, and his place was taken by a young teacher fresh from Teachers' Training College, bubbling with enthusiasm and full to the brim with Picasso, Paul Nash, Matisse, and Sir W. Russell-Flint. Young Mr. Pep was full of ideas, full of drive, and full of the joys of painting and drawing. John began to flower in the art lessons as a result of this new teaching, and he soon became teacher's pride and pet.

John scraped through his General Certificate of Education, and began the two-year course for his Advanced General Certificate of Education.

Soon John became the bright boy in the Advanced G.C.E. art classes: this was not difficult to do, as there were only three boys taking the examination in art.

John failed his Advanced G.C.E. but with a Distinction in Art. James Margaret by this time was beginning to realize that his son would not turn out as he had hoped. The boy wanted to go to art school, and James saw no future in it.

The army wanted John at this point in time, and the

dreamer put on army clothes and marched backwards and forwards across the parade ground at the barracks in Canterbury. The army did not understand dreamers who wanted to go to art school, and John did not prosper: in fact the sergeant in charge of the training platoon was far from proud of John Margaret, Private 172436E—he called him a 'twerp' or some such name, perhaps the name was a trifle more vulgar.

John fired his machine-gun at other soldiers' targets, he dropped his rifle on parade, he was to be seen marching across the parade ground in the opposite direction to the rest of the platoon, and he was hopeless at dismantling his machine-gun.

John wanted a girl friend. But he couldn't seem to find one, and he felt very inferior to the other chaps who all had girls in Canterbury. One day he looked up, and saw a girl's name and address written on the wall. Accompanying this information was further information that said that 'Mary was a smasher'. John wrote down the name and address, rose from his seat, and eventually walked out of the cubicle, closing the door, which registered VACANT once more. He wrote to Mary Williams of 7 Dock Rock, Luckam, a letter of the most friendly nature, but no answer ever came.

So he went on dreaming.

The army was very pleased to find that John was rather too blind to be any use to them, and a medical discharge soon followed. John had been nine weeks in the General Service Corps by the time he got his 'demob' civilian outfit, and three of those weeks had been spent sitting on a mattressless bed in a quartermaster-sergeant's office, eating Naafi mince-pies.

John went back to school to get his Advanced General Certificate of Education. He passed it the second time, and applied for an ex-service grant from the army to enable him to study at the local art school. A wonder as it may seem, John obtained this grant, and began to study at the art school.

Eventually he became a student at a large London art school in South Kensington, and began a life as an art student proper. Real art students do not abound at the provincial art schools. Real art students are mostly to be found at the big London art schools. A real art student wears coloured socks, has a fringe and a beard, wears dirty jeans and an equally

dirty seaman's pullover, carries a sketch-book, is despised
by the rest of society, and loafs in a coffee-bar. A real art
student lives in a low-rent bed-sitter with paintings stacked
in it, talks about painting most of the time, thinks he is a
genius, doesn't wash, adores classical early films, and despises
Jayne Mansfield, eats very little, thinks five pounds is a
fortune, and is to the rest of society sordid and parasitic.
John became a real art-student, with the embellishments of
a curly pipe, very long black finger-nails, a sloppy walk, and,
horror of horrors, patent-leather shoes.

By now James Margaret had disowned his son, and Ethel
Margaret had sadly taken to an orgy of knitting, communicating with her son in secret.

.　　　.　　　.　　　.　　　.

Some time before Betty's party John sat on a 'donkey'
in a dirty, large, well-windowed painting studio, at his art
school. A crescent of students surrounded a nude lady, and
they were all painting her. John kept glancing at Vera
Browning. Now Vera Browning was a 'stunner' by art-school
standards. She wore bright-yellow woollen stockings, sandals,
and a long skirt of orange that tented around her ankles.
Buttoned up to the neck, and fixed closed at this point by a
cameo brooch, she wore one of her father's discarded striped
poplin shirts, rolled up at the elbows. As fine a collection of
bangles as you ever saw spread from her wrists to her elbows;
and a long pony-tail of hair hung down from a point two
inches outwards from the back of her head. At the point where
the vertical pony tail began, a dirty-yellow rubber band
existed. As we said, Vera was a 'stunner', a girl to make art
students enter into a Rake's Progress. Somewhere under the
severe lines of her father's shirt-front a fine bosom existed,
but nobody could see that. She walked like a boat on a stormy
sea, and her eyes shone with the perpetual gaiety of the
imbecilic. John was head over heels in love with her.

John went and borrowed a tube of ivory-black oil-colour
from Vera, and returned to his 'donkey' in a state of fever.

Vera glanced coyly at him, and he painted a taxi over his
painting of the nude lady, so disturbed by Vera's glance was he.

The time came for the nude lady to take her rest. She stepped with black-soled naked feet on to the floor, descending from her model's throne, and cast a flowered and tawdry dressing-gown around her plump shoulders. All the students left their paintings, as she sat down on the edge of the model's throne to read a newspaper, and they gathered in groups to talk about this and that beneath the great expanses of glass windows. A few of the students stood singly, two of those being John and the tempting Vera. Vera, being very perceptive and knowing things with that Woman's Intuition, had sensed that John was attracted to her: she could tell by the way he blushed and quivered when he reached down beside her for the tube of ivory black, and she could tell by the way he could not manage to say 'Thank you' when she helpfully reached down for him and handed him the tube of paint. Yes, she knew did Vera—women can tell these things. She walked across to John, and John, seeing her coming his way, smiled with delighted terror.

As she came up to him, John glanced at her beaming eyes with ill-concealed admiration. To him, the eyes that to her father were like an ecstatic owl's, that to her brother in the R.A.F. were like drunken searchlights, that to her labourer landlord were just plain daft, were eyes that promised a world of delight unimaginable, eyes of a goddess, eyes that were marvellous to behold.

John's head sang, and entered Heaven as he talked to her.

. . . . .

One year later we find John and Vera walking hand in hand, both clad in duffel-coats, along the King's Road, their minds fused into one shared mind, their eyes bursting with joy. Now and again their faces would tend to become fixed, and their smiles fixed also, giving them an imbecilic look characteristic of art students, who are not of this world. Vera walked with a kind of perpetual 'glad-eye' look in her large eyes, and passing shop-girls sniggered at the couple walking on air.

John's father had by now completely turned against his son: John's visits to his parents were endured by Ethel and James in a strained atmosphere, and even Ethel felt her love for her only son turning to a suspicion that John was going barmy.

The relations between John and his parents were not helped at all by the surprise visit that John and Vera received in their love-nest, from Vera's father, who, upon finding that his daughter was living in sin, went angrily to see John's father. The two fathers met, and spent an indignant evening together, cruelly judging the two young lovers. It was a summer's morning when Vera's father made his visit. The morning sun spread its pale golden rays through the window and over the breakfast-table where sat Vera and John, John in his pyjama trousers and a bare chest, and Vera in a Victorian nightdress picked up at a junk-shop. John and Vera lived in a single room in a large Victorian house: in this house were many other rooms, all let out as bed-sitters. The front door of the house was never locked because of the many people who used the house. Vera's father located the house and walked in the front door, asking a person descending the stairs which room belonged to John Margaret. Receiving his answer, Vera's father ascended the stairs, and reached a deserted landing, off which were two bed-sitting-rooms. Turned-out furniture was stacked on the landing, and wallpaper hung from the walls in curved strips, above which were exposed bare areas of plaster. A double-door entry led to the room Vera's father wanted, and the doors though shut were unlocked. On one door panel was a piece of pasteboard with John Margaret's name on it. From behind the double door came the hysterical, silly, happy, laughter of a young woman playing with love. As Vera's father stood on the landing, a couple of arty people came down the stairs, a boy and a girl, with early morning and bed in their eyes. They looked curiously at the unfamiliar figure, and went on down the stairs muttering to themselves. Vera's father was the foreman of a railway repair gang; a large uncouth man, dressed in his best clothes. His hair was greying and short, his skin white, large-pored, and coarse. He opened the double door.

John had finished his corn-flakes, and Vera was filling his plate with bacon and lots of fried bread. John looked at the opposite wall on which hung a painting he had made of Vera— a nude painting—as bacon travelled from a point above his

ear to the plate in front of his bare, scraggy, young chest.
When John rose in surprise from the table, as Vera's
father entered, he looked very undignified in his pyjama
trousers, bare feet, and bare torso. The wearing of pyjamas
in bed was an isolated habit kept from the days when he lived
a bourgeois life with his father and mother.

Vera's father looked at the scene with agony. He then
looked at the painting of Vera. From then onwards he just
blew his top for about an hour, and left with his daughter,
who soon came back to John, a day later.

. . . . .

Vera and John went to Betty's party, with a crowd of
arty folk all cramped together in the back of an ancient van.

Now let us examine another character at this party:
Bernard James Bussey.

Bernard Bussey had made frames, distributed paint to
the students, and had worked in a little room amongst all the
painting studios in a large art school in the south of England.
He had been happy working in that capacity for a number of
years, until a gnawing doubt became active in his mind.

He began to take a great deal of notice of articles in the
papers and magazines about such subjects as the 'spiritually
dead little Londoner who travels on the 9 a.m. train to London
with an expressionless, same-as-the-rest face, to do a monotonous job all day that he had done for tens of years, finally
to return on the 5 p.m. train, sitting in the carriage with all
the other little men reading their newspapers, the expression
on his face weary, spiritless, and devoid of individuality'. Now
Bussey did not travel to London every day, for he travelled
from below London, southwards, but his train times were nine
and five and he saw himself in the article.

Another kind of article in the magazines that hit him
deeply was about the Man who never Lived. The Man who
never Lived was always a tiny cog in vast machinery created
by Real Men. The Man who never Lived was spineless, gut-
less, non-individualistic, the servant type, and the man who
lives in the shadow of his boss all his life.

This kind of article dealt also with the Man who is a Law.

This man Bussey felt he was definitely not and he squirmed when he read about The Man who is a Law, who is a leader of men, a creator, an individual, a force, a dominant man, a captain of industry, a man to leave his mark upon the world.

Bussey scratched his few strands of brown hair on his bald pate, surveyed himself in the workshop mirror—in the parts that were not covered with glue splotches—and saw a not very reassuring sight. Which kind of man was he? mused Bussey, and the answer seemed much too obvious. Bussey looked again in the mirror and saw, flanked by two enormous brown glue-marks, a weedy little man, bespectacled, balding, dressed in overalls, part of a student's frame in one bony hand. His face seemed too insubstantial to bear the weight of the great beaky nose that was the only proud and impressive thing about Bernard.

Bussey laid down the piece of frame carefully and opened the door to a student, who was dressed in a smock covered carefully on every inch with paint-brush wipings. The student was proud and impressive and Bussey found the sight rather disturbing: it reminded him of the articles he had read. The frame-maker felt that the student might become an Individual, a Law, a Great Man, a Force, and a Creator. The student felt that he would become just that anyway, and he imparted that feeling to all who surveyed him—and he made sure all surveyed him: his beard was forked like a Viking, his bow-tie was vivid, and his eyes the eyes of a man who felt he was something to be reckoned with. The student took a frame and walked impressively away down the corridor. Bussey closed the door of the workshop with its Brigitte Bardot photographs on its back, and surveyed himself in his mirror again.

He braced himself and looked as commanding as possible, holding his nose high and his shoulders square. Then he set about making a name-plate for the outside of his door. A few days later the workshop door was graced by BERNARD BUSSEY in white on green, the passing students smiled, and within the workshop Bussey felt for a while a man of some importance.

.   .   .   .   .

Bussey sat in the carriage with his bowler hat on and his high-class newspaper in his hands, reading.

'*Are you a servile disgrace to the name of man?* What will your Life have meant when you lie on your death-bed and you look back at its lack of achievements? Are you a Man or a Mouse? Have you wasted the gift of Life, or taken it and used it to some Purpose?'

Bussey paled under his black bowler, and read on:

'How many times do they call *you* "Sir"? How many times do you call *them* "Sir"? Can you feel proud of what you have done with your life, or has your life been a *waste*?'

Bussey recoiled and hid his face in his high-class paper, quickly turning the page.

He got out of the train at Buckley-on-the-Water, and queued up before the ticket-collector. Big Men before him in the queue handed in their tickets and the uniformed collector said, 'Thank you, sir'. Bussey handed in his ticket and the collector said nothing. Bussey went and had a drink at the Lion and Rabbit public-house.

. . . . .

Bussey dreamed that night that he was being interviewed on a TV programme called *Success Story*. The interviewer asked him many questions and Bussey could not find any answers. The programme was a miserable failure, and the sheets of Bussey's bed were wet with his sweat when he awoke next morning.

. . . . .

He determined to become an Individual. All the students he served were Individuals. He would learn from them. They all despised bourgeois conventions, and Bussey felt he must find a way of life that was unique, anti-bourgeois, and individualistic. He began to play the trumpet in secret, very quietly, to bring out his creative side. He began to cultivate eccentricities.

About a year later, Bussey had taken to writing short stories, all unpublished, painting bad paintings, wearing a flowered waistcoat, and wearing a beard and no hat. He did not clean his shoes, his collection of Brigitte Bardot photographs had enlarged vastly and spread over all the walls of his workshop, he carefully let his morning egg slip from his spoon to his waistcoat and just as carefully left it on the waistcoat for all to see, wore his hair around his ears rather long, and talked to the students about Darwin's Theory, Expressionism in Painting, The Glorification of the Individual, and his new collection of flowered Victorian lavatory-pans. He now felt he was living individualistically, that his life was Personal, and that he was a Character.

The next step was to throw in his job as a frame-maker, and to live a more individual life. But this took courage and some time passed before he did so.

．　　　．　　　．　　　．　　　．

Bussey like many Little Men had saved a great deal of his earnings, and when he threw in his frame-making job and became a writer, he lived on these savings. His writings were naïve and did not sell, but he felt he was happy, he felt he was living a life that sprang from his person, from the Essential Bernard Bussey. He wrote as well as he could, and now and again, when he wrote short stories that were from personal experience, they had a small degree of worth. Here is a story Bussey wrote in his little arty flat decorated with student paintings in well-made frames:

'Fernando was pretty, curly haired, and a weak sort of person with an eye for flowered skirts, flouncing curls, and eager female eyes. Was it bad to be fond of women as Fernando was? No. Certainly not; but Fernando was weak and not the master of the situation, a pretty mouth with roses carefully applied to its moist surface causing him to lose his balance. That was not wrong in any moral sense but it was certainly bad for Fernando, but that is a moral issue anyway.

'The young man sat in his room steaming in front of his gas-fire. Outside lay the streets full of pretty faces and stalwart men. Fernando was afraid of the men and in another way afraid of the women who made him blush in agony when he entered the streets. So he smoked a small cigar and thought of his painting which he did at a nearby academy. For many hours he sat thus "till the fire popped out". Setting his teeth, he put on an overcoat, looked in the mirror to see if he was a presentable figure and blundered into the street, desperately trying to control his faculties. Teeth gripping always helped him face the people in the thoroughfares and so he smouldered his eyes in an effort to appear manly and gritted his teeth. Smoking a cigar made the teeth gripping rather difficult which added to his confusion, but he felt much more self-possessed with a cigar—like all we males do.

'The rain dripped down, the pavements shone and Fernando made his tortured way along. A delectable piece in a glamorous plastic mac and chi-chi umbrella suddenly came along very much aware of her charms. She gave Fernando no quarter, once she saw he was trying to control his natural reaction to such a phenomenon as she, but flounced her skirt at him and lighted her eyes. The nearer she came to him the more she played the temptress, delicately moving her lovely mouth so that he would think of how he would like to kiss her. Fernando desperately tried to get a grip on himself. He glared like a madman, he bit right through his cigar and put an awful lot of energy into the business of standing upright as she walked past him. If only he could look her in the eyes with an experienced look and arch his eyebrows at her teasing. But Fernando had hot blood in his veins, no blasé maturity and a lot of love. So he floundered and the light laugh she gave as she walked by, just a little bit jeering and very exciting, caused him to blush like a flame and blunder onwards.

'Did I forget to tell you it was Christmas Day? Oh . . . how very remiss of me. I am very sorry. Yes it was Christmas Day and all were happy but for Fernando who hadn't got a girl and hadn't even a friend. Father Christmas was around somewhere too giving presents to little girls and boys. He saw Fernando and, though he was a grown man, Santa Claus decided to give him a present too because he was really such a baby, blushing and needing someone to help him when pretty girls came along. Santa thought for a long time about what to give Fernando—a wrist-watch or a bicycle didn't seem quite adequate really, but what was needed was really obvious, though Santa did think it was rather a big present for one little boy to have. You see, Fernando wanted a nice, big, lovely, real, live girl for Christmas. It was obvious to anyone if they really thought about it. But Santa rarely gave real people as presents and it took a lot of thinking to effect such a change of policy. But after a while he took one out of his sleigh. She was a nice girl called Gillian whom Santa had brought along just in case someone needed one for Christmas and he dressed her in lovely clothes with a pretty red mackintosh over them all to keep out the rain. Just then Santa realized he hadn't given her any background, so he gave her a background. Just like that. Lovely wasn't it?

'Santa Claus put Gillian the Christmas present down in the street and waited for Fernando to come along.

'Fernando walked on through the rain and was now frowning at everyone, instead of gritting his teeth or glaring as he had done before. He knitted his brows very fiercely and felt very self-possessed indeed. He quickly thought of all the military leaders he had seen in photographs and modelled himself on them. He walked along, knitting his brows, sticking out his jaw and pushing his lips around his little cigar in a most belligerent manner. Flashes of inspiration like this came to him every now and then causing him to have faith in himself and become self-assured. "Confound all these lovely girls!" he thought to himself fiercely. "I don't need their soft caresses and tender ways. I am much too fierce a chap for that really." And because he wanted to believe such a thing it became reality—for a while.

'For sometimes Fernando had a really splendid time practising his new personality on all the girls who passed him, looking at them as if they were all rather silly really, not lovely, soft, and delectable, but just silly little shop-girls really, who didn't understand the greater life of the fierce and aloof males like he was. He stamped along, scowled, bit his cigar, narrowed his eyes, and looked fiercely in all directions. In fact for a while he thoroughly enjoyed himself—like a child with a new toy. But it would soon end—this act—like all acts do when the play is finished, and Fernando wouldn't allow himself to think of that.

'Santa Claus had put Gillian down in front of the ironmonger's store and gave her a pretty lace handkerchief to hold in her hand until Fernando should come along. "When he comes," said Santa, just a little bit indistinctly because of his great white beard, "you, Gillian, must pretend to drop your handkerchief . . . it will get dirty but don't mind because I'll send you another one from Greenland. Fernando will pick it up and give it back to you, blushing because he's shy. But you must not laugh . . . instead you must say thank you very nicely and say that it is very kind of him. Then ask him if he knows of a shop where you can buy a new one. The nearest one is just round the corner and off to the right. He will then pause wondering if he has the courage to show you the way by accompanying you. You must look just a little bit unintelligent about then and go just a bit nearer to him so that your soft hair brushes his cheek. Then smile very beautifully and in a friendly way . . . not coarsely mind you . . . he will then blurt out in a sudden spurt of encouraged valour that he will show you the way. Then, Gillian, you must encourage his every advance . . . let him ask you out eventually and become his girl." Gillian smiled from under her sweety-pie mackintosh head-cape, clutched her handkerchief in anticipation, and waited as Santa stole away.

'Gillian started as Fernando turned into her street. Thinking of battles and domination of mankind, Fernando took the stub of his small cigar and stamped it underfoot . . . fiercely and carelessly . . . what were girls to him . . . by jiminy . . . he was a hard-bitten chap . . . not a namby pamby. He had a bit of a struggle as he approached Gillian because she was really the nicest girl he'd seen and looking very sympathetically at him too. He immediately thought of what Eisenhower and Churchill would do in a similar circumstance and thought grimly about the Korean warfare as he passed her by ignoring the dropped handkerchief. Back in his room, his mask of aggression abandoned, Fernando thought back about his walk. He began to remember the girl who had looked so nice. He then remembered the fact that she had dropped her handkerchief. He knew a chap who had had that happen to him and suddenly he realized what he had missed. Far from fierceness, he began to cry and didn't stop until it was time to go to bed.

I'll bet Santa Claus cried as well and Gillian too for it really was sad, wasn't it? . . .'

Bussey lived for quite a while writing and being bohemian. He got rather dirty and his beard grew untrimmed. His spectacles became covered with greasy marks, and he began to drink rather too frequently. He had moved to the Centre of Things and lived in Chelsea. He actually had a mystery and ghost story published, in a cheap periodical of a tatty nature called *Seventeen Ghosts a Month for One and Sixpence*. He received five pounds for this.

Then Bussey hit a new low.

Bussey was unmarried and childless, but he wished deeply to become a father. The young men of arty dispositions that he met in pubs were fathered by Bussey when he could so impose himself upon them; and Bussey did not feel his father-frustration so keenly, when he was giving worthless and pompous advice over a pint of beer, to an art student, whose parents had disowned him because he had taken to painting, living in sin, and to wearing jeans and a beard. The art students bore Bussey's attentions bravely because he bought them drinks.

Bussey's life was pathetic. In trying to make it better he had made it far worse. There was no real purpose to his life at this stage, and he subconsciously looked around for something to do. He was at a loose end, like so many bohemian characters in Chelsea, and Depravity entered his life with very little opposition.

He met a grubby little student of painting in a public house and bought him drinks. The little student was greasy from head to toe, had a ragged fringe of hair on his forehead, a great, dirty, roll-neck pullover, and crumpled, tight, slept-in, drainpipe trousers. The student's eyes were brown and lustrous, his chin stubble-covered. Parentless, the student readily accepted Bussey's fathering, and moneyless, the student eagerly accepted Bussey's drinks, food, and bed.

So Bussey was to be expected to go no further in Depravity? We are sorry to point out that Depravity breeds Depravity, and Bussey went from one low to another, just as Brady had managed to do.

Bussey soon lost his little homosexual, for the little student found a better parasitic life elsewhere. Then the ex-frame-maker became lonely and sad.

Martha was small, skinny, and rich. Totally unattractive, she lived in Chelsea, painting hopeless paintings and frequenting the public-houses. She was about forty-five, looked ten years older, wore very similar clothes to the little student once fathered by Bussey, had a sad desire to be loved for herself and not her money, was known to the police for her drunkenness, and rode around Chelsea in a battered Ford Thunderbird.

Bussey met her in a pub and began to love her for herself. This was a completely new thing for Martha, and she couldn't take the joy of it in a balanced way. She drank even more, took Bussey to America with her for a year, and returned with him to Chelsea, a wreck of a woman who looked seventy, drugged herself, and lived solely on toffees.

The effect on Bussey was devastating. He loved Martha for some obscure reason and was faithful to her. But it was her money that transformed Bussey. She was generous with it and gave him all he needed. Bussey dressed expensively, was perfectly well groomed, grew a pot-belly, and covered his head with a false array of hair. He bought himself a small publishing business and published his own books, and some better ones by others as well. The publishing business began to prosper, mainly due to its solid financial backing. Bussey became proud and dignified. He had found at last Individuality and a Personal Life, and he was doing something unique with his life. People began to respect him and the 'Sirs' came thick and fast towards him. Martha died, left him her fortune, and he became a man to be reckoned with.

Bussey in his prosperity still loved his Chelsea, and still went to the pubs and mixed with the greasy art students and the penniless bohemian painters and their wives or girls. A cigar between his lips, the money from his wallet flowed freely over the bar. He really felt he was something, and he seemed to be loved and respected by one and all. He didn't realize that he was buying *everything* he got out of life. The girls who slept with him were well paid one way or another, and they cared not for the essential Bernard Bussey. The young men who flocked around him wanted his generosity or they wanted their books published: little was their concern with the essential Bernard.

. . . . .

Bussey felt he was on top of the world. Such a superficial thinker as he was could not see beneath the outward show. He believed that he had found all he wanted. When he read magazine articles, about little clerks going up to work on the 9 a.m. train, and returning monotonously reading their evening newspapers on the 5 p.m. train, to eat their dinners in their similar box-like, semi-detached, suburban dwellings; little servant clerks with no original thoughts in their brains who did what they were told; identical unambitious slaves wage-bought and used by Real Men; men born to be bossed, men who could not live without orders . . . when Bussey read about them, he no longer felt himself one of them in any sense whatsoever. In his own estimation he was one of the Forces in Society, one of the Creators, an Individual, and a full Person. But though he superficially appeared to be a Big Man, he was essentially a characterless man, no better than the ten-a-penny clerks. Money was the only thing that made him different from the clerks. Bussey was like so many moneyed people who appear often in the gossip columns of the popular Press, people falsely regarded as characters, people who without their money would be boring and common-place. Those lucky moneyed people could do things that poor people could not do; they could buy other people and create stirs, but basically they were often characterless. Their extravagant actions made news and they were hailed as original people—really only as original as their bank balances allowed them to be. Big parties, easy business ventures, and careers helped along by 'connections' and money.

Bussey was as happy as he ever could be, however. He revelled in his self-deception. He would have a kind of un-deserved happiness as long as he kept Martha's money.

'Easy come, easy go', they say. If Bussey had earned his money the hard way, if his prosperity had arisen from his personal strivings, then it would have taken a strong person to wreck him and render him penniless. But he had not the character to hold his money in the face of a strong greed for it.

.   .   .   .   .

Bussey attended Betty's party in his heyday, surrounded by arty girls who fawned on him and arty men who brought him drinks and lighted his cigars.

Bussey's publishing firm lost money initially as was to be expected; and then, when Bussey began to publish other people's writings and not only his own unsaleable stuff, a bit of money started to trickle in. But what really made his publishing firm gain money instead of losing it was Bussey's accidental discovery of a good author, whose books were well reviewed by the critics and bought in multitudes by the public. Bussey started by publishing most of what was submitted to him, and without knowing it he began to publish the work of a fine author: it was sheer accident, and not judgment on Bussey's part, that made Bussey's publishing firm prosper. Bussey did not know a good book from Betty Brown's *Pre-Marital Confessions*. And then he only published the best-selling *Confessions* because it amused him to publish pornography. It was not with a shrewd knowledge of what kind of pornography would sell wildly, that he published *Confessions*.

So the money came in from the fine author's work, and from Betty Brown's lurid penmanship as well.

Bussey employed a couple of readers, and good unknown authors began to submit their work, which was recognized by the readers, and published successfully.

Then Bussey published a book called *The Circus* by a broken-down clown. This book was, unknown to the 'readers', full of libellous material about recognizable persons, and seven people took Bussey Publications to court, and they won in court, so that Bussey had to pay up. This left Bussey merely well off, and no longer rich. The publishing firm packed up, and Bussey sold his car and bought a smaller one.

It was at this time that he met Vivian. Vivian was nineteen and a gold-digger. She bled Bussey without mercy, and

Bussey in his foolishness paid and paid to her. She twisted Bussey around her little finger: in fact she twisted him around all her fingers.

Vivian was blonde, heavy-chested, sensuous, and generally glorious. She posed for pin-up photographs and modelled for painters in the nude. Heavy rosy lips and baby-blue eyes, shoulder-length hair, and a dress-sense both undignified and blatantly sexy, were some of her assets. She was a tart by nature, and very intelligent about how to make money out of her charms.

The gullible Bussey was completely taken in by her, and he readily believed that she was in love with him.

He began to worry when his bank balance became dangerously low, but he was sure Vivian would sell some of the things he had bought her, so that they could go on existing in comfort together.

But when she found out that he was nearly broke, she decided to leave him.

Bussey opened the door to Vivian who was in a tight scarlet dress and high-heeled red shoes. He embraced her, and was surprised to find her unresponsive and cold. She sat down and, playing with her arm bangles, said cruelly: 'I am leaving you, Bernard; leaving you for good, you old bore. I have got all I can from you, and now I'll drop you and look for another rich mug. You can't complain . . . after all you got your money the same way as I got it from you. You got it from a rich sucker by playing the love-game. You had better be a good loser and smile because there is precious little else for you to do. See?'

Bussey was paralysed with astonishment and pain. He could not believe what he heard. She went on mocking him, and gradually he began to accept the situation, and to realize that he would be left with nothing, that he would become a nonentity without his money or a glamour girl. He realized that in a matter of minutes, when she had left the room, he would be just as he was before he met Martha. He felt he could never go back to his old life. When his money had started to dwindle he had worried because subconsciously he realized that the money had been responsible for his glory, although he did not admit to himself consciously that that was so. But some instinct had warned him that without his money he was to be nothing in this world. However, he felt that as long as he had Vivian, whom men looked at with desire in the street when she walked arm in arm with him, he would be a proud man, a man who had something that the pre-Martha Bussey never had. As long as he had Vivian he would be envied, and an envied man is a man who is above the rest.

Now he faced not only the loss of his money but the loss of Vivian.

She passed him as he stood there, and opened the door. The door closed, and Bussey remained for one quarter of an hour without moving. Tears began to run down into his beard, and he bent down on the carpet in abject misery, his hands to his weeping eyes. Naturally he thought of suicide, but it takes either a dramatic man or a courageous man to kill himself, and Bussey was neither. He just cried and cried and became ill as the days passed. His will to live had gone, and he just collapsed. Eventually he went to hospital, and existed there for years until he died.

When he was dying he remembered something he had read long ago: 'What will your Life have meant when you lie on your death-bed and you look back at its lack of achievements?' As he lay dying he felt that part of his life had been worth living; but he felt, with a dying man's sudden honesty about himself, that he was not the cause of his life's moments of notoriety and moderate glory. And as he had desperately wanted to be the Cause of his success, the realization that it had all been due to Martha's money, and not been due to him, was a realization that made him die a very sad man.

·　　　·　　　·　　　·　　　·

At the party was another sordid result of being lionized in youth, and the promise not being realized. With a large horse-face, a beautiful pudgy nose, pale melancholy eyes, and curly golden hair in abundance, this man was a homosexual. A sensuous mouth, well-modelled and sensitive, the line between the lips as finely drawn as the similar line drawn on the mouth of a Botticelli youth. Heavy, gold, silken eyebrows, and thick horn-rimmed spectacles, a nervous thin body, and a ladylike manner. He squirmed and looked coy, his large horsy face touched with the classical carving of Michelangelo. His flesh was creamy white, and a peculiar smell rose from him. Wherever he went he was accompanied by a bodyguard, similar in appearance to Michelangelo's David, as well-muscled as Mr. Universe, handsome, curly-haired, sandalled, with jeans, and an open-necked shirt revealing a white string vest, and bulging pectorals swelling like the supported breasts of a woman. They both sat together at the party, smoking cigarettes in long cigarette-holders and holding each other's manicured hand.

In the room was a handsome, young, champion wrestler, as broad across the shoulders as a normal-sized rifle, dressed conventionally. Spitefully the painter-homosexual left his protector, and sat down by the wrestler, talking coaxingly to him: disgusted, the wrestler left the party. The homosexual returned to his boy friend and bickering began, the boy friend was spurned and hurt, the homosexual selfish and vicious. The bickering went on for a while, white whisky being consumed by both. Knowing he was in the wrong, the homosexual felt guilty, but he refused to apologize, and he hid behind a barrage of daggered remarks aimed at his muscle-man boy friend: the homosexual was feeling very bitter because the wrestler had snubbed him, and he took it out on his boy friend. The boy friend became drunk and evil, taunted by the homosexual's verbal spears. Finally the boy friend could take no more jeering from the horse-faced man, and he slammed his fist into the homosexual's nice mouth. The mouth was the pride and joy of its owner, and as its lower lip split three inches open the homosexual screamed with pain and violated vanity. The party was wrecked, and the fighters were bustled out and into a taxi.

Now this party that had built up in Betty's room, casually and for the most part uninvited, was a typical Chelsea party. I have shown it to you, as an introduction to Chelsea's arty society. You may not meet many of the participants again, but you will have absorbed the atmosphere of the 'Left Bank of the Seine' colony that is in Chelsea, and it is necessary for my story that you should be aware of Chelsea.

9 The weeds that grew in the Park at night

and between the pavement blocks of the Bayswater Road

IT WAS dark, the double-decker bus dominated the traffic on its way to the many lights of Piccadilly. Brady sat on the empty top-deck of the bus, looking down through the lighted darkness at the many people on the pavements below. He felt criminal and lonely, the four five-pound notes in his coat pocket seemed to him to be visible to all the people below him, such was his extreme consciousness of the twenty pounds, and such was his feeling of guilt connected with the money. He intended to spend them that night.

Brady, I must explain, was no more the man you met at the beginning of this story. Now Brady was broken and disintegrated: he had lost his self-respect, and was a slave to his impulses, lost, worn, partly terrified. It seemed sure to him that sooner or later his wife would find out about Esmerelda, and then his life would come falling down about him. He was soon to lose everything, so he felt he had nothing to lose by weakly giving in to impulsive desires, such as the one he was now concerned with gratifying with four five-pound notes.

Brady walked many miles that night, up Piccadilly, around Hyde Park, down the Bayswater Road, back again, through Hyde Park again, and round and round the familiar streets of Chelsea. He met some of the people from Betty's party as they were leaving and then went to see Betty. She talked to him for a while in the entrance hall of the house, the front door open to the black street, and finally decided to let Brady sleep in her bed for the night, as she was sleeping elsewhere under the hospitality of a bearded friend. Brady fell asleep in most of his clothes, the cut-out photos on the wall above his head. Betty returned in the mid-morning, gave her friend Brady (whom she had known in his Chelsea days) a breakfast, and Brady went away into the bustle of London.

Night came again with its romantic dark, electric lights, and people released from the day's work: Brady wandered among those people, unshaven as he was and with twenty quid in his pocket. He had phoned his wife and explained his absence carelessly, with an excuse that would still the active suspicions of no wife but one with undying faith in her husband's purity and honesty. But as it happens Brady's wife did not doubt Brady's excuse mainly because she was afraid to doubt it, afraid to allow herself to think that her husband was starting to deceive her.

Brady wandered up Exhibition Road, past the dignified, dusty, and imposing façades of the Victoria and Albert Museum, the Science Museum, and the Branch Post Office. The road was quiet, with an occasional car running down the wide road. Brady reached the iron gates of Hyde Park, and feeling as if every passer-by must realize the nature of his mission, he turned right, down the road which led to the barracks, and then on to Hyde Park Corner gates. Self-conscious and guilty, Brady crossed over to the Serpentine side of South Carriage Road, and went down towards the barracks, keeping himself badly hidden amongst the trees.

Slowly, an expensive flashy car cruised down the road

past him, its aerial swaying in the wind of the car's movement
forward. Quite a few cars passed him slowly, the drivers' eyes
peering to the opposite side of the South Carriage Road.
Frightened by what he saw on the other side of the road,
Brady strode into the Park towards Rotten Row, and walked
across Rotten Row, sand getting into his shoes, as his feet
sank into it, and he stumbled desperately across. He made
his way to the bridge over the Serpentine, looked at the black
reflecting water, and walked down the Ring towards Lan-
caster Gate. He stopped suddenly and crossed over the Ring
into the slight privacy of the trees. A standing figure on the
pavement had caught his eye, a figure dark despite the lamplight shining on it—a result of racial origins and a dark-brown
coat. Brady watched, as did another man nearby, as a policeman wheeled his bicycle over to the dark figure, which moved
reluctantly away down a turning towards Marlborough Gate,
after a brief conversation with the symbol of English Police
Supervision. Brady was disappointed, because he had liked
what he saw, but soon the figure returned and stood as before,
leaning against the fencing. Brady quivered with nerves, and
trembling, crossed over the Ring. The dark figure was looking
straight ahead across the Ring, but it was very aware of
Brady's slow approach. Brady felt like a collection of bar
electricity wires, vertically crossing each other and jazzing
currents all over him as he moved forward. Frightened, Brady
got nearer to the dark figure, noticing its languid, graceful,
leaning form; queerly dignified, considering that the figure
somehow radiated a message, for any observer to see, which
was 'for sale'. Brady got to an intimate nearness, almost
passed in front of the figure, and then tensed out, 'Hullo'. The
dark face replied without emotion and with toughness blended
with humanity. After an efficient and brief conversation,
during which Brady surveyed the Negroid face, Brady moved
away and the figure began to pose in the same position again,
waiting.

Brady did not know whether to foul himself or not. In a
way he did not want to spend the twenty pounds; he did not
like the idea of getting rid of so much money so fast, and the
elements of decency in him revolted at the idea of bathing in

117

the sewers. After all he had not really meant to get into the mess he was in with Esmerelda, and to spend the twenty pounds would be a calculated act of disgrace, which he felt would be far more blameworthy by his personal standards than his somewhat accidental involvement with Esmerelda, started when he was tired and not himself.

He walked down the North Ride to Marble Arch, passing other men walking through the night on the same errand as himself, and he avoided the standing figures, that were like goods in a darkened shop window, lighted only by the light from distant street lamps along the Bayswater Road, on the other side of the Hyde Park railings, that separated the North Ride from the Bayswater Road. The time was well before the Christmas of 1958, before Wolfenden's recommendations had been made into laws, and Brady crossed over to the railings and viewed the indistinct figures lined up along the Bayswater Road, figures that walked over to cars that had stopped by them, figures that returned across the pavements to stand waiting again, or figures that got into the cars that then moved off.

Reaching Stanhope Place Gate, Brady saw two women talking together: a large black woman with a loose, thrusting, brown jaw and a receding brown forehead, bowed silken legs, and a slip of a white girl, vicious in appearance, hard-faced, and delinquent.

Brady followed them to Marble Arch, where he emerged from the shadows and comparative privacy of the Park into the violent glare of the beginning of Oxford Street. He passed a couple of teddy-boys lounging by the park gates, and walked through the illumination and noise, to the head of the Bayswater Road, where he saw the two women again. They separated: the hard slip of a girl with her knuckle-duster finger rings and armoury of bracelets, usable as weapons against men as vicious as herself, going to the Stanhope Place Gate where she stood waiting. Brady walked after her, half-revolted, and half-attracted, by the unsensuous, inhuman, little rock of a creature. But Brady wanted warmth, so after spying on her for a short while he hurried down the Bayswater Road, in the Kensington Gardens direction, after the large black woman, who was talking to a man in a temporarily stationary car.

118

She stood with her hand on the open metal door of the car, leaning over, talking to the driver, in a classical pose of her profession. She slammed the door, the car moved away from the kerb without her, and she moved into the centre of the deserted pavement, and began walking on again, her bowed legs on high heels, her primitive face slightly visible to Brady behind her.

Brady was a little distance away; and eager to catch her before another car owner drove up to her, he started to drive his feet forward, cracking his metal-based shoes on the pavement, faster sounds than the leisurely clicking of her high heels ahead of him, to the side of the bushes and railings bordering the Park.

As he caught up with her, she very slightly turned her head, seeming to be in a bad temper. Brady had not the courage to do anything else but walk right on past her. Brady had walked many miles that night, and although he was tired, he was getting used to the business of walking, of pounding the flesh of his feet in the shoes, on stretches of uncomfortable grey stone. Brady's legs were toughening up; he felt he was becoming part of the streets; he felt very isolated from the decent citizens in the houses along the roads he traversed, for his sense of guilt separated him from the rest of mankind: it was just him and the people for sale—he even classed himself with the men who organized the people for sale—for he felt he was on the side of The Fallen Angel too.

As Brady walked he got harder physically but weaker mentally: he was becoming mentally tired, and his mind began to work in a way it would not normally do. He began to feel an increasing resentment towards the large army of sentries all along the Bayswater Road, and in the Park. Why should he spend his twenty pounds on one of them, or two of them? His principles deserting him because he was tired, he determined to treat criminal sale with what he thought was justifiable robbery. He would knock out the person for sale, when he had bought the stuff offered for sale, and when he had devoured it: then he would rob the unconscious person's purse, and run away. He pocketed his spectacles for the sake of incognito, and combed his little hair forward. He retraced his steps to a bit of waste land he had passed, and walked amongst the rubbish there until he found a small length of piping; this he pocketed, and then he made his way to the main streets, and eventually to the Bayswater Road.

Does it puzzle you that a man should become so criminal in such a short space of time, or do you remember the pressure that had been put to bear on Brady in his recent past, realizing that when a man feels his world is breaking up it is far far harder for him to remain a decent person? Brady felt the world was against him, and naturally his reaction was to turn against the world in retaliation. Without the happenings of adultery with Esmerelda, the subsequent threat to his marriage and all it stood for, and the murderous attempt on Esmerelda's life, Brady would have found it easy to remain a decent man. But now all seemed broken, and Brady lost faith in life, and turned to evil.

The road was wide, the pavement was wide, and ahead of Brady stood a small pathetic woman, alone on the vastness of the pavement, calling after the figure of a soldier. Brady went up to her, and she told him that the soldier had stolen her handbag. She couldn't call the police, she said, because she was a prostitute, and she felt they wouldn't help her much because she was on the streets for illegal purposes. Apparently the soldier had walked with her for a while, linked arms, then taken her bag and walked off, sure that she would not call the police. Brady did not know whether to believe her or not: she had no handbag, he observed, and later he found she had no door-key—two points that made him tend to believe her story.

Brady arranged details with her, and they got into a taxi, the woman giving the taxi-driver an address. She was ill by the look of her facial flesh and her weak eyes, and she seemed frail of body; she looked like a woman who had risen from her sick bed, to walk the streets, to get money to pay the rent. Her forehead was bulbous and she was dressed in a medium-tone brown coat of no great quality: there was nothing about her that suggested that she was a very successful prostitute, for all her clothes were bad, and could have been purchased at a second-hand shop. She had no particular charms, and

121

there was a look in her face that indicated she was morally weak, and had been from girlhood: Brady supposed that she had never known a life based on solid morals. Later Brady found out, from her own lips, that her mother had been a prostitute: on hearing that, the thought flitted through Brady's mind that there were lives that were so sordidly cheap and empty, that it was utterly depressing to realize their existence, even if the man who realized their existence was in the mess that Brady was in.

The taxi stopped in a deserted dark street, of ordinary small, cheap houses, and Brady quickly paid the taxi-man, the taxi turning in the empty road, as the pair went in at a gate and stood before a bleak, closed, front door. The little prostitute worried and complained, because no one answered the knocking she made on the door. They stood outside in the night, facing the sordid, little, wooden door, until a sleepy man opened the door, and let the pair in. The man didn't seem to know how to treat Brady in the circumstances, and Brady gathered from the conversation between the man and the street-walker that she was a relation of the family housed therein. For a brief moment they milled around in the small entrance hall, with its coat hanger of many coats; a stairway leading upstairs, and beside the stairway a passage leading to the back of the ground floor. The man went off up the stairs and Brady followed the prostitute down the dark passage, to a little room not much wider than the bed it contained. The woman asked for her money and Brady gave her seven pounds, feeling he would take it again very soon. As time passed, and matters proceeded, Brady found himself coming under the will of the woman—a peculiar thing! Eventually he found himself on the inside of the bed, the prostitute insisting that she slept on the outside of the bed, far from the wall. She put her money beneath her pillow cunningly, and turning off the light, prepared to go to sleep. It seemed as if she did not trust Brady: it seemed as if she sensed from his manner that he was up to no good. Brady could not get out of bed, and get his piping to hit her with, and he felt he could not lean over and knock her unconscious with his fist, because she might arouse the house if his first blow was not successful: the house was so small and thin-walled, and seemed to contain so many people, judging by the coat hanger's many coats, that Brady was sure the slightest scuffling noises would bring help to the woman. Brady gave up his idea, and woke the woman, telling her he was going. As he dressed in the light of the lamp by her head, she oddly told him that she could not stop him going, as if she either wanted to continue bossing him about, or wanted him to stay for company. He looked at her bulbous weak-looking forehead on the pillow, with the light shining on it, and felt he could not attack her: anyway, his resolve had left him. He left the house, and hurried down the street, wondering about the family that allowed a prostitute to work amongst them.

The taste for sordid night-life was now Brady's. The following night he stood in Piccadilly in the large house before the wee small hours of the morning. He walked far and in the wee small hours returned to empty Piccadilly to find that most of the ladies had gone home, some of them with customers.

A lorry drew up in the middle of the road, a man jumped down from the driver's cabin on to the roadway, and took a dark-haired young prostitute back to the crowded cabin with him. She got in, and he after her. Men on the sidewalk watched silently as a commotion arose in the cabin of the lorry and the girl pulled herself, shouting, from the cabin to the road and ran, not stopping, till she was out of sight far down the road, and around a corner. A man who had been watching hurried after her.

Brady stood for a long time, and then walked for miles, returning to the Piccadilly area to wait and watch. A huge American car pulled up, and a girl with blonde hair, a large face, and a light-coloured suit, with a very frilled, ruffled, white blouse issuing from the suit at the bosom and neck, and a loose manner to her, got out of the car by clambering leggily out and gave the driver a cheery, good-natured goodbye. She looked around her, came up to Brady, and asked him if he wanted a nice girl. Brady stiffly said no—she asked him if he was sure; and Brady, although he was not sure, nervously and curtly said he was sure.

Brady walked up Old Bond Street and into New Bond Street, and noticed two similarly clad black girls, walking carelessly together, singing. They were young, had tight black trousers, above which a wide, black, shiny belt squeezed in the waist, above which a white sweater hugged the torso. One had a round face and full, brown, merry eyes; and the other had a more introspective face, more bitty in facial appearance, more carefully carved facially. Brady watched them by looking in a large glass shop-front, which was unlighted, for he did not want them to see his interest. The street was deserted.

As they disappeared from view, Brady wondered if they were prostitutes, as they seemed so uninterested in him or the occasional men who passed them in the empty street—a street packed to overflowing in the daytime.

He stood on the pavement, looking at the road; a red sports car came along the road—a new car, chromium fittings gleaming. One man driving and a huge man beside him with a large impassive face, one arm resting on and over the door of the open car. With great fascination Brady recognized the big man as Reg White, heavyweight boxing champion, presumably looking around London when the fans were in bed. Brady admired the man tremendously: admired the way he had stood up to Sam Bartlet, a worthy holder of the world heavyweight boxing crown. Brady walked from Berkeley Square and saw the two black girls again. A bespectacled, moustached business man walked rudely in front of his wife, who tried to keep up with him. As the two black girls sauntered showily by, the man jeeringly and appreciatively whistled at them. One of the girls asked him if he had lost his dog, at which the man told them angrily that they had better watch out. Brady supposed the man was drunk.

Brady followed the girls eagerly, his person filling with passion. He finally went over to them at a spot in Bond Street, and stood between the two glamorous pieces, asking their terms. They told him that they were purchasable, as a pair, and not singly. Brady baulked at this, but eventually accepted. They each grasped one of Brady's arms in an arm-link, and the trio walked towards Berkeley Square to find a taxi, Brady feeling rather sheepish, feeling that he presented a ludicrous picture—he had never squired two girls at once, and did not feel equal to the rôle forced upon him: the girls went on singing gaily, unaware of his embarrassment.

The girls found a taxi, and seemed to know the driver. They got into the taxi, either side of the bashful Brady, and the taxi didn't start for a while, a further embarrassment to Brady who sat between them silently. He asked the quieter of the two, the slightly introspective one (comparatively), what she did during the daytime. She answered that they hung around the cafés, having fun you know. Brady was staggered at this indication of the kind of life they led. The taxi stopped in a road of Victorian basemented houses, with railings round the tops of the basement steps: apparently the girls lived in a basement, for the round-faced black quickly ran down the steps to open the door. Brady paid the driver but gave no tip, so the girl beside him cheerily paid the taxi-driver two shillings extra.

Feeling that he could not keep up with the incessant merriness of the two girls for the night, and feeling that the whole thing would require far too much forced high spirits on his part, Brady suddenly dashed away from the taxi, and the girl who was by now following her friend down the basement steps, and he sped round the corner, wildly racing down another wider street. He charged past a walking group of young men and ran on. He saw a taxi approaching and hailed it desperately. But the taxi-driver ignored Brady, probably thinking Brady's behaviour too extraordinary, maybe thinking Brady was a thief on the run. Eventually Brady slowed down and began to walk. When he got a taxi he wondered what the black girls must have thought about his behaviour, unprecedented in their experience, no doubt. But he was glad to be rid of them: he was so easily dominated when he was tired, and he knew that the two girls would have combined together and dominated him, if he had stayed with them that night: it was just as well that he had run away—they were too high powered for him, with their terrifying confidence and gaiety. But he never forgot them: they were such an amazing phenomenon.

It is obvious to you, dear reader, no doubt, that Brady did

not really wish to indulge himself with prostitutes. He did not know what he wanted. He was unhappy and unstable, and just at a loose end. All these experiences with buyable ladies that I have written for you, that happened to Brady, were the participations of a restless and sad soul, and it is significant that only once did Brady sleep with a prostitute, and even then the physical indulgence was subsidiary. Take an animal for example. Give it a home and security and it will grow tame. Take away its security and it will grow wild and anti-social. Much the same thing was happening to Brady, whose security had disappeared. He was growing wild, wild and purposeless. Brady was afraid, afraid of the uncertain future, and his fear was dictating his actions.

Brady phoned his wife, and invented an extension to his lie about how he was being occupied. Brady's wife put down the phone, and crumpled her forehead, afraid to admit the truth to herself, preferring to live in a false world of blind trust. He went to his bank and drew out some more money, meeting Bernard Bussey outside. They went and had a cup of coffee.

Brady went once more to Hyde Park: there in the after-noon light he watched the line-up outside the barracks, in company with the lorry-drivers sitting in their parked vehicles, who were also watching the fun. Brady wandered

 towards the pros-titutes and came very near them, but, like Joyce's hero Stephen Dedalus, in most cases he shied away from the final contact.

10 The blood-bath in the Chelsea bed-sitters

THE night eventually came and Brady found himself by the side of a grim, great, London railway station, a fair-haired, black-eyed girl of nineteen with long, fair, curling hair beside him: they were looking for a hotel, and eventually found one that overlooked the great station. Brady and the tall, flat-chested, fair beauty, entered the hotel and mounted the stairs to the reception desk on the first floor: there stood a leering little man with the visitors' book in front of him, and a figure behind the desk with his back to Brady and the girl. As Brady signed the visitors' book with the name of J. Storey, and the girl obediently added Mrs. J. Storey, the figure with its back to them turned round. It was the monkey-faced, heavy-browed man, out of a prostitute and fathered by a dustman. What he was doing there Brady could not guess: perhaps he was a friend of the receptionist and was there some-times, in the hope of becoming involved with some rich, single

127

lady staying at the hotel, that he might fascinate by his 'devastating charm' if he stood at the reception desk long enough. But why he was there was irrelevant: the important point was that he had recognized Brady, and his eyes lit up with threatening and a leer. Brady and the girl were escorted to a small room, looking out over a dressing-table to a view of the bleak, windowed side of the great station. The girl went to have a bath and Brady's request for the room keys was answered by a promise to bring them up.

Brady stood alone in the room, looking at the white lacy curtains and the white washstand, when a knock sounded on the door. Brady opened the door and the monkey-faced man pushed himself in, the keys in his hand. His business was explained very briefly: he asked Brady for a thousand pounds for silence, concerning Brady's night out with a prostitute: no payment resulting in secretly taken camera shots of Brady mounting the hotel stairs with the girl being sent in the post to Brady's wife: Brady remembered that the stair lights had seemed to flash as he went up the stairs, and that the little hotel employee had later seemed worried about something. Wanting time to think, Brady arranged a meeting and the man left. Brady turned out the lights, and lay in the bed looking at the lights in the windows of the high station wall across the narrow road, which lights kept the bedroom of Brady's illuminated. Brady waited for the fair-haired girl with the absurd rectangular eyes to return from her bath.

The next day found Brady in a room in Chelsea with the monkey-faced spiv: a room with a balcony that was in the same street as Betty's room, the room of the party. Brady saw Browny Hair walking along in the road below, walking to Betty's door up a few stone steps. Brady turned and faced the man with him in the room. The furnishings in the room were slick and contemporary and there were arty touches here and there. Brady had decided upon a course of action: he stepped near the scarred face of the gigolo, and drove his fist into the grinning demanding face. The man toppled bloodily backwards into a chair, and Brady drove the side of his hand across the man's eyes. Waiting for the blackmailer to rise, Brady then grasped his black, greasy, straight hair and cut

128

the man's face with the side of his hand; the side of the hand hardened by banging it on the wall just previously. Brady was not enjoying the attack, but it had eventually to render the man unconscious and badly hurt, or Brady's plan would not work. Brady knocked a few front teeth out, and as the man heaved himself groggily to his feet, Brady balled his fist, dropped the fist to the carpet, lined up his knuckles with the tired man's neck, and with all his strength swung a punch into the neck between the jawbone and the Adam's apple: the jaw broke, the man choked for breath, and became unconscious. Before he left, Brady put a note on the table which read: *Send me the photos, a signed statement that you tried to black-mail me, and a promise not to reveal anything to my wife—or—I shall continue this beating on a more brutal scale.* As Brady stepped on to the pavement, he saw Browny Hair on the other side of the road. Browny Hair rushed over, legs and arms waving, and passionately began to praise Brady's paintings.

Next day Brady phoned his wife, and was told that a package postmarked CHELSEA, had arrived for him.

But after sending the photos the monkey-faced man, whom we will call Slick Ape for the purposes of identification, changed his mind. From his hospital bed Slick Ape made a phone call. Slick Ape was determined to revenge himself: his missing teeth hurt not so much physically as mentally—his vanity was touched. His appearance was everything to him, and false teeth were a definite drawback for a gigolo. In his private room at the hospital, Slick Ape received the homo-sexual's bodyguard, who rolled his handsome shoulders as he entered the room; his pectorals now bulged beneath a striped T-shirt, his biceps were carefully revealed by high rolled shirt sleeves, and high leather boots were on his feet. The body-guard Michelangelo might have created received his instruc-tions and went away, a cheque in the pocket of his leather zip-front blouse, which he carried over his shoulder—he was very aware that the bent arm, necessary to hold the leather garment on the muscled shoulder, was very fine for showing off his activated biceps muscle: homosexual as he might be, he still enjoyed the admiration of nurses; in fact, girls were very much enjoyed by him.

I   129

Brady was found in the Chelsea streets by the Michel-angelo's David. who told him that the horse-faced painter-homosexual would be pleased to see him. Brady went to a room with the bodyguard of the past, and was surprised to find the horse-faced man absent. 'From a photographer friend,' hit Brady's ears, at the same time as a hard blow knocked his glasses into a corner of the room. Brady closed with the muscle boy in a confusion of arms, bodies, and legs: but the muscle man was master of the confusion, and Brady landed hard on his back on the floor of the room. Brady rose and picked up a chair. The muscle man held the chair and kicked Brady in the stomach: Brady doubled up and his head was knocked back by a long punch. As he lay stunned on the floor, Brady tried to think. He thought this: he was no match for the muscle man: he realized Slick Ape was behind this, and he realized that the beating would go on and on. What was he to do? He thought dizzily of paying the muscle man to stop; he had fifty pounds in his pocket, drawn from the bank for prostitutes. The muscle man interrupted his thoughts by heaving him to his feet, and battering his face. Brady kicked hard at the muscle man's lower stomach: the muscle man crumpled and Brady crashed his hand on the back of the curly-haired neck. The muscle man went out of this world. Brady then smashed the room to pieces, and left all the furniture broken and the sheets ripped to shreds. The muscle man stirred; Brady went over to him, helped him to his feet, and then hit the defenceless man on the point of the jaw: the man screamed and Brady left him whining.

.   .   .   .   .

Brady went home and went on painting and visiting Esmerelda. Four weeks passed and Brady went up to Chelsea again. He walked slowly down the street of Betty's room and the Slick Ape's room, adjusting three pennies in the spaces between his fingers just below the knuckles of his right hand. He quickly put the coins in his pocket, as he saw Bussey in the street. Bussey asked about Brady's injuries, and Brady invented another Lambretta accident. To his wife Brady had given the lie about a mix-up in a road in Chelsea with a careless butcher's boy on a cycle.

As Bussey went on up the road, savouring his titbit of newly acquired gossip, Brady knocked on the door. Slick Ape answered the door, and they went to his room with Brady menacingly behind him, adjusting the home-made knuckle duster in his hand.

As this is a serious novel, obviously destined to become a classic in English Literature, I will spare my reader the sadism that ensued; for we must deal with profound issues, like the subject matter of the Wolfenden Report, and the penetrating character-study of one of England's finest painters; leaving the cheap action-packed blood and thunder passages to the pulp two-and-sixpennies. But, before this gem of English literature is put in the university study-lists, it must sell a few copies, so that is why we descend to writing passages for the vulgar masses and why we must entitle this chapter— Chapter Ten: 'The blood-bath in the Chelsea bed-sitters.'

We read, however, *The Imp of the Perverse* by Edgar Allan Poe, and *Sanctuary* by William Faulkner. We come to the conclusion that violence and horror *can* be ingredients in novels of classical status. Then accidentally we re-read James Joyce's great egotist work, about Mr. Bloom, and we feel that there are no limitations imprisoning the creative urges of us great great writers. So, since we can apparently give the vulgar masses what they want, and still get our great book put on the bookshelves of the Hall of Fame, we will tell you, blood-thirsty reader, what Brady did to the Slick Ape. This following stuff is strictly X certificate, not for children or persons of a nervous disposition, and must surely make the book sell millions, as well as giving the artist, who makes the picture on the glossy card-cover of the two-and-sixpenny editions, an eye-catching scene to depict, making it blaze from the bookstalls seductively. As that artist must have a terrified doll on a bed in his picture, we obligingly have introduced one: she was in the Slick Ape's room when Brady and he entered.

She lay on the rumpled bed, putting on her high-heeled shoes, a glamorous deep-curved-neck blouse of shiny silk revealing her charms. Brady hit the Slick Ape with his armoured fist, and the girl cowered against the pillows, her red mouth open gapingly, and her hazel eyes also open to an enormous size with horror, her red-nailed fingers clutching the low neck of her blouse with terrified trembling. (We can see the copies selling like mad, but what will the critics say?) The Slick Ape opened his lipless slit of a mouth and pleaded for mercy, but Brady went on mercilessly knocking the man over on to his dolly, who bawled hysterically, her silken legs kicking beneath the Slick Ape. Chairs crashed to the floor, the Slick Ape slithered across his dressing-table, knocking hair-oil bottles and brushes to the floor, blood over his face. The girl rushed to the door, but Brady pushed her back threateningly. (The author can visualize, in his mind's eye, a schoolboy reading this book in his bedroom, delighted with terror.) Brady wrestled with the Slick Ape on the bed, the dolly scurrying from the bed, all bangles and thin arms. Brady swung the man into a chair, picked up a hair-oil bottle, opened it, and emptied it over the pulverized face before him. Brady lit a cigarette and waited, chest heaving, for the man to recover. (The author confesses he is worried: how will the university professors of English Literature justify this chapter ten as great literary art? But we think: If the fifth forms want it—they must have it.) Brady threw away his cigarette and resumed his beating. The girl wandered brokenly round the room, her blouse torn, revealing her glorious creamy flesh.

At this point we feel we have done our duty by the schoolboys, labourers, and excitement-starved clerks of this country. We feel that we have jeopardized our claim to great literary recognition, and that we may not, now, get the Nobel Prize for Literature. We see ourselves sadly paying in our royalties at the bank to an adoring bank clerk, while the bank manager looks disapprovingly from the doorway of his office. We see that as we leave the bank, an errand-boy excitedly points us out to his friend, and a book critic spits at us as we pass him. Such self-sacrifice must surely be rewarded in the Halls of Heaven. But we are sad. We did so want to be another Faulkner or Joyce. What will our old headmaster say?

Having put down our pen for a couple of hours, during

which time we have contemplated whether to be, or not to be, a great writer, we have come to the conclusion that if our story is to be serialized in those boys' weekly papers, *The Coldstirrup* or *The Tramp*, we might as well give over completely to writing for the degenerates of the fifth form, and be done with all this worrying. Why not, while we are about it (and it's no trouble at all, I assure you), give Slick Ape a blue, steel, snub-nosed automatic, which he draws on Brady; and let the Doll attack Brady from behind, with a miniature ladylike stiletto, drawn from a pocket on the outside of her gleaming satin-covered corset? (That ought to make the fifth form sit up, and fail their examinations.) But do we want to be accused of contributing to the juvenile delinquency of England? We will never get our knighthood that way. On the other hand, royalties are very nice in abundance, you know.

Now if we were having this serialized in *The Coldstirrup* we could build up the tension to breaking-point, tantalizingly finish the chapter in mid-air, and go on with the story in next week's edition of *The Coldstirrup*. That would get the errand-boys in a state. Let's give James Brady a snarl of sheer animal fury, a tense wince of the Humphrey Bogart kind, and get Brady to heave the mattress from the bed, in a hail of fire from the Slick Ape's automatic, revealing a sub-machine-gun lying on the coils of the bed-springs, which Brady seizes and fires at Slick Ape, filling the room with gun-smoke and repeated thunder. Ape at this point dies gorily by his dressing-table, perfume from his shattered scent-bottle dripping down over him, and a shattered mirror above him, brokenly reflecting the image of the Doll changing her colours diplomatically, by embracing Brady, who is tough with men but weak with dollies, like Humphrey Bogart in *The Maltese Falcon*. (Crikey, chaps!) We had better pretend that nobody heard all this, or the police will rush on the scene, and spoil the appalling romance between the Dolly, lovely in her split blouse, and Brady, tough as nails, a sub-machine-gun dangling from one bloody hand, as he embraces her with the other hand. As Brady, smeared with blood and lipstick, throws his great black machine-gun on the bed-springs with a clatter, the door slowly opens; and the girl glances over her bare, delicious shoulder at the terrifying sight now in the doorway. Tough as he is, Brady cowers by the bed in fear. Continued in your copy of *Coldstirrup* next week. Be sure to get your copy. Order now. (Red hot, man! I'm getting this next week, Smitty. Look out! Here comes the Head!)

Spotty Jones rushes to the newspaper shop on Thursday, excitedly purchases the new copy of *Coldstirrup*, and on the way home, opens the magazine up at the right page, and reads as he walks. The chapter is entitled 'Killer Casey comes to Chelsea: Blood, Sugar, and Gunsmoke in the Dandy Ape's room.' Spotty Jones wipes his brow with his handkerchief, and rushes to Scruffy Smitty's house. They both begin to read, eyes aglow, heads together; Smitty smoking a crumpled fag, and Spotty chewing gum:

Killer Casey comes to Chelsea: Blood, Sugar, and Gunsmoke in the Dandy Ape's room.

('Gor!' ejaculates Spotty. 'Crumbs, man. This is Great.')

'In the doorway stood Killer Casey, underworld friend of the Slick Ape. In his black, artificial hand, he held a huge Lüger automatic, with a long silencer on the end of the gun. Dolly screamed and Brady leapt for his machine-gun. [Now we must not get our hero, Brady, killed by the burly man with the broken nose, one eye, radiation burns obtained at Hiroshima, and bullet-proof vest.] Brady leapt behind a wardrobe, that he pushed quickly from the wall, and drove machine-gun bullets into Casey's face. Casey falls in a heap of death. Blood pouring from his nose—he had bumped it on the Dolly's face in the embrace, and he was always getting nosebleeds—Brady called the Dolly a two-faced asterisk, for no apparent reason, and rushed from the scene, the Dolly crying after him, "Come back, Jimmy." ["I don't think I can stand it," Spotty cries to Scruffy. "Pull yourself together, man," growls Scruffy.]

'Brady leaps into the road, and sees Bernard Bussey racing along the street, and Betty rushes from her door across the road. Breaking the window glass with the machine-gun, spurned Dolly—there is nothing worse than a scorned woman—scrambles on to the balcony, sending a shower of machine-gun bullets after Brady. Betty falls in a pool of gathering blood, and Bussey died on top of her. Brady escapes in the Slick Ape's yellow Rolls-Royce, tyres squealing round the corners, going at seventy miles an hour down the Kings Road. [Spotty faints, but Scruffy reads on, tough as iron. The two boys read on, Spotty having recovered, till they come to the last few paragraphs.] Brady is now fighting it out with Killer Casey's gang in a street in Chelsea. Bussey's lady lies in a lake of red in the gutter. The horse-faced homosexual cries brokenly over the dead body of his bodyguard. Browny Hair lies over the bonnet of Slick Ape's Rolls-Royce, which has crashed into a Victorian house, its back wheels up in the air, the front down in the basement, railings smashed round it. All the constituents of Betty's party lie around, battered and mutilated. The Rooster stumbles down the street, his stuttering equalling, note for note, the machine-gun explosions, as bullets rip into his body; he falls flat on his face in another pool of blood—there are twenty people lying in pools of blood by now.

'Brady fires a machine-gun over the body of a dead gangster, right up into a window on a fifth floor: a gangster falls from the window, to impale himself on the basement railings below. Brady smiles, revealing broken teeth, covered with blood. Bullets spray from a nearby basement. Brady jumps in a nearby car, swings it round, and drives it at the basement, jumping out Chicken Run (*Rebel without a Cause: James Dean*) style, as the car smashes down into the basement. Jumping into a juke-box-like American car, with rocket rear tail fins, Brady switches on the glaring great headlights, which send white-yellow beams through the dusk, and getting quickly into top gear, he roars the engine, and hurls the vast chromium car at the seven gangsters firing from behind an overturned Austin baby car. As the two cars crash, the cars explode into a sheet of petrol flame; Brady jumps out in time of course, and rushing around the wrecked cars and flame, he fires his machine-gun at the escaping gangsters. Brady escapes from the scene with Dolly (now practically naked, bless her) in a Jaguar, and retires to a room in

Bayswater. As they enter the room and close the door, necking in the dark, they see a cigarette glowing in the darkness, and the faint light from the street shining on an old Colt six-gun pointing at them.

'The dim light shines on an artificial black hand: "Killer Casey," whispers Brady, horrified. "But I killed him!" The girl screams, of course, as a belt of flame issues from the gun, bullets crashing into the door.

'To be continued in *Coldstirrup* next week. Be sure to get your copy by ordering now. Is it Killer Casey? Will Brady live? Don't forget to get next Thursday's copy of *Coldstirrup*, with its free lucky Elvis Presley signed charm badge—a relief model of a machine-gun, the kind used by the Americans in Korea. Get your copy. Don't forget.'

Spotty and Scruffy sat stunned.

.　　　.　　　.　　　.　　　.

But we must ask you to let us write for the Nobel Prize, and you must ignore all that the spotty boy read, because we can't think how to pull Brady out of his latest difficulty alive. He is bound to be killed by Killer Casey. Another reason why we feel we can only write a literary masterpiece, is that we cannot find an explanation for the return from the dead of

the very dead Killer Casey. Well, if we are not the type to write for Spotty, we must surely be the high-brow type of writer. Is not that so? Surely. I ask you—I ask you —rather anxiously.

11 The red, red lady

JAMES BRADY had beaten up Slick Ape, *and not in the manner described*. After the beating, Brady spent more money on prostitutes, stayed with Esmerelda for some nights, and began painting again on a twelve-foot by six-foot canvas, which showed a naked skinny man presenting a naval dress-sword.

The day previous, Brady had arranged with a chappie on the telephone that a lady reporter should call, to report material for a Cuban art magazine. Since Cuba was in a civil war at the time, the rebels winning and Batista fleeing, Brady was a little doubtful about the point of the reporting. He waited in the morning for the reporter to call at the arranged time of 11 a.m.: Brady's alarm clock showed 11.15 a.m. and he was not worried because he was experienced regarding the punctuality of photographers and reporters: they always treated Brady casually, for they thought he was eager for the publicity they could eventually give him, with their photos or articles. At 11.20 a.m. the door-bell rang.

Brady reluctantly and apprehensively clattered on his steel-based shoes to open the door, which when opened revealed a trio of characters. The lady reporter dressed in an expensive red, shiny, leather, thigh-length coat, tight crimson jumper, red shiny satin skirt, and red, pointed, high-heeled shoes with a star on the front of each shoe. Also, a very small, bespectacled man, with a yellow hair-fringe, big Punch cigars, high mauve-leather boots under mauve striped trousers, a duffel-coat of mauve, and a scarf, together with a hunched, smiling, pleasant appearance. The lady reporter's car driver completed the trio—he was tall, and held his large head high, had hazel, moist, and pleasant eyes, a long coat of a peculiar shiny texture, and a great love of Brady's small boy.

Brady was bowled over by the crowd, and especially by the Jewish woman reporter, who had lots of dyed hair falling over her red-leather shoulders, a lot of crimson lipstick over a large gash mouth, a bulbous nose, great black eyes which were black discs ever moving. She drank a sip of tea, left the rest in the cup with a smear of red on the brim, leapt on to a chair in stockinged feet, and began to question Brady as if she were a Hyde Park orator.

Brady found them quite an endearing crowd. And especially liked the little, horn-rimmed-spectacled, fringed chap, who was the lady reporter's shorthand man; who was described to Brady by the creative lady as the one who 'types' (he recorded and typed while she gathered the information); who was delightfully Chelsea and bohemian; and who kept himself very much in the background as he took shorthand. The extravagant personality of the Jewish reporter perplexed Brady, who watched her shiny red-leather coat moving in and out of odd corners of his crowded studio, her on-and-off red shoes, her dark appetite-full face, her black-disc eyes, with a hypnotized obedience. She talked hard and listened regarding art, and told how she couldn't find in all London a dye that would enable her to match her hair with her coat: she descended from standing on a chair with great caution, for fear her red silk stockings should tear or ladder. She was not what one would call attractive, for her peculiar charms were laced

with ugliness, and she was a devouring character. But she
obviously had great, overpowering, sexual appetites like other
Jewish ladies, and was a personality too bizarre for Brady
ever to forget, an egotistical, real person; and such people
Brady reluctantly respected somewhere deep down in his
mind. Brady always responded to the intimate humanity of
Jews; although he had a typical English reserve towards the
gushing power and general nature of Jews, towards whom he
was suspicious, like most other Englishmen who are afraid to
relax with Jews. As the lady reported, Brady became less and
less reserved and within himself, his speech becoming rapid,
humanity filling his eyes. In the bedroom the Typer and the
Tall Car Driver Person crashed toy cars with Brady's son.
Towards the end of the session both the Typer and the Car
Driver Man became irritated by the reporter's orders for them
to move a painting of a toy bus-conductor's hat away from
her, to bring a seat out into the front garden, and to get
Brady's son to shoot his toy Colt revolver at her feet looking
at her face at the same time. The two attendants did not seem
to be completely in sympathy with their red-haired, black-
eyed, red-coated, red-skirted, red-shoed, and red-chested
genius, agitating about with her many questions.

No newspaper would employ her for she was beyond any
editor's comprehension, and it made no difference that her
articles were good free-lance, her 'reporting' was completely
original. By acting in the most egotistical, exhibitionistic and
unconventional manner she made her 'subjects' forget themselves by making them concentrate on her, and the 'subjects'
then forgot their natural reserve with reporters and revealed
themselves almost completely, which revelations were copied
down unobtrusively by the yellow-fringe man. The circus she
brought with her (or seemed to do) distracted the person
being interviewed, and thereby helped to make the 'subject'
forget himself. Really it was all a very clever and calculated
procedure, depending for its success on its outward appearance
of madness and carelessness. But Brady was aware that the
group made money, for they were all expensively clad; and he
almost forgot Esmerelda and his chaotic activities with her in
the present chaos.

Out in the garden went the lady, gabbling enormously and listening without appearing to do so: when she was really listening with great attention and the Typer was writing shorthand intensely, she covered these activities up by dancing around madly and pointlessly—over the flowers and around everyone—and by playing hilariously with Brady's child, who reacted happily. The sad-eyed Jewess got colder and colder, the red of her mouth (some of it had smeared off by now on tea-cups) blending with the raw-red cold patches on her otherwise sallow, shiny face. Brady, his wife, and little boy sat down on a wooden-topped low wall talking to the reporter: Brady leapt up and examined the seat of his trousers for a tear, for he had sat on an accumulation of projecting nails, happily banged in by his son—a hammer and nails would keep him quiet in the garden for hours. The Jewess fiddled with her red hair, with frozen fingers that bled with deep-red nail varnish on the long wide nails of her fingers. But she suffered for her reporting and carried on her act enthusiastically. However, her cavorting did not seem to warm her up and she got colder and colder: she was obviously one of those women who are very sensitive to cold, and who get extremely distressed at the slightest lowering of temperature. Brady, his wife and child, were not bothered by the cold and Brady's mouth activated unreservedly, much to the concealed delight of the visitors who were all for the 'Freedom of the Press'. In all the calculated confusion Brady did not notice that the Typer had filled sixty pages with shorthand. The Jewess prodded her dyed hair with frozen fingers, looking unhappily out of a face blotched with cold, and cut open amidst greasy gore from her handbag.

Back in the studio Brady went on talking with no reserve at all by this time, so that the reporter had to do nothing but listen and try to warm her frozen person. In the background the Typer worked on silently. Coat gleaming brightly as it moved and folded with the quick movements of her body, she high-heeled in her tight skirt with short steps to warm her hands by the fire, and below her skirt showed dark-white petticoat frills, as Brady babbled on uncontrollably. A heavyish figure, with shoulders rounded by the heavy, glossy, red leather; shoulders curving down the leather arms from thick, red greasy locks of hanging hair, she was absorbed in her work, concerned with nothing but the success of her reporting work, and even her cold state was put in its place and received little attention from her mind compared with the attention her work was receiving from her devoted self. She was a handsome woman in a way, with too much character for the business of sexual attraction to be accomplished easily, however. Brady felt attracted and repulsed, by her heavy dark energy and nerves. Not an essentially likable woman, but characterful, and the creative, artistic type. A woman of misery and the satisfaction of her lusts. Earthy, vital, vigorous, and powerful: needing friends to lean on and to help her; but the kind of person who is a source and a force, bringing her own personal, unhappy, strong atmosphere with her wherever she went. So black was she, her eyes so melancholy, with the obvious dynamism and devouring sexuality of many Jewish ladies. She was about fifty-five to sixty years old, experienced and full. Like two other similar female Jews he knew, she had the same dark disc-like eyes that opened directly on to the intimate very-human soul that was hers; and she was like the other two female Jews in that she courageously lived her life on a selfish egotistical basis, flouting conventional behaviour so that she could live as she wanted to, even though such flouting caused her misery, and hate from English people around her. She readily told Brady that she was of Israelite origin and in a sad way—proudly. As she told this to Brady, she didn't look at him, but smiled a strong golden smile to herself and the Car Driver Man. They do what they want to do, because they must live that way, thought Brady about Jewesses in England, but they get much pain from the uncompromising egotistical lives they lead, lives with such queer morals by English standards, lives that have, however, a lot of love for others in them, and a vast embracing humanity laced with toughness and fatalism. Such contradictions, such warmth, such darkness and melancholy, thought Brady. But Brady was wrong about her morality, for she was happily married and strictly moral, unknown to him, but his thoughts went on.

Such Jewesses puzzled Brady with his ingrained Church of England English morality—puzzled him like Roman Catholic ladies, swamped in high moral principles, who could easily commit sins and chant, fingering their rosary, after a purging confessional, emerging spiritually healed. If Brady broke the laws of his morality he became a broken man, with no chance of healing, but those Jewesses could sin and go on and on, seemingly unscathed. Brady wished he was like a Jewess in that respect, able to retain his self-respect after he had sinned. Theoretically he had no morals, but when in reality he was immoral something made him suffer, something in him made him ashamed, and he lost his self-respect and became worthless in his own eyes: as it was with the Esmerelda affair. Such confused and maybe faulty thoughts Brady entertained: all of this chapter is Brady's thoughts, though I have put them down in a way that may make the reader think otherwise: true and false those were Brady's thoughts. Brady realized that his feeling of guilt over his first act of adultery with Esmerelda had been his undoing: if he had not felt so guilty he would not have got so chaotic later on, and subsequent actions—the result of his unbalanced guilty state of mind—would not have happened. Guilt made him exaggerate his first adultery into a frightening crime he dare not let his wife know about; guilt made him afraid of Esmerelda's blackmail—her blackmail wouldn't have worked if he had not felt so guilty; guilt made him go to Hyde Park and guilt led to Slick Ape's blackmail. If only he could have looked in his mind, at his first sins, with less exaggerating drama, one thing would not have led to another. Confused thoughts of Brady's were those you have just read; maybe not so confused—maybe. Perhaps he saw himself clearly, and if he did it did not help him at all.

As the trio left, the red lady clutching her cold hands to her leather-covered chest, Brady thought back about the origins of his present chaotic life, He had had lusts he had frustrated because he was too 'decent' to have a little fun behind his wife's back. His morality, a morality subconscious and not intellectual, a morality he didn't believe in but lived by despite himself, had been the ruin of him. If he had not let those lusts grow in the cage of his silly self-discipline, if he had had his fun behind his wife's back as others would have done, the lusts would not have multiplied and become a danger caged—the gorilla; then when Esmerelda came on the scene the break-out of his lusts—his gorilla uncaged—would not have been so destructive to him; and if he had not been so morally ashamed then he would have been better off. He was easily blackmailed because he thought his wife would have the same outraged morality as he himself had about his adultery; she might have forgiven him—she might have—he would never know. If he had been easier on himself, if he had not judged himself so harshly morally, the Esmerelda affair might have ended in his wife's forgiveness, and not led on to a murder attack, a full affair with Esmerelda, life with the whores, blackmail by the Slick Ape, and the vulgar brawls that followed. So Brady reasoned, as he cleared up the foot-squashed paint tubes that littered his studio.

A weaker and looser morality, less self-judgment over moral matters and things like the Lambretta accident, the poor shooting with the shotgun in Norfolk, the fireplace business, etcetera, would have saved Brady from his present messy life. But there is no fiercer morality than that embedded in the bones of a Church of England Englishman, a morality injected into him from birth, a morality intellectually rejected at sixteen but adhered to subconsciously for a lifetime: no crueller morality than such a one, no morality more destructive, for it destroyed Brady. Principles had fought battles in his mind, conflicts had cut him apart. These truths I give you, my reader, and they were not Brady's thoughts.

Brady pulled a letter from the rusty, iron-gridded letter-box and, opening it, he read it. It was from a single girl, a friend of his wife and himself. It ended so: '*Love from Jenny. XXXX from Freddie (you know how boys love his golden eyes).*' Freddie was a homosexual, his girl joked about it, as in her letter to Brady, and by this slack moral attitude on her part towards her boy-friend's homosexuality, she kept her liaison going on happily. But Brady's subconscious, ingrained, strict morality was not so elastic as Jenny's was, and it did not give elastically to the pressure of the beginnings with Esmerelda, as Jenny's slack morality gave elastically to the pressure of her boy-friend's homosexuality, thereby preserving her happiness and the happiness of dear darling Nancy-boy Freddie.

Jenny had other boy friends. Her Fred had his boys. A Brady-like morality would, under such strain, cause fireworks but Jenny's slack morality just expanded like elastic to embrace the situation, while Brady's deeply ingrained (but intellectually disowned by him) morality was like cast-iron that, given the knocks Jenny's morality had survived, would crack forever never to mend.

When he was younger, newly married, and fresh out of art school, Brady had gone to Sicily for a couple of months, and had lived in a cottage, a half of a peasant's house, by the sea, near a place called Cefalu, which had once been the scene of ghastly black-magic ceremonies presided over by a man who named himself The Beast 666: the abbey of The Beast 666, with its obscenely painted walls whitewashed by the police, was very near Brady's half of a house. Brady painted the sea and the olive-trees; watched the olive pickers kneeling and collecting—a soul-destroying monotonous task; avoided the huge hornets that could kill a man; brought water to the house in a jar, from the sunken tap right beside the railway line, and it was whilst standing in the sunken place wherein was the tap, as the train passed a few feet away in the frighteningly lonely night (there were bandits in the nearby hills, and a free murderer allowed to live in Cefalu), that he saw a snake slide beneath a rock in the shallow water at his feet; collected drinking water from the alternative tap amongst the grape vines in a peasant's backyard, until the peasant caught him eating the grapes as he waited over the ten minutes it took for the slow tap to fill his jar, which caused a row in which Brady insulted the non-English speaking peasant who had made a pass at his wife, with English words collected from the gutter that the peasant didn't understand; rode around on a broken old Lambretta that always needed repairing; swam in the blue sea; walked on the beach; left the speaking of Italian to his wife; found worms in his butter; saw by night in the house by oil-lamps; garaged his old Lambretta in the chapel by the side of his house—each little dwelling had a chapel; swam in the storm-swept sand-coloured sea, which hurled stones and rocks around in its wild waters; watched the proud-breasted, sensuous, high-heeled, Italian girls in the village, and the boys holding hands; walked amongst the emotional peasants in Cefalu; and loved so much the soft, sun-drenched beauty of all that was Sicily.

Brady found out later that Sicily was not Italy, and the peasants were Sicilians. English people want to go and die in Italy; in the land of softness, sun, and warm people: Brady understood this, and he too loved the hot blue skies, the rich beautiful people with their sexy girls, dark-haired and glorious, and the dusty sleepy roads and decorated carts; for it was so easy to fall in love with Sicily.

Behind the village of Cefalu rose a huge rock, and the village had its harbour from the sea filled with boats. Just outside the village was the Jolly Hotel, one of many across Italy and Sicily; and outside the hotel were parked ostentatious, vast, American cars that rocked on their springs as they moved on the bumpy roads.

It may seem peculiar to my reader that Brady remembered all this while thinking of Moralities. But my reader will find out why, very soon. Before he began to think of the morality of a girl and a man he met in Sicily, Brady remembered more of this wonderful island. He escaped for a while from his troubles into a world of beautiful exotic memories, memories started off by remembering that girl and her lover who once lived in a house near Cefalu.

The man was a tall handsome Italian who had a wife in Paris: he was educated and fine. He lived for a while with the Scottish girl in Sicily, and one day he went back to his wife, leaving the crumpled bedclothes on the bed in the large rented house in Sicily. The man and the girl suffered because of the parting, but they were undisturbed by their immorality. Now Brady knew he would have felt terribly guilty if he had been in the man's place, a wife left in Paris. Why? Why? Why had he such a conscience?

Tormented, Brady concentrated on remembering Sicily again, and escaped from his tormenting thoughts about moral issues, by visualizing in his mind's eye the peasant as strong as a horse, who carried Brady's trunk, so heavy, on his back for a mile down a rocky path to Brady's dwelling—Brady visualized this scene, and these others:

The girl crossing a street in Palermo, a vision of sensuality with breasts so high and so far from the ribs, that Brady kept his eye upon her by running across the square from his companions, as she turned down a side turning, hidden by people then briefly revealed again—a sight that made Brady weak and full of yearning.

The girls in the mountains outside Rome, going to wash clothes in the stream, in high-heels, dignified, their fine breasts visible from Brady's position, hundreds of yards away.

The film starlet living with her lover in a peasant-house high up in the soft hills outside beautiful and elegant Roma: Brady thought wearily of morality again, for the loverman had a wife in Argentine, and the Starlet was divorced three times.

The party in the French School at Rome, an old building at the top of the Spanish Steps: Brady had watched the wealthy French painting students throw wine bottles at the dining-hall walls, and he had thrown glasses from the high window into the fountain far below.

Brady filled his mind with memories, and thereby banished worry:

Rome with its buildings; the mountains around Rome; the tinny bus careering through the dust, full of people, out of Roma to Anticoli in the mountains. The village of Anticoli on a hill, squalid, sordid, dirty, wonderful, charming, and a dreamworld. The chickens on Anticoli's rotten, winding, sloping paths, chickens and chicken food on the paths. Filthy and dirty. Sun and clear blue skies. Peasants staring at the tourists. Dirty lira notes, so many of them. Prostitutes at night around Mussolini's vast central station in Roma. Roma in the early morning. The Lambrettas, the crowds, the fights to get on the buses, the cheap cigars, the horrible garlic meals, the fine espresso coffee.

The hundreds of cats in the ruins of the Coliseum; the way the lire disappeared. The peasant house in which an American had hidden during the war; the peasant had betrayed him to the enemy, who came and took him away one day: a year or two later an American plane roared low down the valley and dropped one bomb on the house.

Tormenting thoughts interrupted the memories: if he had not been feeling so guilty about his first adultery with Esmerelda, then he would have hoped his wife would forgive him, as well she might; he would have gone home from Esmerelda's bed and confessed to his wife asking her forgiveness which she probably would have given then (not now, however), and Esmerelda would have found her blackmail powerless to influence her catch. So thought Brady, as he tried to remember the jack-boot kicking Sicily into a battered lump, as he tried to think escapist thoughts that were ousted by thoughts on the subject of Morality.

Shall we think together for a minute, dear reader? Imagine Brady confessing his initial adultery with Cracked Esmerelda, to his wife. *Brady with a slack morality*—this is a hypothetical Brady of course—*confesses to his wife.*

Now his wife was easily influenced, and would be influenced by Brady's guilt, and strict and subconscious morality, into judging him by the standards he used to subconsciously judge himself; *or* she would be influenced by our hypothetical slack-morality Brady, into judging him when he confessed, by his slack morality, forgiving him easily. His wife listens to Brady apologizing for his unfaithfulness, and she perceives no great self-criticism or feeling of guilt in Brady. It is easy for Brady's impressionable wife to accept Brady's slack moral attitude, and when he swears that the affair will not ever happen again, she forgives him with a motherly smile. *Now imagine our real Brady*, filled with a feeling of guilt, asking forgiveness from his wife, who is impressionable enough to judge Brady by his own moral standards. Something in Brady's cringing figure, a figure lacking self-respect, a figure condemning itself, makes Brady's wife immediately judge him as harshly as he judges himself, and he is not forgiven. Brady's self-condemnation comes across to her, and she judges Brady as he judges himself: she finds it too difficult to judge Brady by a slack morality when he is all the time judging himself subconsciously by a stern, punishment-fearing morality, absorbed by him in his youth from parents who absorbed it in their youth.

What it all boils down to, dear reader, is this: If Brady had had a slacker morality way back in the hours when he first met Esmerelda, if he had not had his deep-down, subconscious, strict morality ruling him, and producing a destructive feeling of guilt, then things would not have developed from the day he first met Cracked Esmerelda, into the state of affairs Brady now found himself in, which state of affairs he tried to forget for a while by remembering Italy and Sicily.

It is difficult for us, dear reader, to explain these matters clearly to you, because of the contradictions in Brady's mind, and Brady's self-realization may seem to be an impossibility. But though the mind-doctors work from an opposing premise, self-realization is no help to some people, and their problems still live and get worse despite clear self-realization, realization of the original causes of those problems. Then, dear reader, you may find the contradictions in Brady's mind hard to accept. You may not feel that Brady could have an intellect that accepted a slack morality, and that at the same time he was ruled, despite himself, by a stern morality lodged immovably in the marrow of his bones. Please believe us, dear reader—Brady was like that; and if he listened to his mind, and acted accordingly with immorality, then he became torn within himself, unsettled and unhappy, because he was acting against the laws of conduct deep within him, which laws he only found true inner serenity by obeying.

12 Final chapter on Esmerelda

B RAD Y went again to see Esmerelda. He had not done so for quite a time, and she had been getting pretty neurotic in his absence. She had begun to paint weird paintings, very dark, of herself with staring eyes, the eyelids stretched open and away from the iris, above and below, leaving large areas of white revealed around the staring iris and pupil. Her mouth in the paintings was open, and her hair wild and uncombed. At the art school people were getting worried about her unkempt appearance. In her room she painted, besides the self-portraits, a series of elongated pictures of lavatories. She painted in the lavatory, much to the disgust of her landlord, and some paintings she did from drawings made in the smallest room in the house. Her landlord, a usually unsociable recluse, who didn't have much to do with his neighbours, began to talk to them excitedly about his barmy lodger. One day she stood painting in the lavatory and then decided that if the water was running into the pan from the cistern, it would be a better sight to paint; so she began to dab with her

149

brush and pull the chain alternately. This drove the landlord mad, and he came rushing up the stairs, to engage in a verbal battle with the wild-eyed girl standing amidst the pipes, lavatory-pan, water-tank, palette, paints, and propped-up elongated canvas. She yelled about subject matter being irrelevant, and shouted something about Rembrandt's flayed ox carcase on a hook; and he shouted about writing to her employers. She turned her back on him, and pulled the chain again, dabbling furiously at her canvas as the water poured down the white glistening sides of the pan. The landlord stumbled down the stairs muttering about lunatic asylums. Once more the chain was pulled as he slammed his kitchen door, and he heard through the door a shout about 'Rubens's pornographic "Rape of the Sabines"—Great Art—Subject Matter irrelevant and Painting is the aim, you old fool!' He began to make a cup of tea with an unnatural calm, as the chain clanked and the water hissed every half-minute, and he later sat down with his cup of tea, turning over the pages of a large book called *Great Masterpieces by Peter Paul Rubens*, which Esmerelda had lent him in a kind moment long ago, in an attempt to find 'The Rape of the Sabines', to see if there were any lavatories painted in it.

He mounted the stairs and shouted up to the girl who was dark against the light from the lavatory window: 'There are no conveniences in that painting by Rubens, my girl.'

Esmerelda laughed in a superior way, and said, 'Look at Hogarth and look at Breughel, my good man!' pulling the chain with exaggerated dignity.

So great was her frustrated passion that she kissed Brady one thousand six hundred and ninety-seven times during his visit, and he left in the morning an exhausted, ulcerated person.

(Humour, my dear readers, a contrast for you after the wearing seriousness of the second half of Chapter 11.)

But let us look in on Brady's visit. He mounted the stairs, his footsteps noiseless in the greater sound of clanking chain and churning water. Esmerelda heard his steps as the water stopped flowing, and she turned, brush in hand, paint on her face, dressed in messy jeans and dirty sweater with roll neck, to greet Brady with the leer a hungry tramp gives at the sight of a good meal of steak-and-chips. Brady recoiled, but was rushed into her bedroom, and smothered with passion, paint that came off on his face, lipstick, and an enveloping dirty sweater. Esmerelda did not let up until the frustrations of lonely time were banished by a feast of love. Then, seating the naked man in a chair, she began to paint him. Her face was contorted and furious, as Brady half an hour later asked for a rest. The tension between them for the next hour was extreme, her face demanding, mad, and angry. When after one and a half hours Brady got up, she leapt on him and pushed him into the chair, the contact with him changing her anger to more suffocating love-making. Brady kicked out accidentally, as she dug her elbow in his bare stomach, while she wiped her mouth over his unwilling face: the painting on the kicked easel came crashing down on to Esmerelda's back, covering the sweater with paint. She dragged herself muckily away from Brady and smashed her fist in his face. She was also angry with him for not responding to her loving. She then slammed her palette down on Brady's head, and knocked him unconscious with the pot containing her paint-brushes. No wonder Brady left in the morning an exhausted, ulcerated person.

When Brady recovered, the matter was smoothed over, but Brady realized Esmerelda was going round the bend, and as he left in the morning he was not only an exhausted, ulcerated person, but also a person who dreaded the thought of his next visit to the lunatic asylum he had just left.

The next time Brady mounted the stairs in the old man's house, the lavatory was empty of paint and painter, and he found Esmerelda painting in her dirty underclothes, a painting of a dead pigeon which lay in front of her, crawling with fleas. She had lost her job at the art school, as a result of weeks of frantic, violent behaviour, including vicious verbal attacks on members of the staff and hitting a student when she, Esmerelda, was in a temper. Esmerelda had saved some money in the post office, and was living on that. She was getting worse and worse as the days passed, and our hero found her in an unwashed state, plates on the floor, food scattered half-eaten

beneath the bed, and somehow the blankets had got covered
with green and red paint, now dry. She sat in pink silk knickers
that were paint-smeared, greasy, dusty, and utterly filthy.
Dried egg was in dribbles from her chin to the cleavage between
her breasts, which were bare. On her legs were black stockings,
unsupported and unmended. Her hair was all over her face,
and her dirty feet, beneath the stockings, were black. In-
congruously on her wrist was a bracelet, and from her neck
hung a rosary she had found in the street. As she rose, scattering brushes to the floor, and pressed herself to him, Brady
felt sick. He looked into her eyes; they were lost, unintelligent,
and weak. Brady's hand held her back, and his fingers smeared
into an accumulation of cold cream. He wondered how it had
got on her back, as he felt his fingers sticky and revolting. The
room was in chaos, and the floor covered with rubbish. In
the middle of the floor was a chamber-pot of yellow urine,
which Esmerelda took to the lavatory, giving Brady a slack
smile as she did so. She did not clothe herself as she left the
room. Brady felt very very sad. He looked at her painting.
Behind the painting of the pigeon was a man, disembowelled,
on a table. A little figure of Esmerelda was painted standing
over the man and on her face was a mad smile. The paint
itself was very thin.

Esmerelda came in holding the chamber-pot in the crook
of her arm, its wet brim digging into her breast: Brady was
nauseated. She slopped around the room aimlessly, and then
decided it was time for a wash. She trailed a towel from her
hand to the dirty floor, and went to the bathroom; washing
herself with the bathroom door wide open, and the bathroom
light glaring on to the corridor. Brady had never seen her
quite as slummy as this, and he did not know what to do. He
realized she was getting weak mentally, because of the strain
of holding him against his will. She returned once more, her
hair lank and wet, trickles of undried soapy water coursing
down her breasts and over her stomach: he noticed that her
navel was full of dirt, and that her pink knickers were sodden
with wet in parts from careless washing: her feet were still
black he could see, as she changed her stockings. She plastered
her mouth with lipstick, smearing it on to the skin round her

lips. Kicking a plate out of the way she drew on a skirt, and pulled on a shirt over her bare breasts. Brady watched her cook some bacon, in a frying-pan full of fat containing pieces of burnt matter in it and a matchstick, as she combed her hair with a comb, dropping long hairs into the frying-pan. Brady ate his bacon on a plate she had picked off the floor, with an unwashed knife and fork, on a table covered with lovely little and big pools of tea.

A stain of dark fat on her skirt, she ate with her hair ends brushing her food, eating a mixture of bacon and lipstick, until her lips were not covered with lipstick, and bacon grease shone on her chin. She drank her tea nervously, clattering the cup down into the saucer and talking very fast in a high-pitched voice, the words jumbled into each other, so that Brady missed their meaning. Wiping her chin with her long hair, she stared hungrily at Brady as he finished his meal, a meal he did not enjoy, needless to say. She bent her head, and looked at the table, her hair falling like a cloak over her face; she moved her finger in a pool of stale tea, pushing a wet slug's trail of tea out from the pool towards the edge of the table by her chest. When the trail of fingered tea reached the table edge, she jammed her chest against the table, ran the tea-wet finger-tip up across her chest, where it was revealed by the open shirt, and giggled hysterically. Filled with a pity that surprised him, Brady took her to bed and comforted her, soothing her hysteria.

In the early hours of the morning, amidst the paint-covered blankets, she collected herself, and threatened Brady fiercely, saying that if he did not come again, she would go and see his wife.

Before Brady left to walk down the street, below a lightening sky with a moon in it, she clung to him naked in the bed crying piteously. Brady kissed her and promised to come in three days' time. He left the visit for ten days, and then once more entered her room.

She sat before her gas-fire, her duffel-coat over her shoulders. As she rose to greet him the duffel-coat fell open, revealing her torso clad only in a vest, brown with lack of washing, that hung in a loop from between her breasts. A black petticoat with a great gash in it hung from her waist. Her hair had been treated with hydrogen-peroxide and was golden in colour. Dark tired patches ringed the undersides of her staring eyes, a glass of beer was in her hands, and a cigarette drooped from her loosely-open mouth. She spilled beer over Brady and herself as she embraced him, her arms round his neck, the beer-glass in one hand and the cigarette in the other hand. As she pushed her crazed poor face into his unwilling face, the glass slipped from her fingers to the floor. She had run out of money, and had been on the streets. She had met a drunk and had been beaten by him: a dark bruise she showed to Brady on her thigh. Her toe-nails had been painted and the varnish was peeling off. Ear-rings hung in her hair, and the powder was thick on her dirty cheeks. She laughed weakly and defensively at Brady's astonished face. And she muttered some silly nonsense about preferring to earn her money, rather than sponge on him. She would not need him if she could find her sex on the streets, thought Brady.

She patted Brady on the cheek with artificial prostitute tenderness, and called him 'Dearie'. Brady wondered how she had picked up prostitute's clichés in such a short time. 'I've got to go out soon for a few hours, Duckie, but I'll be back at one o'clock, and I'll see you then.' She pulled on a satin blouse of black, and a skirt of the same colour and material, slipped into high-heeled shoes, and put on a plastic mac. Then she made up her face, hung an imitation gold chain from her neck into the valley between her greatly exposed breasts, and poked Brady in the stomach playfully. Brady was rocked on his heels, stunned completely by what he witnessed. She left the house.

Brady sat down on a chair, and looked at the newly acquired clothes lying around the room: clothes designed to attract men; high-heeled shoes and low, loop-necked, silk or satin blouses. The clothes looked in direct contrast to the clothes Esmerelda used to wear: the duffel-coat and the red wool stockings, and sandals or low-heel shoes. In a corner, just visible behind a roll of drawing-paper, lay her discarded straw basket. (Or was it a wickerwork basket? Brady didn't know the difference.) How, Brady wondered, had she earned enough money in the ten days from his last visit to buy all these clothes; and how could she change from an art teacher, arty and duffel-coated, to the cheaply sophisticated tart she now was, during a mere ten days? But mad people can change in the way Esmerelda had changed, very easily.

Esmerelda had realized desperately that she needed money, had thought of an answer to her problem in prostitution, and had quickly changed into a prostitute. Her mental unbalance somehow destroyed her inhibitions, and she walked with the other whores by the docks, picking up their mannerisms, attitude, and talk. But underneath she was not one of those girls, although superficially she was identical with them. And it was tragic when she began to realize that fact, and when she began to see herself as Brady was seeing her now. The result was as tragic as can be, and it was announced luridly in the Sunday papers.

After selling herself many times in dark corners by the docks, filling her shiny black handbag with many pound notes, and getting more and more unspruced and wrecked-looking, she finally quitted the task of calling after passing men: 'Do you want a bit of pleasure, ducks?' (they felt like ducks in the pouring rain but it was a bit unnecessary to call them that), emerged from her shelter, and went home. The rain had kept most of the other whores at home, and she made the most of being left in full charge of the shop, as it were.

She was very wet, and down the back of her mackintosh were a few great patches of mud. Her shoes were covered with mud, and her black satin skirt hung creased and lopsided from her waist. Her blouse hung out on one side from the waistband of her skirt, her face was streaming with rain, and her hair hung heavy with water, plastered to her forehead and the sides of her head. She moved her thighs in a loose slack way as she walked clumsily in her high-heeled shoes, her mouth hung open slackly; and she seemed to be all thighs—her consciousness being in her thighs. Her stockings hung in circles around her legs and ankles, and her plastic mac hung from her shoulders in weary vertical folds.

When she came in, Brady was sitting looking at a book

of reproductions of Leonardo's work. She flopped down on the unmade bed, pulled out a collection of notes and coins from her handbag, put the money down beside her, and said: 'Hullo, sweetheart, I hope you entertained yourself while I was working.' She pulled off her mac, shoes, stockings, skirt, and blouse; dried her hair on a towel, and sat before the gas-fire, herself on the floor, her yellow hair fluffed out, a cigarette hanging from her mouth, her thighs naked, and the dirty vest hanging from her shoulders and breasts. She rose, leered tiredly at Brady, and fished out of her mackintosh pocket a crumpled, black, torn petticoat which she threw in a corner: then she put on her duffel-coat, and turning up the gas-fire jets she sat down in front of the fire again.

When they went to bed, she fell asleep immediately, and Brady left her sleeping as he left in the early hours of the morning. He never visited her again.

Some weeks after, he read of her suicide in the newspaper that he read as the church bells rang. He cried with pity for her. He did not know it, but she had burnt her diary, and everything she had that connected her with him, in a period of decency.

13 Lily

BRADY lay in bed reading his *Daily Clarion*, about how Garth's body was inhabited by the mind of another, and about how Belinda was reaching the puberty stage, when stiletto-heeled knee-length boots crashed up the front garden path to the front door, and his front doorbell rang. His eyes blurred, and the lids sticking together with the substance sleep issues from the eyes, Brady realized bad-temperedly that he must rise and shine, for Lily banged on his door, and told him it was disgusting that he should still be in bed when his model had arrived. Lily had a cup of tea in the kitchen with Brady's wife, as Brady slid into pre-laced shoes torn off the previous night, jammed his feet and legs down into the crumpled tubes of his jeans, punched his way down the sleeves of a pullover, and charged into the lavatory to sit down and quickly plan his day.

As he came into the kitchen, he looked down at a head of straw-coloured hair, and then had presented to him a mouthful of friendly, grinning teeth. Lily showed him changes of clothes she had brought for her posing, and suggested she posed in tiny shorts, and a hat like a busby that had not grown very tall. Though he felt he could make a painting of any subject, Brady suggested that she was perfectly well dressed for posing as she was—in those boots; a huge black belt with a huge yellow buckle of brass, over which a red woollen jersey bulged where it was constricted by the belt; black stockings stretching whitely over bent knees; and a heavy black-and-green skirt.

Lily bought paintings; was writing a book about a girl who wished to find completeness; had bought a house in Cheyne Walk, Chelsea; had just had twenty gallons of paint, a leather skirt, and jacket stolen by burglars; had a baby son called Boulder; was twenty-one or two; held her high-backed head high and backwards, so that her jaw slanted forwards, and her brow and combed-down hair slanted back to the high crest of her head; had a mouth and its environs that protruded forwards; was in her late teens a vision of child-like loveliness spiced with fresh sexuality; was now more mature mentally and more lovely; was lively; mink-coat scorning; in love with her husband; in love with motherhood, creating books, creating films, Brick Lane Market, and Roger Vadim— Brigitte's former husband.

Brady posed her on a stool with a green revolving seat. Lily always told her friends, who came generously to pose for Brady, that Brady loved painting petticoats. So whenever any of Lily's friends posed for him they always fixed him with eyes that hid their laughter, asked him if he wanted some petticoat showing, and hitched up their skirts a trifle, revealing red-ribbon-gathered lacy frills, which he obediently painted, wondering behind his moist brow why so many of his models went through this little petticoat procedure.

Lily hitched up her skirt over knees that showed white and bulging beneath in-fashion black stockings, and pulled out layers of noisy, crackling, stiff-white petticoat hem. Loading his paint-brush with flake white, Brady bent down, knitted his sweaty brows, and painted the petticoat on his canvas, while Lily laughed to herself at some secret joke. Brady wondered what the joke was.

Cool white paint was brush-dragged over the hardboard simulating the folds of her petticoat, while beads of perspiration ran over the artist's forehead. He was secretly, very secretly, in love with Lily, who was to his eyes, and to the eyes of others, a dream of loveliness become reality. She was indeed charming with her golden hair cascading in wavelets down from the crown of her head, her Renoiresque appearance, her vivacious manner and her prettiness and elegance. Brady's secret love was not expressed in cow-like glances from behind his spectacles or in the sending of anonymous billet-doux, but was expressed by the rivers of greasy perspiration that coursed down his fat neck. Brady's love for Lily was purely romantic and it was a love of admiration that existed only in Brady's mind, stayed unexpressed, and never crossed the gulf of reserve between them. His love was like a pretty poem which he might have written being too shy to show it. As perspiration puddled the floor from Brady he felt sure she would know the reason for his embarrassment—which was his secret love—but of course she had no idea at all.

Lily rested for a while, and asked to be allowed to paint a bit of Brady's painting. Brady gave her a blank, white space to play on; and she dashed across the floor with a brushful of red, and painted three little red leaves quite carefully. Saying she enjoyed painting in Brady's studio, she rushed across the room again, filled another brush with black and, rushing across the room once more, she painted two black leaves below the red ones. Brady stared perplexedly at what she had done; and she, happily smiling, hit her fierce sharp heels across his floor, and mounted her revolving seat again, filled the scene with layers of petticoat frills, and uttered from her forward-pushed mouth, which was approached on either side by little curls combed on to the face from below each ear, the words: 'Shall we start again?' Brady gave one last puzzled look at the red and black leaves, and picked up his dirty old brushes.

When Lily was seventeen she had purchased for forty pounds a self-portrait by James Brady. The forty pounds had been saved carefully and she was very very pleased with her purchase. It was a painting of Brady dressed like a labourer, with an open-necked shirt, shirt-sleeved arms, an old waist-coat, trousers that seemed to be at the point of falling down; and a bulge-out of shirt between the points at the base of the too-small waistcoat, and the downward curve of the beltless waistband of the sagging baggy trousers. Brady had an open mouth, no spectacles, and long hair, in the self-portrait, which was dark with much Prussian blue used: the white shirt sleeves seemed very white against the rest of the dark painting. Behind the figure, on the right upper side, was a window show-ing a cloudy sky, which sky Mr. Ruskin Spear, R.A., had said looked like an explosion.

While Brady was listening to Lily talking about her picture, the phone rang, and a woman very nicely asked him and his wife to a few drinks with a few people. The woman talked with an utter weariness mixed with a blunted eager-ness, as if her husband and grown-up sons had unwittingly battered the points of her will down over the years: on the phone she seemed very tolerant, perpetually tired, and generous—a very nice person. She wanted Brady to come to the gathering, because her angry young sons were fed up with the dull people who always attended her parties, and they wanted—she thought—a few angry young men to attend her parties for a change. She was so nice on the phone, and she said that Brady and his wife could bring their son, who could smash up the whole house if he wished to, that Brady nearly felt like going along. But he did not.

Back to Brady painting while Lily talked.

Lily took the painting to her flat in Eaton Place, and put it on the wall by the side of her bed. She adored it. It was a symbol of working-class energy to her. At the time she loved working-class vigour. It was a sex symbol. It was a symbol of a way of life. In the vigorous brush-strokes she saw expressed a way of being, and a way of seeing, that inspired her. It made her see life visually, as if every part of it was tremendously exciting visually.

Every morning when she woke up she would look at it for a spell. Every visitor she had to her flat would be shown the Brady painting.

One day she had a bath, wrapped a towel around her nakedness, and went to her bedroom. Incidentally the bedroom had a huge low window in one wall which overlooked a vast drop to a hard courtyard below. But to get back to Lily's story: she entered her bedroom and saw a man, presumably a burglar, standing in the room. She raised her arms in shock and surprise, and stood there naked, her towel fallen around her feet. Then she realized that the man was her purchased Brady self-portrait. She was pleased, because the incident impressed on her the reality in the painting, and she sat down on the bed and laughed.

She got married romantically and happily, and was very much in love. Then she wrote to Brady and asked him to paint a wedding portrait of her and her husband. When she first saw the real Brady she was not disappointed, and they became friends and she posed for him often in the ensuing years. Brady respected her and poetically fell in love with her from a distance, and she was a great admirer and purchaser of his paintings.

Brady went on painting her, and the confidential atmosphere weakened his reserve, and made him tell her in confidence the story of Esmerelda and the story of the Slick Ape. She sympathized, but of course could not make his burden any lighter for him.

So much for dear Lily, dear reader. You complain, do you, that you have read all the book, and you consider the part about Lily irrelevant to the story of Brady's fall down the slippery slope. You say the passage about Lily is like the Hooptedoodle chapters in John Steinbeck's *Sweet Thursday*— irrelevant and unjustifiable, even if it is inspired. But hold on, dear reader—wait a minute now! What is this book about? Brady's character surely. And doesn't that part about Lily reveal his character a bit more. You read it again, our friends. Brady *was* that painting, you know. Brady could have been the chap Lily admired on her wall before she met him. We are responsible for our lives and what we become: Brady could have gone from strength to strength, but he chose to collapse. When Brady painted that self-portrait he expressed in paint his strengths, and Lily admired the expression of them. Brady could have continued to be as fine as he was when he painted that: he could have cultivated his assets. But he went the wrong way instead and indulged his weaknesses. I disagree with you, reader: no Hooptedoodle there about the Butter-flies all drunk at Pacific Grove: in fact the passage about Lily serves to point out the tragedy of Brady's break-up, by reminding us that Brady could have lived Fine. Oh, dear thoughtless reader, do I have to explain it all to you? Shall I write a key to this book, like the key written to explain James Joyce's wonderful masterpiece about that Homeric character wandering around Dublin?

Now, dear reader, I'll present you with another small event in Brady's life. And you will have to work out unhelped whether this is relevant to our story or whether it is Hoopte-doodle. I'm so angry with you that I might even write irrele-vant Hooptedoodle just to be cussed. And I might even write some more Hooptedoodle later on. You settle down and enjoy the book and don't be so darned occupied with picking holes. If you enjoy the book that's good enough, isn't it?

After all, if you want to pick holes, go and read a part of William Faulkner's noble novel *Sanctuary* which I'll quote for you; remember Faulkner was given the Nobel Prize and *Sanctuary* is considered to be his best work. Now get your fault-finding mind on this: 'Popeye appeared to contemplate him with two knobs of soft black rubber.' And a page later: 'Popeye's eyes looked like rubber knobs, like they'd give to the touch and then recover with the whorled smudge of the thumb on them.' In 1949 Faulkner pretentiously said, when he received his Nobel Prize, that his literary creation was: 'A life's work in the agony and sweat of the human spirit, not for glory and least of all for profit, but to create out of the materials of the human spirit something which did not exist before.' Hooray!

We have to be tolerant to enjoy literature, dear reader. Now if you have learnt tolerance you can go ahead and enjoy the reading of the one great (and we mean great in the aesthetic sense) book, that the egotistical James Joyce wrote about himself.

You can pick holes in the greatest, but it won't do you any

good. We do hope you have learnt tolerance, because you will need it while reading our charming little literary piece.

Here is the event in Brady's life promised a few paragraphs back:

Brady stopped his Lambretta in the deserted main street, and went into the shelter of a shop doorway with his wife, to look at some dressing-gowns through a large piece of plate glass with SALE spread over it from the inside. Brady glanced down the road: huge shop-fronts mostly lighted, stretching down a night-enclosed street, with nobody around but a crowd of larking teddy-boys shouting in the echoing street with new-found manhood, swaying and menacing, laughing and purposeless; the ghosts of shopping crowds fled from the cold, uninviting, unselling street; no high, helmeted, dark-blue policemen walked slowly, lonely, and watchfully, down the pavement; most of the shop-fronts shouted visually the word SALE. Brady coldly looked at the formal glass frontage a few inches from his face; cold unfriendly tiles beneath his feet. He stood in a street of glass frontages which displayed raincoats, trousers, shirts, overcoats, and boys' leather helmets. Teddy-boy yells clamoured down the street: yells that grew bigger against the façades of SALE written plate glass; yells that bellowed and enlarged as they came along the street in great, long, curving challenge, clattering on the mighty shop-fronts. The teddy-boys revelled in their mastery of the street.

The street light shone, as they passed it, far from Brady, on a youth of middle height with dark, glowing, excited, fightful eyes, pushing crêpe-soled shoes out in front of him, a drape of shiny coat slacking forwardly downwards to his forward-pushed pelvis from curved, sloping, backward-positioned shoulders. They swayed darkly as they came along past the unbending verticals of the shop doorways: they were still a long distance from Brady and his wife.

The new generation trying to find a place in an established world that would not let them in. A new generation full of youthful power and aggression; fighting angrily and mystified in an attempt to find their feet in a hostile, resentful world, that turned its back on them. They owned nothing but their

Tommy Steele, black-leather, motor-cycle, Black Jack, wind-cheaters with white piping on the zip pockets breasts-positioned; their dandy-tight tapering jeans; their bumpy suède shoes; and their crew-cuts or sideboards; and they grasped ruthlessly at the chance to own a huge main street of a town, for the length of time it took them to walk slowly and menacingly from one end of it to the other, when the thousands had deserted it for the night: it was small consolation to own the street for so short a time, but they made the most of it, and their bellowings of triumphant possession crashed into the empty and large shop doorways and across the wide, grey, desolate, road surface. Brady was not wanted in their street.

Brady crossed the pavement to his Lambretta, and a shout said: 'Get away from that bike!' He mounted with careful self-control, and slowly moved chuggingly out of the street in first gear, leaving them to make the most of their fiercely defended kingdom.

Born in the World War II, and raised when mother worked all day in a factory, and father was at war. Developed in post-war years of too much intellectual understanding and tolerance by their elders, who were too tired of the recent war to stop teddy-boy aggression with force, for the elders were bellyfull of force. And anyway, Freud started the understanding, over-tolerant way of thinking; in which fertilizer the weed of teddy-boy aggression grew large, prickly, and poisonous—a weed that needed a sharp fierce scythe, unblunted by too much understanding, to cut it down, so that a flower could grow in its place.

14 Mrs. Tunkle

A CAR door opened on the road side of the parked car, and Mrs. Tunkle stepped on to the road, the car door projecting out across the road. Brady was driving his Lambretta at forty miles per hour, on the pavement side of the road, and was heading straight for Mrs. Tunkle's opened car door when he saw it barring his way. He was immensely disappointed when he hit the door, and so was Mrs. Tunkle. Mrs. Tunkle was proud of her car, and she surveyed its smashed yellow door with concern, as Brady picked himself up, and staggered brokenly towards his crushed Lambretta: fortunately Brady was not seriously injured. Brady was indignant and furious, and said to Mrs. Tunkle: 'You didn't look to see if anything was coming before you opened your car door!' Mrs. Tunkle ignored Brady and spoke to the policeman. Brady raged and examined his torn clothing.

After the court case Brady and Mrs. Tunkle shook hands, and Mrs. Tunkle invited him over for cocktails.

Mrs. Tunkle was forty-two, childless, dark-haired, and eccentric. Her eccentricity took the form of an obsession, an obsession both weird and completely lunatic. She had always wanted children, but her husband had a loathing of children, for he was a very precious individual, who could not bear the thought of children scratching his period furniture or damaging his darling collection of rare flowers in his garden. So he forbade her children, and she suffered within, and her suffering changed to a hidden madness. In every way but one, Mrs. Tunkle was sane, and to everyone she seemed flawless. Nobody realized the insane part of Mrs. Tunkle, and Mrs. Tunkle was unaware of her flaw. It is surprising that Mrs. Tunkle's flaw was not noticed, because the resulting actions due to that flaw were very notable. Perhaps the fact that Mrs. Tunkle's madness manifested itself in different countries was the reason for nobody noticing the repetitive events. She never told her husband of these events when they happened abroad.

Now my reader will be irritated to an extreme by his author's inconsiderate withholding of the definition of Mrs. Tunkle's manifestations of madness. So my reader must get himself in hand and keep a stiff upper lip, because he won't find out yet awhile.

Denied a child Mrs. Tunkle became bitter, resentful, and a cancer developed in her mind. She felt Life owed her a child, and she began to hate Life for its meanness. Devoted to her husband, she refused to blame him, although the blame was obviously his. Subconsciously she groped around for a way to get her own back, on Life identifiable with Society and with People. Unknown to her conscious-self she found a way of revenge. The way was always the same, and its repetition in her life puzzled her, but somehow she accepted its repetition, and took no steps to stop it happening again and again.

Now before we hit you, dear reader, with Mrs. Tunkle's one and vast eccentricity, we will describe her for you.

A vast chest hung from a bony upper rib-cage and her dark hair was flecked with white. Like many childless women Mrs. Tunkle was very motherly in appearance, with great hips, a kind smile, and a generous, friendly face. Her eyes glowed with consistent warmth. Big blobby drops of amber hung from her ears, suspended on tiny link-chains of gold, while around her long neck ran a string of wooden beads, which dangled on her maternal chest, encased in a flamboyant floral dress, a chest that hung its coverings down to her waist.

Mrs. Tunkle's eccentricity was this. She opened car doors carefully, exactly at the moment when a car would be coming at speed directly at the spot the door would open on to. She did this deliberately, but as soon as she had done it, another door—a door to a compartment in her brain—closed, and the responsibility for the act became closeted away in the compartment in her brain. By causing these car or motor-cycle accidents she hit out at Life around her, and she felt Revenged, revenged for the cruelty Life had inflicted upon her by leaving her childless.

If the Eccentricity had been more conscious it would probably have been more organized and therefore unlikely to injure the Injurer. However, if the Eccentricity had been in the consciousness and not in the subconsciousness, it would have been checked by Mrs. Tunkle's sense of Right and Wrong, and therefore caused to be non-existent. But because the Eccentricity was so subconscious, and so caused by a warped part of her brain, it injured the Injurer as well as injuring the People around Mrs. Tunkle, whom she wished to repay for the wrong she vaguely and subconsciously imagined they had done her. Mrs. Tunkle, in her attempt to injure, injured herself, because of the confusion in her mind. The way she injured herself was as follows:

On holiday in Carlisle in Cumberland Mrs. Tunkle stopped her car in Vander Streer, a street that ran from newly erected middle-class dwellings to similar buildings in the process of erection and then out into the country. She stopped her car in the part of Vander Street that was surrounded by all the paraphernalia of building houses. Just before she stopped the car she had passed a happy woman glorying in her advanced pregnancy. Although Mrs. Tunkle didn't consciously realize it, she was deeply affected by this reminder of her childless state.

Eva Tunkle waited in her stationary car. The pregnant woman passed on the pavement of newly laid blocks, her face beaming with the ecstasy of a hugely filled womb, her great distended stomach bulging monstrously beneath her maternity dress, and her fat milk-filled breasts bulging on top of her ballooning middle. Mrs. Tunkle observed her, and deep within Mrs. Tunkle's mind little worms formed quickly and writhed around with evil irritated movements. Eva Tunkle's eyes became vicious and insane, and she observed the approaching cars in her driving-mirror. When the door she opened was smashed closed again, by a fast-moving car, Mrs. Tunkle's hand was crushed, and she lost a thumb. Her husband was too busy with other things to inquire into the exact details of the accident. No one was injured, but Mrs. Tunkle had injured someone else's car and that was her intention. She had struck out in Revenge and certainly revenged herself: it was a messy kind of revenge, however, because Mrs. Tunkle suffered more than anyone else. There was quite a lot of money to be paid to the owner of the passing car, her car door was broken, and she could never bring herself to use nail varnish again—it looked so ridiculous on a broken hand.

Again on holiday, this time in Rome, Mrs. Tunkle observed a woman suckling her baby by the roadside. Mrs. Tunkle promptly stopped her car, opened the door, dashed round a motor-cycle, and watched it break up her open car door. It cost her quite a lot of money, but she had Hit Back once more.

The brain is a peculiar thing and very complex. Mrs. Tunkle craved a child and to be denied one was an unhealthy thing that twisted her brain, so that a cancer of insanity dwelt in an otherwise sane brain.

. . . . .

Brady wasn't very good with cocktails and Mrs. Tunkle's drinks soon intoxicated him. Mr. Tunkle was away in Holland buying a bulb or two, and Mrs. Brady was in bed with 'flu.

The great painter was rather weak in the mind at this stage in his life, the experiences with Esmerelda having wrecked him considerably. Drink loosened his brain even more, and by 11 p.m. he was looking at the maternal Mrs. Tunkle with amorous eyes behind misty spectacles. Mrs.

Tunkle drank more than usual, and she began to think of her need for a child, with special reference to Brady.

Brady stared at the ceiling through the bottom of an empty upturned glass, held high and to his lips. He filled the glass with whisky, and surveyed Mrs. Tunkle primitively. His eyes saw not the wrinkle-encased eyes and the bony upper chest. He somehow did not see the fallen bosom, the greying hair, the somewhat ageing face, or the thick waist and massive arms. As whisky, gin, and soda water streamed over his tongue and down his throat, he peered amiably through the electric light at an image part real and part of his intoxicated imagination. The real part of the image he saw was carefully selected: all he saw that was real was a bulging bosom, an equally bulging posterior, a pair of amorous eyes, a black satin dress, and The Eternal Female.

On the other hand Mrs. Tunkle felt basic biological urges stirring within her. Smudged with whisky and gin, thoughts about adding her little contribution to a future generation spread around her brain. The vicious, little, white worms in the secret closet in her brain changed form and extended and criss-crossed, till they became the lace on the canopy over a pram, in which resided a little baby remarkably like Brady and very derivative of Mrs. Tunkle: Mr. Tunkle's features were sadly absent from the baby face in the pram.

Perspiration cascaded down Brady's face, his hair shone wetly, and steam rose from his sweaty paws. His love-thoughts collected together into one passionate active idea: he gazed steadily at Mrs. Tunkle's beaming mouth and eyes, his glass slid from his wet hand to the carpet, and he advanced towards her. Mrs. Tunkle's heart swelled redly, and she waited invitingly.

Somehow Brady went backwards instead of forwards, and he slid along the table covered with bottles in an ecstasy of love. Murmuring tender words and choking passionate utterances, he embraced the table and buried his drooling mouth in the red exterior of a bottle of wine. His glasses slipped down his water-covered nose, to drop into a glass of gin. The table creaked under his weight as he spread over its delicate construction: the table gradually split across, and

Brady fell slowly to the carpet amidst torn polished wood, many bottles, and a few glasses. A distinct atmosphere of primeval passion hung around the collapsed assemblage, and Brady fell asleep dreaming dreams decorated with red ribbons, and dreams that it would be most inappropriate to decorate with red ribbons.

The smile slowly vanished from the lady's face, and she gazed stupidly at the sight before her: Brady's knees were bent, his backside raised in the air above his heels, and his head resting on his arms. A bottle of good red wine rested precariously on his upper backside, its contents pouring slowly and richly over his bulging buttocks. The sight sobered Mrs. Tunkle very rapidly, the pram canopy of white lace changed quickly into writhing, vicious, white worms, and her once-amorous mouth set hard and bitter.

She took a torch and went into the garden to look at her husband's fine flowers. Then she returned, and regardless of her carpet poured ice water over the gallant artist's head.

.   .   .   .   .

Brady stirred at 3 a.m. and switched on the light by the bed. He lay fully clothed on the bedspread of Mr. Tunkle's bed. He gazed at a picture of Mr. Tunkle in his air-raid warden's outfit that hung on the far wall. Then he tumbled down the stairs, and began drinking again.

Hearing his descent, Mrs. Tunkle rose from her bed, put on a dressing-gown, and went down. In her mind were white worms in a closet and a muzzy idea about sending Brady from the house with indignant insults buzzing around his ears.

Intoxicated once more Brady gazed fondly at the stern Mrs. Tunkle, who was attired in a red silk dressing-gown, her hair around her shoulders, and her big chilblained feet spread over the carpet. His heart went out to her.

He stepped over to the revolting and unfriendly lady and apologized profusely. His words were golden and endearing, pleading and tempting. Mrs. Tunkle was surprised to find that the white worms were now golden and had pink bows tied round their now happy, little, cherubic faces. She accepted a drink, had a few more, and perched her ample posterior on the arm of a chair. Her dressing-gown belt slipped untied, and the dressing-gown opened to reveal a cascade of golden silk nightdress. Brady's mind raced, accelerated, and charged down-hill completely out of control. Down went the drinks, this time to their intended destination, and Brady's mouth hung open in a ghastly fashion. Mrs. Tunkle began to convert, in her imagination, her husband's study into a nursery. The little white worms in their closet became gleeful little babies, who broke open the closet door, and tumbled out with big blue eyes sparkling.

Brady raised his eyes to the uncovered window and gazed drunkenly at the starry heavens, as he tried to uncork a soda-syphon. The cloudy sky had cleared, and the moon beamed suddenly as a small cloud moved from over it. Then another small cloud covered the moon, revealing the silvery gold disc again as it passed. But when another cloud passed over the moon, it revealed to Brady not the moon but his wife's disapproving face in the sky. Brady looked away, gulped down some more liquid, and turned his eyes upon Mrs. Tunkle's love-sick smile.

An enormous distance seemed to separate Brady from his objective. Just one action, just one piece of initiative on his part, and Paradise would be his. But he could not bring himself to make his thoughts reality. It was easy to imagine Paradise, but so hard to reach out and own it. So they stayed, on opposite sides of the room, wanting each other, unable to take each other.

As the sky began to lighten ever so slightly, Brady, his mind roaring with excitement and passion, hypnotized the gorgeous Mrs. Tunkle with his heated eyes, and resolutely moved over the carpet towards her.

She rose from her chair, her mind alive with carry-cots and nappies, and cast her dressing-gown to the floor. She pushed her bumpy reddened toes forward across the carpet, looked as girlish as possible, and waited.

Brady looked happily at the devastating delight in golden gleaming silk, with parallel horizontal rib-cage bars from the neck down to the lacy neckline. As always his spectacles slid from his nose and his ears, and he blundered forward.

Only one yard between them. The moon beamed approval in the lightening sky, the clock struck four, and Major Tunkle smiled pompously from his photograph over the fireplace. A cat wailed in a ghastly fashion in the garden, and Mr. Tunkle's prize tulip bed suffered considerably.

Mrs. Tunkle placed a thumbless hand on her silk-covered bosom, and ran her other hand seductively through her hanging hair. The tulips were flattened, and the cat's wail was long and horrid.

Brady stood at the Gates of Paradise, one and a half feet from the glorious Mrs. Tunkle, who closed her eyes in delight. 'Eva . . .' choked the famous painter, 'we will be so very very. . . .' His words were covered by a new and gathering searing wail from the garden, a scurrying and a cat's cry. The tulips sprang half upright, and a car roared down the road. A cat ran along the outside window sill, and a cloud covered the moon. Golden silk curving and gleaming poured into Brady's eyes. He stood inches from the Doors of Paradise and raised his hand flutteringly and hysterically to the huge golden doorknob.

'*Ring, ring, ring!—ring, ring, ring!—ring, ring, ring!* . . .' The telephone rang cruelly from a nearby table, cutting the atmosphere of amour viciously and severely.

Mrs. Tunkle picked up the phone, her face ghastly with agony. 'Mrs. Tunkle? This is Mrs. Brady. . . . Is James there please? Is he all right?'

'One minute, Mrs. Brady.'

Mrs. Tunkle put down the phone, and slowly put on her dressing-gown, tying the belt securely. Returning to the phone she picked up the instrument and said:

'It's all right, Mrs. Brady. James got rather intoxicated, and he is sleeping in my husband's bed. I'll tell him you called when he wakes. Is that all right? Yes. Oh yes, he is. Goodbye, Mrs. Brady. Goodbye.'

Mrs. Tunkle marched out of the room and went up the stairs. Brady heard her lock her bedroom door. He put on his overcoat and left the house dispiritedly. He walked till 7 a.m. and returned home.

.　　.　　.　　.　　.

Two days later in Scotland Mrs. Tunkle parked her car by the side of the road, one hundred yards from a baby-supplier's shop, a shop that sold everything for babies from nappies to prams. She purposely waited for a Lambretta this time, and the little white worms writhed feverishly, their closet door open wide.

She swung the door open wide and leapt out on to the road, missing the Lambretta by inches. The car door was ripped from the car, and the Lambretta went across the road and into a shop-front. A big American car hit Mrs. Tunkle squarely and she landed on the pavement in front of a pram containing a baby. That was the end of Mrs. Tunkle, and she walked through the Golden Gates of Paradise.

.   .   .   .   .

Returned from Holland Mr. Tunkle stood in his garden looking mournfully at his ruined tulips. On the garden wall a female cat lay contentedly, a look of sunshine in its half-closing orange eyes. Mr. Tunkle drowned the kittens when they came.

15 The Battle of Flodden Road

CAMBERWELL; art students, from Camberwell Art School, and out of the Oval Underground station; local youth from Camberwell; a photographer; five bands in a big barrack-room hall lit dimly, girders bare across roof; on the tickets it said: 'Jazz Night, two bars, three-and-sixpence entry charge, Friday 22nd March, 8 p.m. to 2 a.m.'; Territorial Drill Hall; teddy-boy and art student dance; five bands; one band was Tim Castar's Blue Chinas from the Sardo College of Arts and Crafts, Little Wingleston; one band was a steel band of Negroes and had steel, primitively decorated, drums; another band was 'The Teetotallers Seven' old-time jazz band with Edwardian and Dickens characters playing washboards with thimbles, and playing trumpet, trombone, clarinet, pedal clarinet, tuba, banjo, piano, dressed in ancient clothes picked up at junk shops; the T.7 loved by art schools—The Royal College, Goldsmith's College, Camberwell Art School, Chelsea Art School, St. Martin's Art School; big dance held in the hall in Flodden Road, Camberwell; teddy-boys everywhere; dancers danced and danced—stamina; teddy-boys well-armed were there to get drunk and have a smash-up.

Electricity Out was the name of a girl, tall, willowy; dressed in rude tight pants from waist to low-heeled shoes, pants were purple with black irregular-edged spots, 1920 orange coat with birds and animals on it; pointed chin, charming tense grin, black-encircled, vast, beautiful eyes; a beauty girl with long, uncurled, orange-yellow-dyed hair, black jumper; twenty-one; much admired by girls and boys of her type, not admired by middle-aged labourers and housewives; up-curving cheek-bones curving into verticals of hanging hair; white face; a fairy face with a sad-happy soul in its enormous pale sometimes, black other times, eyes; a fringe to the eyebrows of separate down-pointing verticals; a personification of the new generation—the part located in Chelsea—she talked to the teddy-boys grouped on the dance floor. She talked to teddy Ferdy Cramp, 'a nice boy' who was a boxer; she liked the teddy-boys she talked to—before they began to get rough.

Big barn-type doors in one wall of the hall; arty girls dancing, pony tails swinging, lank long hair flying, bare feet pounding and shuffling, rhythmic, black-tight-encased legs, serious eyes, open mouths, sweaty brows, dirty feet, dirty necks; one girl a Bournemouth existentialist with four jumpers, black eyes, black fringe, round, plump, impassive face. Leader of the teenage teddies—a thirty-year-old cockney, criminal type, pasty-looking, out of job, on the loose, little black eyes, like currants poking out of a bun, pop-out and glisten at you, eyes, aggressive, big head, long chin, lined grey lower-face, (didn't worry Mr. Out), tough fighter small, leading poor young teddies astray, rot man.

The Teetotallers Seven played 'Jolly Old Boating Pals Together' and jazz numbers in their own inimitable style; T.7 member Joey, in tattered leather coat falling to bits— holes and patches, blond teddy-bear-short hair, amiable chubby face, thirty, small, lovable, adored by 'dollies'; Mr. Out, spectacles, fringe, sideboards, secretive, characterful, curved nose, well educated, Bachelor of Science, silvery-brown blond hair, greasy hair ends over stiff, high, white,

shiny collar—he had trouble with collars before the dance, for they all fell down into the slop-pail below the doorless clothes cupboard—shoulders forward, backside out, tight trousered legs, the man was permanently crouched, looked like typical bank-clerk-turned-bohemian, but a very free and creative spirit lurked beneath this deceptive appearance, striving for a personal individual way of life, reacting against suburbia birth and upbringing, deceptively meek, has guts, tough as Old Nick when the occasion demands, sweet, charming, alive, intelligent, job in day, band at night, Electricity Out's beloved husband, good with Lambrettas, printing, collector of battle-axes, phonographs, old gramophones, pressed flowers, first edition Byrons, Brigitte Bardot photographs, shrunken heads, and toy steam rollers—he was playing in the band, finger-tips sore in grandma's thimbles, bent feverishly over grandma's washboard; Mr. Reg Parker blowing trumpet, black beard, black, smiling, expressionless eyes, waiting for his Delhi money to come through from the sale of his father's houses in Delhi—has been waiting for Delhi money since he was six, sells vintage cars and repairs gramophones in meantime; Electricity Out dances around outskirts of band, beauty girl, teddy-boys leering, people-hating teddy-boys in dark suits come from backyards lit by light through back-window curtains, where in those backyards they took a chain from an old disused bicycle, cut its parabola on the chucked-out rain-cleaned table, and polished a line of undulating links four feet long, folded it up, put it in the pocket of an Edwardian jacket, and planned its terrible usage—no more a swinging leather belt with the brass buckle cutting into a face.

The Teetotallers Seven stops playing, tries to get to bar, teddy-boys in solid block at bar treading on T.7's toes not letting them through. Most of the bands had left by now. Mr. Out goes to lavatory amongst glistening white tiles, white row of wash-basins, long mirror above them, pipes, and coat racks: three teddies come in and carefully bolt the door. 'Look, Mr. Out, why I do believe the door is bolted!' says one near to quailing-bellied Out, advancing on Out, who knows his fate and shows his knowledge with calm eyes behind spectacles, his back to the tiled unsympathetic wall. Ding, ding, ding, a teddy-boy clangs his knuckles on one basin after another, his waving aggressive head held laughing high, blood lust in his stupid excited eyes. Mr. Out's glasses fly from his face and skid over the slippery floor-tiles into an enamelled white urine-channel along the base of a wall half up with urine goals. Mr. Out crumples and slips down amongst raining blows and pounding arms, pulls himself upright, fights back gamely, blood on his high, white, shiny collar, blood from his curving nose, a shattered wrist-watch on his arm end. Three teddies bustle furtively out of the door. White tiles, perpetually running water over the intact glasses, white, glaring, cold room, Mr. Out on the floor collecting himself and his glasses. Mr. Out washing himself at a basin, peering above the running tap at his battered reflection in the long mirror, blood swept from the inside of the basin collected by a curve of water down into the drain hole. Mr. Out returns bloody-faced to dance floor and plays his washboard regardless of beating—tough stuff Mr. Out, and we ain't being facetious.

A bicycle chain up in the air, down across a skull. It all started when those nice teddy-boys suddenly changed to brutes and began to charge others with chairs, legs forward, and then they threw bottles at the bar and had them returned. A hand raised above the heads, a bicycle chain in the hand, the chain extended high in a metallic linked line above the holding hand; down comes the chain across the leader's skull, leaving a wound that is a long curving line from back to front on the side of his head, blood flowing down to his ear. Electricity and other girls hide in cloakroom, the Teetotallers Seven forming a cordon aroused in front of the cloakroom door. Teddies flung bottles at the barmen, and tiny girl Vivian in her bohemian set of clothes—black trousers, black jumper, bare dusty feet, and a leaden medallion on a chain hanging from her neck down between diminutive covered-by-jumper breasts—went mad and nearly killed a teddy-boy in her fury: another gutsy character Vivian, the art-school queen. She didn't hide from flying bottles and she met them by throwing bottles back: strong stuff. Chivs, sharp scalpels, flick knives, cutting up teddies. The leader wailing piteously amongst his blood. They were 'nice boys' when electric Electricity (don't doubt her name—she was called that) talked to them, they thought her one of them, asked her what she did, asked her why she wore those clothes. Up swung a bicycle chain, links polished and gleaming, down across a Tony Curtis haircut.

As the fight subsided the Teetotallers Seven began to play again, to try and pull things together, and re-establish the dance. They played on like old soldiers: the Windmill played through the war and never packed up, and the Teetotallers Seven played through the remains of this dance-hall war, re-establishing the morale of the frightened dancers. After all why shouldn't the Teetotallers Seven play through fights? They were derivative 'musically' from the bands who played in the late twenties in Chicago clubs, so why shouldn't they imitate those bands, 'courage' bands who played on when rival club-owning gangsters had gunfights amongst the dancers and music in those Chicago clubs?

A photographer had tried to take pictures with a flash-light camera, but the teddy-boys had smashed up the camera. Rightly scared another photographer had left, trying to hide his valuable camera from teddy-boy eyes as he retreated into Flodden Road.

Other teddies banged on the big barn-type doors, clattering. The police came and put water on the leader's wounds. A steel-band Negro afterwards walked around the hall moaning and banging a stacking chair on the floor, as a T.7 man advanced on him with a glass of beer in hand.

Never forgotten—called Battle of Flodden Road after Battle of Flodden Field.

Electricity and others one day in Soho at night meet the same nice teddies who ask, 'Did they remember that little bundle down in Camberwell?' They ask nicely, but Electricity in her pink, tight, rude pants and sailor top with sailor's number on it is frightened, so she gets away as soon as she can.

Walking through Camberwell on the night of the Battle of Flodden Road, James Brady wandered into Flodden Road around about the time when the battle was about to commence. One of the teddies standing in the road on the outside of the barn-type doors was challenging a mate to play Chinese roulette: he held the gun in one hand, spun the six revolving chambers with the fingers of another hand, so that the chamber with the bullet in it got lost, and then handed the gun to his mate, telling him to point it at Brady who was passing, and telling him to release the firing hammer, saying there was a one-to-six chance of Brady getting killed. Brady ran hard and Elvis Presley animal voices jeered after him as he ran: 'Move it, four eyes, move it. . . .' As Brady slowed down out of sight, he listened for a shot. Surely the teddies would keep banging the firing hammer down, and keep spinning the six chambers in the old Colt revolver, and surely they would fire the single bullet soon. But no shot was fired. Brady stood waiting for quite a while in a dark side-street, smoking a cigarette, but he heard no explosion. Perhaps there was no bullet in the gun, he thought . . . perhaps the teddy was just doing it all, to put a scare into Brady, thought 'four eyes'. 'Four Eyes' felt suddenly very sick with himself and ashamed: he was sure the teddies had made a fool out of him with an empty Colt revolver. A clock struck two in the morning in Camberwell.

Now my readers will be pretty exhausted by this description of the Battle of Flodden Road, and I propose to entertain them and relax them with the gentle and soothing little story of the ghost of Eliza Cromwell, which story may also serve to extend the knowledge they have gained about the character of Mrs. Out.

Oliver Cromwell: gravestone in a garden, of his unhappy daughter; she haunts Electricity's house; Sidmouth Street— half a dozen old, melancholy, ghostly houses set back from road, with church in ruins opposite due to be de-holied and pulled down; Cromwell's daughter seen in garden of Electricity's house in Sidmouth Street; people in downstairs flat left due to ghost; Electricity sits at night—when husband playing with band—in her flat afraid to look up, in the lonely room in the haunted house; she feels the house is being watched; the site of Sidmouth Street houses was once a graveyard—now people walk in the gardens with a few remaining gravestones on the side; offices on ground floor of Electricity's house which are empty at night making house lonely; Eliza daughter of Oliver

Cromwell; Electrical Percussion Equipment Limited offices on ground floor; Duke of Bedford's estate; everybody in road believes there is a ghost there; when the gardens are locked at night on a misty summer evening they have seen Eliza walking; Electricity like a Botticelli or Leonardo girl; giggling-mouth split-faced Electricity.

Mr. Out and Electricity, being married, slept together, in a not-too-large bed; Mr. Out, glasses off his now naked face, would sleep on the outside, and Electricity in a Victorian nightdress would sleep on the inside by the wall, and over the bed the kittens would roam, sometimes in the night. Electricity rolled while asleep, and Mr. Out would shift over in his sleep, when rolled upon by the larger Electricity. Rolling Electricity, shifting over Mr. Out, until Mr. Out fell out of bed, to wake up and re-enter the bed, whereupon Electricity would awaken, and want to know why he was coming to bed so late and what ghastly immorality he had been up to that kept him out till such an hour. They never saw the ghost on such occasions, for such occasions were not conducive to the appearance of ghosts.

PART TWO

16 Cornwall lunacy

JAMES BRADY felt life was at an end. A barren, hopeless, and empty feeling was constantly with him. He no longer had any direction in his life, no purpose, and nothing to strive after. His life was meaningless.

He wished to think things over and to think them over in a place that did not stink of oil-paint, in a place that was lonely and the breeding-ground of philosophy.

But Brady's mind was loosening up. Thoughts did not link as they should, in his mind. He was becoming remote. With very little money in his pocket he caught a train to Cornwall and arrived there at night. He found that the ticket for the journey had cost him most of his money. Wandering around in the night, with his large case in his hand, Brady unsuccessfully looked for a place to sleep.

    .   .   .   .   .

Soon we find Brady wandering across the cliff-tops, across the grass, his case in his hand, gazing at the sea, much in need of a shave, and with a tear in his trousers. He had slept in many queer places on recent nights: he had come in desperation to a stack of hay, and tearing out a hole in the side of the stack, he had tried to sleep in the hole, with the out-torn hay spread over him—prickly, poking into him and up under his chin, and comfortless: he could not sleep in that hay-stack because he was afraid of rats who might be in the stack. Another sleeping-place he found was a water-supply control 'hut' of concrete, on the edge of a ploughed field, dark-brown and furrowed, beneath a dark sky, star-studded and intense. The concrete place housed control mechanism and water-pipes, was inside as small as the smallest lavatory closet, was strongly doored and locked, and had a tiny window six feet up in one thick concrete wall. Brady uprooted a wooden bar from the fencing around the concrete 'hut', and tried to 'crowbar' the door open, by inserting the wooden bar in the surrounding gaps around the door and prising with all his strength. But he could not open the door, and he threw down the bar, and went round to the hole in the wall that was a kind of window. He put his hands on the lower border of the hole, and struggling, eased himself up, and into the window, head first and body afterwards. The window sides dug into his body, as he hung there in the window, his head and arms inside the tall narrow 'hut', his pelvis and legs dangling outside the hut, and his belly and chest in the tiny window. He was not the happiest of men at this moment, and he did not feel that life was 'just a bowl of cherries'. He looked down into the 'hut', and drawing a box of matches with difficulty from his hip pocket, he lit a match, and illuminated the collection of controls and large water-pipes. He dropped the twisted, charred, black spiral with the black knobbed end down into the darkness; eased the match-box into his trouser pocket; and, stretching out his hand, grasped a high-up pipe just above him and some feet before him. He pulled himself laboriously into the 'hut' and dropped down amongst the machinery, to light another match. He looked down at the machinery around his feet, at an empty pail there, at some old sacking, and at the dead chicken he had thrown through the window before he entered. Here follows the story of the chicken:

HELL IN A HAYSTACK

Brady was hungry and tired. Also he was highly depressed; felt himself an outlaw from society because of his adultery with Esmerelda, who had committed suicide somewhat because of him, and whom he had tried to kill; and had become anti-social and unbalanced in his mind. He passed through a town, and walked on down the road that led out of the town and into the country. It was getting dark. To his left he saw a plot of unkept land between two houses: a stretch of land about an acre in area that was not fenced where it met the pavement; and on the side of the land, where it ran along the side of a fence separating it from one of the houses, was a chicken run. Brady walked off the road and across the grass to the chickens. After he had hit the chicken with a piece of wood, it didn't die, but ran wildly in the wire-netting-sided area, squawking horribly. Filled with fear, afraid that the occupants of the house would hear, Brady's eyes filled with a desperate madness, and he sloshed away hysterically at the racing bird.

He stuffed the dead chicken under his coat and on his chest, held his arm over it in a way calculated not to arouse suspicion, and proceeded at a brisk march down the road, the dark fields either side of him vague in the half-light, the horizon a pale-blue. He felt a mounting of his fear as two labourers approached on bicycles, but they passed him unsuspecting, and bade him good night.

Brady walked wearily on into the countryside, looking for a place to sleep, and a place to cook his chicken where the fire would be unnoticed. But there were no trees and no shelter, and when Brady saw the concrete 'hut' he turned to it, for it was the best place he could find, it was getting quickly dark, and he was so very tired.

Having got into the concrete cubicle, Brady began to wonder how to cook the chicken. He had abandoned the idea of sleeping in the concrete 'hut' when he saw the machinery contained therein. But he thought that he might be able to roast a small part of the chicken in the 'hut', for his fire would not be seen.

He had left his case under a hedge a day before.

All Brady wanted was a few pieces of eatable chicken. It

190

must be explained that he had come down to Cornwall to get away completely from his life as a painter, his life with all its horrid memories. So he would not try to get any of his money in case his wife found out where he was, and the privacy of his wanderings became destroyed; his belongings of value he had sold or pawned soon after his arrival in Cornwall and the money had been quickly spent.

All Brady wanted was a few pieces of eatable chicken. So he spread some oil from a can in the hut, over the sacking, put the sacking in the pail, put the chicken on top, lit the sacks, and waited hopefully, his tired brain numb with weariness.

Brady hoped that just a few bits of flesh would become roasted, and that he would be able to tear them from the chicken, and slightly ease his hunger.

The 'hut' filled with smoke, and Brady pushed himself out of the window, and walked across the furrowed field, looking back at the smoke pouring from the window. He lay down in a furrow, too dispirited, aimless, and exhausted to go any further, and stared at the black starry sky. His unwound mind, revved up to screaming pitch by tiredness, intensified everything, and the sky seemed very near his face, very powerful, and like a Van Gogh sky, he thought. But he could not sleep, and had to wander brokenly onwards over the fields.

Queer places he had slept in, before he wandered with his case in his hand, over the cliffs that ran raggedly down to the wonderful sea. Queer places indeed and a queerer one to come. As he looked over the sea from the cliff-top he felt he had resolved nothing, he had thought out no solution to his troubles, he had found no answer to the problem of his wrecked life and smashed self-respect, and he knew it was because he had had so little time to think, for all his energies and time had been spent looking for places to sleep. He espied an old pill-box, used during the war, built on the cliff-top, a double-roomed concrete edifice, now housing only a broom, a fork, and a spade.

But let us show you the queer places he had slept in before he found the pill-box.

Brady walked past the large, concrete, one-storey building that stood in a field, the building by the side of the road, his

mind eager and expectant, as he glanced out of the corner of his eyes at the potential sleeping-place. He hoped nobody would notice his interest in the place, which contained a load of china telephone-wire attachments, and a load of hay.

He walked on further in the evening, amidst the trees, along the country road, and went into a public-house where he purchased a box of matches; and then went out into the road again: the warmth and friendly lights of the pub interior contrasted with the lonely, dark road outside.

Feeling absolutely criminal, he retraced his steps, and came to his coveted sleeping-place.

He got in quite easily; and made a fire with some of the hay: rather a rash action this, because the light from the fire could be seen from the road; but it was quite late when he made the fire, after exploring the interior of the building, and he was very cold anyway. He felt pleased at first with the place; but when he settled down to sleep on the hay piles, and the fire went out, he felt very cold, and he began to worry about rats that might be in the hay. After trying to sleep for an hour or two, he re-lit the fire with some expensive telephone wire matter, that was inflammable, and sat miserably looking at the warming flames. He didn't sleep that night.

.   .   .   .   .

On another occasion he found this queer sleeping-place:
James Brady came to a village at midnight.

There was a church, and attached to it was a side building in which was a long table: Brady wondered much later if it could have been a snooker table.

He went down the side passage, between the dark church and the attached building, and stood looking at the locked door to the side building. He forced open the lock of the door, entered the longish room, closed the door, and stood in the complete darkness. He groped around and found the table, which he mounted, and he decided he could sleep upon it. He lit some pieces of paper, which burned so rapidly that he was not able to find out the nature of the room from their brief flames, which burnt his holding fingers. In the blackness he lay down on the table and slept fitfully.

As the dawn broke he slipped out of the church-side building to the road, and walked through and out of the sleeping village.

He found a water-pump, and was drinking from it, in the new morning, when a man on a cycle, on his way to work, asked him if he had had any breakfast. The man gave the dishevelled Brady a currant bun, which Brady received with paralytic gratitude.

Brady passed through another village at noon that day, and went into a shop to buy a loaf. He looked so much like a tramp by now that the woman in the shop would only hand over the loaf after Brady had handed her the money: she suspected that, once he had the loaf in his hand, he would rush from the shop without paying for it.

The man who had given him the currant bun passed Brady, soon afterwards, and angrily told Brady to get a job.

It almost goes without saying that, by now, the police were aware of Brady's wandering existence, and that they kept their eyes upon him. However, they did not know of his concrete 'hut' entry, because the water-supply controls needed infrequent attention; and they had not had any news of theft, given by the owner of the chickens.

.   .   .   .   .

Brady stood on the pavement of the town watching the passing traffic. A coachload of Saturday cricketers passed slowly on the other side of the road, and Brady saw eyes in the coach laughing at the sight of him.

He walked out of the town and up a hill. He walked past houses on either side of the road, until he came to a building site with three-quarter-erected houses. As it was the week-end, the site was deserted; and there was no watchman guarding the houses for some reason. Brady returned to the empty houses at nightfall and built a fire which blazed its light out of the glassless windows—but nobody came to turn Brady out.

He slept quite well that night, and descended to the ground in the early morning, to wash his face in a pail of water from a tap, his toilet being performed by the roadside, in front of the uncompleted houses.

He went on his way refreshed, and clean from his neck to where the hair on his head began to grow. His hair was full of dirt from haystacks and many other sources. His socks were full of grease and dirt, and sweat and dirt together was embedded in the clothes that touched his skin. But he felt clean because of his face-wash in a builder's bucket.

As he walked out of another town, some children jeered at him and threw stones at him. He chased them into the back garden of a house, where they hid, while he stepped into the lady's kitchen and complained. She promised to speak to the children, and saying, 'I'm sure you will!' sarcastically, Brady strode out of the kitchen, round the house, through the front garden, and out on to the road, where he continued his destinationless journey.

He came to a few houses situated on a long lonely road. He walked past a trio of housewives standing in the road, a hundred yards along the road before the houses. They stared at him with hostility as he came towards them. He passed them while he was looking at an old, black, ruined house; his mind being full of thoughts about the possibility of sleeping in the ruin that night. One of the women divined the nature of his thoughts, and loudly said that the ruin should be taken down as it encouraged tramps to sleep there.

So this is Brady, scorned by children and housewives, tramping the country roads in rags, observed by the police, and going nowhere in particular; just trying to work things out in his mind.

. . . . .

Brady walked through the night, along the main road by the sea, ahead of him an accumulation of lights in the black, which indicated that a town was there. It was a seaside town and Brady walked along the deserted promenade, big guest-houses with balconies on one side of him, and the dark mysterious sea moving in the darkness on the other side of him and somewhat below him.

He looked at the sheltered seats spaced regularly along the

promenade, and went to one to bed down for the night. But as usual his sleep was far from pure, deep, and untroubled. He spread his body on the hard wooden seat; and his legs felt like pieces of hard wood, as did his arms, elbows, neck, and head; and all those pieces of painfully hard wood, angled on the hard wood seat-bars, resulted in the direct opposite to a rest on a soft pillow, on a soft spring mattress, and within soft embracing sheets: he looked enviously at the guest-houses. A couple of lovers sat on the seat on the other side of the glass partition in the middle of the seat shelter, and later they went away. A policeman came, observed, and departed.

'The sergeant said that we don't want you here and you better get out of this town quickly. Do you understand?' Brady looked up at the dark, uniformed, helmeted, unsympathetic, and heavy figure, standing in the darkness on the sea front. 'If you start walking up that road . . .' the policeman said, pointing to a road leading away from the sea, 'you will come to some crossroads with a telephone-box located at that point. I advise you to do that. Wait there and a van' (the policeman described the van) 'will come along. Hail it and they will give you a lift. Come on, you'd better do that, for the sergeant doesn't want you here. Be gone from here when I next pass this shelter.'

Brady watched him go.

The traveller picked himself up, and crossed the main road that ran along the front, then he began to walk away from the town and into the night-enveloped countryside.

After a number of miles he felt like an inhuman thing dragging along the road: he forced himself, his weary legs, along the dark road; utterly tired was he, lonely, and miserable. He began to worry about not getting to the crossroads in time for the van. He had walked robot-like for several yards before he realized that one shoe had come off, and that it lay behind him in the middle of the road. But he was too weary even to stop, let alone turn, retrace his steps, bend, pick up a shoe, put it on a tender swollen foot, turn again, and walk on. He wanted only that comfortable seat in a van, with a human being; transportation with no other purpose than that it gave the luxury of an enclosed space, comparative warmth, and

protection from the bleak, lonely, cold night. He wanted the mothering protection of being in a van that roared comforingly, its lights beaming into the night he found so desolate and impenetratable. The van became a haven of rest in his mind.

But, when he reached the crossroads and waited for two hours, there was no van. The policeman had tricked him in an effort to get him out of the seaside town. His mind hardened with desperation and extreme tiredness, and he went back along the road, to find his shoe, and walk back to the seaside town. Why, he thought, should he not be in the town?

The morning came, and he rose from the shelter by the sea, looked at a workman going to work along the sea front, and walked in the early pale sunbeams into the town. As he walked, stiffly and gaunt, many eyes on his queer, desperate appearance, the people in the streets multiplied. He saw the policeman on the other side of the street, or thought he saw him. He glared at the policeman and the policeman's eyes shone with laughter.

He stood in front of a corner guest-house, guests in seaside clothes passing him as they came out of the hall of the house, past its open front door, and into the seaside town

He stood later by a coach station, and he looked enviously through the sunshine, at the people gaily getting into the coaches and at the destination lists. How he longed for the comfort of a coach seat on a long journey.

.   .   .   .   .

The corn grew in the fields and the cars passed on the road. A sunny day died into twilight and darkness. Brady walked into a field to a lean-to shed made of corrugated iron. Within the shed, majestically, resided a farm mechanism of some kind, upon which Brady placed a piece of corrugated iron, and in turn upon which Brady placed himself. The cold was cruel and the dark hours passed.

A rider and a white horse passed, and Brady undiscovered lay quiet and still. The horse stopped, and Brady went to see. Brady peered round the edge of the shed, and saw a white horse standing riderless by a wall; its rider, a blond young farmer, his back to Brady, urinated on the wall in the mist-wet darkness.

The horse and rider rode away, and Brady was left to his silent lack of comfort and no sleep.

· · · · ·

Brady called it a pill-box. He drew on its walls, with burnt wood, huge Picassoesque bulls. It had a door in its concrete wall and Brady slept well there for a few days, the sea beyond the edge of the cliff in front of the entrance to the concrete look-out place. His suitcase was now with him. He stole potatoes from a field, borrowed a box of matches, and tried to cook the potatoes, with little success. Nobody bothered him, and a few holiday-makers passed him as he sat in the sunshine in the entrance to the rough concrete 'home'.

Brady had a long carving-knife in his suitcase: he had bought it when he first arrived in Cornwall, because he wanted a knife to cut and spread, when he sat down to eat the accumulation of purchased food he had obtained at the beginning of his Cornwall journeyings.

He thought wildly in his hunger about killing a cow with this knife, a cow that was with others in a field behind his concrete 'home'. He planned to do this act at night: he felt so remote from everybody, that he imagined that nobody noticed his existence on the cliff-top; and that he would be able to kill the cow, take it to the concrete 'home', slice it up, and not be caught for his crime. Such was the extent of his madness, brought on by isolation, hunger, tiredness, hopelessness, and the memory of his previous life.

He closed the door, barred it, left his suitcase within, and pinned this note on the door: *Please do not enter. By order of the Borough Council.*

He wandered away.

· · · · ·

A few times the police had stopped him, and questioned him, and once he had had to show the contents of his case to a constable on the grassy edge of a road.

He stepped from the curving road into a thickly treed

jungle that dropped steeply from the roadway. It was again night-time, and he wandered lower and lower from the road level, into the trees and bushes. A steep bank rose from the roadway, and then the ground dipped rapidly down to where Brady stood.

A police car roared by on the road above him, its lights beaming, and Brady thought they were looking for him. He stood terrified in the jungle.

The car roared round the crescent again, and Brady lay down to sleep.

The moon was a white disc in the sky, the trees stretched high above Brady's wakening face to criss-cross their upper branches blackly against the moon. Tangled prickly bushes jabbed into his lying body and curved over him. A wall of brick, aged and beautifully textured and coloured, rose beside him.

The torchlight shone its narrow beam on his bearding face, and he stared into the beam and up to its source. She was young, about nineteen, bedraggled and dirty, ragged and wild. Far away in Atwood Lunatic Asylum the nurses waited for her return.

Her face was heavy and full, red, and somewhat bloated. She was a coarse-looking girl, full-lipped, and heavy-browed, of middle height, with a bulging figure, full wide hips, full bosom, and large splayed-outwards feet. She said something inarticulately, and stood there in the tangled strands of the bushes: immobile, simple-minded, and with eyes showing the innocence of a child, and also showing the coarse maturity sexually of a slum housewife of twenty-seven with six children. She pushed her tangled, long, brown hair from her face with a red heavy hand, licked her shapeless great lips with an equally shapeless, great, red tongue, leered toothily, and scratched herself.

Brady rose from his bed of wet leaves and sticks, scraped against some barbed stems, and stood upright, looking with amazement at the girl. He had lost a lot of weight, and was haggard and gaunt; his hair sticking out spikily, matted and clogged, full of dirt, leaves, and twigs. He combed his hair with his fingers.

He clung to the powerful bulging form, and the two moved awkwardly against the bushes. Bestiality was in him, and his actions were unhindered by inhibitions. The girl was also like an animal, and she grunted and made sounds with her mouth to be found in no dictionary.

They fell to the ground at the base of the mossy-green, crumbling brick wall, spiky stems bending under the weight and flying released up and quivering. Her coat base spread out on the ground its silken lining revealed. Brady's arm slowly dragged down against the wall and crumbling particles fell from the wall, dislodged, upon the mad girl. Her bulging staring eyes, whites enormous, watched the top of the wall, where the moon was cut in half by the line of broken glass up there. Her mouth leered open gigantically; and back went her chin, from which ran down saliva trails along her stretched heavy-muscled neck.

Her mouth contracted and set fiercely. Her eyes became covered by the lids, and a mean expression was within them. Her brow became muscle-corded and ridged. Words of no meaning viciously spurted from her mouth. Brady saw a golden cross on a golden chain hanging on her violently heaving breasts, gold metal on her dark green dress.

Sanity briefly blessed his mind, and he decided not to do what he had intended to do. He rolled from the girl and lay disappointed and sullen. She rose with a swirling of coat and dress, became calm, lay down by Brady, and went to sleep. When Brady awoke she was gone and rain drizzled down upon him. He climbed to the road, jumped down, and began to walk in the rain along the middle of the road.

.   .   .   .

He walked to the farm along a gutted muddy track, past sheds and barns, eventually to confront the bespectacled farmer, who was once a policeman. The farmer asked Brady if he had any money, and when Brady said, 'No,' the farmer asked Brady to wait. Brady had asked for a job.

The two policemen came after hours of waiting. They took Brady in a car to a place far away, and the car entered through a large gateway, and travelled round large bleak buildings.

The doctor told Brady to undress, and he examined Brady from behind his desk. Brady dressed in a nightshirt was led to a bed in a long room, and he fell asleep within the bed.

The following morning Brady watched the male nurses polishing the ward floor. In the next bed was an old man, too senile to feed himself. In another bed was an old rector, who encouraged the cat that was not in existence to cross the ward. At one end of the ward were the padded cells, and in one of them a youth, strained by his school examinations, imitated aeroplanes all the day long.

Word got round that two patients from the women's section were to be led through the ward that afternoon. Great excitement prevailed.

When the startled women came, old Fred jumped out of bed, bare feet slapping on the polished floor, his white night-dress billowing, gay imbecility gurgling from his ancient mouth, his urine pot crashing from its place on top of his bed-side locker to the floor. He rushed between the beds, urged on by the delighted screams of the others in the beds, his old arms flailing, his feet slipping, pursued by a male nurse, who tried to conceal his amusement. Old Fred was a favourite with the male nurses. He was led gently back to his bed.

That night Brady lay awake. Old Fred got stealthily out of his bed and crept over to behind the male nurse, who was reading at the table in the middle of the ward. 'I'm the Man in the Moon come to chop off yer 'ead!' wailed Fred. The nurse gave Fred a stern talking-to and led him back to bed.

Brady signed himself out after three days, and when he had walked out of the town he decided to go back to his family. He had worked nothing out in his mind, he had no plan formed which he could use as a basis for his life from then onwards, and he was as distressed as he had been before the Cornwall period, and the period in Atwood Lunatic Asylum in the county of Barleywall which adjoined Cornwall.

He walked back into Cornwall.

.   .   .   .   .

Brady worked in the clay mine for one day. It had been difficult to get the job, but a sympathetic director had been kind. The men gave Brady some food from their lunch packs, and Brady worked amongst the great dips and towering walls of clay. Hoses of water threw great jets on to the wall, and rivers of clay-water ran around Brady's feet. Brady worked to control the directions of the rivers, blocking the rivers and changing their courses.

She stood at the top of a sloping wall of clay, her clothes torn, her figure covered with mud. Brady wondered how she had got there. The men saw she was mad and walked in a group to her. As they came from behind her she saw them and then saw Brady. Yelling to Brady as if they were dear friends she ran down the sloping mass of clay, sliding and rolling. She picked herself up, dripping and grey with clay, and clambered towards Brady. Her feet splashed into rivers and the grey water covered her in spots and blobs. Carelessly she rushed through the rebound shower of water, that cascaded from a clay wall, where a hose jet hit the wall. She fell headlong into a mass of clay and water, arose, and lunged lovingly at Brady. They fell together into a pool of grey water, the men milling around them.

Brady said later that he had never seen her before and they believed him.

Brady slept that night in the youth-club room in the grounds of the vicarage, as he had done on the previous night. He had gained the vicar's sympathy when he walked into the vicarage the previous night, and the vicar had let him sleep in with the billiard-table and the chairs, in the room reached via metal stairs.

The following morning Brady departed.

.   .   .   .   .

Very strong was she and very desirous of freedom. The man left to guard her was young and weak of will. They waited for the mental-hospital van by the roadside. He accepted her amorous and secretive caresses, for she was not the clay-covered figure of hours before: she had on a man's shirt, man's trousers, man's shoes, socks, and suit-coat; and her hair was washed and clean, as was she all over. She hit him with a rock and ran away, escaping successfully.

She slept in the bushes by the roadside, and in the morning she just sat and watched the passing cars, thinking she would ask for a lift later on. Brady came down the road and she joined him. Her necklace was lost and she had decided to talk coherently. Brady liked her and responded to her advances. They left the road very soon after meeting, and they travelled together only by night.

.　　　.　　　.　　　.　　　.

The cave was large and hidden. The sea was spread with sun and dotted here and there with little boats. High in the arching blue heavens a ball of yellow fire was. Holiday-making families walked high above the cave: they walked on the grassy cliff-top. Stones and boulders stretched from the hidden cave-mouth to the sands which ran yellow to the tubular breakers. Two exploring children entered the cave, played some way inside for a while, and went away. . . . The liner came in from the horizon and disappeared beyond a screen of cliffs stretching out to sea.

The cave was dark within; and a pool of water lay still in the cave, from the entrance to far back in the cave, where the cave floor rose and spread hard and dry, for a long way further into the cave.

The day had been hot, and as the sun wallowed in a glory of dark-fire red and purple, the girl slipped with Brady from the cave, running naked down the now brief beach, to merge with the warm and lovely sea. They swam together far out from the shore; and Brady experienced poetry he had never known in his sanity, but now found with his madness: it is true that the mad mind finds great beauty sometimes, due to its characteristic uninhibited state, great beauty that the sane mind is too inhibited and fettered to absorb.

The sun lowered still further as they swam towards it: swimming were they in the long band of light that was the reflection of the sun in the sea, a wave-broken band of light that stretched from the sinking sun, across the sea, to the shore. Nobody saw them at this time, at the day's end. As the sun sank even lower, it changed to crimson, and the band of reflected light they swam in changed to fire across the water.

SWIMMING BY EVENING SUN

Bratby.

Their arms rose from and dipped into the red water, and little flurries of white foam tailed by their feet. They kissed together amongst the fire on the horizon, turned, and swam back to the shore, swimming right down the band of flame in the water; till they rose from the sea, and ran nakedly across the sand and stones together to the cave. Within the cave their laughter rang around the rock walls.

They dressed in clothes washed previously in the sea and dried in the sun, and climbed the cliff, to walk along the edge of the cliffs. Above them the mackerel sky was purple and red.

Also previously Brady had pawned her watch, and with the money had bought a supply of food, part of which they cooked on a fire that night: a fire made at the very end of the cave, above which a hole led conveniently up through the rock to the outside air—through this hole the smoke from the fire escaped; and so the cave did not become filled with smoke as did the 'chicken-roasting hut of concrete'.

They ate well, and they relaxed in the cave, lazily smoking cigarettes, feeling that life was good. All was romantic and idyllic.

Many days passed secretly in this manner.

Brady's wife back at his home received a letter from Brady, which cunningly explained his absence, and the lies put her mind at rest.

Then the money ran out. About a week passed and hunger was ruling. Tempers became frayed and all was far from romantic and idyllic.

Brady got back from an evening swim and found that she was not in the cave. He began to worry and the night came. She returned as the clock on the town-hall tower showed twelve, and as she stumbled down the cliff, she glanced at the far away, but visible, tower, apprehensively. Brady guessed how she had got the money: she had previously cut and sewed her male attire until it fitted her and did not look so masculine; and also Brady remembered Esmerelda's last days. He looked at the money she handed him, and felt he was no better than a Stepney pimp living on a prostitute's earnings. He slept that night as far from her contaminated person as possible.

But they lived on the money for the following days, and when it was all spent Brady began to realize that the hunger would rule again unless some more money was obtained.

He also began to worry about their being discovered. The cave was very well hidden, and on a very remote part of the beach. But he felt someone must have seen them when they were swimming in the evenings. They kept in the cave by day and very seldom walked on the cliff-top, but Brady was sure people must know of their existence there. And then there was the fact that she was sure to be looked for by the police, who must have been notified of her escape by the asylum authorities, notified about her peculiar dress (now altered somewhat, however), and notified about her assault on the clay-mine labourer.

Though Brady did not know it, no one had taken any notice of their infrequent appearances outside the cave, no one had seen them go to the sea or return from it (though they had been seen in the sea, and dismissed as holiday-makers because their nudity was not visible), no one knew they lived in the cave, and no one had reported seeing them to the police.

The police thought Brady had left the county, and the police and the asylum authorities imagined that the girl had left the county also.

The men who had given the money to the girl had naturally spoken to no one about her.

So Brady and the girl remained undiscovered, though Brady worried nevertheless.

Brady weakened and let the girl go for more money. They lived on the money for a while, and the girl earned some more. She then went to a shop on the near side of the nearest town, bought some clothes, changed into them in a women's public lavatory, disposed carefully of her former clothes, and returned to Brady. Her new appearance excited Brady and his love for her became stronger. She dyed her hair a deep red, began to wear much make-up, and altogether changed her appearance. Brady grew a beard, trimmed it carefully, trimmed the hair on his head, peroxided his beard and hair, and did all he could to alter his appearance. Then he, too, went shopping and bought new clothes.

She went to the cliff-top and earned a large sum of money, far more than on any previous occasion. That night they gorged themselves with food, finishing up their supply as best they could. In the morning they destroyed all the evidence of their stay in the cave, went out together in broad daylight, and went to the railway station. They caught a train, travelled to a very far-distant town, and rented a bed-sitting-room as husband and wife. That night she earned more money, the rot set in, and they began to live fairly happily and comfortably.

She was mad, of course, although not as barmy as she had seemed to Brady the first time he met her—at the base of the mossy, glass-topped wall, when she had acted so queerly. While she lived with Brady in the bed-sitter she talked coherently, and could do things like cooking and sewing well enough, but her madness showed in her reasoning, which was completely illogical and irrational. However, she loved Brady, was lovable because of her affectionate nature, and she was pleased to do things for him. So, as Brady's mind had become very uncritical in these days, he accepted her wholeheartedly. Only now and again, when periods of real sanity came to him, born in the comparative calm and order of this new existence, did he see her for what she was: but during these periods of critical judgment he also saw himself clearly, saw how he had become debased; and therefore felt he was in no position to judge her, and he felt he was a fitting mate for such a person.

She had got better mentally since the early days soon after her escape from the mental home: the mental home had encouraged her mental illness rather than tending to cure it, for the constant association with other mad people had aggravated her mental illness; and now that she was living amongst sane people, meeting them in the shops and so on, she improved mentally because of those contacts, and because many people who only knew her superficially treated her as a sane person. Nobody got to know her very well and so nobody found out her true mental state. Some of the men she slept with realized that she was abnormal, but they were the only ones who did, besides Brady.

Dressed in expensive clothes, with a new self-respect, with

a man to love her, and with every-night confirmations of the fact that she was attractive, she became quite beautiful. Remarkable changes can occur in women, especially if they become loved, for then they flower.

She gained a new poise. Her previous coarseness became slightly refined, and she took great care over her appearance.

Brady was pleased with her.

But he was older than she was, and the young seek the young instinctively.

The young labourer she slept with one night was simple, but handsome and virile. He wanted her permanently and she responded to him eagerly.

Brady knew nothing about this, until the labourer called at the bed-sitter one night, and carefully and kindly explained to Brady that the girl would be leaving the bed-sitter. The labourer left Brady stunned.

Brady watched her making the supper and asked her when she would be leaving. With the kindness of the simple-minded, she stood close to him, her full bosom against his chest, her hands in his, and tenderly told him that she would be leaving in one day's time. Brady clung wretchedly to her and began to cry. His life with her had been very happy, and he could not bear it to end. Her generous soul was deeply touched by his tears, and she comforted him as well as she could. His words meant little to her at times, because she could not understand them, but she was quite able to understand the situation generally. Brady began instinctively to play on her emotions, and realizing that his spoken reasoning was futile he discarded it. He cried greatly, made love to her, and played ruthlessly and fully upon her pity and inherent motherliness. The girl was confused and her loyalties became hopelessly divided. She became hypnotized by Brady, as he pleaded with her. He felt he was succeeding, and with an awareness of his gaining power, he tried harder and harder, as the girl became weaker in her desire to live with the labourer. She promised to live with him for another month, but Brady knew that, as soon as she was with the labourer again, her mind would regain its desire for the young man, and the promise to live with Brady for a month would be broken.

Brady knew he was hypnotizing her somewhat, and that us soon as she was out of the room the power of his hypnosis would weaken considerably. He went on pleading, and playing carefully on her emotions and sympathy. He wanted her never to see the boy again, for he knew that was his only chance of keeping her. He fought a great battle that night, and his winning was a triumph of will, cunning, and intelligence regarding the make-up of the human being. They packed a few things in parcels, and caught an early-morning train to another town, hundreds of miles away.

The girl started all over again in the new town and things seemed to be going well. . . . But unknown to Brady she yearned for the labourer and one day sent him a letter.

The labourer came to the town the following week-end and stayed at an hotel. He saw the girl, and she returned to Brady, resolved once more to leave the older man.

It had been quite a number of weeks since Brady had fought his 'battle', and he faced the new one with a new spirit refreshed, and courage. But he was unable to vary his tactics, and she knew what to expect, and she had hardened herself against his pleadings, tears, play with her emotions, and his reliance on her sympathy and mother-feelings.

He played his game, and then the realization that he had no chance at all began to dawn on him. He saw in his imagination, the future without her, and self-pity welled up within him. He looked at her set face, felt her hardened resolution, and began to hate her. Her attitude put him on his own, and his selfishness dominated him.

The atmosphere tensed and Brady's hate became great. He beat the girl and she left in the morning intending never to see him again.

17 Final disintegration: the soggy brain

BRADY began to wander again. He searched for years for the girl, walking the streets of many towns at night, in the desperate hope that he might find the girl standing in a dark doorway.

Soon after the girl left him Brady wrote to his wife:

Dear Wife of Mine,

You will perhaps never see me again. If you want a divorce I will be as co-operative as possible. If you do not want a divorce please write to the above Post Office address, and I will arrange with my bank that you shall be paid one thousand pounds a year indefinitely. This amount should be enough to keep you and the child fairly comfortably.

There is a store of many of my paintings at 18 Barnett Street, Chase Park, S.W.3. Eighteen Barnett Street is a warehouse, and the paintings are kept dry and cared for. My bank pays the cost of this storage and the paintings can remain there indefinitely. The value of the paintings there is about £42,000. I shall probably not paint any more paintings, and therefore that figure of £42,000 will probably increase, as the years pass and people realize that I am painting no more: rarity will put the prices up. If, my dear, you want more money than the twenty a week, you can go about the business of selling those paintings in the two main London auction houses. You see I must pain you by leaving you, but I want you to be completely unworried financially.

One day, if you will then allow me to, I might return to you. Our marriage has meant a great deal to me, and I am only leaving you because I must do so and because I am unworthy of you. I am not leaving you because our marriage means nothing to me.

Dearest wife, I have deceived you, and I have become a man with no self-respect. My mind has become very weak, and altogether I could not bear to inflict my degraded person upon you and the child, by continuing our marriage. But, if for any reason you wish our marriage to continue in a legal sense, I will be very honoured and grateful, and I hope one day to return to you, when I have sorted myself out, pulled myself together, and become again a proper person to be your husband.

You have not deserved the injustices I have done you, and I feel very badly about that. One day I will perhaps be able to make up for it all, by living with you again in a marriage of respect and loyalty from me to you.

If, my darling, you wish to find another man to love, during this period of my absence, I cannot blame you, and in fact wish you to do so if you can find happiness thereby.

On the other hand, if you quite understandably wish for a divorce, I will realize that I completely deserve that, and I will do everything I can to co-operate. However, I do ask this one favour from you: please let me see the child once in every few years, and if I could be allowed to see you once in every few years also I would be very grateful.

I hate to think of what pain this letter will cause you, my dear. But I am not fit for you in my present state, and I have no alternative but to send you this sad and cruel letter.

I will send the boy and yourself birthday and Christmas presents, if I may, through the forthcoming years.

I am crying, my darling, as I pen this letter, crying with self-pity and sorrow for yourself.

It would serve no purpose for me to tell you what has happened to me since my breakdown from self-respect and dignity commenced. It would only pain you. But so that you will know that my breakdown has been real and complete, and so that you will realize that I cannot be with you until I am a better man, I will just tell you that I have sunk so low that I have been put, some time ago, in a lunatic asylum.

Goodbye, my darling, goodbye for ever or perhaps for just a number of years.

Thank you for our marriage—thank you from the bottom of my heart.

I love you and the boy.

May you be happy, despite my cruelty,

> **Love,**
> **Jim.**

Poste Restante,
Cranbury Post Office,
Cranbury near Verystand,
YORKSHIRE.

What cleansing of himself, or what betterment of himself, Brady hoped to attain, by roaming round the country, looking for a weak-minded whore, it is difficult to understand. But he meant the letter when he wrote it, even though after posting it he immediately went on with his searching.

.   .   .   .   .

Seven years later Brady wandered down by the river in the darkness. The *Cutty Sark*'s masts reared high into the sky, and its bulging black sides loomed up beside him, as he walked around the preserved vessel. A few people walked into the lighted under-river tunnel across the open space surrounding the wonderful old boat. The Venereal Disease hospital for undisciplined sailors was set back from the road that led from the boat to Greenwich Park. On the road, stationary, red, double-decker buses waited.

Brady walked down the steps, and he walked around the base of the gigantic tea-transporting vessel, that had once raced its cargo to Britain across the deep heaving sea. The boat was set in a deep depression, and Brady walked below ground level with awe in his admiring eyes. He ascended the steps again, and looked at the seats beneath the wall on one side of the square, seats illuminated by lamps high above them: Brady looked, as he rose step by step from the hole containing the *Cutty Sark*.

He stopped on the top step and grasped the railing, staring at the seats. His mind became filled with electricity, and he shivered with violent nervous quiverings. He then became aware of the cheap drama of the situation, and his mouth grinned stupidly and tensely for a brief moment.

He stared at the girl standing brazenly by the seat illuminated by the lamp.

With trembling fingers he tried unsuccessfully to light a cigarette in the wind. Throwing the white tube away, down into the hole, he walked towards her.

The skin was drawn tightly over the bones of her face, and tired sacks of fallen skin hung darkly below her dead eyes. Youth had deserted her very quickly and left her drained and prematurely old. The powder resided obviously and sordidly on her blossomless cheeks, and the various kinds of make-up on her face caught Brady's eye before any other aspect of the face did.

He looked at the girl before him, appalled and horrified. Had he spent so many years looking for *this*? She smiled at him, like a skeletal ghost plastered with paint and powder, as deserted of Life as the *Cutty Sark* which lay behind her; but without the ghostly grandeur and proud magnificence of the vessel, whose masts towered, silhouetted blackly against the moon-lighted sky.

Brady could not move, could not tear himself away from where he stood, could not take his eyes from the disappointment before him.

People laughed as they looked at the pair, people laughing as they walked along the road that led to the lighted tunnel, a road one hundred yards from Brady and the girl.

The girl stepped forward a step and looked eagerly at Brady, for he was a find indeed, a pile of gold in a wasteland devoid of love, comforts, and warmth. She hoped that their old life would begin again, but she knew inside her that the chances of that happening were small, because she had often looked in the mirror in her room. Her smiling, voiceless mouth, smeared carelessly with cheap red, was pathetic in its entreaty.

Brady wanted her to be her previous self so desperately, now that he had found her after so many years of dispirited weary searching, that he tried hard to find traces in her of the attractiveness that had once pleased him. But he could see no beauty at all, only wasted and drained ghosts of the things that had once been full of life, and young.

With an inner realization that it was hopeless to do so, she came body to body with Brady, laid her red-nailed hands on Brady's arms and made to kiss him, in an attempt to re-establish the old relationship. This so nauseated Brady, who was tired with the tiredness of so many pointless years of searching for another version of just this kind of reunion, that, as her sexless red lips touched his, for the first time in his life he fainted.

He found himself in a slummy room, lying on a bed, when he came to. She was making him a cup of tea. He stared hopelessly around the sordid room, wondering how he had got there. She told him: 'You were on the ground, darling, when all of a sudden some nice sailors came up, and when I told them you lived with me . . . a white lie, darling . . . they put you in their old car, and brought you up here. By the way, darling, that boy left me some years ago, and we can live together now if you want to.

'Oh, I gave the sailors five pounds, or they would not have helped me. But they were very nice. I was able to give one of them a little pleasure when he got up here, and he gave me two pounds, so it only cost me three pounds really. Hee, hee, ha, ha.

'By the way, Sylvia shares this room with me, and she will be back soon. She is a nice girl—you will like her—very pretty she is and so she makes more money than me. But neither of us makes very much down here by the river—all the sailors go up to Piccadilly.

'What's Sylvia like, dear? What do you want to know for, eh? You've got me now, dear.

'Well, Sylvia is young, you see, about nineteen. She is clever, you know, reads books, and is always buying them. All the clever men like Sylvia, you know. Oh and she's religious too. I'm religious now and we both go to church. Sylvia's got a nice Bible she pinched from the church we go to. I want to be Roman Catholic, but I'd have to go in the confessional every day, being a girl who helps these poor men all the time. I sometimes help them for nothing, being a Christian girl. Another cup of tea, dear? Why did you faint like that? I had the shock of my life when you fell down like that. Oh Sylvia— well she's got a nice big figure and luvly eyes has Sylvie. Luvly eyes. There was man wanted to marry Sylvia—nice man he was—worked on the buses. But Sylvia wants to marry a—forgot what she said though—she wants to marry a intellactil, or is it a inectuactil? A man who thinks all the time, like you do, it is she wants. Oh yes, that's it—an intellectal! Now you lay off Sylvie. She might like you, you being one of them intellecticshall men.

'Well, she will be in soon. Why do you keep asking about Sylvia? Well, here's a photo taken of her when she went down to Bognor with that man whose wife wanted a divorce. He committed a dultery with Sylvie so that his wife could get a divorce. He was ever so nice, Syl said, and she had to stand up in court and say that she had committed this dultery. A dultery week-end gets a girl about twenty pounds. I frown on it really, being a Christian, but Syl said there was a Bible in the hotel bedroom, and the sea was luvly, so I suppose it was all right, her committing a dultery.

'Oh you are interested in Syl, aren't you, you terrible old man? Well, here is a picture of Syl with that city councillor. Well, Syl got it taken secretly, when he didn't know, so she could get money out of him by blackmail. He was very fond of Syl was Henry. Nice chap, but smoked too much. That was when we lived in Crounge.

'A nasty thing to do? Oh well, I suppose it was. But he

had lots of money and could afford it. No, Syl didn't get any money—he sent a man to beat her up but Syl just sent me out and . . . well, you know . . .

'Here's another one of Syl—we have lots of Syl—I don't know though why you are so interested in Syl. You are going to stay with me, aren't you, darling?

'Oh well, they help in the business those pictures. And we sell them too.

'That's Syl at Blackpool. Ooh! She was so rich when she came back from Blackpool. And this one's of Syl when she lived by the camp. Made a lot there too she did. Syl's been at it since she was quite young, you know. Keeps her young, she says, though she's got a long way to go before she stops being young. Funny things Syl says sometimes.

'That sounds like Sylvie now. She hasn't got a man with her, by the sound of it. Now you keep off Sylvie. Please, dear, it might not be good for Syl.'

.   .   .   .   .

Sylvia was reading. Brady sat by the fire in an after-dinner stupor. Sylvia and Brady then went to bed, because it was Saturday evening, and Sylvia had to go to church early next morning.

The next morning Sylvia kissed Brady goodbye, and putting on a hat, went off to church. On the way to the church she met a fishmonger on the loose, and she had to go to the later service. She was a conscientious girl who worked hard at her job. Coming home from the church, with Mrs. Jacks, the baker's wife, and Mrs. Sladosh, the wife of the crane-driver, she talked to them earnestly about the Government and cooking. But it was a good day for work, and she left her respectable companions, to walk down a side turning in which she had noticed an old customer standing. He had a mate, and so she went home with six pounds at two o'clock in the afternoon.

Sylvia liked to hobnob with (comparatively) the swells, at and after church, and to do this her profession had to be concealed. So Sylvia felt it safer to change towns every so often, and she and Brady would do that every month.

Brady felt these days none of the mental turmoil of the days of Esmerelda, when he was fighting the weakness growing within himself, and when part of his mind judged him. He felt none of the guilt of those days of yore, none of the great mental activity brought on by the sudden awareness of his fall from grace and the initial stages of his degradation. As the years passed he began to accept himself; to accept the new Brady: a Brady with no self-respect at all, who could live off a prostitute without the slightest stirrings of conscience within his brain, without the slightest self-criticism, and without any self-distaste. His pride was gone, and the consequences of the Breakdown were being lived out.

His wife had not divorced him, and he could have started his life with her again if he had chosen to. He could have started painting again, and continued his career again quite successfully. Perhaps he would have had to lie to his wife, about what had happened in the years when he was away from her, but perhaps she would have understood and forgiven him.

But the rot had set in and he was unable to do these sensible things.

At one point in the progress of the degradation he had piled contempt for himself upon contempt for himself, until he could bear it no longer, and his mind had reacted by slowly killing that part of his mind that had the powers of self-judgment, leaving him free of the agonies of self-contempt, and leaving him uncritical of himself, free to live a life of muck in a state of untroubled mental peace. But that part of his mind that had died was capable of rebirth. At various times that rebirth was made, and the young baby was a great trial indeed, but the baby was a sickly child and soon died.

. . . . .

Sylvia and Brady had not saved any money, and when Sylvia was put out of action by the last months of her pregnancy, and the months of caring for the very young child, Brady had to draw money from his bank to keep them with. He hated to do this because he had an obsession—the desire to keep his former life completely disconnected from the present one: the obsession was caused by hidden ghosts of the contempt he had once had for his degraded life, ghosts that had the power to cause an obsession of this kind; caused by the hidden desire in his subconscious not to contaminate one way of life with another any more than it already was contaminated.

Brady's child suffered from the lack of mother-love: Sylvia soon left it by itself for long periods of time while she went off soliciting. Brady cared little for the baby and when Sylvia left it at home he was always out of the house. Subconsciously he wished that the baby, which represented the making of a permanent thing of Brady's life with the whore— the baby established firmly the reality of their life together— would die, and he felt that if any carelessness on his part would cause the baby any illness then that would be a good thing. So he almost tried to neglect the baby, and this attitude, together with Sylvia's lack of concern for the child, caused the child's eventual illness and then death.

Sylvia had grown older by then, and she was beginning to see the sordidness of her life, now that the youthful physical desires for it were disappearing. This realization of the mess she was cultivating, and the boring regularity of her sales to all and sundry, made her bitter.

When the baby died, although she cared not for it, she felt the death underlined the hopelessness of her life; and she wished the child had lived, thereby making her life seem fruitful in one way at least. So she disliked the baby's death, and blamed Brady for it. She told him that he should have stayed in and looked after it, when she was out earning the money. And in this way bitter nagging of Brady became gradually habitual, and arguments became part of their life together. Consequently, Sylvia's life with Brady lost some of its charm for Brady. Sylvia had lost her youth to a certain extent, although she was still comely. The result was that Brady's tranquillity, and slack love of his life with Sylvia, disappeared; and as his mind became irritated into life again, within that newly activated mind (a mind previously apathetic), the child symbolizing the powers of self-judgment became reborn, amidst cruel labour pains, to grow strong and energetic, making its existence very surely known: a difficult child, a child that needed a great deal of attention.

Sylvia came in exhausted and flopped down in a chair. She smiled after a while at the thought of church the following morning, for she loved her church attendances—they purified her and she felt so dirty so often. She could act the part of a lady for a change when she was at church, an act that was hard to perform when she was at work beneath the moon. There had been a long break in her church attendances, and she had missed those attendances very strongly: when she had become obviously pregnant she could not bring herself to go to church, because she would have had to talk to the ladies about the embryonic baby's father; and the lies she would be forced to tell, to conceal its illegitimacy, would have been a strain upon her; even though she lied easily to conceal her profession. When she had the child, and her breasts were milkful, she still did not go to church. But now the baby was dead, and they were in a new locality, she felt happy to go to church. She was a mixture of contradictions as are many of her type: and although she could live with some disgraces quite happily, deceiving herself amazingly, she could not stomach the disgrace of having an illegitimate child, or deceive herself about it, especially when she was in church. Her life was a constant self-deception: prostitutes could not live without self-deception, for they would naturally feel themselves the filth of society if they were honest with themselves: the ladylike and proud heads of prostitutes are supported on splints of self-deception.

Sylvia looked at Brady, who lay in the bed, wakened by her noisy entry.

'Well, had an easy day, mister? Eh? I went out just after dinner and have been on the go ever since. What the hell have you done today, mister? Why do I keep you, I wonder—-you great lay-about? Most of the men I go with are better than you. Do you hear me? Why don't you keep me, instead of my keeping you? When I was pregnant, and when we had the kid, you found some lolly somewhere. If you could get it then why don't you get it now? Where on earth did you get it from anyway? You secretive old lazy slob. I bet you could get more if you wanted to. What did you do before you linked up with me, and before you met up with that old wreck I used to live with? Have you lived off women all your life? What a parasite, to be sure, you are! Why don't you tell me about yourself?

'Why don't you get out and leave me alone? If any man asked me to live with him, I'd do it like a shot, I swear it. But they don't ask me any more. I sometimes wonder why I turned them down in the old days when I was living with you. I suppose I thought I loved you. Goodness knows why.

'I'm getting so used to living with you I suppose I can't bring myself to leave you. But I shall, I promise you. I'll just think hard about what little use you are to me, until my mind sets hard against you, and then I'll not come back one night. If only I could get a man to live with me. I get lonely without a man in my home. You keep me company I suppose: that is why I still live with you. But if I leave you I could get a room somewhere and bring the men home for the night—that would keep me company—except for the days—I'd be lonely during the days. Blast you! Move over, slob—I need some sleep!'

The nagging ceased, for a time; then, as the room filled with morning light:

'Can't you even make me a cup of tea? Any decent man would make me breakfast. But you just lie there and wait for me to get up and make . . . blast you! . . . Go and make a cup of tea! Get out, get out, get out and make me a cup of tea for a change.

'Well, what an achievement! Thank you, mister. Not a bad cup of tea either. I suppose life without you would be lonely. No one to speak to in the mornings and afternoons. The men I give myself to don't make very nice company because they treat me like a whore. It's nice to have the company of someone who doesn't buy me.

'But you *are* wet sort of company, aren't you? You add up to nothing, mister! *Wet, wet!* Oh hell, I've got to go out tonight. What a life! Keeping a slob with money from selling myself!

'I suppose I need not go out tonight in the ruddy cold. You can't imagine how awful it is to have to stand waiting in this cold weather at night, while the men roam around you,

224

trying to decide whether they like you enough to lash out a couple of quid for a "short-time". I doubt if you realize what a hell of a bore it is to have to wear those shiny clothes all the time, and to keep your top-coat unbuttoned even in the cold weather, and also to keep an everlasting bed-time look in your eyes. No, you have no idea of what I have to put up with—just to keep you, so you can laze around, smoking cigarettes all the time, idling your useless life away, while I get older and older. Sure I'm still nice to look at, and will be some more years yet, but just how loyal will you turn out to be, you slob, when I get quickly old like the girl I used to live with did? You didn't want her when you saw how rapidly she had aged because of this life—did you? *Did you?* Answer me, for Pete's sake! Don't just sit there with that look on your silly face. Say something. Yeah, you did not want her then, did you—and when I'm like that, you'll drop me pretty fast, and go and find someone else, that is, if you can, which I doubt: what have you to offer, I'd like to know, you miserable old punk?

'Just why should I continue this life like this, just so that, when you choose to, you can leave me old and flat—yes flat, that's what I'll be, like she got to be—and clear off to find another life to your liking? If I am sensible I'll get myself a young feller—but he will leave me when I get quickly old, I suppose. Oh hell! A girl's youth goes so quickly in this game, especially if you go on working as hard and regularly as I do. How many years of youth have I got, I wonder? I don't look so bad now—my reflection in this mirror looks O.K. I'm not as young as I was, but I've got a long time till thirty, and thirty ain't old, or is it? I'm not blooming like I was when I first saw you. This life saps you—takes the freshness out of your skin, takes the champagne out of your eyes, and takes the bounce out of your figure. Damn you, man—damn you!

'Yes, and when my figure starts to get scraggy and my chest sags down, when my face gets lined and grey-looking, when my hands get veined and ridgy, and when I don't swell voluptuously any more—and it's all starting to go that way—when that happens, Buster, just how easy will it be for me to earn money? Maybe I ought to save. Yes, it will be awful

then, when you have left me, and the money is hard to get. I
hate to think of it.

'But there are quite a few years yet before I get like those
not so old, but old-looking, wasted tarts that stand around,
not getting anyone, by the docks. They calculate—I know
cos one told me, the drunken bitch—that the sailors off the
boats have not seen a dame in weeks, being in the boat for
so long, and they come off the boats ready to take anything.
But as I said, there are a few years yet for me before that. I
must do something: save hard, or—if I could only do it—get
married. That would be the answer: to get married to some
decent lad before the work drains me. Ha—that's it! Marriage.

'You! Would you marry me? No, I can see by your face
you wouldn't. Perhaps you are married already. Are you?
Might even have ten kids for all I'd know about it—you
swine.

'Anyway you'd leave me, married to me or not. What I
want is to marry a young man now, who loves me. If I got
married to a man who would keep me, I could stop the "game"
now, and I would then keep my youth longer; and anyway
he would keep me when I eventually lost my youth. If only
I could get hold of one of those decent boys who go to the
church. Then he wouldn't know I was a pro.

'But how can I get my claws into one of those boys? I
would need to plan things very carefully, and put a lot of work
into it. I know! If I got one of them churchy boys interested
in me, so he took me out sometimes, then one time I could get
him to take me into the woods, and then get myself in the
family way by him. You see. Then, being a chap with principles, he would feel he had to marry me. Heck! That's a beauty
of an idea—oh damn you, you old louse—that would solve all
my problems. Look out, you church boys, here I come, and
let's see just how churchy you are when I get you involved
with my plan.

'Now who is there at All Saints? Who is there I can work
on? If there ain't nobody there, I can move to another town,
and try another church. But wait. There is John Bradshaw.
He likes me. I have never given him the come-on. I'll bet he
would respond in a big way if I played with him a bit. And

his father is quite wealthy too. And then again, he is the sort of chap who is as churchy as they come: if he got me in the family way, he would know only one course of action, and that is wedding bells, an old boot, and all that junk. No, it's not junk really, for it would be rather nice to have a white wedding.

'Gosh, I've never thought of wedding bells and a honeymoon. Rather lovely. And then a nice house and maybe a servant. He's a clever boy that Bradshaw kid. Easy meat I'll bet. Clever at his job, but not so clever at resisting dear old. Sylvie.

'I'll do this in a big way. I'll buy new clothes for my visits to the church, and really doll myself up—in a nice way, of course—but with lots of sex under the old respectability stuff. That's how those respectable girls do it: they dress real dignified-like, but flaunt the sex like mad behind the refinement. How can I lose? How can I lose? I could lose by being too obvious. Sylvia ain't so dumb. She can see that. I must play it slow and restrained, but give Bradshaw enough to make him dream at nights. Sycollogy, that's the thing. I know a thing or two about men's minds—I ought to, I've spent most of my life with men.

'The thing I must do is to concentrate on acting the lady. Dignity, poise, and refinement. I do read a lot. That will help—they will think I'm educated like. Yeah. I'll concentrate on them things, and let the sex stuff take care of itself. I can build the sex side of my appearance and presence up later, but I must concentrate on those things that don't come natural. I speak O.K. No trouble there. It's all the books I've read that makes me speak educated.

'He doesn't know what is in store for him.'

Brady could hardly believe that it was over: that her nattering had concluded.

.   .   .   .   .

Brady's brain was irritated, by her recent bouts of continual nagging, and spoken thoughts directed against their relationship together. And the irritation in Brady's brain yanked his brain from its slough of previous inactivity, into an active state: the thoughts he thought were painful. As a result of her talk of leaving him, he was forced to think of himself without her, to think of himself as an isolated individual. And as he pictured himself in his mind's eye as an isolated individual, he began to see what an undignified person he had become. His old contempt for himself was given new life, and his disturbing thoughts urged him to do something about bettering himself. He began to think about painting, and eventually returning to his wife.

For quite a while, as Sylvia's nagging increased, Brady was tormented by his thoughts. He was forced to think, for there was no peace now in his relationship with the whore, and his mind was always irritated into activity. He began to discipline his thinking once again, after such a long period of slack thinking or non-thinking. The mechanism of his brain began to work again, the wheels going round rustily, and squeaking with protest after lying idle for so long, the power driving the mechanism coming from the dynamo of Sylvia's irritant and unceasing nagging. His thinking became more and more disciplined, as he used his brain more and more, and his thinking began to gain a new strength. He realized clearly that if his wife would have him back, and it was possible, for she had not divorced him, then he could start his life all over again in a very satisfactory way indeed. He wrote to his wife:

My dear wife,

Do you remember my last letter to you? In it I said I would try and make myself whole again and then ask you to take me back. Well it seems that I did not try too hard to make myself worthy of you again. But I think I have recently improved, and I am asking you to have me back.

Love
Jim.

Dear James,

Why did you not write that letter sooner? What did you think I would do in your long absence? Did you think I would just wait for you, doing my knitting, and bringing up the boy? Have you been without a partner for this length of time? If you have then you surprise me, for I found I needed love and companionship while you were away.

I hated the idea of appearing in a Divorce Court and that is partly why I have not divorced you.

Of course I would like to see you, and for you to see the child, now grown very big.

Your paintings are still in the warehouse. They must be worth a fortune now, because your work is now a rarity and sells for great amounts of money.

Your wife.

Brady was at first discouraged by her letter, but he soon felt differently. He was changing; and his enormous contempt for the broken Brady urged him to re-establish himself as a self-respecting person, whatever the obstacles. The same profound power that drove him down and down to eventual Breakdown Complete, now drove him in the opposite direction. His confidence became unlimited; and Sylvia knew not the man who slept in her bed, for he was not the man she had been living with: he was a man she could not fathom, a man with a purpose—a strong purpose.

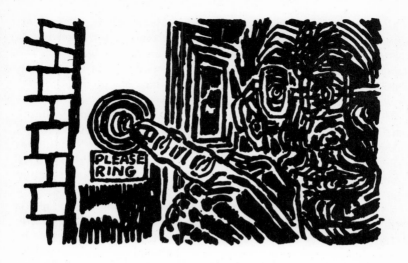

18 Repair

BRADY stood for a long while at the end of the road, her letter with the address on it held in his hand. No. 72 it was, and he counted the houses carefully until he located the house that must be 72. He watched the house for a long time. He calculated that she must own the house, and he waited in the rain.

When he came out of the house, Brady saw he was a small and tender man, with not a great deal of power to him. Brady felt reassured and smiled.

Brady's mind had improved enormously, and it was disciplined and strong now. There were obstacles to surmount, and he needed power to get past them.

The man walked down the road towards Brady, Brady pulled his hat over his eyes, and bent his head down, and the tender little man passed by, glancing suspiciously at Brady. Brady now knew that his wife's Comfort in the Husbandless Years was gone from the house. He walked up the road to No. 72 in the pouring rain.

It was a Victorian house with a balcony on the first floor, and below the ground floor was a basement, set deep below the garden level. Brady walked between the hedges from the gate to the porch, and stood for a while before the door, sheltered from the rain. It was just like a film he thought cynically: *The Return of the Wanderer.*

Hesitantly he pushed the bell, and heard it ring, echoing within the old house. The door opened and a boy stood in the doorway, his hand on the side of the door. The boy's eyes opened in wonder at the man on the doorstep, and he shyly asked Brady to come in. Fascinated, Brady watched the boy go up the stairs to find his mother.

Brady stood in the dark hallway for a long time. Beside him, on the wall, hung one of his early paintings of his wife, the paint on it applied cruelly and without any love for the essential nature of the paint. His wife's blotched face looked down at him, her face strained with the efforts of posing. Brady looked expectantly up the stairs, and saw another of his paintings, on the wall where the stairs turned: a painting of his child when a baby, holding a nippled bottle of milk in his pudgy, unformed, tiny hands; all painted with great blobs of paint too large for the tiny size of the painting. A door opened on the floor above him and voices broke the silence. Brady pulled himself together. He looked up, and a woman stood in front of the painting of the child, a woman standing tall on the bend of the stairs, looking at him, a woman he could hardly see in the half-light. A band of light that had illuminated the painting of the child played on the side of her face, as she half-turned from the darkness, lighting the blotched forms of her familiar face: a face Brady had caressed long ago, a face that Brady had looked upon many times, long and intensely, as he painted it with blobs of ugly paint during the years that were now no more.

Somehow he felt she had gained in dignity, and his self-assurance temporarily deserted him.

.   .   .   .   .

He opened the warehouse doors and went inside, out of the rain that poured in the street. It was rather dark inside, and he searched for the light switches. Clicking down the switch levers, all of them at the same time, with a brutal stroke of his hand, that left his hand burning, he gazed around him in the blazing illumination.

Vast canvases towered around him, long ribbons and weals of paint stretching from staring heads to ill-proportioned feet. Ladies in various stages of undress, lividly painted, were spread, ridiculously, and somewhat pornographically, across six-foot-long areas of canvas, their eyes staring, their foreheads corrugated with enormous worry.

Hundreds of pounds of paint expenditure, hundreds of pounds of models' fees, and hundreds of pounds of canvas purchase, transformed into thousands of pounds of valuable paintings.

Brady stood close to a monster painting, looking along the painting and not directly at it, so that he saw a vast width of paint in mountain ranges and valleys, stretching away from his near face to the other end of the long canvas.

As he looked at those paintings that were visible—some of them were lined up front to back and therefore unseeable—many memories came flooding back into his mind, swamping him with nostalgia. He longed to paint again, but first he had other things to do.

He sat down on a box, and his eyes on a painting before him, he began to think things out.

He knew now that his wife wanted him back, but she could not bring herself to discard the Tender Man.

Then his thoughts, caused by the paintings before him to change direction, concentrated on the business of getting his old studio back again into working order.

He switched off the lights, closed the large doors, locked them, and tramped off in the rain.

.   .   .   .   .

'And so you see that, my dear Jim, just because you choose at this time, convenient to yourself, to return and partner me again, things cannot be rearranged, suddenly and drastically. It is selfish of you, and I cannot hurt Percy, just so that you can pick up where you left off when you left me years ago. I just cannot do this to Percy, who has been such a dear—I cannot throw him away as you seem to want me to.

'I don't know what I would have done in those awful years if Percy had not been with me. And I am grateful to him. I cannot tell him to leave me: it would be inhuman of me—an act of cruelty comparable to the act of cruelty you performed when you left me.

'I know Percy has not the legal right to me that you have ——because you are my husband. What the position as regards divorce is now I do not know: I have not gone into the matter. But as far as I am concerned Percy has more right to live as my husband than you have. We have got to know each other very well, Percy and me, and we harmonize; also Percy and the boy get on very well together, and Percy takes the boy fishing and cycling.

'Look, Jim, you must accept the fact that I cannot live with you any more. It is Percy that I have to consider, good, dear Percy. It isn't that I don't feel for you—I loved you once, and my love lasts, though it is nowhere near as strong as it was when we first got married. If it was not for Percy, I would start living with you again; even though we are now like strangers to each other; and my attitude to you would be very much influenced by the injustice you did me.

'That makes me think about what other injustices you might have done to me, that I did not know about. I remember finding your behaviour very strange in the time before you finally left me: you were away many nights at that time. Oh I know you gave me reasons that I accepted, but now that I know that you left me soon afterwards, I often wonder if you were telling me the truth about those nights and I have a right to be suspicious of you considering what has happened —your going away.

'Anyway, before I lived with you again—which, as I said, I cannot do because of Percy—I would expect you to tell me all that has happened to you in your absence, *and* to be honest about the time before you left me. I would be honest with you about my own life in your absence, although there is very little to tell. I met Percy when he came to do a plumbing repair job and he was very kind. I got to like him so much and I was so lonely that eventually I said he could live here, first as a paying lodger and a companion and later as—well, as my lover. Oh I know Percy is not the great man, as some folk thought, and still do think, judging by the prices your pictures change hands at, you are, James; but he is a good little man and can teach you a lesson in loyalty.

'I wonder, since you returned—I wonder just what sort of person you think I am, James. You take me much too much for granted that is certain. You must think me a very odd woman, if you expect me to fall into your arms as soon as you return after deserting me, and then throw over dear Percy, just like that, when he has meant so much to me. No I suppose I never really knew you, James, and I suppose you never really knew me: you couldn't have known me properly, because, if you did, you would know that I wouldn't live with you again, if it meant throwing Percy away—I don't do things like that, James, because I cannot be as cruel as you seem to be able to be. Yes, cruel: even cruel regarding Percy, who you would hurt terribly, if you could get me to discard him.

'I suppose you thought you were being *generous* when you gave me one thousand a year—I suspected then that you thought you were perfectly godly in doing that. It was the least you could do to salve your conscience, to make yourself feel that you were not utterly swinish in leaving me. But then it *was* nice of you to offer me a divorce with your co-operation, and to say that I could sell those paintings, I must give you that, James.'

'And now, wife of mine, listen to me.

'What happened? I have weaknesses like so many of us. They began to rule me, and I did things that made me unworthy of you. I realized I was not fit to live with you any more, and so I left you. It would have been really cruel of me if I had stayed with you and inflicted my decaying person upon you, making you live with a man who was breaking up hideously. It might have seemed Cruel, but in fact it was Kindness. In kindness to you, in consideration for you, I removed my odious self from your life, doing the best I could to see you all right financially, and hoping that I could put myself to rights and then return to you.

'I don't want to hurt Percy, you know that, but since I did what I considered to be the honourable thing and the right thing all along, I feel that I deserve to start being your husband again: if this happens to hurt Percy, no one is more sorry than me, but sometimes a person has to be hurt, so that someone else can get his rights in life.

'Would you blame me because I found weaknesses in myself—a *very* human thing to happen—and upon finding them did the best thing possible: that is, went away and tried to fight those weaknesses in private, so that the pain you would experience, if you saw those weaknesses in action, would not be inflicted upon you.'

After hearing his wife speak with such finality, Brady had realized that to win her back would involve a hard fight. He determined to abide by the old saying that 'All is fair in love and war,' he would use any means that came to hand, in his attempt to win his wife from Percy—in this battle he fought with words. He spoke not only the truth, but he spoke lies. He said anything that would further his cause. He felt that the end justified the means. He threw lie after truth, lie after lie, and truth after truth, at his wife, in a desperate attempt to win her back; for winning her back was the first step on the ladder to the regaining of his old, worthy self.

'Just why do you think I came back? Just on a sudden selfish impulse? No! It has been my intention all these years to return as soon as I was fit enough to return, and not before. I only postponed returning because I had not made myself whole: as soon as I made myself whole, I came back. I stayed away for *you*, my dear, and not for myself. I so respected you that I could not cause you to live with me when I was disintegrated. I could not inflict upon you my unwholesome self.

'Some of this I wrote to you in a letter. Have you forgotten that letter? Why not get it out and read it? You will see then, that that what I say now links up with what I wrote then.'

She got the letter from a drawer and read it, glancing at Brady now and again.

'Well, James, it says in this letter some things I had forgotten, but I must admit that the things said in the letter link with what you are now saying.

'How long were you in the asylum, James? What does this mean about deceiving me?'

Brady wormed his way out of difficulties, and went on with his persuasive talk. He could see that he was making headway, even if it was only because he could talk more than his wife. Brady began to feel as he had felt when he persuaded the lunatic-asylum girl to give up her lover: he felt a growing confidence in his hypnotic powers, in his great energy, and in the power he had—born of need—for a reinstatement of his marriage as a basis for his new life. Percy's tenderness and goodness became forgotten as Brady piled on the persuasion, as Brady talked incessantly, and as the wife grew tired.

.   .   .   .   .

Percy bent down below the wash-basin, and angled his large spanner on the pipe. The housewife's talk hardly penetrated his ears, for his mind was occupied with his problem.

Percy's life had begun when he met Brady's wife, and from then onwards he had been a happy man. Now he knew his happiness must end. Brady's wife had talked to him, and he knew his relationship with her was finished. He had not the persuasive power of Brady, and his virtues were overshadowed by the personality of the stronger man.

He turned on the taps, showed the housewife that the job was done; and he packed up his bag of tools.

.   .   .   .   .

Percy sat down in the hotel room and wrote to her:

My Darling,

Thank you for so much happiness. I am sending the boy my fishing-rod. I won't be seeing you again, for I have no place in your life now, and I am only in the way. I'll give up my job here, move away and get another job.

Please remember me,
Tenderest Love,
Percy.

Hotel Roger,
18 Saverton Rd.

He moved away and settled in another town. For some reason he could not get another job, his personality was not a pushing one, and perhaps that is why. His money ran out and he felt so much that his life was pointless that he robbed a man one night on a common. When that money was gone he tried again, only this time the man he tried to rob turned out to be a strong man physically, who took Percy to a policeman. Percy managed, peculiarly enough, to get a job when he got out of prison. He existed for a year in great depression and loneliness. Then he went on a holiday to Scotland.

He stood on the mountainside, looking down the steep slope beneath him that dropped down into the rocky valley. He took out his wallet and looked at a newspaper cutting. It was a review of Brady's recent exhibition of paintings. Reproduced by the column of print was a painting by Brady of his wife. Percy looked at it for a while and then threw the wallet and the cutting into the valley. He wanted to follow the wallet that grew smaller and smaller as it fell, but he had not the courage.

He lived a long time did Percy: if you can call it living.

.   .   .   .   .

Brady watched the television happily with his wife.

'See that chap, dear. Do you remember—I suppose that is a silly thing to say, but—do you remember that chap Percy? Look how like Percy that chap on the telly is. Bloody wet that Percy. Sorry, dear, I didn't mean to hurt you. Still he wasn't up to much, was he?'

Brady's wife looked at the side of her husband's face for a moment with hate.

19 A man's weaknesses are always with him

BRADY slashed on the paint, dribbles of turpentine-thinned colour running down the bare canvas, the paint-smeared handle of his brush making his fingers discoloured and oily. He tensed himself into concentration, knitted his brows, set his mouth, felt the acid digest the lining of his stomach, and drew a fine and sensitive line down the side of his model's face on the canvas, fixing her all the intense while with a look of agonized scrutiny. As the hairs of his brush dragged the paint down the side of the painted chin on the canvas, and the carefully painted line appeared below the painted imitation of her chin, the model, disturbed by Brady's intense stare, moved her head nervously: Brady was forced to discontinue his line, which was going up the other side of her face on

239

canvas, and the acid ate painfully away at the stomach wall.

She sat there, an art student from a neighbouring art school, her long hair dropping down in rats'-tails from her pale brow.

Brady gave up in exhaustion, and wrote out a cheque for the girl. This cheque the girl received delightedly, for it meant a meal with meat that night instead of a meal of potatoes and cabbage. He watched her sign a receipt for the money, the afternoon light playing flatteringly on her relieved face, the red hair now tied up behind her head.

.   .   .   .   .

She had posed for Brady a few times before; and like most art-student girls she used any middle-aged man she came across, as a father-confessor; and if she couldn't find a middle-aged father-confessor she would make do with a younger one.

The second time she posed for Brady she gave him the job, and poured out at the poor man a non-ceasing torrent of confession, and imagined and non-imagined troubles.

Brady tried to paint the falling waves of her red hair; the well-formed breasts on her chest, that, glowing whitely, existed in a mist of very fine perspiration and reflected light; the Existentialist hips and thighs; and the brutally formed face, with its open, discharging mouth. Yellow hair was at the roots of the red.

She told him that there were five men in her life, and she didn't know which one to choose. There was the sixty-year-old car-driver who drove an American millionaire around London: the car-driver was a father-substitute, a man determined to have his one last fling before he became sterile. He was a man whose figure had become formed by the seat of his car. He gave her a feeling of security because of his maturity and fatherliness: she was seventeen years old.

Secondly there was the sixteen-year-old art student who had a very serious adolescent crush on her. He did not worry her very seriously. But subconsciously she revelled in the complications of her life, for it made her feel alive and kicking, and furthermore she would have been very bored without her confessionals.

Thirdly there was the crippled art student with the small, deformed figure, black beard and long, girl's hair, whom she was attracted to as a nurse is attracted to her patients: she was attracted by his pathos. The fourth man was much in the background: Cardew from Brazil, who was a sailor and who made infrequent appearances.

The fifth man was the one whom she wanted most. She really had no troubles at all: all she had to do was to choose the fifth man. But that was much too simple an answer, and it did away with the confessionals, which would never do! The confessionals really meant more to her than the lovers who justified the existence of the confessionals.

The fifth man was called by her Pretty Paul. Pretty Paul was an old man, white-haired, naive, white-bearded, childlike, and with features so delicate and fine that one could hardly believe he was of this base and vulgar world. Pretty Paul wrote poetry and painted paintings for Christmas cards, paintings that were intensely detailed and precious in appearance. He had never married, was lonely and remote, and was just a little mad in a harmless other-worldly way. Rosalina felt protective and motherly about this fairy creature. He was a somewhat devitalized lover, but one must expect that of a man of sixty-eight: Rosalina found him relaxing and she found she could put him in her imaginary worlds without the fear that he would suddenly become real and earthy thereby destroying her poetic escape world which remained successfully superimposed upon reality.

Her confessionals became habitual when she posed for Brady. He began to realize her basic moral weakness, for her talk betrayed her because of its comprehensiveness. He also began to realize that he could become the sixth man if he tried to do so. This realization disturbed him.

. . . . . .

It lasted six months, then she got tired of it. She wanted Brady to leave his wife, which he would not do, and weighed down by her troubles and the complications of her young life, she wrote Brady a terminating letter, and went on with her life, anxiously wondering if she would have a baby She went back to Pretty Paul.

20 Rosalina

FOR a while Brady suffered with love-sickness after the girl
Rosalina had left him. He bought a record-player, and some
Elvis Presley and Louis Armstrong records, and tried to forget
her and work, while listening to the passionate sounds of 'I
Cried For You' and 'Heartbreak Hotel', and the deep emotionalism of the Negro's trumpet. But the records did not help
him to forget: on the contrary the romantic crying emotionalism of the sounds pouring from the incised black discs
heightened his yearning for the departed Rosalina.

He placed the black disc on the red turntable and watched
the pick-up arm rise inhumanly like a snake from its resting-
place, swing across to the edge of the disc, and subside into
the opening sounds of Louis Armstrong singing 'Chloe';
waves of emotion poured into him, and in his mind those
absorbed waves of emotion enlarged and multiplied, as he
listened to 'Through the smoke and flame, I gotter go where
you are', and further heartfelt wailings after the girl Chloe,
lost in the swamp. Overflowing with weeping romantic emotion, Brady's mind was as soggy as the swamp in which

Chloe was lost. He changed the record to 'Blueberry Hill', but it did not make things any better.

· · · · ·

Brady put on a bowler hat, dyed the moustache he had grown for the occasion, put on dark glasses, wrapped a scarf round the lower part of his face as naturally as possible, dressed in unfamiliar and seldom-used clothes, and hired an open sports car.

He parked the car on the other side of the road to Rosalina's art school and sat in the car amidst the dense rush-hour traffic, to wait for her to come out of the building, disgorged with all the other laughing, scatter-brained art students at six o'clock. Cars swung round the parked car, and Brady watched a sloppy couple of interwoven art students flop out of the art-school doorway and romance along the pavement, early out of lessons. Buses and cars churned past him in a thick mass, obscuring the sight of the art-school doorway.

Just before six o'clock the street became filled with idiotic arty girls and unreal arty boys. Brady watched carefully and then saw Rosalina coming out by herself. She crossed the road right by him, her head in the clouds, and walked slowly along the pavement, by the side of his car, unaware of him.

Although he had not intended to, he called briefly to her, and she turned and came over to him.

· · · · ·

He extended the period of hire of the car, and drove the car through the evening traffic, the sunlight whitely shining on all the surfaces of the streets, dazzling Brady, who peered forward with half-closed protected eyes. She sat beside him, saying nothing, her face expressionless with terrible, controlled emotion, looking straight ahead of herself, looking at nothing. All-enveloping white sunlight bathed them both as they drove into, and out of, and in, a world governed by the Sun God. He could not see what was happening in front of him: a congestion of massed cars and a confusion of traffic signs and signals, enveloped in shop and house façades, became impossible to understand, because of the turmoil of sunlight and reflected light that activated and hung like a mist around those objects somewhat ahead of Brady, glancing in beams from the chromium fittings on the cars. Brady drove forward, straining his eyes, not understanding what was ahead of him. He found himself crossing over an intersection, cars roaring towards him in the confusing light. He accelerated and roared away safely, along a carless road, the angry shouts growing fainter and fainter.

.   .   .   .   .

The sun was orange amidst a mauve patch low in the sky that divided the soft, fading, orange of the sun's face by a horizontal bar of violet. The rest of the sky was blue and white, and between Brady's car and the lowering sun, naked trees bordered the road darkly.

Brady talked to her as he drove along the country road. She replied now and again, trying to pretend that she was in a mental agony because she had broken her promise to Pretty Paul, a promise never to see Brady again, but Brady knew that really she was intrigued by the sudden appearance of Brady and the long car-ride with him. However, she could not just accept the excitement of the situation plainly and simply: it was characteristic of her that she needed to complicate the situation by inventing non-existent troubles: perhaps the pain she made for herself acted as a foil, setting off the delights of the new contact with Brady, thereby helping her to intensify the delights at the cost of the pain.

The car sped on; and across the fields the sun was hidden in dark-blue, low on the horizon, above which were a few horizontal ragged bands of pink, surmounted by a vast clear sky of blue, across which an isolated band of white cloud was drawn, just off vertical. Black in the sky a bird flew, and Brady listened to Rosalina's worryings, as the light began to go and the car's wheels turned rapidly on the dusty road.

.   .   .   .   .

The car's headlamps beamed out into the darkness, and on the horizon, where the sun had got lost, a few lights twinkled where houses were. The car's headlamps ceased and the car was motionless by the roadside in the darkness. A cigarette lighter flared and was extinguished, and two red dots glowed for a while. An hour later the headlamps illuminated the hedges again, the car's engine roared, the car turned in the road, and with the sound of gear changes, the car moved rapidly away.

Some time after, the clouds cleared and the moon shone down its silver light, which showed a pool of water in the road into which oil had dropped: rainbow circles shone in the pool in the moonlight for a while, and then the moon was covered again by clouds, and all was darkness. A drizzle of rain began to fall, increasing to pelting rain, and the storm began. Lightning branched across the sky, and momentarily the swollen pool on the road was revealed, rainbowed with wonderful radiant colours. Far away in a town ablaze with artificial light Brady said 'Good night' to Rosalina, who walked away from the car thinking hard about her promiscuity, worrying herself silly. She turned beneath a street-lamp, waved to Brady, and walked away, past street-lamp after street-lamp.

In her room the light from the naked bulb in the ceiling shone down on Rosalina crouched over her table. She clenched and unclenched her hands, and her worrying intense face was low in the shadows at her not too exuberant breast, shadows enclosed by her arms, her head, and her falling hair. She lifted her agonized face to the naked bulb above her, the light shining down on her clearly revealed face, and the tears on her cheeks shone insipidly, smeared and abundant. She was enjoying herself. She wailed stagily, and waved her arms with agony. Then she talked to the lamp above her for hours, worrying and worrying, for she had nothing better to do, and it did conceal certain truths. To conceal from herself that she was simply a tart, a promiscuous girl who was loose, she hid in masses of intellectualism, kidding herself that she really wanted to be a good girl, which was untrue: she was essentially a weak girl who subconsciously delighted in promiscuity and then wallowed in self-reproach. She loved her self-reproach, because it made her interesting to herself, and, on occasions, interesting to those who had to listen.

Switching off the naked bulb, she walked across the

darkened room to the curtained window. She drew back the curtains, and opened the window on to the night without. The light from the street-lamp outside the window eased itself with difficulty into the room, and Rosalina stared down at the lighted road and the lighted cars that rushed along it. Below a man looked up at the leaning girl winged by the two open halves of the window, white lace on the lower parts of them, dirt smeared on the panes of misty glass. She spread her tormenting thoughts in their nagging multitudes out into the night across the park that lay greenly on the other side of the road in darkness, and way over the roof-tops and lights beyond. Her mind felt freed and not imprisoned in her aching cranium as it had done when she sat in the curtained room: she felt that her mind was everywhere, above all the things she could see with her eyes. She worried over her disloyalty to Pretty Paul that her outing with Brady represented, and smiled with a sudden gaiety at a teddy-boy who glad-eyed her from the street below.

Brady opened the door, switched on the hall light, and went to the room that now contained his record-player. As he sat in the darkened room, the signal light glowing redly on the record-player, the end of his cigarette being a twin to the signal light, and the hall light causing a bar of yellow light below the door, the circled disc issued out Louis Armstrong singing and trumpeting, 'Don't Fence Me In'.

He opened the bedroom door and clicked the light switch. The resultant blaze of light revealed his wife sitting up in bed, waiting. She closed the lids over her cynical eyes that ceased staring at him, slid down beneath the bedclothes with her back to where Brady would lie, and tried to go to sleep. Brady put on his pyjamas, killed the light, and went to bed: he lay for a while in the darkness, thinking.

Rosalina, later on, looked finally at the street outside the window, the street-lamps having gone out and the lighted cars having disappeared. She drew in the halves of the window, and closed the curtains: thereby blocking out the moonlight.

Her continued complicated mental activity had eventually finished, and loose subconscious thoughts now took their place. Darkness ruled over all.

21 Rosalina II

ROSALINA went to school the following day and waited for Brady to make the next move. Brady did not make any move relating to Rosalina. This left Rosalina very puzzled, and gave her food for thought: so she thought—massively. Apart from thinking about Brady she worried about everything; and as she considered herself to be an honest girl she worried if she ever felt she was being dishonest or untrue. One of her worries at the time was concerned with the deception she was practising regarding the dyeing of her naturally gold hair: she felt herself a very unworthy person because of this and every time she dyed her hair she suffered agonies of self-reproach. The result was that she tried to ignore and forget the existence of her red hair and always shied away from the re-dyeing evening, so that the roots of her hair often became very yellow indeed and she looked very peculiar with her red-and-gold hair. But somehow the appearance of her two-coloured hair was attractive: not to beauty parlour experts perhaps, but to Brady and less cosmetic-conscious males. Why she dyed her hair in the first place is not very clear: she certainly had an obsessional, twisted motive somewhere in the dark, mysterious channels of her mind, but the original motive was lost there, and only the demanding force that resulted from that motive remained, urging her without reason now to keep her hair red: she felt the compulsion to dye her hair but the reason for dyeing her hair was now hidden from her conscious mind. Then there was another worry that turned Rosalina's mind into agonized chaos: she was not happy about her thin hips and thighs. Thin hips and thighs were fashionable, especially in the Existentialist circles that she moved in, but Rosalina was illogical, and she wanted Rubenesque hips that were fat, curvacious and bone concealing. So she had torments on this score. She would look at dumpy women with envy, and look at her very attractive figure in her mirror with loathing. She tried to get fatter by eating more, but her nervous, active disposition kept her thin and wore the fat away so that she still remained lithe and beautiful in her figure. Her face she was pleased with, although it had been carved by the Almighty out of a very unmanageable stone and his chisel must have been blunt.

Now Rosalina liked to terminate her love affairs herself. This was a subconscious thing with Rosalina, but it was a powerful thing. She did not like the way things had turned out. It had been all right the first time when she had broken with Brady, but when Brady took her up again, and then apparently dropped her, she did not like it at all, although she would not admit it to herself. Instead of admitting to herself that she felt slighted, she worried and worried about what she described to her girl friends as her motherly concern over Brady, who she said was only keeping his distance because he knew she was involved with Pretty Paul. She worried over what she said was Brady's need for her, and her worryings became so complicated that in the end she did not know what she *really* wanted, and she began to work against herself: she confided to Jane and Olga that she thought it best if Brady found another girl friend, and she persuaded Olga to go and see Brady, ostensibly to get a job modelling for Brady, but really to cause a love between the dark and morose Olga and Brady. Brady found the tall Olga very depressing; he painted her twice, and then went on painting his other models.

Rosalina felt very disturbed when she heard that Olga had been rejected, and she felt she should begin worrying over Brady's need for her again, which she did.

In fact Brady was quite happy; he knew that he could have Rosalina whenever he wanted her, a knowledge gained from his success with the car-and-country incident, and he was taking his time, waiting for the need for Rosalina to rise within him again. He listened to Elvis Presley, undisturbed.

Rosalina became obsessed with the idea of Brady's dependence upon her, and read Pretty Paul's love poetry with only half her mind. Pretty Paul realized that something was wrong, and began to forget to trim daily his pretty white beard—a sure sign that he was disturbed.

.   .   .   .   .

Pretty Paul sat in the cinema with Rosalina, his head hidden completely by his duffel-coat hood, muttering to himself about the standards of beauty accepted by the masses, and looking disapprovingly at the film-star girls on the screen before him, and looking approvingly at the girl beside him.

The people later flooded out of the cinema, Pretty Paul and Rosalina pushed along with them. Rosalina went into a nearby chemist and Pretty Paul walked on ahead: he hid in a deserted street that was on their way. Rosalina came sternly and with dignity out of the chemist's shop and began walking. As she passed the hidden Pretty Paul he swept out upon her, his duffel-coat hood behind him bouncing, and his duffel-coat billowing from his upraised arms, passionate poetry, composed during the waiting, pouring from his mouth, his face red with the mounting blood beneath the skin.

This over, they walked down the street, Pretty Paul kicking a stone before him along little lengths of pavement and dragging a stick along the brick wall to the side of him. Rosalina hardly noticed, for she was concerned with the important things of life; she was worrying.

.   .   .   .   .

Brady went past the parked Lambrettas, motor-cycles,

and beat-up old cars, with mild trepidation, glancing at an old taxi painted orange with 'Been all the way to West Germany', 'Only Cost Two Pounds', and 'Blew Up in Naples, Italy' painted on its sides in pale-blue, which was parked by a veteran Rolls-Royce. Brady passed a disciple of Brigitte Bardot, who was drawing a tree, and he walked into the building.

The 'Life Room' was dirty and dark and the nude Negro model's skin looked like old potato peelings. The floor was black, smeared, and occasionally dotted with bright-coloured paint from past upset palettes and paint fights. A photograph of Elsa Martinelli was pinned on the wall beside a reproduction of a Matisse. The Negress rolled her dog's eyes at him disagreeably as he entered, and ran a red tongue over her black ape's mouth, casting her eyes down again to continue looking at the array of electric-fires around her 'throne'. The air was thick, foul, and heated, and nobody looked up from their paintings as he entered. At the far end of the room, blocked out from Brady's searching eyes by two angled screens, was another nude model; surrounded by dirty ancient easels, and dirty young students, who painted dirty coloured paintings, on canvases which once were virgin white. One of the young men raped his virgin-white canvas by brushing across it some broad strokes of black: he stood back and surveyed what he had done with justifiable distaste. Brady came up to the high screens, upon which were many pencil writings and pencil drawings, and looked fully at the second painting assembly, observing through his misty glasses that the model was graceful, pale, unhealthy, white, elegant, and male. The male nude model looked with female spitefulness at Brady, wriggled coyly, and put his nose disdainfully in the air. All was silent and concentrated. A fancy waistcoat, a huge black beard, and a pair of glaring sensitive eyes sidled up to Brady and asked him what he wanted. Brady spoke to the man, trying to see what was beneath all the hair, and the man pointed to Rosalina and then to the door. Brady went over, touched her back, and then left the room.

A bell clanged throughout the corridors, and the miserable, gloomy, and silent walks became shattered with voices, and

charged with duffel-coats of all colours; bouncing and long
necklaces; carried easels on the shoulders of bearded Christs
in jeans and pullovers; Lollipops and Dowdy Doras; sandals
and sketchbooks; potential great painters (perhaps), and
potential teachers who thought themselves potential great
painters or just great painters; dead-pan morbid-looking Jills
and Janes in ever-so-long grubby skirts; father-confessor tutors
dressed like their male students, except that they were
cleaner and more expensively dressed than the boys; dumpy
Mary and long tall Cecilia; angular Arthur and sad small
William; paintings, with pale-pink nudes against tasteful
backgrounds on them; and Rosalina alone in the crowd. 'I
say, Mary—coming to the school dance? You're not? But
why? Blast your father!' . . . 'I love your pony-tail, Helen—
it suits you.' . . . Then gruffly in contrast to the shrill: 'Oh,
cokernuts to Leonardo, haven't you heard of Bratby? He
can't paint portraits? Oh, cokernuts, haven't you seen his
portraits of Jean? Well, it may look like just thick paint to
you . . . it looks . . . marvellous to me. Oh, cokernuts! You're
up the creek, boy . . . up the creek.' Rather more than gruffly:
'Matisse has got form, you know: not so obvious as Picasso's
early figures, but you look again and you'll see that Matisse
has form in his paintings—three dimensional form and the
other kind of course.' Girlie sounds: 'Stoppit, Jimmy.' 'Did
you see that black model staring at me? 'Orrible old cow.'
'That model on the other side of the room: queer as they come:
too many queens in this monarchy!' 'Oh, of course he's in love
with me. Why shouldn't he be?'

Hysterical high-pitched crescendos of girlie giggling
laughter cut across bellows of masculine amusement, and
Rosalina was silent as she walked.

Softly and female: 'I'll give you this woman's address . . .
she'll get rid of it for you. . . .'

'Daddy doesn't know, and he would chuck me out of the
house if he found out.'

'Can you raise ten quid?'

'I'll have to find it somewhere, won't I?'

Brady waited in the entrance hall, looking out of the doorway at the girls and boys mounting their Lambrettas, and a

large bearded gentleman getting into the decorated taxi that had been to West Germany and that had exploded in Naples, Italy. Looking through the doorway Brady watched the students pour out of the art school into the busy street, students mixing with housewives and bread-earners, Lambrettas dodging around buses, and the taxi making its glorious way into the road.

Brady was buffeted and elbowed as the students milled in the entrance hall. A wet landscape-painting smeared over Brady's trouser-leg unnoticed by Brady and the owner of the masterpiece. To his confused and embarrassed delight, Brady became entangled with a glorious example of art-school glamour, who accidentally dug her plump elbow in his glass-covered eye, which event did not delight him: however, it was at least a minute before she disentangled herself from Brady, and became swallowed up in the throng, holding her painting high above her head, as she went out of the doorway into the wild life outside; and Brady felt it had been a satisfactory encounter.

'Are you going to put in for the London Group, Joey?'

'Oh yes, sales are good there, you know. By the way, did you see the Bratbys there last year? He really is a rotten painter, you know—can't draw hands at all—and those colours are all as unrelated as bits and pieces in a dustbin. Of course the bits and pieces in a dustbin come mostly from the kitchen, and Bratby is a member of the Kitchen Sink School of Painting, so I suppose there is a relationship there somewhere, especially as Bratby's paintings look as if the contents of the dustbin and the kitchen sink had been emptied over them.'

'Oh dry up, for Pete's sake, will you!'

'I know, Jill—we can go to the opera tonight. How's that?'

'What a good idea, Fransie!'

'Louie, I won't get my Intermediate Exam if I keep coming to the pub with you chaps in the evenings.'

'Of course you will, Barty.'

Brady was squashed up against the wall and didn't know where to put his arms.

'Now listen, you half-wit: Bratby is a marvellous painter; he has painted anything from your dustbin to your kitchen sink, and with the passion of Soutine and the drawing of Kokoschka.'

'Well, I don't see his work like that. What on earth is the point of squeezing paint out of a tube down the canvas in long thick lines? Why it looks as if he was icing the canvas with an icing squeezer. He's mad . . . quite mad.'

'Coo-ee! Judy! . . . Oh blast this crowd! Oh there you are. This is like the crowds on the Underground. This building is too small for the amount of students it contains. Alfie Chase criticized my drawing today in his Life Drawing class; that man makes me squirm when he puts his wet paw on my shoulder, and bends over me to redraw my life drawing. Do you know what he said to me, the great fat heap of egotism? He said, "Well, you can't draw yet can you: don't worry for you have not been drawing long," . . . and I've been drawing for two years now. Oh I hate that man. The last time I . . . he came over . . . towards me lecherously. . . .' Her voice lost its continuity as she went out of earshot.

'I put sand and cigarette ash in my paint—gives the paint such an interesting texture, and stabilizes the paint too!'

'. . . sort of painting that my Aunt Fanny would think was marvellous, but like most Aunt Fannys she thinks painting reaches the heights with—well—Highland-cattle pictures. People like . . .'

'Oh hmm! I think Brown will pass his Intermediate, you know. I suppose his life drawing might let him down, however. Be glad when the new annexe is opened. You know Brown . . .'

'I say, Mr. Silverstone! Can I have a word with you, sir, please?'

'Of course, Brown. I was just talking to Mr. Sayers about you. Coincidence. What is it now?'

The crowd began to thin out rapidly, and Brady was not buffeted any more.

'Well, sir, it's about my Life Drawing. Do you think it will pass the Intermediate, sir? I know it's my weak point and I'm very worried about it. Can I miss Miss Dyer's Perspective class, and do an extra Life Drawing class instead? I'm pretty good at Perspective, sir.'

'No, I don't think you'd better do that Brown. I say, Sayers—when that annexe is opened, then perhaps we will not have so many elbows shoved at us. Just like being in a football-ground crowd these days. Too many people in the Intermediate classes. Sorry, Brown, where was I? Oh yes. Well, Brown, I think rather than switch classes for the sake of your Life Drawing, you might improve it by talking a little less during the Life Drawing class to Miss Doris Bateman. Or better still, if you are on such good terms with Miss Bateman, get her to pose in the nude for you some evenings, and draw her—draw her, I said, Brown! Fine figure that girl has—probably be a very good model, Brown! Don't you think so, Sayers?'

'Oh yes. Quite.'

'Well, sir, thank you, sir. Then there is my composition, sir. How about that?'

'I think I'll be going now, Silver, old chap.'

'O.K. Bye-bye, Sayers. Have a good time. Tell Bratby I think his last exhibition stank, will you. The chap shouldn't be allowed to exhibit except in Russia. 'Bye, Sayers.'

'Well, I won't tell him that, Silver. Goodbye.'

'Well, Brown, your comp is fine, except that all the female figures in your compositions look remarkably like Miss Bateman.'

'Well, I don't think so, sir! By the way, sir, I think John Bratby's paintings are terrific. I went five times to his last show.'

'Bratby, my child, is the biggest charlatan since Picasso. I hear he paints those huge pictures of his from six inches away from the canvas: how can he compose them? James Brady is bad enough, but John Bratby is the end. Funny how they paint so alike.'

'Yes, sir. Thank you, sir. Goodbye, sir.'

'Goodbye, Brown. Can I help you, sir? I have noticed you waiting here all the time I've been talking.'

'. . . Pablo Picasso is the greatest genius in painting of the twentieth . . .'

'. . . seen Janet's new hair-style? Suits her down . . .'

'. . . and he drank himself silly last night in that Soho pub. And then this queer came up to him and said: "Hullo, darling. Buy me a drink?" And he bought him one; and talked . . .'

'. . . that's James Brady! I know him—I posed for him. I suppose he's waiting for Rosalina. She's keeping him waiting on purpose, I think. She is . . .'

'. . . I come here quite often to learn to paint, you see, Agnes. These students don't like us evening students. They think we are horribly bourgeois. Yes they do. I heard one say so. I think the room is over there. You enquire at the office.'

'Sorry to keep you waiting, Jim. How are you?'

'Hullo, Rosalina. Like to go for a walk?'

'All right.'

.   .   .   .   .

'Now look, Jim: I have promised my poet. I can't sleep with you. It's unfair of you to ask me. He has been good to me and I won't be unfaithful to him. That last time in the car was very wrong of me and I don't intend to do it again. I promised him that I would be his and nobody else's. . . . What? Go to a hotel in Wales? Are you mad? Well, for a start what would your wife say about you staying away for the week-end? . . . Well, she must be trusting if she will accept a lie like that. Going off for a week-end's painting in the Land of Song. That's a good one. I suppose it would be nice over there. How would we get over there? . . . By first-class carriage? I've never seen the Singing Land. Gosh, it would be lovely. No, I won't! I won't be untrue to him! I won't!'

.   .   .   .   .

'Are you comfortable, Jim? . . . Here, read this book of poems by Lord Tennyson. . . . Haven't you read him before? . . . Yes, they are lovely, aren't they. . . . I wonder if I can get some sleep before we reach Wales. I'll try. Good night.'

.   .   .   .   .

'Did you see the way that boy leered at me when I asked

him where the hotel was? . . . Oh damn! I've broken this tooth-cleaning glass on the washstand. We must get out in the morning before the woman comes to make the beds. Come to bed, Jim.'

    ·   ·   ·   ·   ·

'It's nice having breakfast here with you, Jim. Pass the marmalade, will you? Oh, James!—I've just remembered my Pretty Paul again: I can't go on being unfaithful to him—poor Pretty Paul—I so much want to remain true to him, for he is absolutely faithful to me. We made a pact—Paul and me. He would be true to me and I would be true to him. No, you mustn't say that: it isn't easier for him to stay faithful just because he is aged. That was a nasty thing to say.

'This hotel is a wonderful place right here on the valley-top, isn't it, Jim? Pretty Paul would just love to stay here. Now what's the matter? Hey! Where are you going? What? Well, I can't say I'm sorry that I keep mentioning Paul, can I? No, I won't say that! Come and sit down and finish your breakfast: people are beginning to stare. . . . That's better. Now, have another piece of bacon and for goodness' sake stop leering at my chest: your face reveals every thought you have and people are laughing at you.'

    ·   ·   ·   ·   ·

'Well, Jim, we are pretty comfortable in this sleeper, and it was a lovely visit. Oh, look at that silly man grinning at us from the corridor: does he think we are a honeymoon couple then? Pull the blind down, Jim, will you. . . . I suppose all this must be costing you quite a lot.'

22 Rosalina III

'No, Jim, it is very wrong that I have been away with you for this week-end. I shall have to tell my poet. I cannot lie to him. He is bound to have tried to see me while I was away, and he will want to know where I have been. I am not going to invent lies about this. Goodness knows what his reaction will be. I don't want to lose him. . . . Oh look, here is a reproduction of one of your paintings, here in this book: *From Sickert to Bratby*. It's jolly good, Jimmy. Here are some reproductions of Bratby's work. Aren't they like your work, Jim? Either he has copied you or you have copied him . . .'

'I haven't copied Bratby and Bratby hasn't copied me. We are both of the same generation, moulded in the same moulds, taught by the same generation of painters and both expressing the tensions and unrest of our atom-bomb-threatened age—no wonder we paint alike. It's just like Michael Ayrton and John Minton: they both painted similarly during the Second World War. We have our differences though: Bratby is a better draughtsman than I am, and I have more humanity in my work. Oh, and he doesn't sell as well as I do, and he'll probably get a knighthood if he doesn't blot his copybook: the pompous social snob! I met him once: he's such a blasted egotist, you know, and thinks he is the best thing that has happened to England since Turner. Now he's writing a book, a novel: who the hell will read that? I won't, that's for sure: that's for damn sure. I don't think we had better talk about him any more. He makes me sick. Why he even thinks he's better than Sickert! I heard him say so once. Just a bloody show-off: riding around in that Rolls-Royce and his Ford Thunderbird—I bet he can hardly afford it. Oh perhaps he can—I forgot that Unesco building job he got— he must have got a lot from that I suppose. Why, his little wife paints better than he does sometimes. Very good she is, a subtle talent.'

'You are just jealous that's all. Oh look at those cows! When do you think we will reach London, Jimmy? . . . What will he say when I tell him I've slept with you. Oh dear— what a mess.'

'What will he say, Rosalina? Why he'll probably write a poem about it such as:

'My voice wails about Rosa in Wales:
Oh why do I hear her awful tales?
I'm not so young as I used to be,
But why she went I just can't see.

She stayed in a gay and loose hotel,
After Paul had treated her so well.
Oh how I cry about my dear,
And shed not just a single tear.

She said she'd be my love for ever,
But not for long stayed on the tether:
And at a call she ran away,
And by the mines and rocks did stay.

'Why, Rosalina, our week-end will be a fountain-head from which poetry streams, and your poet will drown his sorrows in the doubtful depths of his art. No need to worry, my girl, you should feel proud—look what you're doing for him.'

'Very funny indeed! Sometimes I hate you intensely. How can you make fun of him like that? . . . He won't beat me, because he's not that sort, but he'll feel it very deeply, the poor thing. Oh why am I always in such a mess, why is my life so complicated?'

'Look, the train is stopping, this must be pretty near London by now. That accident on the line, that we had to wait for the clearing-up of, has made us very late. I suppose it will all be in the papers. I'll lean out and buy a paper from that chap on the platform.'

'I try so hard to simplify my life but it is always complicated like this. I mustn't see you again, Jimmy, I must be faithful to one man—my poet. People get the wrong idea about me and they think I am a loose girl. Look at that man getting in the train, isn't he just gorgeous! Yes, people think I'm promiscuous and loose, but I'm really a good girl.'

23 Breakdown—repair—as new—and Rosalina

BRADY stood in the big room in which Bratby's paintings towered to the ceiling. A vast triple-mirrored sideboard covered one wall, and lying across the table-part of the sideboard was Esmerelda. Rosalina poked the fire meditatively, and Sylvia, old and shrunken, talked to the other prostitute in this wise: 'That copper nearly took me in last night, dearie.'

Brady's wife handed round coffee and cakes, and then all became still; Brady's wife leaving the door just a fraction unclosed, as she left the room with the tray. Brady opened the windows wide; and the door, at the end of the room far from the windows, blew open with the through-draught created. Esmerelda, wakened from her sleep by the draught of cold air, descended from the sideboard, and danced with Rosalina, Sylvia, and the other prostitute: round and round Brady's old Lambretta, that he had been painting pictorially. On the seat of the Lambretta was a broken watch, and across the handlebars lay a shotgun. Then they all danced before Brady's painting, an enormous painting of a breakdown lorry: the only Brady painting in the room—the rest were Bratbys.

Esmerelda told Brady that her suicide was faked, and Brady looked at his painting with worry and puzzlement. He opened the huge doors in the wall and looked out at the pavement outside: he beckoned, and the breakdown lorry lumbered over the pavement and into the room. Brady closed the doors, dismissed the driver, and paid him by giving him a copy of *The Secret Life of Salvador Dali*. Then Brady picked up his brushes and went on with his painting of the breakdown lorry. Esmerelda hindered him by hanging on to his back, but she helped him in other ways. Sylvia read a very profound book, the other prostitute looked at herself in the mirror, and Rosalina rocked her baby in her arms.

Brady went close to the breakdown lorry, which was being driven away through the big doors, which were open on to the street. He had now finished his painting, but wanted to have one last look at the lorry: he climbed on to the back of the lorry, and, to his acute dismay, the lorry carried him away with it, through the streets. Brady, looking very old, with white hair and a lined face, lay on his back on the back of the red breakdown lorry, looking up at the passing house-tops and second-floor windows.

The lorry came to a standstill in the repair garage, and Brady descended from it. Somehow he became involved with the garage owner, and eventually handed over repair costs in a confused state of mind: he felt it easier to give in than argue further.

He walked away with his receipt, and looked back at the garage with its sign across it: REPAIRS.

He returned to the big room to find it full of glorious Brady paintings, devoid of Bratby paintings, devoid of Esmerelda, Rosalina, Sylvia, or the other prostitute, and with no enormous breakdown-lorry painting to be seen. The objects in the room were very costly, and his wife greeted him with a loving kiss. 'I heard you sold your latest painting of me for seven thousand, my dear,' she said.

'Oh, was that my one hundred and seventy-seventh, or my

one hundred and seventy-eighth painting of you, dear?' asked
Brady. 'Are the children all in bed? I think I'll go for a ride. Is
Henry in the garage or in his private rooms? I'll go in the
Bentley, I think. 'Bye, dear.' He glanced at the watch he had
had all his adult life, and rang for Henry.

Cruising round Piccadilly in the Bentley, Brady observed
the alterations that had been made to the Circus in his lifetime,
examined Eros from the sculptural appreciation point of view,
and never noticed the ladies standing around in the Circus of
Love. He looked quite young for his age, and felt very contented. His life had been steady, his wife had been constantly
by his side through life, and his career had just reached a peak
—he had been given the Order of Merit.

He looked out of the Bentley window and saw Esmerelda,
Sylvia, and the girl from the looney-bin, selling their wares;
but he glanced away again, for he had never seen them before.

On the way home Brady passed the garage with its sign:
REPAIRS. He waved to the mechanic standing outside, and the
mechanic waved to him. Brady looked hard: he had seen that
face a lot once, he thought. Why, the man looked very much
as he had looked in his youth! Oh well!

.   .   .   .   .

'Wake up, Jimmy! Here we are at our destination. You
were not allowed to sleep for long, were you?'

Brady looked sourly at Rosalina, and stood upright in the
rocking compartment of the train. He took his coat off the
bunk and put it on.

'I'll leave you outside the station, Jimmy. I am going to
phone my poet, and get him to come up to London and have a
good dinner with me. Give me a few quid, Jimmy. I must put
things right with my poet. Perhaps after a good dinner he
will be able to take what I have to tell him about the Land
of Song. . . . Thanks, Jim. Oh five pounds. Thank you, darling.
Thank you.'

'I feel awful, Rosalina! That cat-nap I had left me feeling
awful!'

24 Rosalina IV

THE station roof towered high above: arched grandly, and smoke-darkened. Brady passed the engine's huge wheels, that were motionless, and glorious to look at. Crowds surged around him and Rosalina, as they walked to the ticket-collector, who was standing by the gateway in the barrier.

'I had a dream, Rosalina—when I had that cat-nap, it was. The most peculiar dream!'

'What was it about, then?'

'Tickets, please! Tickets, please!'

'I've got to pay extra on this ticket, haven't I?'

'Yes, miss. Five and twopence.'

'Go on, Jim. Don't wait for her to pay: hand in your ticket and let's get by.'

'Have a cup of tea with me, Rosalina, before you go. I'll tell you about my dream.'

'O.K., we can get one over there. Come on. Oh wait a sec. I'll phone my poet first. Just wait here a few minutes. Have you got four pennies? . . . Thanks.'

'Unk . . . Unk . . . Unk . . . Unk.'

'Now then: S.X.Z. 1.4.6.7. . . . Hullo, is that you, dear? . . . This is Rosalina! Oh damn! I forgot to press button A. . . . Hullo, dear! Rosalina here! Look, I'm in London! Would you like to have dinner with me? I'll treat you—and to a jolly good dinner too! I've got something to tell you too! It's jolly important! Oh wait a minute! There's a man opening the door. Can't you see I'm using this phone-box? . . . No, I won't be long! No, I'm not going to be ages! But I've only just started phoning! Hullo, dear! Sorry about that! Some chap thought I might use the phone for the next hour or something! Will you come up? . . . Good! Meet me at eleven o'clock at the Crown and Ant, South Ken! Kisses to you, dear! Bye-bye!'

'Oh! There you are. Come on, let's go and get that cuppa.'

'Two teas, please.'

'There you are, sir. Sixpence, please.'

'Let's sit down here. . . . Well, I dreamt a funny dream all about myself broken down; and a breakdown lorry that took me to be repaired; and then it was all about myself if I had lived a steady life and no messing around.'

'Why, what sort of live have you lived then?'

'Oh I've lived pretty wretchedly at times.'

'Well it sounds a funny dream to me.'

'It was, I assure you. Makes me think though. Makes me think what might have happened if I had lived strongly and cleanly.'

'Hey! Just what kind of life have you lived then, for Pete's sake? I don't like the sound of that. Perhaps I'm just the most recent of a series of girls you have slept with during your marriage.'

'But you are different, Rosalina!'

'Oh sure. Look, you make me sick. I'm going and don't try to see me again, or try and get me to come on any more dirty week-ends.'

'Don't go, Rosalina! Oh hell!'

Quarter-dried paving-stones glistened in the early-morning light, beneath the dark verticals of the lightless lamp-posts. Steps far out on to the pavement, leading up to shabby doors. Broken window panes. A near street going down to a crossing road, and rising up as it right-angled away from the crossing road into the distance. A man holding his forehead as he shaved the side of his face with rapid movements: seen by an open window. A boy swinging on the high, horizontal bar of an old lamp-post. Housewives together in an open doorway that opened right on to the pavement. A children's playground: a couple of boys fighting: little girls singing: two girls swinging a rope while another skipped over its moving, curving arc. Ruined houses around a waste plot of ground: a boy running across the plot. A gaunt face with staring eyes and wind-blown hair. A road made of little rectangular blocks. A pretty girl, out on the pavement, standing on a chair, washing the window. Children squatting on the step of an open doorway, by the pavement: a dog jumps round them, out of the house, and down the road. Milk bottles, in many crates, the crates piled on the pavement. Long, long rows of identical houses: houses undetached and welded together into one stretching monotonous block. An old woman, weary, sitting in her door-way. Big-feet teddy-boys at the corner of a street. Children on a rubbish-dump. An old man in braces and shirt, poking clean a drain with a stick. Grim, rectangular doorways, flanked by grim, rectangular windows: above, railinged balconies: no decoration to relieve the grimness and austerity. Children swinging on ropes suspended from a pole. Brady wandered in the back-streets of Liverpool, Stockport, Salford, and Manchester. When Rosalina left him, he phoned his wife, gave her a few lies, and caught a train north. After about a week of wandering he returned.

.   .   .   .   .

Four things were causes of Brady's next crack-up. One was the dirty week-end with Rosalina, with the preceding Rosalina activities: prior to the advent of Rosalina, Brady had been straightening himself out and getting a more balanced attitude to life, but Rosalina undermined all that! Secondly, there was the dream: this hit him behind his guard—it made a profound impression on his subconscious—and it made him feel he had 'missed the boat' in life, such feelings making him think that, as he had messed things up, there was no point in avoiding further messy situations. It must be remembered that the dream and its after-thoughts came to a mind that was tired from lack of sleep, and therefore the mind was vulnerable to the infiltration of depressive, defeatist thinking. Thirdly, there was the dispirited wandering through the back-streets of the northern places: the previously described scenes were very depressing, and they contributed to his low morale. When he wandered past the rubbish dumps and the austere, horrible, and barren stretches of house façades, his mind was still tired —even more tired—and the whole atmosphere around him was of hopelessness, which easily depressed such a weary mind: a tired mind is weak and easily influenced; powerless to reject, and entirely absorbent and vulnerable. Fourthly, there was the fact that Rosalina had left him. But she had left him in a certain way: she had left him when she was despising him, and this led him to despise himself, while at the same time he was battered by her violent leave-taking at the station tea-and-buns counter.

Brady was strongest when he was in familiar surroundings, and backed up by reminders of his achievements. For a while he had been away from such a setting, and he felt lost and consequently weak and demoralized.

If he had gone home, settled down again, had a good sleep, thought things over quietly, and collected himself, he might have recovered. But he did not do this, unfortunately. Instead he kept away from his wife and home: the cure for his illness. And so he became gradually worse.

This account of Brady's life that this book contains is not the story of a breakdown that gets gradually worse and worse, terminating in some final chapter of subsequent great depravity, such as suicide. The breakdown is not like a hill that falls from its summit rapidly to a stinking ditch. It is more real than that: life is not always so simple in its form. Brady's breakdown was comparable to a hill that falls from its summit gradually to a swamp on a very low level below sea level, and then on the other side of the swamp, where the swamp is murkiest, the ground rises very rapidly in a steep wall to a height equal to the summit of the hill, at which height the ground is covered with green grass. Then the ground descends again, once terraced, to another low level, to rise again, and then fall violently at a cliff-face far down to the cruel rocks below. There is the line on your graph paper.

25 From below the terrace, down

. . . . .

Brady is comparatively young, and he stands on the fresh green grass on top of the hill. He holds his wife by the hand. Gradually, as a man turns into a werewolf, Brady's appearance begins to change to that of a gorilla, who lets go of Mrs. Brady's hand, and stumbles down the sloping side of the hill, which becomes more and more slippery as the ground descended. We notice that the gorilla has a companion by now, and they both stumble down the slope together: some way down the slope the companion falls down, and rolls over, dead: in her hand is a key to a cage, and as the gorilla stumbles further onwards we see that she is Esmerelda. The gorilla reaches the swamp at the base of the hill and squelches around in its murky mess. He doesn't try to extricate himself, and gets over to the far side of the swamp, which is putrid and foul. Suddenly the sun rises; and, werewolf style, the gorilla changes back to Brady again, in the gathering light of morning: the darkness is over, and Brady climbs a steep ascent from the putrid swamp side, quickly reaching the top of another hill, where he finds his wife standing on the green grass. With a sidelong glance, back down at the swamp, he sees the nuthouse prostitute and Sylvia wading around in the swamp, sinking deeper and deeper. Then Rosalina joins Brady and his wife, and his wife turns away to look at the view from the hill, while Brady and Rosalina walk down the other side of the hill (the side furthest away from the original hill), in the growing dusk, Brady changing once again in appearance. They reach a terrace of grass, and Brady finds Rosalina has walked away along the terrace, and his wife has joined him. Brady gets out his portable painting-easel, and begins to paint the view, but his wife turns away, as Brady completes his transformation, and Brady abandons his work, and stumbles down the hill-side, as the setting sun he was painting in the

half-light goes out of sight. Eventually he climbs up again, to another hill-top of grass in the daylight, where his wife awaits him. But he goes too near the edge of a cliff that descends from the hill-top on its other side, and he falls down, in a moment, to his death on the wickedly sharp rocks at the base of the cliff.

.   .   .   .   .

ROSALINA had moved. She now lived in a little room in an old Greenwich house overlooking the park: the house was owned by an ex-dancer now turned probation officer; he had bought the house with the savings from his forty pounds a week earned by his dancing on the stages of music-halls. Her landlord was large, and an Italian: blue-eyed and well muscled (he now did weight-lifting and had demonstrated the contractions of his muscles to Rosalina on one occasion, saying that, as she did anatomy at art school, she might be interested to see how his rectus-abdominals bulged into ridges and how his lattimus-dorsi muscles looked when 'separated'): fierce, and with a kind heart beneath his fabulous pectorals. The house was divided up and let out to various people, while the landlord and his wife lived down below: the landlord was often to be seen in the garden, rolling the lawn, in a leopard skin, or grunting as he raised his weights. When Rosalina told Brady all this, Brady seemed dimly to remember something similar, but he could not place it, and he dismissed it as the invention of his disturbed and chaotic mind.

Brady found it difficult to make contact with Rosalina but eventually managed it, and re-established their relationship.

In her ceiling Rosalina found a trap-door that led up into the roof: there was a tiny room up there, and Rosalina sometimes painted, by standing on the ceiling beams and banging her head on the roofing beams—a not very profitable activity. She got her landlord to break a hole in the brick wall in the attic room, and he placed a window frame in there, with window glass fitted in it. She curtained the window. One day she mounted the steps to the hole in her ceiling, and began to paint in her little room. She stepped back to view her painting, and fell through the hole, and down the step-ladder. She was luckily unharmed.

Brady worried over his now lengthy association with Rosalina. The fact that he was sure he had heard from someone before the things Rosalina had told him about her landlord, or that he had experienced them himself at some time in the past, made him feel that perhaps he was going mad: sometimes he doubted his sanity, for his lunatic-asylum experiences undermined his confidence in his sanity.

The distaste Rosalina had felt at the station for Brady, because of his past life, soon disappeared. Like a child, she lived in the present, and she could not be bothered to hang on, in her mind, to somewhat sordid revelations in the past, which she was happier forgetting. What her worries were, and what their magnitude was, did not prevent them from being forgotten because of new eventualities of a gay and charming or intriguing character. Sometimes her worries lasted for a long time, especially if they were anchored to, and springing from, such a phenomenon as her poet; but it was surprising how quickly some great epic worries were transformed into her history, by the advent of some new enthusiasm in her life. In this way she was like a child, who will cry with sounds that tear her mother's heart to ribbons, for half an hour or more, and then when given the joy of toffee will suddenly forget her great woe, and start loving life again. It was not that Rosalina's worries, when they were alive and kicking, were not all-embracingly intense and consuming; for they were of the great magnitude of a child's short-lived woes; but sometimes they were as soon forgotten as a child's tragedies.

Rosalina was very contradictory. Although she had hated Brady when she heard what he had to say in the station, her attitude to what she had heard, and what she subsequently imagined, soon changed to a delight in the existence of evil and depravity in Brady's past. Her imagination was boundless, and Brady became the Devil incarnate to her, which tickled her fancy enormously. It must be remembered that she was young, and her mind had all the contradictions, the strivings after a principled way of life, and the complete irresponsibility, of a mind not yet properly formed or disciplined. The guilt she felt, urging her to try to live according to high principles, when she knew that she was living loosely, caused her worrying bouts. Because she was young and had no formed principles she was obsessed with morality and fierce in judgment; and intellectualization about morality became an enormous thing, quite out of proportion, in her mind: and then suddenly her moralizing would cease with ludicrous abruptness and she would start acting like a tart again: after which she would have another bout of enormous moralizing which would worry and distress her, until the *cease-fire* occurred again—when she would *dismiss* and *relax* (not by the sandbags but by the pillows). Rosalina was essentially young, and she had the perplexity of youth: youth does not understand itself, but it tries to understand itself with all the great energies that youth possesses, making a titanic fuss about problems that adults have solved long ago and since forgotten that they solved them in some cases. But a middle-aged man in love with a seventeen-year-old girl cannot laugh at her worryings because he knows they are the exaggerated, strivings of youth, and thereby ignore them. The worryings are real to the girl and she will act accordingly, and so the worryings become part of the life of the older person and part of his worries also. So it was with Brady and Rosalina. Rosalina felt pulled towards a high moral standard, and also

271

pulled towards a low moral standard, and she did not understand it all, at all! And Brady, and Rosalina, and the Poet, suffered.

Rosalina was groping for a set of principles on the one hand, and on the other hand she was lured into acts of delightful depravity and exciting immorality. She was therefore divided within herself. Her unsure and unformed mind groped around, and found moral principles and also found the influences of depravity: with the lack of selection, common to all young people, her mind accepted all that it came across in its groping, the result being that her mind became confused and divided, because the two opposing influences could not exist harmoniously together in her mind and they created discords that made her very unhappy. Which influence she would eventually live with, and which influence she would eventually discard, is unknown to us. Deep within her lay the answer: the answer lay in her essential make-up. Perhaps she *was* a tart as we have written, and perhaps she was not one really, only a girl who was experimenting with the parts of life. She was at this stage in her life, both a tart and a good girl, and the battles between the two girls caused her great worryings. So many contradictory things were true about Rosalina. At times she became completely drawn over by the depraving influence, and became for a while indistinguishable from a tart, wallowing in self-reproach. At other times she became completely drawn over to the other side of life by the good influence, and her self-reproach was then utterly real. The thing to remember about Rosalina was that she was *young*: and her youth explained her apparent contradictions and changes of personality. All we write about Rosalina, however contradictory some of it may seem, is true. Like most young people she was a Jekyll-and-Hyde creature, and not yet mistress of herself.

Sometimes Rosalina was sincere in her mental agonies, and sometimes she was insincere.

Brady became more and more involved with her gigantic intellectual periods of mental activity: he became related to every worrying thought that lived during those periods of intense strain. And he became as exhausted, during those periods, as Rosalina herself became. Every leave-taking, Rosa-

lina decided, was to be the end of their relationship. And so for
hours, before he left her after every meeting, Brady had to endure the task of persuading her to continue the relationship.
Always this task was done in an atmosphere of great emotion
and many tears; and battle after battle of his mind against
hers was fought wearily by him. She seemed to need the battles
in some way, and Brady felt that she could not live without
them. They were like her confessional orgies: they were orgies
of argument. Perhaps they were a safety-valve used when her
nervous energies accumulated to a certain total amount that
she could not healthily contain, her orgies, confessional or
argumentative, were perhaps an outlet for surplus nervous
energy. Whatever they were, Brady had to endure these leave-
taking marathons of argument; and they wore him down:
though he always persuaded her to see him another time. She
argued not only that her disloyalty to her poet could not go
on; but she also argued that she didn't want to live for sex,
but for a life of the mind; and she argued that she was cheating
Brady's wife—in fact she argued anything at all, providing
that she felt it at the time. She could not simply leave Brady,
after having a good time with him, by kissing him goodbye
and departing: she seemed to find it absolutely necessary to
kill all the pleasures of the meeting, in a masochistic way, by
rowing and crying for an hour or two with her head-scarf on,
her make-up newly applied, and her basket in her hand. Needless to say, she had to re-do her make-up before she finally
went.

Brady found it very difficult to separate his thoughts from
hers: once the hypnotist himself, Brady found himself somewhat hypnotized. When he was away from her his mind was
filled with her worryings; and he found no peace; and could not
view her, in his mind, objectively. The great power of her
worrying intellectual assaults, was that the millions of worrying attaching thoughts were mixed with great emotion and
tears: this combination penetrated to the innermost corners of
Brady's consciousness, and stayed there, taking over his soul,
and depriving him of his ownership of himself. Her hold on his
brain was far greater than his hold on the brain of the prostitute had been: because, when he was away from Rosalina, he

still heard her voice battering away at him and he still felt immersed in her tears and wailing emotions. Nothing could have been more destructive to Brady than this state of affairs: at the beginning, when he first met Rosalina, he had been able to hold himself apart from her—now he was like her twin, linked to her, though miles and miles separated him from her. His strengths seemed to be deserting him, and she seemed to be taking possession of his soul.

Brady could not give his whole attention to his painting and he could not concentrate. He walked out of his studio and caught a bus to the park gates. The chestnut-trees grew in rows along the sides of the park approach. Brady walked through the tall, ornamental iron gates of the park, and as he progressed the ferns fell beneath the blows of his feet, and he passed by where the squatters had lived in their caravans in 1949. He walked off the road and crossed more fern-covered ground towards a group of deer which stood between him and the exit gates. He advanced with caution. He looked at a stag that was crowned with the spiking glory of its curving antlers: two prongs that curved forward, over and above the proud stag's brown-haired face; and two prongs that rose upwards from between his ears, to bow grandly outwards, giving birth spikily on the forward side, to terminate in small forks pointing inwards on high—in the manner of the upraised claws of an attacking and angry crab: and he felt scared as the stag faced him. The stag moved slightly towards Brady, though not very far from the rest of the animals: its demeanour seemed very menacing. Brady crossed to the road again, and went by a roundabout route to the exit gates.

He crossed the road outside the park gates and walked the pavements to the dancer's house. He rang the doorbell and was admitted by Rosalina.

As soon as they were in Rosalina's room she began to involve Brady in her worries: he was no longer a father-confessor: father-confessors have to be remote and undiscovered, reserved and unfamiliar, because 'familiarity breeds contempt' and no girl confides in a father-confessor whom she has heard pleading for her body. No, Brady was no longer the priest in the box: instead he was dragged into the turmoil of her mind,

and thrown about in the nagging chaos of her intellect. **Brady**
tried to shield away the arrows of her worries, while **he en-**
deavoured to make love to her. The love-making they indulged
in subsequently was strained and miserable: she went on
worrying him with words even when they were in bed. This
kind of life was ruining Brady, and he felt very disturbed
indeed mentally: he remembered how he was sure he had heard
about her landlord before she told him about him, and this
helped to make Brady sure he was on the verge of insanity.
But it all ended pretty rapidly.

Brady received a letter, when he had been at home, after
the just-described events, for about two days. It was from
Rosalina, terminating the affair.

It is true that Brady had made it impossible for her to
conclude the affair in his presence: he would have pleaded
with her so much that she would have given in to him.

When Brady finished reading the letter, he took it out of
the room where he had been reading it secretly, a room that
contained his wife and son, and took it to the kitchen. He laid
it on the kitchen table between his hands which did not touch
the letter, leant his shoulders on his straightened arms, bent
his head, and cried brokenly, on and on and on.

26 Rosalina and reincarnation

BRADY began to teach at the England College of Art, the
greatest art school in the British Isles. He had a temporary post
which was to last one year, and he taught painting and drawing to students who were too advanced to care about his
teaching: Brady found himself crawling to the students and
pleadingly asking them if they wanted any teaching, please.
The school was like most art schools: dirty and gloomy. The
gentleman in charge of the painting school of the England
College of Art was a person of great presence, handsome,
weighing fifteen stone with his pockets empty, and weighing
seventeen stone with his pockets full. He looked something
like Brady, but far better looking, and they once went to a
party together as Tweedle-dee and Tweedle-dum. This gentleman had made a fine reputation as a painter of beautifully
painted dragons upside down in ponds of an indescribably
beautiful green colour being watched by nicely painted lamp-
posts: the paintings were done in the style of Modigliani and
Turner, and they sold like hot cakes. At his home the gentleman had the most wonderful candle-snuffer Brady had ever
seen. This man had a vast humanity, and was very well chosen

for the job of guiding the lives of the painting students, to whom he devoted his life. Brady admired him immensely and with just cause. Brady's admiration for the man had been enormously strengthened by 'The Rescue of the Action Painter'. Now the gentleman tolerated Action Painters in his painting school with a generosity that was indeed great: he didn't like their work (for who did or does?), but he allowed them to continue walking or cycling over their bitumen-covered pieces of hardboard, even though they ruined the room they conducted their circus in. One day when he was walking by the River Talestotell with Brady, on a winter morning, the gentleman espied one of his Action Painting students trying to get an Action Painting into a rowing boat. The student afterwards told them that he wanted to row the painting to the middle of the river, and dump it in the river; so that he could return after two weeks with a swimming-champion friend, who would dive in, and bring the river-changed painting to the surface, and into the boat: the purpose of all this was to alter the texture on the painting, by exposing it to the ravages of the depths of the River Talestotell. Brady and the gentleman watched the student struggling with his so far comparatively unravaged painting and the boat. When the student slipped and fell into the river, the painting falling on to him and covering him with bitumen and shoe-blacking, the observers soon realized that he could not swim. So the gentleman dived fully clothed into the empty-bottle-infested water, and rescued the horrible Action Painter, who had been shouting his war-cry of 'Pollock's great and wonderful!' as his head disappeared beneath the River Talestotell.[1] Brady felt this was a marvellous action, and Brady never forgot his admiration of the gentleman.

Brady tried hard to enthuse about the uninteresting paintings that he had to criticize, but he spent most of his time in the gentleman's studio within the school building, where he watched his double painting a picture, watching with enormous admiration, for nobody else, he felt, could paint dragons up-ended in pools of green water. The gentle-

[1] Jackson Pollock was a great American Action Painter who was one of the originators of the art.

man, though very like **Brady**, was a glorified version of our hero and a really handsome man.

The entrance examinations occurred in the New Year, and then the interviews followed. Brady sat with the other members of the teaching staff of the painting school, who were all seated on comfortable seats in a semi-circle in the interviewing room. The student to be interviewed would enter the room, ushered in by a porter, and take a seat in the semi-circle, and then be put quickly at his ease by the kind addresses of the members of the teaching staff. Fred Bailley of Stockwouldton School of Art sat in the corridor outside, with all the other frightened students, awaiting his turn. The porter, an enormous fellow in a biscuit-coloured overall coat, came out into the corridor and bellowed: 'Mr. Frederick Bailley of Stockwouldton School, please! Come this way.' Fred went through a small room full of the paintings belonging to candidates for entry, and into the interviewing room. He was put at his ease, and the questioning began. 'What do you think of Picasso's Blue Period?' asked an elongated version of the younger Degas. 'Well, sir, I think Picasso was just groping around in those days, and although the work was very good, I don't think he had found his true—er—er—*métier*—sir.' And so the questioning proceeded. Other students came and went, and the day wore on. The porter went out into the corridor at three o'clock, and bellowed, 'Miss Rosalina Frend, please!' at the waiting line of students, sitting amongst tables bearing examples of their paintings and drawings. Rosalina got up and went through to the interviewing room, dressed in her very best clothes: a suède jacket bought specially for the occasion, a skirt of red, and high-heeled shoes.

Brady had not properly examined the list he had been given, a list of the names and schools of all the candidates to be interviewed; and Rosalina's entry was a surprise to him. When she saw him she hid her feelings and began to answer the questions. 'You are a student of Mr. Silverstone, aren't you. And I think Mr. Sayers taught you, didn't he?'

'Yes, sir—that is right.'

'Why do you want to come to the England College, Miss Frend?'

'I want to be a painter. I must be a painter in this life because I believe I was a great painter in my previous life. I believe in reincarnation, you see. A long time ago I believe I was a buffalo, and in the year 12 B.C. I was an orange—that is why I use that colour in my paintings so much.'

'Quite! Who were you in your last life, Miss Frend?'

'I think I was Leonardo da Vinci, sir.'

'Splendid.'

Brady watched her, his mind in a frenzy. When his turn to ask a question came, he forced himself into a controlled state, faced her directly with a reddened face and blurred eyes, and said, 'Don't you think that you have done enough painting already if you were Leonardo?'

She looked at him with sudden disdain and answered: 'Leonardo did very little painting really because his interests were so diverse. As his reincarnation I hope to do in my life all the painting that he did not find time to do—that I did not find time to do.'

Brady was astounded to find that since he had last seen her, since she had written that final letter, she had found a new intellectual phenomenon to occupy her energetic brain with, even though it was quite in character for her to do so. 'What makes you sure you were once Leonardo, a buffalo, and an orange?'

'Oh one just knows these things, Mr. Brady.'

Brady wondered how he had had the power to ask her the questions, considering he was in such a confused state of mind at the sudden appearance of her in the interviewing room.

A question from a tiny man with a hook nose, and lips that looked as though they had been chewing gutter-rubbish, followed: 'How are you going to continue on for Leonardo, when your work before us now, over on that wall, is very Matisse derivative?'

'I have only just realized that I was once Leonardo, and up till just recently I was sure I was the reincarnation of Matisse. But that doesn't matter, does it?'

'Oh of course not. Of course not. It doesn't matter at all, does it, Mr. Zeigler?'

'Why, no! No.'

279

They all felt very embarrassed except Rosalina, who sat there with absolute self-assurance. She seemed to have forgotten Brady's presence, and seemed to be unaware of the turmoil of emotion heaving within him.

'Miss Frend. How do you account for the fact that though the orange, the buffalo, and Leonardo were masculine in each case I suppose, you are feminine?'

'Well Leonardo was an artist, and artists are very feminine, for that is why they are artists: if they were completely masculine they would not be artists. So you see I am a reincarnation of the feminine part of Leonardo; and if I am not, and I am not sure I am sometimes, then I believe I must be likely to change my sex—I feel that is very possible, you know.'

The interviewers gaped at her unhappily; and Brady·felt distinctly sick, for how could the cause of his romantic pains, his obsession, be not a woman, but really a man? Brady could not see, because of his emotional turmoil at that moment, that all this was merely another expression of Rosalina's youth, and that soon she would discard completely all this reincarnation rubbish: her conviction deceived him.

'By the way, sir, if you accept me for the England College and I change my sex in the second or third year of my studentship here, will that be all right? I am rather worried about this, and I meant to tell you before.'

Everybody seemed to be extremely unhappy by this time, Brady most of all, but Rosalina seemed in quite good spirits. It was amazing how she managed to inflict her mental activities of the moment upon whoever she happened to come across.

'No, there would be no trouble there, Miss Frend You need not worry about that. But I think we feel that the college would be of limited use to you if your future as a painter is so assured. I think the best thing we can do for you is for me to write to the Director of the National Gallery and let him know that you are the reincarnation of Leonardo da Vinci. I'm sure he will be extremely interested, and keep an eye on you.'

'Are you laughing at me, sir?'

'Of course not. I am a believer in reincarnation myself. I am convinced I was a tear-drop once.'

'Very funny, I'm sure. Those who mock at reincarnation will get a great shock when they die, and are reincarnated.'

'Well, Miss Frend, I think that will be all, thank you. We all enjoyed meeting you, I'm sure.'

A chorus of backing for that last remark came from the interviewers in tones of utter non-conviction. Rosalina departed, and the interviewers exchanged cynical glances, lighting cigarettes rapidly to calm their shattered nerves. Then, after listening to Brady, who argued in defence of her—because he naturally wanted her at the college—they sent a porter to recall her for further interviewing later on in the afternoon. Then they went off for mid-afternoon coffee.

Brady did not go for coffee but wandered around looking for Rosalina. When he found her she tried at first to be distant. But Brady had some small success and they both went back to the interviewing room together.

The gentleman in charge said: 'Miss Frend, Mr. Brady has persuaded us that you deserve a place in the college. But we must ask you a few more questions, and also I do not want you to feel sure you have obtained entry. We must think about it very deeply. Now tell us—if you are Leonardo reincarnated, why is your painting not of a far higher standard? Leonardo was painting gloriously at your age.'

'I have been working against myself: as I said, I thought I was Matisse reincarnated, and I spent all my time working along similar lines to Matisse. Now that I know my true origins I shall work in the style of Leonardo and my development will surely be rapid. . . . Don't you think?' she added with failing self-confidence.

'Do you think your impending change of sex will interrupt the development of your work, when it occurs?'

'There will be no interruption in my work at all because of my change of sex. It will be completely natural, and I shall not have to go to hospital: I know it will be like that some-how—my well-formed breasts are getting smaller and smaller as the days pass, I am sure!'

At this, the assembly stirred uncomfortably, and many

sly glances were cast at the delicate swellings on her chest. Aware of these glances, Rosalina deflated her lungs, and tried to look as masculine as possible, with a distinct lack of success.

'Oh dear!' said the gentleman in charge, looking down his handsome cheeks.

'Look at the hairs on my legs and arms!' she cried eagerly, demonstrating the limbs in question to her utterly embarrassed audience. '. . . Masculinity will soon envelop me and these are the first signs.'

Her observers looked at her attractive and normally haired arms, and then looked at each other questioningly.

'Why! I even bought a cigar yesterday. I have not smoked it yet. . . . But *I will!*' she added with too much determination and little conviction.

The interviewers wondered what they were letting themselves in for, and also wondered why Rosalina had come to the interview in a nice feminine skirt and high-heeled shoes. They looked at her noticeable womanliness with appreciation, very distressed at the thought that she might soon be Roger Frend, striding around the college in trousers: although they had very little confidence that such a change would occur. But they felt that even though they had not much faith in her beliefs, they had some faith in her paintings, and the at present misdirected strength of her character; which strength, if directed towards the improvement of her painting, might result in the creation of some very good paintings. After all, they felt, her Leonardo madness would at least mean that all her attention would be on her painting, which was a good thing. They let her go, and the day's interviewing terminated. Brady followed her out and talked with her as they walked through and out of the England College of Art.

'Can't we start all over again, Rosalina? I have been so miserable without you.'

'Jim, get this straight. I am not interested in sex any more —not until I become my true self and then I shall start going out with girls.' She looked fiercely at Brady, as if daring him to laugh at her. She need not have worried, because Brady didn't feel like laughing.

'What about your poet—and the others?'

'My poet and I are living together as brothers now: he quite understands—I think. He still writes poetry about me, but he writes not about Rosalina but about Leonardo, his brother.' Brady thought glumly that the only way to continue the Brady-Rosalina link-up, was for him to try hard to change into a girl, and this thought did nothing to dispel his depression. But an idea occurred to his battered mind and he embarked upon a ludicrous campaign to get Rosalina to love him again.

'What will you do if you find yourself painting Florentine masterpieces and they sell for fortunes—Leonardo?' Brady asked, with as much sincerity and femininity as he could muster.

'Well I shall be rich then, won't I?' she answered, with a suspicious glance at Brady.

Brady flounced his trousers and looked coyly at her. 'Suppose I change my sex, Leonardo: will you let me be your girl: will you give me a chance anyway?'

She turned and stared at the hip-waving Brady and blushed. She tried to quell him with a look of disdain, but she had to retire within herself, looking very embarrassed, as a passing man gave her the glad-eye. Her act did not last very long under the attack of Brady's act. She had kept herself from sexual pleasures for a long time, and she subconsciously yearned for them, so when Brady treated her as a girl again later on, she responded quite readily. Brady wondered as he kissed her how she would try and explain herself then to the interviewing board.

Oh yes. It really did happen, dear reader. It really did happen.

.   .   .   .   .

Brady threw back the sheets and blankets in a curving sweep of curling brown and white, away from his naked body. He angled one unhealthy-looking leg over the side of the bed, placing the ugly reddened foot on the floor. Then he repeated this procedure with his other leg, and hauled his repulsively naked torso and the rest, up and out of the bed. He looked down at the mound of blanket and Rosalina, and went over to a table upon which resided a cigar. He picked up the cigar, roused Rosalina, and offered her the cigar mockingly. She grimaced, and turning her back on him, wrapped herself in the sheets and blankets again, and tried to go to sleep.

'Why don't you want to smoke your cigar, Leonardo?'

'Oh shut up, do—I'm tired.'

'I say, that's a forest of hair you have on that arm sticking out from under the blanket.'

'Go to hell.'

'I'm only being pleasant. Shall I put the kettle on so you can have some hot·water for shaving with? I'll put out your razor and shaving brush in the wash-basin, shall I, sir?'

'Look, just because you have got what you wanted, there is no reason to kick me when I am down. Can't you see that I was sincere when I talked about reincarnation and sex-changing? Just because I have not properly achieved the sex-change yet is no reason for making fun of me.'

'I'm not making fun of you. I was only trying to help, Rosa.'

Now that Brady had slept with Rosalina, he ceased to play up to her, and to fawn and plead. All the pain he had experienced, because of her long rejection of him, caused him to feel the need for revenge, so he mocked her mercilessly. He felt he had her at his mercy now.

'Leonardo was accused of sodomy, Rosa, old man: and as you have just loved with me, and I am a man and so are you, and you are Leonardo, I think Leonardo has practised sodomy once again.'

Rosalina leapt from the bed and began to attack Brady. Brady's vicious verbal attack did not cease however: he had to hurt her a great deal to make him feel even with her, for he had been made to suffer a great deal by her, ever since he had received her letter.

Eventually Brady left Rosalina. He left in a queer state of viciousness, laughing cruelly to himself, while she cried brokenly.

·   ·   ·   ·   ·

Rosalina cried for a long time after Brady left her. She was in a terrible state of mind. How could she accept herself?

Every thought she had at that moment indicated that she had made an awful fool of herself, and made such a fool of herself in front of the interviewing board, too. She cried wildly for days until eventually a calm settled upon her. She gradually admitted to herself that her imagination had been getting the better of her, and that she was neither going to change her sex nor be the reincarnation of the greatest genius that ever lived. But calm though she had become, she was not balanced correctly in her mind, for the strains she had experienced had disturbed her mental equilibrium greatly. She also reacted to the realization that she was female after all, by an exaggerated acceptance of her womanliness, and she became for a while a nymphomaniac. It was during her nymphomaniac period that she saw Brady a great deal, and she dragged him down with her. For a long long while Rosalina was utterly loose morally, and there were no periods of self-reproach or moralizing, as there had been in the past after periods of looseness.

27 Nymphomania and Rosalina Frend

ROSALINA walked down Oxford Street in bare feet, pink jeans, baggy pullover affair on her torso and arms that covered her hips, bare ankled to the calf-length jeans, and with a great square ornament hanging from her neck on a chunky chain —the ornament bouncing out from, and into, the slight concavity between the full mounds of her full breasts under the heavy non-furry material of her smooth-surfaced pullover. With her was a Negro art student dressed in appalling clothes and dressed in masses of dirt: his very long tightly curling hair spiralled out from his head in spiky squirls, making him look just like a golliwog in a child's toy collection. People stared, people muttered, people yelled, and people giggled at the pair, but Rosalina and Bobo were unaware of that for they were in a world of their own. They strolled into a coffee-bar after a newspaper photographer had taken pictures of them without their consent. The Negro Bobo drank his coffee from an extravagantly wide cup, wishing that he could meet the photographer on a dark night on Hampstead Heath. He fingered the flick-knife in his corduroy-coat pocket. The couple got on the Underground to Hampstead; and Rosalina and Bobo sat down in a carriage, much to the disgust of the surrounding people, who eyed Rosalina's dirty bare feet with contemptuous and unconcealed looks of hate.

The couple went down into the Hampstead basement room which contained two more Negroes—Bongo and Joseph. Bongo was pushing heroin into his armpit with a hypodermic syringe and squealing like a stuck pig. Joseph was merely drunk and pouring beer down his throat from an upended bottle in the air above his ceiling-raised ape's face. Blankets had come off the disgustingly filthy bed, and lay amongst the floor rubbish in mounds. The room was indescribably squalid, with windows brown with dirt and old tins of ointment everywhere—Bongo had a skin disease. Rosalina and Bobo began to drug themselves and someone switched off the light. The dim light that had managed to penetrate the windows revealed Rosalina's feet undersides on the end of the bed amongst the folds of the crumpled sheets—feet undersides that were horny and black. Feet undersides of a dirty pink belonging to the Negro Bobo were beside hers. Long after, in the early morning, Rosalina got up, cleaned part of a window, drew out a crushed and unopened letter from the pocket of her jeans, opened it, and began to read:

Dear Rosalina,

    I have been unable to find you: where are you? I am writing to your art school in the hope that you will get this letter: I imagine you do not go to the art school much nowadays because you are waiting for the England College autumn term to start in October. My heart yearns for you and I am sorry I mocked you about reincarnation and sex-changing. It was only that I loved you so much that I could not bear the thought of you feeling you were no longer female, because I loved my Rosa and not Leonardo reincarnated. Oh, please see me, Rosa. Please let me know where you are. I saw you from the top of a bus going through Hampstead: you were walking along with a Negro chap with long hair. I could not call to you as the bus window was not open, or near me. I got off at the next stop and ran after you but then you disappeared. I don't want to offend you: but I was very worried to see you in such a state for you looked terrible with your bare feet in the puddles, and that awful Negro. Come back to me, my Rosa, and we can live decently and I'll buy you some more clothes and some nice shoes. If you still want to be a man I'm willing to live with you as brother and brother, just so that I can be near you. I love you so, Rosalina. My wife is ageing and I need you so much. Please write to me.

I saw Bratby the other day: he seems quite a sincere chap and I must say I liked him.

I'm having an exhibition in London in September of paintings I did of you and some others.

Please write, my Rosa,

Love from

Jim.

Rosalina balled-up the envelope and letter and threw it across the room. The ball landed in an open tin of pink ointment and stuck there. Rosalina went over and began to pet Bobo.

．　　　．　　　．　　　．　　　．

It was night-time and Bongo had run out of heroin. He ran out of the room and up the basement steps into the lighted street. He ran down the street. Joseph ran after him protectively. Rosalina turned to Bobo and began to make love: Bobo threw her to the floor and her face smashed into the side of the bed. Bobo kicked her and went out.

Brady was wandering around Hampstead looking for his lost love when Bobo came out of the basement swearing: 'I dun mo' fo' dat Rosa dan she deserve. . . . I wan' to live with somebody else now. De good Lawd will understand, won't you, Lawd? Ise ain't goin' no mo' with dat Rosalina. She talk too big: she always talking 'bout morals and mo' and mo' talk. I wan' get away from dat Rosalina, and 'way from dat squiffy Bongo and 'way from dat Joseph—*Right away from here dis Bobo am a-goin'!* I wan' to fine a white gal who don' talk so much 'bout things I don' understand. I goin' leave art school. I ain't no good at makin' pictures. Nobody very nice people at dat place. Wish I was back in Jamaica in de Wes' Indies, I wan' be back in Kingston in dat Jamaica where all de black people are. I wan' go out fro' Kingston harbour in ma boat, ma li'l boat, like I don' used to do. Hell! Dat Rosalina talk an' talk an' talk—she made me wan' go far 'way back to Kingston and to Montego Bay, where ma fader dun live, poo' ol' man. Hell! Dat Rosalina. I wan' to drink dat fine Jamaica coffee again an' get away from dat poo' silly Rosalina.' Brady swung round and looked at the back of the retreating Bobo. He recognized Bobo as the Negro he had seen with Rosalina when he saw them from the bus. 'Damn dat Rosalina . . . talk, talk, talk, dat Rosalina. . . . Oh hell . . . Rosalina . . .' drifted along the pavement to Brady's ears, as the spike-haired Bobo went gorilla-wise flopping away down the road. Brady looked towards the basement railings where he had seen Bobo come from. He went through the open gate, down the steps, below the railings, and down to the door of the basement flat.

Rosalina had picked herself up after Bobo had gone, and washed herself in the dirty wash-basin in the foul bathroom. The washing had cleared her mind and she came back into the main room muttering: 'Filthy bloody niggers. Why do I stay with them? Why have I got like this? I ought to clear out and start living decently again. At least then I wouldn't get beaten up by the filthy niggers. I don't like Bobo James any more. He doesn't understand me when I talk sense, anyway. I want to talk to someone intelligent for a change. All that Bobo can talk about is how he went over to Santiago in Cuba, when he was seventeen, and how his boat got caught in the fringe of a hurricane. I hate the filthy state I have got to, living with these niggers. Niggers, niggers, niggers. . . . I hate them, the golliwogs!'

Rosalina cleared the table by sweeping the empty bottles and old ointment tins to the floor, scraped a chair across the floor, sat down at the table, and head in cupped hands began to soliloquize: 'They can't talk on my plane and it's very depressing to have no one to talk to. Why on earth did I start this living with niggers? I've lost my poet for good now. I suppose I could go back to Brady, the old wet. But I hate him for the way he jeered at me about my reincarnation beliefs. Where's Jim's letter now? Oh there it is. What a mess—all this ointment on the letter. Yes, he says he will have me back. That would be fine after this squalor. Brady can talk to me intelligently anyway. Ugh, this pink ointment! It might be very very nice if Jim would buy me a flat and buy me some nice clothes. I don't care about his wife now—the old cow. If Jim would have me, and I think he would, according to his letter, I could have a nice time. Of course, I don't know how he would treat me, now that he knows I have lived in filth with niggers. I would not be able to defend myself, if he chose to treat me with no respect. If he didn't treat me right, then I'd have to leave him. Oh what a slum this room is. I suppose Bongo and Joseph will soon be back in a terrible state. I suppose Bongo won't have got any more heroin unless Joseph lends him the money. Bongo will try hard to persuade Joseph to loan him enough money. What hell it will be when they return! I hate Bongo and Joseph. Now that Bobo has gone out, I suppose Joseph when he returns will try and rape me. If I leave this room for ever now I could avoid all that hell and go and ring up Brady.'

Rosalina went to a cupboard, got out an overcoat and a pair of shoes and a skirt; and began to dress for leaving. A key turned in the lock of the main door, and Joseph came into the room: 'Hey you, Rosalina! Dere's a white man with glasses on outside. What he doin' out there, Rosalina? He have a bald head with no hair on it at all, you know. That Bongo gone crazy wantin' dat stuff. I left him waitin' by de pond fo' de man who sells it to him. He ain't got no money fo' to buy de stuff, anyways. De man won't give him no stuff to put under de arms. Dat Bongo is sure crazy now—wantin' dat stuff. He' walkin' round de pond, all de time talkin' to hi'self. Dat Bongo wave his knive at me when I tell him to come on along home like a good fellah. I want no mo' to do with dat man. He don' fear de Lawd like I do. He will burn in de hell-fire, for sho'. De devil will poke him with his fork and Bongo will cry in de flames. I left him by de pond. Why dat man outside, Rosalina? Shall I go on an' show him white-trash can't stay roun' black folks do'? I 'member when I was in Savanna la Mar, an' a white-folks man was outside my pappy's do'. My pappy go out an' make his white face all red

291

with blood. My pappy very strong—big black man! My pappy say to me: "Joseph Israel Jonathan Saul John!—De white folks are trash. One o' them pistol-whipped my brudder an' I never fo'give de white folks for dat." Say, Rosalina, why you all dressed up? You goin' out Rosalina? You ain't goin' with dat white man, are you? If I let you go with him Bobo will kill me, fo' sure. Are you goin' with dat white man, Rosalina?'

'No I am not! I don't know who he is, anyway. But I am leaving this hell-hole and you won't stop me, Joseph. If you lay a hand on me I'll tell Bobo that you tried to rape me, and you know what Bobo will do to you then. Just let me go, Joseph, and if you are afraid of Bobo then run away yourself. Now get out of my way, will you!'

'Now, Rosalina, you ain't goin' nowheres. Now come here like a good li'l girl, Rosalina chil'. Ol' Joseph ain't so bad. He'll make you happy so you think you're in de heaven of de Lawd in de blue sky. Don' think youse goin' out of de do', Rosalina, cos you ain't! Now don' be like that, honey-chil'! Why! You hurt Joseph then! Now if you hurt Joseph any mo', Joseph will hurt *you*! No tellin' what Joseph will do if you bite him again. Ise a God-fearin' black man, and I loves de Lawd my saviour, but if you bite me again, Rosalina, I'll lan' you a clump so hard you will not look pretty any mo'. Why, you look so pretty in dat coat, Rosalina, I sure do like you, Rosalina. Why, you bitch! Why you hit me with dat thing? Now de blood is on my po'r face. Come here, you li'l Rosalina. Joseph will teach you, Rosalina! Aw God! Aw wah! Aw . . . wah . . . ah! I can't see now. Oh Lawd!—Ise so hurt—I can't see! Oh help me, Lawd, I can't see!'

Rosalina bolted out of the sordid basement flat, and out into the street, where she met Brady. They caught a taxi, and Brady had his Rosa back again.

.   .   .   .   .

'Why, Joseph, what's the matter wid you now, boy? Why your face all bashed up like that, man? Has dat Bongo gone crazy cos he can't get no heroin an' beat you, or sumping? Huh? What de matter wid you, boy? And where dat Rosa o' mine. She in de bathroom having' a bath? Why, she never have no bath, jus' like me? Where is dat Rosalina? Hey, answer me, boy! Where Rosa?'

'Sure don' know de answer to dat question, Bobo. All I know is dat she hit me with dat umbrellah she never used but kept in the cupboard with her nice clothes. She bit me, too, Bobo.'

'Why, Joseph? Have you been foolin' wid my girl? You been foolin' wid my li'l Rosa-honey, have you? Is dat why she don' hit you and den run away? I tell you, Joseph, you bad nigger you—if you dun fooled wid my Rosa-baby, you better get ready for de biggest beating youse ever had. Sho'! You dun try an' sleep wid my Rosa befo', din' you? An' I made you ill for dat, din' I. If you bin foolin' aroun' wid my Rosa jus' now, I sho' will mess you up, man. I sho' will.'

'Look heah, Bobo. I jus' try an' stop yo' Rosa fro' goin' away. She all dressed up in dose bes' clo' of hers, an' I say: "Rosa. You goin' away? Cos Bobo won' like that at all. You better stay heah." And Rosa, she hit me wid her umbrellah so's I cannot see fo' a while. Outside the do' there was a white man with no hearh on his head. I tol' her not to go but she dun go jus' the same.'

'You lyin', Joseph. I knows you. You waited 'till I wus away, an' you take yo' opportunity, and you try to make de girl an' she hit you an' she run away. Dat's my girl, man, an' you knows it. I gonna make one hell of a mess o' you, boy! One hell o' a mess! Yes sir! All dat stuff about a white man sho' don't deceive me, mister. Ise no fool. Ise no man wid a brain like dat Bongo. Ise Bobo, an' I know what I know. You goin' to get hurt, Mr. Joseph—you sho' are! You sho' are.'

'Now listen, Bobo. Now look heah. I din' try nothin' wid yo' Rosa. Honest I din'.'

'I'll jus' cut you up a bit, Joseph, so's you'll 'member not to mess wid my girl. And then you go 'way. See, boy?'

'Please, Bobo. Please. . .'

. . . . .

'You there, Bobo? You there, Bongo? You there, Joseph boy? Yoohoo! You there, Bobo? You there, Rosalina? Where are you all? Oh, there you are, Bobo. Why, man, you sho' look worried an' funny-looking, Bobo. Why, yo' face am all ill an' sick, Bobo. Hey, let me come in, Bobo. You sit down here, Bobo, an' rest—you sho' look like you need a rest, Bobo. Why don' you talk, Bobo man?

'Hey? Jumpin' Jehoshaphat! What dat Joseph doin' on de flo', Bobo man. Look hearh! Joseph's face is all in a mess. Man, look at all dat blood. Hey, Joseph boy—you O.K. down dere. Let me wipe some o' dat blood off of yo' face, Joseph— you mus' be knocked out. . . . Aah—Oh oh oh owah! Jesus, he's dead! Oh my God! Oh my God! My God! You killed him, Bobo! You killed him, man! Ise gowin' to get de poelese. You rotten, Bobo. Joseph was O.K. Why did you kill him?'

'Ah no, Bildad Jones—you musn't get de poelese. I don' wan' to die. I don' wan' to be hung high on de rope above dat trap-door. I wan' to live a long life, Bildad. You musn't get de poelese. Hey, come here you, man.'

'So you goin' to kill me too, Bobo?'

'I got to. Bildad—you will get de poelese iffn I don' kill you. I got to kill you wid dis knife, Bildad.'

'But we are friends, Bobo. You won't kill me.'

'Iffn I get rid o' yo' body, and also de body o' Joseph, an' I think I can do dat you know, den I will be all right. I will tell ev'ryone dat Joseph has gone away. I got nuttin' to lose by killin' you anyway, Bildad: if I don' kill you, man, you will get me hung. Come here, Bildad, Ise goin' to do it now.'

'Steady now, Bobo. Hold it now, Bobo. You dun killed someone already. If you kill me too you will sho' go to hellfire, fo' de good Lawd will not have yo' in his golden heaven. But de good Lawd might forgive yo' fo' jus' de killin' o' po' ol' Joseph, iffn you killed him in de heat o' de moment. But yo' got no chance on Judgment Day iffn you kill me too. When you go up befo' de Lawd on Judgment Day an' he's sittin' on his golden throne, he'll say: "Bobo: You killed two men. Iffn you jus' killed one fellah I might have forgiven you. But you killed two po' men. So down to Satan an' the Fiery Pit you go, Bobo." An' de Lawd will rise up in his anger an' his glory; an' he will get his angels to throw you down to the evil Satan. P'raps I won' go to de poelese iffn you let me go, Bobo: I

don't want to meet de Lawd on Judgment Day tomorrow, fo'
I'd rather wait twenty-thirty years befo' I do dat.'

'Bildad Jones. You speakin' sense now, boy. I 'gree wid
you 'bout dat. You see de Lawd would let de killin' o' Joseph
pass probably because I killed dat Joseph becawse he lie wid
my Rosa. But iffn I kill you, Bildad Jones, dat would be
diff'rent wouldn' it? An' de Lawd would shove me down in
the fire fo' de killin' o' you. No, Bildad, I don' kill you fo' I
wan' to go an' live in de golden mansions wid de Lawd, an' I
wan' de angel Gabriel to let me in God's land on Judgment
Day an' not fo' him to usher me out an' fo' him to point down
to de land dat de bad Satan is master of. But iffn I let you go,
Bildad, will you still go an' get de poelese? Please, Bildad.
Jus' you go on home an' say nuthin' about what you have
seen. Will you?'

'All right then, Bobo. I'll go home an' say nuthin'.'

'You are a good man, Bildad. You go on home an' don'
you tell any o' de boys an' girls 'bout dis matter: don' you
tell Louis, Jack, Ella, or May. Jus' put it out o' yo' mind.'

'I'll do jus' that, Bobo. Now I mus' be goin' away from
dis terrible place.'

.　　　.　　　.　　　.　　　.

'Ma name is Bildad Jones. Ah promised to say nuthin' to
you 'bout this matter but I did that to save ma skin. Iffn I
don' tell you 'bout it, then when de Judgment Day comes, the
Lawd will say to me: "Bildad Jones. You protected that
murderer Bobo and you know that . . ." '

'Yes! Yes! Mr. Jones. But what have you to tell us?'

'Ah wan' to tell you that Bobo has dun killed his friend
Joseph an' the dead man is now at Bobo's place. Bobo goin'
to dispose of de body. Bobo was goin' to kill me when I said
I was comin' to tell you, so I talked to him an' had to tell him
dat I wouldn't tell you: so he let me go. But I has to tell you
poelese gentlemen cos de Lawd on Judgment Day——'

'Quite so, Mr. Jones. Now where is this body?'

28 Heathfield House

IT WAS a place with a surprising number of human touches; it was not as severe and official as you might have expected it to be. There was even a man in a sports coat sitting at a desk, talking to one of those men you expect to find there, about football. Really, one would be surprised at the benevolent, cheery, red, and sometimes handsome faces that were to be seen in the place. A bank of dark-green filing cabinets and boxes partitioned one room, and on a table stood a roundabout filing apparatus which had a central vertical rod, from which radiated criminal-record cards that revolved around the vertical rod if pushed with the hand. Cups of tea were being handed round on the other side of the counter which bore Bildad's arms and black, sensuous, eye-catching hands upon it. On the inside of the counter stood a young man in a black policeman's outfit which was splattered with white metal.

'You just stay here for a while, Mr. Jones. Take a seat and

we'll give you a cup of tea. The flat will be visited soon by some police officers.'

'Ma girl will be wondrin' where I am.'

'You just stay here, Mr. Jones.'

.   .   .   .   .

Bobo went to the art school to borrow a car. The Jamaican had stolen money at one time and with it paid his fees a year in advance. He had wanted to go to the art school, because he knew a girl who studied there, and he always fancied himself as a painter anyway. Lately he had not attended classes very much because he was in need of money and had to look around for it, that occupation taking rather a lot of time. He had been rather desperate and had tried to persuade Rosalina to go on the streets, to earn some money for them, but she had been far from co-operative.

Bobo managed to borrow a rather battered old Ford and drove it back to the Hampstead flat. He waited till nightfall and then went over to the dead body of Joseph, put it in the trough of his arms, and carried it to the main door, Joseph's dead head bouncing and hanging down on his curving neck. Bobo listened carefully and heard no footsteps or cars outside. He ran up the basement steps, and carried Joseph through the opening in the black, spear-headed railings, across the deserted pavement, and into the car, whose door he had purposely left open. Bobo ran back across the squared pavement and clattered down the steps. After he had closed the door, his head reappeared behind the railing verticals, and he ran across and entered his car. He placed his black hands on the steering-wheel, swivelled his head round, and ogled his eyes at the body in the back of the car. The car moved down the road.

Blackheath grass dipped and rose in the moonlight. Bobo drove his car past the prefabricated houses, and past the lovers' cars that were always parked all over the heath in the pre-midnight darkness. Bobo rolled the whites of his eyes around him with exploration: a couple in the front seats of a car disentwined themselves guiltily as Bobo's car cruised slowly past.

Heathfield House was a yellow to yellow-ochre house in decay, that looked out on to the heath from behind corrugated-iron-sheeting, blocked-up gateways. A hill-side road ran down from the situation of Heathfield House towards the back of the prefabs. Behind Heathfield House on a lower level existed some new flats, which looked face to face at the balconied decay that spread across the back of Heathfield House. Heathfield House was at the end of a row of period houses that bordered the heath, and stretching from Heathfield House at a right angle was a row of pretentious middle-class dwellings on a private road. The decayed house was the only uninhabited derelict in the row of period houses. Bobo parked his car outside the house. He walked down the hill-side road; the wall of the building attached to Heathfield House beside him; a red letter-box was set in the wall, and a half-scraped-off election poster, bearing the name Hudson in capitals six times, decorated a blue door in the wall, which door was secured against intruders by a piece of bent, holed metal, with nails in it. He looked for a low wall or fence, but found none. He walked round to the back of Heathfield House: the overgrown garden at the back contained a broken, tilted, wooden fence, some bricks, some rhododendron bushes with waxy, dark-green, spearhead leaves, and a rusty bird-cage: the back garden was enclosed by a very high wire fence with the wire crossing all over it in diamonds, and from one of the vertical metal poles that held up the diamonding wire a long strip of angling rusty metal waved. As he looked at the attached, dark, brick building, through the wire fence, he saw it looming ghostly across the overgrown garden, glass-broken window openings looking strange and high up in the wall. Battered outbuildings were below the strange and wrecked windows. Bobo stood on the pavement of Baizdon Road that sloped down from the hill-side road (Elliot Place), that pavement that ran down to a low area below the back of the house, where the flats were in their neat and miserable austerity. Way beyond the flats a train clattered along a railway line well out of sight of the heath. Bobo walked haltingly, straining to keep himself erect, down to the bottom of Baizdon Road, where he turned left. Here he looked across at the back of Heathfield House, through more diamond-shaping wire, the flats just behind him. The back of the house, at the top of the sloping wasting garden, bulged out monstrously. Across the back of the yellow house were broken, wooden, balustraded balconies, below which more wooden structures in the shape of Gothic arches were greyly and brokenly adding to the fantastic appearance of the back of Heathfield House, with its many broken windows. Bobo found no low fencing, and went back up Baizdon Road into Elliot Place. He walked up the slope of Elliot Place to the top of the hill, where his car was parked in front of Heathfield House. The corrugated iron was blue-grey in parts and rusted to purple and red-brown in other parts. On the wall between the gateways were five milk-bottle crates, above which spirals of barbed-wire stretched across, though not above the corrugated iron. The house had a central part with wings either side of it. In the central part a large doorway was boarded up between two similarly boarded bay windows. Above rose a façade, ugly with shattered glass windows, and surmounted by high chimneys. Bobo got into his car and sat awhile, thinking.

Bobo got out of the car; looked furtively round him—up the road and down the hill; walked over the pavement to the corrugated-iron sheets blocking the two gateways; looked up at the waving tops of the corrugated-iron sheets, where Heath-field House rose dirty-yellow against the dark sky; and observed the yellow gateposts rising from the pavement with 'I love Jean Bassen' written in white chalk upon them. Nobody was in sight. Bobo hauled Joseph's dead body out of the car, sweat pouring from his curving ebony brow, which glistened in the moonlight, his eyes rolling comically with fear—the whites enormous—and dragged Joseph across the pavement to the corrugated iron. There was a large space between one sheet of undulating iron and a gatepost of stone, and Bobo hauled Joseph up from the pavement, pushed him awkwardly through the gap as the iron sheeting clanked, and Joseph's body fell down to the unweeded ground on the inside of the gateway. Bobo pulled the corrugated iron over the gap, fixed the metal securely so that it was sprung hard against the gatepost—set permanently against the gatepost by its own spring pressure—

and lolloped across into his car, driving rapidly away from the house that he knew would not be sold or investigated for a long time. Bobo knew a man who lived in a house near Heathfield House. This man had told Bobo that Heathfield House was owned by a man whose wife had died in the yellow house. Apparently the man would never sell the house that his wife had died in, so Bobo felt reasonably safe: Bobo also knew that the owner of the house never cared to visit the house and never let people go in the house or its garden, because the corrugated iron kept them out. Bobo drove past the lovers in their parked cars, and back to Hampstead.

.   .   .   .   .

It was the following morning and rain had fallen that night. A silver-barked tree curved into the air, splaying out its limbs above: at the base of its black-wealed silver trunk, shoots sprouted out over the upturned face of Joseph, who lay deep in the high-grown weeds, an old brick for his final pillow, a slug motionless on his brown-black cheek. His clothes were wet, and one leg rose into the air, the foot of which rested against the inside of the corrugated iron. On the pavement side of the corrugated iron, a milkman stacked empty, thin-milked, milk bottles into his cart noisily, and bellowed through the fresh air to a boy who was yards further along the road: 'She has two pints, David. Ring the bell for her.' One of the new residents of the Blackheath houses passed on his way to work, giving the milkman a cultured, upper-class, but socialistic ' 'Morning!' He was a member of the new Blackheath 'public-school' set, thirty-four, pretty-waistcoated, and wearing a bowler hat. The milkman returned the greeting and started to mutter into his empty milk bottles as he crated them. A sparrow in the silver, black-scarred tree darted a precautionary look at the milkman's back, and dropped something through the branches, down on to Joseph's black nose, where it splashed disrespectfully.

Bobo slept on through the morning in his flat, encased in the dirty blankets, the Ford car outside in the road, his coat on the floor by his bed, his shoes there too, and all the rest of his clothes on his body.

300

A young man in football clothes, with an overcoat over them, clumped up the hill and past Heathfield House, his heavy, studded, football boots noisily dragging on the pavement as he pushed them along, his thick-stockinged feet within them. Ungainly in his clumsy outfit, he banged himself against the corrugated iron as he passed. Over on the heath a game of football was in its early stages, observed by standing spectators.

The corrugated iron, dislodged by the young man's barging of it, swung from its fixed position, and the gap appeared again: Joseph's foot clattered down the corrugated iron and lay amongst the weeds. The corrugated iron swung backwards and forwards slightly, for a while, scraping the gatepost; causing crumbling, powdering, stone to fall down upon Joseph's leg. A zephyr waved the upper branches of the silver tree, and old leaves dislodged and fell clap-clap over the dead body, one of them completely covering Joseph's right eye. Joseph's body could not be seen from the pavement because of the obscuring weeds and sprouts from the tree base.

That night Bobo returned to Blackheath with some pieces of iron, which he used to fix the corrugated iron in place again, so that the gap was closed. He had anticipated that the gap might have occurred again. The following morning he was visited by the police, but they found nothing, and dismissed Bildad's story, which had been couched in imaginative ramblings and had not therefore convinced them. They did not give the matter much more thought, because they were concerned with the recent finding of Bongo's body in the Hampstead Heath pond.

Through the months that followed changes occurred in the appearance of the body in the garden of Heathfield House. The rains were heavy that winter, and the earth below Joseph became mud, because Joseph lay in a depression in the earth. Joseph sank deeply into the mud that was between two roots of the tree and the weeds grew over him. The rains ceased, the mud hardened, and the flowers began to flower around the body. The shoots grew from the base of the tree in abundance, shielding Joseph's half-buried head. Rubbish thrown over into the garden covered Joseph still more, till all that could

301

be seen was a single foot and an outstretched black hand—
the latter not being visible because of its colour, so like the
earth it rested upon was it. Joseph's gravestone became an
old beer-crate draped with an old silk stocking. In his open
mouth beneath the growths, the high heel of a woman's shoe
was stuck. From a broken branch of the tree, a branch that
hung a yard above the burial place of Joseph, a white brassière
fluttered inappropriately, for Joseph had not been a very
great success in his life with the fair sex, be they fair or
Negroid black.

·　　　·　　　·　　　·　　　·

Joesy worked in a shop in Blackheath village, a collection
of shops located on the other side of the heath to Heathfield
House. She was rather wild was Joesy, and her mother was
worried about her. Joesy was sixteen, a mixture of tomboy
and the other thing that sixteen-year-old girls should not be.
She wore jeans and a pullover in the evenings and had long
gold hair.

Jack was also the worry of his mother's life and of his
father's too. Jack earned his wages for lying underneath cars
and he was not the nicest of teddy-boys though Joesy seemed
to think he was.

Joesy and Jack looked at the barrier in front of Heathfield House and laughed at each other. Jack hoisted her up
over the corrugated iron and she scrambled painfully over it
into the night-enveloped garden. She looked around her, and
Jack swung down into the garden. They lay down side by side
and lighted cigarettes. Jack leaned over and kissed Joesy
and then, cigarettes discarded, they lay together amongst the
flowers, grass, and weeds. Jack felt for her hand and finding it
caressed it lovingly. But it was a very large hand for such a
pretty girl, and Jack, startled, lit a match. The hand was
black in the matchlight and its arm disappeared into the
weeds. Jack leapt up, and they both scrambled over the
corrugated iron. They never told anyone about what they had
seen because they would have had to confess why they had
been in the garden.

·　　　·　　　·　　　·　　　·

Beneath Blackheath were many tunnels, laid many years ago, in the time of Sir Sydney Stowmarket and the Earl of Dartmouth. The tunnels were for the conveyance of water. We have heard stories about them leading down to the River Thames and being used by smugglers. One of these tunnels, in a decayed and somewhat collapsed state, lay directly below Joseph's body. As the years passed, the roots of the tree penetrated deeper until they came to the tunnel roof. The roots gradually penetrated between the bricks of the tunnel roof: the roots swelled and grew longer as time went on, and the tunnel-roof bricks were forced open. Eventually the tunnel roof collapsed, and the earth between Joseph's body and the tunnel dropped down into the tunnel cavity. Joseph's body fell below the level of the garden, and so did the rubbish on the body. More rubbish was thrown over the corrugated iron through the years, and the hole above Joseph became filled up with junk of all kinds, and an entanglement of weeds and flowers. The rain washed earth into the rubbish, and so the garden levelled over. Sixty years afterwards, when the owner was dead and gone, the house was sold: the distribution of the owner's estate was a famous court matter that lasted many, many years before it was settled, and the ownership of the house was only finally settled ten years after the old man had died. We are no student of such matters, but we do believe that it was the most drawn-out case of its kind in the history of the law courts. By the time the house was sold, no trace of Joseph's body was to be seen, for it was well covered over. His gravestone by this time was an old bicycle with only one wheel and no chain, and a battered television set with no tube. They tore down the house two years later, and built flats there; but they left the area just around the tree comparatively undisturbed. The flats were a good financial proposition, because, by then, Blackheath had become a district that was very popular for people working in London to make their homes in. The workmen cleared the garden—cleared away Joseph's gravestone, but they did not disturb the earth by the tree at all: they let grass grow there while the flats were being built; and when the flats were occupied that patch of grass beneath the tree became

a favourite spot for mothers and their children to sit upon.

     .   .   .   .   .

Eighteen hundred and sixty-four. Elliot Place in its heyday. Heathfield House had smoke issuing from its chimneys, and expensive curtains were behind the unbroken glass windows. No corrugated iron filled the two gateways: instead, fine wooden gates hung from the gateposts. No milk-crates were on the wall that in those days had rhododendron blooms showing above it. A beautiful lady in a long tiered skirt with hoops in it stood on the front balcony. The back garden was cared for by a landscape gardener and the flats were nowhere to be seen. A little open fence surrounded the stretch of heath in front of Heathfield House, and within the boundaries made by this fence, gentlemen in top hats paraded, with their ladies in hats that looked like lampshades somewhat squiffy.

Across the heath the Paragon Crescent was in all its splendour; and carriages were drawn by horses, and driven by elevated drivers. Ladies walked from the Paragon to Elliot Place with little sun-shades balanced elegantly on their shoulders.

In Heathfield House lived Sir Sydney Stowmarket, a wealthy tea importer, whose tea was brought to this country by the *Cutty Sark*. He was a typical gentleman of the period, bearded and dignified, with arrogant blue eyes. Sir Sydney was a war hero, and he was often heard to boast over a glass of brandy that he was afraid of nobody and nothing.

Sir Sydney and Lady Jane Stowmarket had a six-year-old daughter called Mary Louisa: Mary Louisa was the apple of Sir Sydney's eye. One day when Mary Louisa was playing with her pekinese dog, on the balcony at the back of the house, her dog's ball fell through the balustrade woodwork, which in those days was painted a fresh grey, and she leant over the balustrade to watch the ball bouncing down the garden below: the ball bounced down the path, over the rose-bushes and into the lilacs: Mary Louisa craned over to see, and laughed gaily, her pretty laughter spreading over the garden below. Her foot caught in the woodwork, and she pulled it hard, to try and dislodge it: her foot came free suddenly, and as she was doubled over, her stomach on the rail, she overbalanced, and fell screaming to the stone walk below. The sun shone down on the dead little girl, her blue dress spread around her, her ringlets of hair golden in the sun's light.

.   .   .   .   .

The flats were fully occupied for quite a long time, and then people began to move out, until many of the flats were untenanted. New tenants stayed for only a very short time. People had heard tinkling laughter in the summertime at the back of the flats; laughter of a little girl; laughter that changed horribly to a long-drawn-out scream; laughter from a little girl when there were no little girls there—when all the little girls were at school.

Also mothers who were pregnant, and who sat beneath the tree in front of the flats when dusk was falling, heard masculine moanings that seemed to come from the earth below them. One pregnant woman had a miscarriage because of the fright she had received.

29 Heathfield House II

ONE day before Bobo came to Heathfield House there was a storm: the worst storm for many years. The winter sunshine had shone coldly across the wasted garden behind the house, and the laughter of a little girl had been heard, laughter that changed, horribly. Then the drizzle came, then the spears of heavier rain, and then the storm. Low in the sky dark-blue clouds hung, and the rain washed the old balconies. All was dark as time passed, and the rain did not cease: streams of rainwater rushed down the sides of the kerbs of Elliot Place, down into Elliot Vale, at the bottom of the hill. Lightning forked across the sky; a lonely figure in a mackintosh hurried past the house: the corrugated iron rattled under the fierce bombardment of the spears of rain: and an old tramp came up the hill looking for shelter.

The old tramp was soaking wet. He looked up at Heathfield House and went round its boundaries: there was no point of possible entry. But the tramp was desperate: he hurt himself on the barbed-wire as he climbed over the gatepost,

John Bratby.

and, with his hand bleeding and his backside showing white through a flapping tear in his old trousers, he looked closely at the house. He went round to the back and looked up at the bulging balconied back of the house: it rose high and pale in the darkness, and it was strange and a memory of days long past. The tramp went to a boarded doorway and with very great difficulty prised open two of the boards. Inside, the room was bare, cold, and dark, but it was dry. The tramp looked around for a cosy spot to sleep in, and not finding one, he walked up the stairs to the first floor. He climbed higher and higher in the darkness, and walked into the building attached to Heathfield House: he looked up at a Gothic window with woodwork in the upper part of it: the lightning gave momentary illumination to the room through this window and the tramp saw the figure of a little girl standing across the room. The lightning ceased and the room was in darkness: the tramp felt the nerves in his shoulders quivering, and he felt very frightened, for the little girl's face had been covered with blood.

He made his way from the room and climbed to a higher floor. Then he made his way back into the main building and looked out at the garden from a broken door that led out on to a decayed balcony. The lightning flashed again and he looked back into the room: there stood the little girl again, her face all broken and with blood on it: sweat poured from the tramp's balding scalp causing a prickling feeling, and he felt a shivering empty fixity around his jaw-bones. He stood where he was, not daring to cross the room. Then in desperation he rushed across the room, terrified that he might bump into her, his nerves screaming, his eyes staring: he rushed from the room and went up to the top of the house.

There he found a little room: he closed the door, put an old, broken, dusty chair against it, and stumbled to a corner, where he stood paralysed. Thunder made the heavens shudder, and lightning illuminated the room: the tramp saw that the room had been a child's room and he saw a child's toys on the floor—toys thick with dust; toys of long ago. The storm seemed to cease for a while; and an opening appeared in the sky, through which the moon shone: the moon's light filtered through the little window and the tramp looked around him. Water trickled down from a guttering. The tramp saw her by the door, holding her ball, and the skin of his back crawled with nerves. Then a cloud crossed over the moon, and in the brief moment of darkness she disappeared. Far beneath him the tramp heard a little girl's voice crying for something: the tramp saw by the moonlight that the little girl had left her ball in the room: the ball rolled towards him: the tramp picked up the ball and found that it was new and smelt faintly of lilacs. The tramp's heart thumped in a ghastly fashion as he heard little footsteps on the stairs below. The stairs creaked, and he stood petrified, holding the ball in his hand: he looked down at the ball and noticed its coloured surface. The footsteps came nearer and up to the door. There was a knocking on the door, and then the footsteps went away again, down the stairs. He heard her go on to the balcony: she seemed to be looking for something: perhaps it was her ball.

He heard a long scream and the sound of a body fallen on the stone at the back of the house. He looked down at the ball in his hands: it was covered with blood. The tramp collapsed and fainted.

The tramp awoke in the morning and looked around the room: it was as he had seen it in the moonlight and lightning flashes: dusty toys lay on the floor: he saw peeling wallpaper, faded and printed with child's toys, flowers, and dancing children: in a corner was a rocking horse, battered and falling to pieces: but the ball was not in the room. He walked across the dust-grey room, and taking away the old chair, he opened the door and went down the stairs. By the morning light he saw rooms full of dust and some with broken furniture in them, as he walked down the stairs. He went out of the doorway, past the dislodged boards, and walked below the balcony. He looked down at his feet: on the stone was an area of rain-thinned blood, being washed away into the earth by the stone pathway, by a stream of water that crossed the stone pathway, water that had its origins in an overfull guttering above the balcony and in the rainwater of the previous night.

The tramp waited until nightfall before he scaled the corrugated iron for he did not want to be seen. As he crossed from the house to the corrugated iron in the lamplight he heard a calling in the house and the closing of a door high up in the old ruin. He clambered down on to the pavement and went away across the heath, looking back at the old house.

.   .   .   .   .

'Where was her daddy? Why was it so lonely in the house? Why were all the people who walked on the heath in the daytime dressed in such funny clothes? Mummy and Daddy must know that the house needed cleaning, and that she, poor little girl, had hurt her face somehow, and that although she could feel no pain, she could feel that blood was there, and see it on her hands when she touched her face. Why was the garden allowed to go to rack and ruin, and what was that funny pink building facing the back of the house? Oh, where was Daddy and why didn't he come when she called so plaintively? Please come, Daddy. Please come and stop your little Mary Louisa's tears, and wipe away the blood. Please, Daddy. Please.'

The little girl stood in the evening, looking out of a front window of Heathfield House, tears in her wide open eyes. Her long golden hair hung in pretty ringlets, and a large, faded, pink bow in her hair was limp with blood. On one side of her face the bones were crushed, and streams of blood were there—blood that moved and yet did not move. She stood looking out of the broken window, but drawn back and to the side, so that no one could see her: she knew she was not nice for people to see: she wanted her mummy to wash her and groom her, so that she would be presentable again, but her mummy did not come: she wiped the tears from her eyes and looked at her hand—a hand red with blood.

She walked through the house looking for her mummy and daddy. 'Where could Daddy have gone? Why, when she loved him so, would he not come when she called? Why were the rooms so dirty and ruined? They could not have left her alone while they went away to the seaside: that could not be the explanation: Daddy would not do a thing like that. Oh please, dear Daddy—come and kiss your Mary Louisa and tell her that you will never leave her again.' Floods of tears poured motionlessly down the little girl's cheeks; and she bent down, knelt down on the floor, bent down her head, and sobbed pitifully, her golden ringlets falling over her crushed face, her dress spread out on the floor around her.

'Nobody is here. She had looked in all the rooms: in Daddy's room where she wasn't supposed to go: in Mummy's room and in her nanny's room. But they were all empty and full of grey dust. When her daddy returned, she would make him promise never to go away and leave her again. He would return, wouldn't he? He had been gone so long—such a long time now.

'Why was everything changed? Why did peculiar things happen? For a long time people she did not know had lived in the house and then a lady had died and the people had gone away. Why was the house sometimes like it had been when Daddy was here, and sometimes all changed with funny furniture in it? When the people she did not know had come, she at first thought it was Daddy returning, and she had rushed down to welcome him: but they were people all dressed in funny clothes and she had gone up to her little room and cried. When they lived in the house they had left the few topmost rooms as they were, and she had kept in the room up there for the duration of their stay: but a woman had come up there.'

.   .   .   .   .

They came to Heathfield House some time after their honeymoon. He was a devoted husband and loved his frail wife with a love that was extreme; selfish, jealous, and devouring. She had been a typist before she got married to Geoffrey Hunter, but that was not because she was of a lower social stratum than he: like most pampered only-children of well-off parents, who were possessive regarding their only offspring and stern disciplinarians, she strained for a life of her own and she wanted to be independent: so she trained to be a typist after her twenty-first birthday, and when trained took a post as secretary to a man who ran a metal-stamping factory: in this way she found the way of life that she craved—a life divorced from the life of her parents.

She met Geoffrey Hunter at a dance. She did not go to dances very often, but this dance was a works' dance at the place that her father had a managing-directorship of, and she went to please her father. Geoffrey Hunter was nothing to do with her father's works, but he was a friend of her father, and her father had invited him along, saying that he would like him to meet his daughter. At first Geoffrey Hunter had not liked her: he found her spoilt, self-willed, difficult to talk to, remote, and tending to give herself sophisticated airs. But for her father's sake he talked to her at the dance, and danced with her. By the end of the dance Geoffrey Hunter had seen beneath the acted sophistication: brought her from the remote hideout in her mind, to a state of being that was more on the spot, and communicatable-with: become somewhat in control of her self-willed ways—this was easy to do because all women subconsciously crave for male mastery: become tolerant of the manifestations of her spoilt nature: and found her basically attractive. Calling himself a fool in his mind, Hunter asked her to meet him again, and they met in Hyde Park by the Serpentine. The spring morning somehow made her more natural and Hunter found her very desirable. As she got to know him better, during the ensuing weeks, she began to relax with him and to substitute a charming natural-ness for her hard, sophisticated, silly airs; a womanly sub-missiveness for her former wilfulness; a grasping friendliness for her former unfriendly stiffness; and a reality of personality for her former remoteness.

They got married in the Church of the Ascension in Dartmouth Row, just off Blackheath, a church that was next-door to the great house that the Earl of Dartmouth once lived in, a house now occupied by the Grey ladies. Coming to the church in the festooned car with her father, she looked out and saw Heathfield House, and she decided, with a rebirth of her former wilfulness, that she would get her husband-to-be to buy that house. On the way back from the church, with her husband, she asked for the car to be driven around Heath-field House, and she then told her husband that they would live their married life out there. Tolerant in his love for her he decided to buy the house, but before he started to contact the estate agents he decided that he would first have his honeymoon: this may seem rather peculiar—but as it happens he was rather looking forward to his honeymoon.

The car, with its ribbons stretching from the radiator ornament to the roof, cruised round the house, down Elliot Vale, and then down Baizdon Road. She looked out of the car, which was bespattered with confetti, and lifted her bridal veil with her newly-ringed hand. The decayed balconies attracted her, and she decided to leave the house in its romantic decay as much as was practically possible, when she eventually took up residence there. Her hand lost its hold of the veil, and it cascaded around her face, blurring her view of the back of the house. That is why, she told herself, that she couldn't have really seen a child's ball falling from the balcony and bouncing down the overgrown garden. As the car turned round at the bottom of Baizdon Road, and made its way up the slope of that road to the slope of Elliot Vale, the old boot attached to the rear bumper clattering on the road, she thought she heard a little girl's laughter. But she immediately forgot this, for her husband began to kiss her through the frail white fabric of her bridal veil. Lost in the roar of the car and the clattering of the old boot, a horrible scream faintly came from somewhere at the back of the house; and the old, unkept lilac-bushes at the end of the garden quivered because of some impact. The gay car drove away across the heath.

After their honeymoon, Geoffrey Hunter and his wife went to look at the house again. They crossed the heath on foot from Blackheath Village, and when they got to the house they unlocked the padlock on the decaying gates that filled the right-hand gateway, and pushing the awkward gates aside, scraping their lower border on the gravel pathway, they went up to the house. Hunter pocketed the key he had been lent by the estate agents, and looked at the house that had lain unoccupied since Sir Sydney Stowmarket had lived in it. The house had suffered from neglect, but its appearance was different to what its appearance was to the eyes of Bobo, when he came to Heathfield House on his unsavoury errand: but Hunter's wife wanted the house to be changed as little as possible, for she was in love with the romantic-looking decay of the woodwork at the back of the house, and many other things about the house that made her think of the days when the house had been in its glory. Hunter unlocked the front door and entered the house with his wife. Sir Sydney Stowmarket and his wife had left the house soon after the death of Mary Louisa, and in his grief Sir Sydney had not bothered to move any of the furniture, etcetera, out of the house, so Hunter found the house full of furniture and full of dust. Cobwebs hung from chair to chair and the wallpapers were faded but still beautiful. The curtains, heavy with dust, were faded to no colour at all where they had been exposed to the sun's rays, and the carpets were still fine although piled high with dust and dirt. Hunter and his wife went from room to room and from floor to floor. A figure in hiding watched them sadly as they walked from room to room: the little girl stood behind the white-grey cobwebs and watched Hunter and his wife laughing in the silent house: Mary Louisa felt their laughter within her and went to play on the balcony: she somehow knew that it would be tragic to play there with her ball, and she seemed to remember that playing there, which she always did, would end in pain: but she was drawn over and over again to the balcony, drawn there to play with her ball. In search of play that would give her laughter like that of Hunter and his wife, Mary Louisa went to the balcony with her ball, looking all the while for her dog. But she couldn't find her dog; so she just pretended he was there on the balcony, as she threw her ball across the woodwork to his imaginary presence.

Hunter's wife went away from her husband in her exploratory wanderings. Hunter, in one of the downstairs rooms, thought he heard female laughter tinkling across the garden, and he supposed that it was his wife's laughter caused by her joy over the house. Hunter's wife did not hear any laughter however.

Hunter and his wife went down together into the cellars of the house. Hunter had no torch with him, and the only illumination that they had was from his cigarette-lighter whose light cast great dark shadows around the cellars. Hunter opened an inner cellar door which squealed on its rusty hinges and they passed through the doorway: the squealing of the hinges seemed very prolonged and so much like a scream of great pain: they turned in the cellar to look at the door which was swinging slowly on its clogged hinges: the hinges grated and squealed as the weight of the door carried the door right round till it was parallel with the wall: had they heard a screaming human sound, they wondered; or had it just been the noise of the door moving by its own momentum, after they had pulled it open wide enough to permit their entry into the cellar, and entered the cellar? They looked at each other, and laughed at the fearful look they saw in each other's eyes, and their laughter banished their fear, and they soon forgot.

They came out of the cellars, their clothes covered with dirt from the cellar walls, and gladly entered the ground floor where there was more light. Hunter decided to look at the back of the house and examine the firmness or possible lack of firmness of the wooden structures attached there: he walked into the garden, and stood in the middle of the once lovely and cared-for place, looking towards the back of Heathfield House, examining from a distance the balconies and the Gothic arched wooden structures below them. He then walked towards the building meditatively, his pipe in his mouth below a small ginger moustache, and his brogued feet pushing through the weeds growing in the cracks of the path. He fingered the woodwork thoughtfully, and cast his blue eyes upwards at the underneath of the balcony above him: flakes of paint fell down on to his ginger curling hair as he shook the supporting beams. The male practical side of his nature prompted him to conceive plans for the tearing down of the old woodwork: but his love for his wife, and the desire to abide by her wishes, made him decide to leave the woodwork as it was; with the addition of a coat of paint of the same colour as it already was—that, he felt, would not alter the appearance of the woodwork, and therefore please his wife—and with a nail here and there, hammered in, to secure the woodwork.

He walked slowly along the stone walk beneath the balconies, fingering his watch-chain. Then he stopped. Something on the stone walk, by his much-punctured brogue shoes, caught his eye. He took his pipe from his mouth and bent down. There on the stone walk was a patch of fresh blood: where were the feathers? he wondered. It certainly must have been a large bird that the cat had killed, he thought to himself, and a bloody killing as well. From behind a smeared and dirty window looking out on to the garden, a little girl watched him, her battered face pressed to the window pane. Then she went away. Hunter did not notice that on the window pane was a mass of gleaming red blood.

Hunter's wife roamed round the dead house looking here and there with delight; wondering what it would be like to live in the house. Careless of her fine clothes, she sat in one of the chairs, after wiping it down inadequately with an old table-cloth she had found in a sideboard cupboard. She imagined herself sitting before a fire and imagined that all was clean and bright. She swivelled in the chair, looked across at the misty windows, that showed a vague view of the garden outside, and thought to herself how wonderful the room would be when the windows were cleaned, and she could sit in a nice clean chair and look out of the windows at the down-sloping garden shown through them. She decided to leave the curtains that were already there: she would have them cleaned of course, but she would hang them up again after the cleaning, for they were part of the atmosphere of the house, an atmosphere that she was in love with, and wished to preserve as much as possible. She looked around for other things she could leave as they were, but for cleaning, thereby preserving the old-fashioned and evocative atmosphere: there were the balconies of course: a great deal of the furniture: and the carpets.

She journeyed from room to room looking for things she could retain. She decided not to alter the garden very much; and not to tidy it up too much, for she felt that if the garden was made neat and ordered, then the whole romantic atmosphere of decay at the back of the house would be destroyed. She would leave the rather aged gates as they were and not even have them painted: perhaps, she thought, she would have the hinges seen to, but that was all. But she reckoned without her practically minded and somewhat conventional husband. She thought also that she would leave the outside of the house as it was, and certainly not have the tree in the front garden pruned at all. Outside in the garden her husband thought practical thoughts as the smoke from his pipe curled around his face: his hands in his pockets, he jingled his coins in his pockets all the while he thought.

She wandered round the house amongst the dust and the objects that had lain there unobserved and untouched for so long: objects unobserved by no one except Mary Louisa that is: Mary Louisa watched in her immortality those objects for year after year, and for decade after dedade. Mary Louisa watched those objects just as she watched from amongst the cobwebs the figure of Mrs. Hunter walking to and fro. But Mrs. Hunter didn't see her. Mary Louisa sometimes walked very close behind Mrs. Hunter, her hand placed on the battered side of her face, amongst the tangled, blood-clotted, golden ringlets of hair, and through the pretty white fingers of her hand blood oozed slowly. The little girl could not understand why Mr. Hunter was there; could not understand why the woman was dressed in clothes she had never seen before; and she could not understand why the woman walked around the house as if she owned it. Mary Louisa forgot about the existence of Mr. and Mrs. Hunter in the house, after they had finally left the house—after living in it—Mrs. Hunter in a coffin and Mr. Hunter with tears on the ginger lashes of his eyes. Somehow Mary Louisa had never felt they belonged in the house, and they had not altered the house very much, so the little girl was able to feel that while they were living in the house they were not really there, and to forget them to a great extent when they departed, Mrs. Hunter to her bed of earth, and Mr. Hunter to his hotel bed—with only him between its clean white sheets.

But to return to Mrs. Hunter and her exploration of the house. Mrs. Hunter fingered the faded curtain hanging over the window, and just behind her Mary Louisa cried silently. Mary Louisa reached out her bloody hand to touch Mrs. Hunter, the frilly cuff of her pretty dress stained with red, but just before her hand touched the woman, the woman moved away. Mary Louisa retired just behind the curtain and

looked with horror and wonder at her hand—which she had
noticed as she reached out to touch—a hand completely
covered with thick, sticky, shiny blood. Mary Louisa wept
brokenly behind the curtain for a long time, for she could not
understand why her hand was bloody—she could not understand: 'Oh, why didn't her daddy come and comfort her?
Why was her daddy away so long? Should she ask the woman
in the funny clothes?' But Mrs. Hunter had walked away into
another room. Mary Louisa went away up the stairs to her
little room. The curtains she had hidden amongst were red, for
that was their natural colour, so the blood upon them hardly
showed. Mr. and Mrs. Hunter left the house soon after, and
crossed the heath to the railway station: Mr. Hunter had his
arm round her waist, and Mrs. Hunter leant her head on his
shoulder happily. Up in her tiny room, Mary Louisa went
to her little dressing-table and opened a drawer. She pulled
out a picture of her father: a little miniature painting he had
given her. On the back was a line written by him that said:
*For my dearest little rose, my Mary Louisa, whom I love with all
my heart. From her devoted father. June. 1863.* She looked at
the face of her father with longing, her tears falling on the
painting. Then she put the picture away in the drawer, and
began to weep and weep.

Some time after, when Mr. Hunter had bought the house,
and when he had had it cleaned and done up, he and his wife
drove in a car to take up residence there. Mary Louisa heard
them come in the front door and she ran down from her little
room, her heart bursting with joy. 'It was her father and
mother come back! Oh how long it had been. But now all the
waiting was over. It was her dear, dear, daddy! Hooray! Oh
how lovely it would be to bury her face in his waistcoat, and
feel his strong hands on her hair, and to hear his soothing
voice, so gruff and yet so tender. Oh! Daddy, Daddy, Daddy
mine.' She flew down the stairs, her hair bouncing on her
shoulders, the skirt of her dress billowing out behind her. 'To
see her daddy's face again. Oh just to see his darling face
again after so long. Daddy. Oh! Daddy.' Her eyes were wild
with excitement and expectation as she careered down the
house. She hid behind the turn of the banisters and looked

down into the hall. When she saw that it was not her father, her heart broke. Mr. and Mrs. Hunter did not see Mary Louisa.

.   .   .   .   .

The woman was bored. She would explore the top floor of the house, she thought. She went up the stairs and on the top floor she found three dusty rooms. She looked at two of them in the pale, winter, afternoon light and went to the closed door of the third: this was a small room and on it was painted in old-fashioned capitals of faded pink the name 'MARY LOUISA'. The door was a faded light-blue, and she found, when she rubbed away the dust from it, that the door-handle was of silver. She must tell her husband of that.

The door was slightly ajar: she pulled open the door which opened only after much tugging, and looked into the room. There, within the room, was a little girl kneeling on the floor, her back to the door. The little girl turned her face to the woman, who saw that it was broken and bleeding. The girl rose, and came towards her imploringly, her hands outstretched. The woman forced the door closed again, and stood at the top of the stairs in terror, looking at the name 'MARY LOUISA' on the door. She ran down the stairs.

It seemed a long way down the stairs: first down the curving wooden and dusty stairs from the top floor to the one below, and then from floor to floor to the ground floor. She stumbled on the stairs, clutching wildly at the banister handrail. She fell in a sprawling heap, and then quickly rose again to continue down the stairs, her hand on the handrail moving fast on the wood and consequently burning. At the bottom of the stairs she turned, stared up the staircase with round wide eyes for a moment, and then scurried to her sitting-room. She sat down in her chair, panting and gasping, looking every now and again over her shoulder in fright, at the door of her sitting-room which she had locked securely. Her mouth hung open for quite a while, and the colour did not come back to her cheeks for quite a while either. Tired lines dropped from the inner points of both her eyes, either side of the nose, down to her cheeks.

The woman said nothing to her husband about what she had seen and her weak heart was not improved by the experience on the top floor. She kept well away from the little room at the top of the house. Her husband and herself went away for a long holiday, and when she returned she felt better. For a long while she did not feel bored, but as the following winter progressed a feeling of boredom would oppress her when her husband was away at work. The days were very long and tedious for her that winter; the tedium only being relieved by the visits of her doctor, and the enjoyment she briefly obtained by reading a novel written by a well-known painter called *Hell's Bells and Buckets of Blood*, a stimulating novel that was very popular at the time.

It was after Christmas and the woman felt very strongly the anti-climax of January: she would sit sewing in the afternoons, while outside the house the wind blew cold and unfriendly across the heath. She was bored to tears, and her thoughts went to the top of the house and the door with the name upon it. Her experience at the top of the house had been so unreal that she had put it out of her mind during the months afterwards. She almost made herself believe that she had never seen the little girl in the old-fashioned dress. She felt it was all so improbable, and she told herself that she must have imagined it all. It was quite stupid really, she reasoned: the idea of a little girl with a battered face up there was quite ridiculous. But her thoughts dwelt on the experience, and she remembered the silver door-handle. Was that also a product of her imagination? she mused. She thought she could go up and see if that was real or not: and if it turned out to be a brass handle, or something other than silver, then she would know that her imagination had played tricks upon her, and that there was nothing in the tiny room. Perhaps, she thought, the name on the door, and the child's old toys in the room, had fired her imagination, and she had deceived herself into thinking that she had seen a wounded little girl. She laughed cynically to herself. She thought still further: was she mad—believing in such rubbish as ghosts? The sight of the girl she thought she had seen was probably some old curtain piled on the floor, with perhaps a red object on top of it: similarly the silver door-handle was probably only some other metal: perhaps she had been drinking a little to dispel her boredom, and her befuddled mind had been so confused that she had not seen things clearly. She would prove to herself that the door-handle was not of silver by going straight up there and looking. She would take up a torch, and just in case she would take up a loaded revolver. She opened a drawer, extracted a small shiny revolver, found a torch, and went up the stairs. She told herself that, when she had proved to herself that it had all been her imaginings, she would get her husband to have the three rooms cleared out; they did not need the space up there, but at least it would stop her silly beliefs, she felt, as she went up the stairs.

The light was bad at the top of the house, because some of the windows were shuttered, and the afternoon was drawing to a close. She stood on the dust-covered landing at the top of the stairs, her confidence deserting her; then she went into one of the other rooms and looked round at the old furniture thickly covered with dust, and the piles of papers yellowed with age on the bare floor-boards. An old cannon stood in the second room, surrounded by piles of cannon-balls, and leaning on the cannon was an old door. In a corner of the room were two carriage wheels, and against the shuttered window was a box containing the dress clothes of a captain of infantry. A mouse ran across the floor and she watched it timidly. She walked backwards and forwards from room to room nervously, as the light began to disappear, casting glances at the faded blue door of the little room: the handle of the door of the little room gleamed very much like silver, and she hastily told herself that even if it was silver that did not mean that another improbability existed behind the door it served to open. But somehow she could not bring herself to go to the handle and look at it closely, and she kept as far away from the pale door as she could. She looked at the door from within one of the other rooms, and she saw that it was decorated with flower painting on its panels, and that it was a very lovely door indeed, obviously made by a father who was very fond of his little daughter. As she looked at the door with the beam of her torch she thought she saw it tremble slightly. She rapidly ran down the stairs, and when she was on the ground floor, she stoked up the fire of her sitting-room, and giving herself a brandy she told herself not to be such a fool.

Some months passed, during which time the woman tried to get her husband to have the top floor cleared out: but her husband never got round to getting the workmen in to do the job.

She felt that her rapid departure down the stairs, just because she imagined she had seen the pale-blue door move ever so slightly, was the result of her nerves; but she would rather have had the rooms cleared out nevertheless, than have them stay above in the same condition as before. She did not really know what she felt about the room above, and she did not know whether she was afraid of it or not.

It was in the early summer, and she was in the middle of another period of boredom: her husband was abroad on business, and even her doctor was becoming a bore with his talk about her heart condition. She was so bored that she took to re-reading the painter's novel, which on second reading she found to be fantastic, ill-composed, weak, and unconvincing. She threw down the book, talked to herself about its lack of relationship between part and part, and gazed wearily at its gaudy dustcover. On the dustcover was a picture of a little girl playing with a rocking-horse. This reminded the bored woman of the phantasm she was sure she had not seen on the top floor, and she idly began to think about the room again. It was so silly of her, she thought, to be so wary of the room. She felt she really should put an end to it all; for she hated to think that she should believe in a phantom, a phantom that probably existed only in her silly mind, and that was in existence in no other place. She rose from her chair with an air of fortitude and no-nonsense and strode to the foot of the stairs. When she reached the top floor but one, she halted, and looked up the uncarpeted flight of stairs that led to the final floor. The sunshine was bright and reassuring and it was not late in the afternoon so there was plenty of light everywhere. But the empty house was peculiarly still and the undisturbed floor above her head had an even greater stillness than the rest of the house: and the upper floor looked so stale and gloomy, despite the sunlight, in comparison with the lived-upon floor that supported her at that moment, which was bright and fresh.

She pulled herself together, and went up the stairs that curved round a little and that got dustier and dustier as she ascended. She looked down at the dust-covered stairs as she climbed, and then looked up: the door of the little room was open! How could that be? she thought hysterically: no one ever went up there, no one at all. But still, perhaps her husband had been up there and opened the door—quite likely, for she *had* asked him to have it cleared; and what was more natural than that he should go up and see what work was to be done before he engaged the workmen? She stood by the open door and looked in at the room. Then she looked down at the handle and she found that it *was* silver.

She walked into the room and looked around at the peeling wallpaper and the decayed rocking-horse. She stood there for a while in the great stillness, the sunshine coming into the room and glittering on the dust particles in the air. She looked down at the floor, and her eyes wandered over the toys in dust that lay scattered around on it. Then she noticed a patch of colour in a corner, and this interested her, because all the colour in the room was dulled by thick dust, especially if it was colour on an object on the floor. The patch of colour was partly hidden by a doll that lay in the corner, and before she went to see what the colour was upon, she looked around and mentally noted that there was no pile of curtaining on the floor that she might have previously mistaken for the kneeling figure of a little girl: but, she thought, her husband might have moved such a pile of curtaining, and he must have done so, because she was determined that she had seen the curtaining. When she saw that the dust on the floor was undisturbed, and she realized that it would be disturbed if her husband had moved any pile of curtaining, she felt a chill come over her.

She walked across to the corner and saw that there lay a child's doll, the kind made many years ago, and she saw with terror that it was completely free of dust. She stood looking at the coloured ball for a long time. Then she turned to the door for escape from the room and from the thoughts which terrified her mind. Her eyes bulged with horror as she saw that the door was closed. Then her eyes caught sight of a light mass on one side of the room. She turned to it in a half-paralysed way, and saw, standing there, a little girl with golden ringlets, in an old-fashioned dress, and with one side of her face crushed and bloody. The little girl's eyes were hypnotically appealing and she walked towards the woman.

The woman looked at the dust on the floor just below her face, and slowly rose to her feet. She must have fainted, she thought: she must have lain unconscious on the floor amidst the dust for quite a long time, for it was nearly dark now: God how her heart was pounding. Oh God! was Mary Louisa still there? She spun round, her eyes searching: then she darted to the corner, but to her relief the ball was gone: perhaps, she thought, that meant that the girl was away for a while. She made her departure in a hectic manner: her heart was pounding extravagantly. When she reached her sitting-room she sat down. Soon afterwards she died of heart failure.

Her husband in his grief shut up the house after her burial, and put corrugated iron over the decayed gates, and wire fencing around the garden.

30 Heathfield House III

AFTER his beloved daughter's death, Sir Sydney Stow-market felt he must leave the house, but he felt that he could not completely leave the district, so he built a house in Dartmouth Row, which was a road that led from the top of Blackheath Hill to the hill that led down to Lewisham. Sir Sydney built a house opposite the house that the Earl of Dartmouth had lived in. It was a house that was about a mile away from Heathfield House, a house he called simply 'Mary Louisa'. Sir Sydney died in that house at the turn of the century and it was sold to a couple of maiden ladies called the Misses Plunkett—Maria Plunkett and Lily Plunkett. Maria Plunkett was rather disappointed in life, for she was a very vigorous lady with a great delight in the sensual pleasures, who had never managed to get married or even seduced: when she and her sister bought 'Mary Louisa' she was a very bitter woman, whose bitterness showed cruelly upon her lined and heavy face. Lily Plunkett was also rather disappointed in life. She had never been very attracted to the sensual pleasures, and at the age of thirty-two had been raped by an officer in the cavalry on Wimbledon Common, which had destroyed her faith in the male sex, and that lack of faith was quite enough to make a woman disappointed in life, be she sensual or not. Lily Plunkett's bitterness showed cruelly on her frail face also.

They lived together, the Misses Plunkett, but they didn't like each other very much, their companionship being the result of their being sisters: Maria Plunkett rather resented the fact, secretly of course, that it was her sister Lily who had been raped and not she; and Lily resented the fact that she had been raped rather than her sister, a resentment she made known to Maria on every possible occasion. When the Misses Plunkett bought the house they were both in their sixties, Maria being sixty-one and Lily being one year older. They had a gardener called Alfie working for them and Alfie was seventy, but a very lively seventy to be sure. Alfie was rather over-fond of whisky, and one day got very, very drunk behind the rhododendron bushes. Lily Plunkett was looking at the rhododendron bushes when Alfie leapt up from behind them, and, clasping her to his braces, kissed her bitter old face with lips that smelled sweetly of whisky. This had such an upsetting effect on Lily that six months later she died. Maria was so disappointed that it had been Lily again and not her, that she lived on miserably for another nine months, and then died also. George Plunkett inherited the house from his sisters. Now George Plunkett was not so old as his sisters, in fact he was only forty-two, and a very racy forty-two indeed. He brought two of his mistresses to live in the house and for the next thirty years the house was gay for the first time. Then George died of thrombosis—naturally enough—in 1934, leaving the house to his two mistresses.

.   .   .   .   .

Daisy Makepiece and Dora Jumper were fifty-seven and fifty-five respectively. What happened to them was never very clear. The existence of the vicarage next door and the existence of a church opposite them was indeed a great strain upon them. They put a little gargoyle on the crest of the gable of the roof of the house, a gargoyle that stuck its tongue out at the church, but that didn't help them very much and they stayed indoors most of the time. By now things had changed in the area since Sir Sydney's time and many more houses had been built.

One day, when Daisy and Dora were in two churchyards sound asleep, waiting for the day of the Universal Resurrection when they hoped to get together with George again, Brady rented the house and brought Rosalina to live there. After a while Rosalina began to forget about Bobo and she began to accept the fact that she was Brady's mistress. She went to the England College of Art for a while, but could not bear the strain of being watched so carefully by the painting-school staff, so she left the art school and at the same time Brady resigned his teaching post. At the England College Rosalina had been subjected to the most severe observations by the members of the staff there, who hopefully waited for her to change her sex, a performance they clearly wanted to witness. She had one day found, as she was painting at her easel, a member of the staff observing very closely the skin between her nose and her mouth in the hope of finding hairs growing there. The disappointment of the staff became very obvious to her as the months passed, and she felt she must either provide the spectacle they desired or leave the school—so she left.

.   .   .   .   .

Brady and Rosalina found an old letter in the attic of the house. It was addressed to Mary Louisa Stowmarket and read as follows:

My dearest daughter,

I must soon die, and before I die I must write this letter to you, which I hope to have the strength to post in the letter-box of Heathfield House, or get someone else to post it for me, if I am too weak.

My wife came to me in a vision last night and told me that you haunt Heathfield House to this very day searching for me. Your dear mother died some years ago. I never knew that you were still at the house or I would have certainly come to see you and comfort you. You must know that I loved you with great devotion when you were alive, and it pains me to know that I could have helped you by visiting Heathfield House but that I never did: now I cannot, because I lie on my deathbed, and death will come to me very soon, and I shall never rise from this bed until the good Lord comes to take me away.

Since you died in that tragic way I have never forgotten your sweet person for one instant. You were everything to me when you lived, and everything to me when you were dead. How I wish I had known of your spiritual existence at Heathfield House, for I would have gone across the heath to be with you and with great joy, and I would have started living there again.

When your mother came to me in that vision, she told me that you were very unhappy, and this knowledge distresses me deeply. Please understand, my dearest Mary Louisa, that I would give anything to be able to come to you and soothe away your unhappiness.

If only I could come to you in spirit when I am dead. But I fear this is not to be so, because your mother tells me that I am not to be allowed to do so for some reason. I shall not question the rulings of the Great Powers.

I have named this house I am to die in, with your name, my darling. I always have your picture by my side. So you see I have always pined for you ever since you died.

When you read this letter I hope it will explain things to you and make you easier in your mind.

Please try and understand, my darling, that I can never see you again, and that you must live spiritually upon this earth without me. I know you will find this hard, but all I can say in comforting you, is that I love you so very dearly, and wish you with all my heart, a life of peace and spiritual stillness.

Please rest, and search for me no more, my darling.

Your devoted father,
Sydney Stowmarket.

July, 1900.

Brady looked up from the letter and laughed cynically, but Rosalina, who had read the letter first, was crying.

.   .   .   .   .

James Brady began to be dissatisfied with his life with the girl, and the separation of himself from her began to take birth. But the final and complete severance was difficult for Brady to accomplish: he had on the one hand to uproot himself from by now familiar ground, and on the other hand to face the difficulty of telling the girl of the impending cut; both acts being uneasy for the somewhat ageing painter.

A great slothfulness was upon him and he could not break free from the self-indulgent life he had been leading. He tried hard to find Spartan resolution, but his mind sat in an arm-chair from which it could not rise. And then he confided in a friend. The friend was a woman, ugly and bitter, introspective and remote—not the perfect advice-giver. But her course through life of protecting her introspective secluded soul from the coarse cruelties of life, had been difficult and therefore thoughtful, and she had gained wisdom in her fiftieth year, from fighting her battles, the battles against those who would threaten the privacy of her introspective and hidden being. Her bitterness tainted the sanity of her advices with bias, but her ugliness made her a safe confidante for Brady on matters of sex. Brady told her of his sloth and she called him a fool with venom in her voice. She didn't stop calling him a fool and Brady went away in an agony, her vicious words ripping into his complacency. He could not get the barbs out of his mind and his armchair was suddenly a fakir's bed. So, with a resolution spurred to a driving and unrelenting force by the little, sharp, starred wheels that were her words, he broke free and went back to his wife and son, where he found the spur wheels dug no more with good horse-sense into his mind.

·   ·   ·   ·   ·

James Brady bought swords. Old swords with long steel blades and wonderful handles; handles that swelled and bellied in a huge, iron, one-piece hand-shield like a section of an orb; blades a yard long, cold dead steel, cruel and associated with battle; blades never sharpened, and blades that had killed how many men. Old swords light-green with age, rusty and encrusted. Old swords in scabbards, dark-rusted metal. Dress swords well preserved, yellow, gleaming, brass handles, with long, clean, gleaming metal blades. Old swords eaten by rust, the blade-edge pitted. Old swords with blades so wide that Brady was made to feel the way they had been used— like an axe. Brady didn't know much about the swords he paid a pound or two for, but he didn't need to know; all that mattered to him was that the swords were beautiful in shape, and so cruel in purpose; their cruelty expressed so horribly by their long steel blades, and shield handles. Brady liked to hold the swords in his hand, and look at the fine shape—the various hand-shields enveloping his clasping fist, from which sprang the long, fine, metal blade. Brady painted the swords, the long blades, the clasping hands, the bare muscled arms, sinewed and grooved. He bought swords from a jeweller's shop that was plastered with judo-class advertisements. He talked for hours with the judo-expert jeweller about jewels, swords, the jeweller's collection of bad paintings, antique guns, and judo: for hours they talked in the jeweller's flashy and customer-lacking shop; the jeweller's wife pushing a pram and child through the shop and out, returning after shopping, pushing pram and child past Brady and into the back of the shop, casting disapproving glances at Brady and her husband idling the hours away, as they talked of Brazilian topaz's superiority over quartz topaz; of judo belts; of the great interest in America about antique guns; of the increasing value of precious stones; of the little value of Brady's giant quartz-topaz ring in its lopsided, cheap, gold setting; of a diplomat's dress suit and sword dated before 1900, at six-pounds-ten the boots, hat, trousers, jacket, and tin box, and six-pounds-ten the sword in its sheath and case; of curling wire, heated, sanded, and hammered into a gun barrel; of rifling of the inside of the barrel to make the bullet spin as it was fired out of the barrel; of this and of that.

The jeweller, a small man of thirty years, swarthy, white-coated, and so eager to talk, a friendly nice man, showed Brady a sword which had engraved on the blade the following words, 'Do not withdraw me in Haste; do not sheathe me without Honour,' written in Spanish. Also the jeweller showed Brady a curving Arab sword with no hand-shield except for a cross-bar: the Arab only used the sword from the height of his horse, to cut at 'pedestrians' in the battle, so he did not need a hand-guard on his sword. Brady glanced to his side, as the jeweller talked away, and saw a net stocking full of pennies for charity. Air rifles were in the window of the shop, and a notice asking to buy old Colt revolvers, Derringers, and swords. Brady faced the talking jeweller again, the jeweller's hands resting on the dark-red piece of velvet on the counter, upon which permanently resided an accumulation of false coins welded together with a nice, polite, jeweller's message on the underside of the queer mass. On the counter also was a box with a hole in it, through which a roll of paper showed, upon which the jeweller recorded sales of his stock, which consisted mainly of tiny brooches, buttons, pins, rings, bracelets, keyholed gold hearts on fine gold chains, and other little pieces of inexpensive jewellery. A woman, a typical working-class Ma with specs, came in and asked about her daughter's brooch that was being repaired. Brady looked around the shop and wondered how the pleasant jeweller made his living, for, although the jeweller said thirty people each day purchased from him, Brady could not believe it, as hardly anybody came in to buy as they talked in the rush-hour in the evening, when people thronged in the streets at maximum; furthermore the profit on sales of tiny brooches of semi-precious stones seemed so small. But the jeweller loved jewellery; and, anyway, Brady was in no position to judge accurately the jeweller's income, against his capital outlay on purchases, and rent for the tawdry shop in the poor area. As the working-class Ma, with her dull nondescript face, asked about Mary's brooch, Brady bent down and examined glad-eyed the glass case of swords beside him.

Brady paid for two swords; the jeweller wrote down the sale in his mahogany box, and wrapped the swords in brown paper, sealing the long ungainly parcel with transparent sticky tape, which parcel Brady manœuvred through the door-way and out into the lighted night, angling the parcel between walking, just-released wage slaves, freed by the hooter: he stood on the pavement edge by his parked Lambretta and swung the long parcel around accidentally into the cowled, pale, virgin face of one of two nuns, passing. That incident over he fixed the parcel on the luggage-bars over the back mudguard of his scooter, by the thick elastic bands with metal hooks on the ends which entwined around the parcel sticking out from the back of the scooter, the handle of one sword sticking out from the wrapping. Putting his foot on the stand, he heaved the scooter forward, kicked the starter down, hurting his ankle, mounted, turned in the gleaming wet road, and roared up the hill, past parked lorries and workers crossing the road carelessly, who let the motorists take care they did not get run over. His precious swords behind him, Brady rode home, eager to unwrap the weapons in front of his wife, and enthuse about them to her tolerant and bored face.

He unwrapped the parcel on the kitchen-table, the swords being placed over a marmalade jar, a bread-board, a plate, and very near an open package of butter. He sandpapered a sword, brandished it playfully at his wife, and greased it with Bengal jelly.

He was careful with the swords, for he remembered what he had read in his newspaper a week previously. Two brothers of teen age had played by fighting a sword battle. They had clashed the great blades together. One brother accidentally pricked the other, and the pricked brother became enraged. The enraged brother, half in anger, half in play, had swung his sword in a broad arc, laughing but angry. As Brady brandished a sword in fun at his wife—but with care—one of the brothers awaited trial for manslaughter.

In the underneath of his mantelpiece he inserted hooks, and from these hooks hung the swords, down, close, either side of his fire in his studio. Above the mantelpiece was a wooden projection, roofing the fireplace bay: from hooks in this wooden projection, which was six foot high, hung more swords, their wicked points three foot six inches from the floor-tiles in front of the fire. One day Brady bent down to tend his fire, throwing on the fire a chunk of coal: then he poked the fire a bit so that it would burn the chunk of coal. Having done this back-tiring task, Brady straightened up sharply and forcibly. Deep into the insertions of the trapezius muscle, on the back of his neck, a pointed blade sank. The sword came off its hook, but remained in his neck. Brady crashed forwards, his head right into the fireplace, his face on the burning, red-hot coals; there lay his bunched body, in front of the fire, a long sword stuck in his neck. The sword had killed him instantly: when his wife found him his face was burnt away.